SEARCHING FOR HEATHER

Eagle Point Search & Rescue, Book 6

SUSAN STOKER

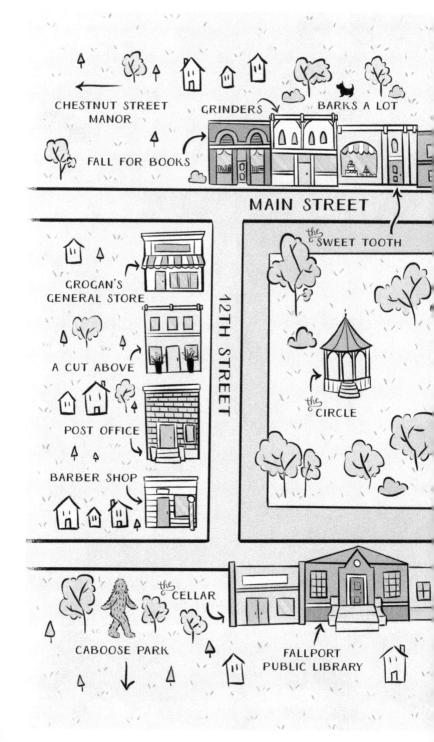

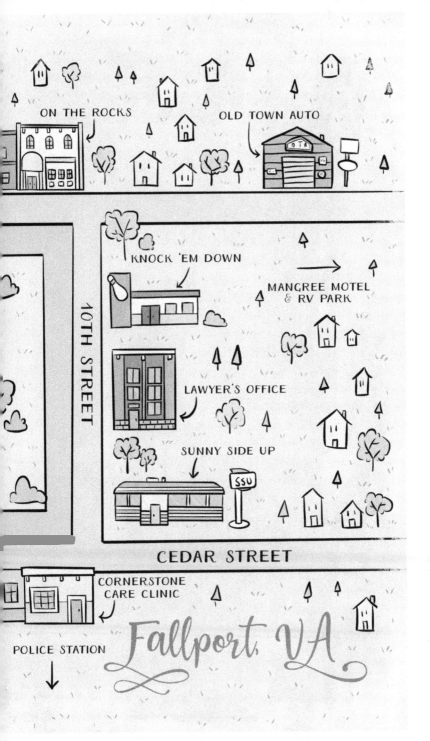

This book is dedicated to Elizabeth Smart. My inspiration for Heather's character. She'll probably never see this, but that doesn't make my admiration for her any less.

CHAPTER ONE

"Any luck yet?" Ethan asked Talon as they walked out of Grinders, the local coffee shop. They'd just gotten back from an overnight search and rescue.

"No. But I'm getting close."

Ethan studied him, and Tal pretended not to see the concerned look his friend was shooting his way. "Have you ever considered that she might not *want* to be rescued?"

Tal sighed. He took a swallow of the hot black coffee, then looked over at one of his best friends. Ethan had literally saved his life. He'd been well on his way to drinking himself to death when Ethan had contacted him and asked if he'd be interested in moving to the United States and joining a search and rescue team he was putting together.

At first, Tal *wasn't* interested. But the more he thought about the offer, the more it appealed to him. He'd gotten out of the Special Boat Service, the UK version of the Navy SEALs, after a mission went not only sideways, but upside down and backward as well. He'd been struggling to find his way, and flying halfway across the world seemed like a great alternative to despair.

Tal loved Ethan like a brother, not only because he'd given him a purpose again, but because he hadn't pried. He'd given Tal the time he'd needed to heal.

But nearly six years after arriving in Fallport, Virginia, and joining the newly formed Eagle Point Search and Rescue team, Ethan was apparently done giving him space.

Tal figured his current nosiness was probably also because he was so deliriously happy with his wife, Lilly. His *pregnant* wife. And Tal had no doubt Lilly was also worried about him, and had probably asked Ethan to check on his state of mind.

All of his friends knew about his quest to find the mysterious woman in the woods, the one who'd helped save Finley and Brock when they'd been snatched in the forest by two drug dealers determined to get information out of Finley. The woman had appeared as if out of thin air, throwing dirt into the face of the guy who'd been holding a knife to Finley's throat and allowing Brock to make his move, getting them away from the threat.

From the first moment Tal had heard about the woman —barefoot, wearing a shabby brown dress, with red hair past her waist—he'd been hooked. He was determined to find her. To thank her. To see if she needed help.

And of *course* she needed help. It was late December in the Appalachian Mountains and the woman was running around without any shoes. But despite his experience, both in the military and with the search and rescue team, so far he hadn't found a trace of where she was living.

Something within Tal wouldn't let him stop looking, his quest becoming an obsession. He hated the thought of her being in the forest alone and vulnerable. He could barely sleep with his need to find her. At most, he was getting two or three hours of restless sleep a night...before the nightmares started. The ones he'd thought he'd gotten over a few years ago.

For his own sanity, and the mystery woman's safety, he needed to find her.

"Tal?" Ethan asked with a frown. "Talk to me."

Mentally shaking his head, forcing himself to pay attention to the conversation, Tal turned to Ethan. "Like I said, I'm getting closer," he told his friend.

"Really? How do you know?" he asked.

"I cheated," he replied without a shred of remorse.

Ethan raised an eyebrow.

Tal's lips twitched as he took another sip of his coffee. "I put out trail cameras," he admitted. "Ever since she took the first bag of stuff I left for her, I've been tracking her. I've tracked her northeast. I'm guessing she's somewhere between the Eagle Point Trail and the Eagle Rock Trail."

Ethan whistled. "That's not easy terrain to navigate."

"It's not. But it's also not too far from where that cult used to live, maybe a mile or two. I figure it's an area she knows well. Especially if she really *is* Heather Brown, and has been living with those assholes since they kidnapped her twenty years ago." Tal felt his blood pressure start to rise just thinking about an eight-year-old little girl being snatched off the street near her home here in Fallport, only to be raised in a cult called The Community, forced to live according to their rules.

From what he'd learned from Simon Hill, the chief of police, The Community had stuck to themselves, didn't cause any problems, and lived a hippie kind of lifestyle. They'd been checked out when little Heather was kidnapped, but no sign of her had been found in the group. Eventually, with the passing of time, and when her parents moved out of the area, the kidnapped girl had been largely forgotten. Most people figured she'd been murdered within hours of being taken.

But Tal couldn't stop thinking about the description of the woman Brock and Finley had seen in the forest. Of course, many women had red hair. That didn't mean *this* woman was the long-lost Heather Brown, but deep down, Tal couldn't help but think it was. Somehow, miraculously, she'd survived being kidnapped and whatever else she'd endured in the last twenty years.

"What's your plan if you *do* find her?" Ethan asked. "You think she's just going to agree to come back to Fallport with you after living who knows how long on her own in the woods?"

Tal shook his head. "No, I don't think that. She's not going to trust me. And why should she?"

"So? Your plan?" Ethan repeated.

"I don't have one," he admitted.

Ethan stared at him in disbelief. "You always have a plan," he said.

His friend wasn't wrong. Tal *did* always have a plan. He was allergic to not having a plan A, B, and C. But the woman he was searching for was an enigma. She didn't do anything he expected. He'd been tracking her with game cameras, but when he figured she'd go west, she went east. When he thought she'd camp next to one of the many mountain streams, she steered clear of water. Which was smart. While being near water was convenient, it was never good to camp too close because of the threat of wildlife.

The woman frustrated and intrigued Tal. She was very

wilderness savvy, light on her feet, and if it wasn't for the cameras he'd hidden along the routes he thought she might take, he wouldn't be as close to finding her as he felt he was now.

"What do you need from me?" Ethan asked.

Tal took a deep breath. He couldn't have a better friend than Ethan Watson. "Nothing. I'm good."

"Seriously, Tal. What do you need? You know we're all willing and eager to help. We want to find her too. Especially Brock."

He knew that. "You know as well as I do if she feels the least bit threatened, she'll disappear, possibly for good. She doesn't trust me, even though she's accepted two more bags of supplies. She's like a feral cat. Willing to take the supplies to make her life easier, but she's so far from trusting anyone it's not even funny. If she's confronted by men she doesn't know, she'll run."

"When are you going out again?" Ethan asked.

Tal was relieved when his friend didn't try to convince him to take anyone else along. "This evening, after I work a shift. Harvey's been cool with the amount of time I've taken off lately, but I don't want to push my luck."

Tal worked part-time at the barbershop on the square. It wasn't exactly a dream job, but it kept him busy between searches. And money wasn't an issue. Tal had saved more than enough to live on during his previous career, especially since he wasn't a man who desired a lot of stuff. He had an apartment not too far from the square, a TV, a couch, a bed...and that was pretty much all he needed. He ate out more than he cooked and spent his free time with his friends...although, over the last year or so, that had tapered off significantly since Ethan, Zeke, Rocky, Drew, and Brock had all gotten married or moved in with their girlfriends.

"Well, we're all here if you need anything. And I mean *anything*," Ethan said.

His support meant the world to Tal. "I don't know how long I'll be gone," he said. "I'm close, I know I am, and that big snowstorm is forecasted for the end of next week. I can't..." He took a deep breath before continuing. "I want to find her before it hits, and that means I could be gone a while," he finished.

"Rocky's wedding is in six days," Ethan reminded him.

Tal sighed. "I know. I want to be there, but..." His voice trailed off.

"But she's more important," Ethan finished.

"It's not that," Tal protested.

"I get it," Ethan said with a small shake of his head. "If I knew Lilly was out there somewhere and a foot of snow was coming, I wouldn't let anything get in my way of finding her and getting her to safety."

"I don't know this woman though," Tal said.

Ethan merely shrugged. "Maybe not, but there's something about her that's captured your attention. Maybe finding her is the key to finally exorcising those demons that have you in their grasp."

Tal pressed his lips together. It was true that events from his past were a large part of why he was so obsessed with finding the redheaded woman. But it was...more than that. He couldn't explain it, so he didn't even try.

"I have one request before you go," Ethan said.

Tal looked at him expectantly.

"I need you to call me at least once every day."

Tal smirked. "What am I, ten?"

"No, you're a grown-ass adult, but you're also my friend

and I worry about you. You're going deep into the woods, by yourself, to look for a woman who most likely doesn't want to be found, and no matter what you might think, she could turn on you. If you check in every day, I'll make sure the others don't come after you, because you know as well as I do they aren't going to be happy you headed out on your own with a storm pending."

Ethan wasn't wrong. Thinking about what his fellow search and rescue teammates would say when they learned which area he'd be searching, Tal nodded. Brock, especially, was not going to be happy.

"And even though you might be in the middle of nowhere at the time, I want you at my brother's wedding, even if it's just via phone. Bristol's gonna cry on her wedding day—and not in a good way—if she thinks you're lost in the wilderness during her ceremony. Not to mention the other women will all lose their minds too. So...call at least once every day, and if you can't get back in time, I want you on the phone when Rocky and Bristol say 'I do.' Deal?"

"Deal," Tal said without hesitation. "For what it's worth...I'm gonna do everything in my power to get back in time for the wedding."

"I know you will. I want you there, and I know Rocky does too. I'd say he'd probably postpone if you're not back, but...nothing is gonna keep my brother from making Bristol his."

"She's *already* his," Tal said.

"Very true. Fine, nothing is gonna keep him from making Bristol his, *legally*. Not even an obsessed friend."

"They're cutting it close with that snowstorm," Tal said, ignoring the "obsessed" comment.

Ethan nodded. "Agreed. I suggested maybe they should

move it up a day, but he doesn't want to stress Bristol out more than she already is. They're willing to take their chances. They don't care if they're the only ones there. But I've already bribed one of the guys who plows the roads around here, and he said he'd bring the officiant to Rocky if need be."

Tal smiled. He didn't doubt Ethan in the least.

Ethan put a hand on Tal's shoulder. "Be careful out there. You have enough supplies?"

"Yeah." He'd already loaded up his larger backpack. It had room for a small tent, his butane camping stove, freeze-dried food to last two weeks, and filters for his water bottle.

But most of the bag was full of things for the woman. A pair of boots he was praying would fit—he'd had to guess her size based on a footprint he'd found in the dirt, near where he'd left the last bag of things for her—another one of his old sweatshirts, more leggings and socks, a pair of cargo pants—again, he guessed at the size—an old copy of *The Lion, the Witch, and the Wardrobe* he'd found in the used bookstore, a deck of cards, several bars of chocolate, a bottle of lotion that smelled like lemon and sugar, a brand-new pocket knife, a set of cutlery, an unbreakable bowl, plate, and cup, a pot, another flint, a brush and comb, bottle of shampoo and conditioner, and some hair ties.

"If at any time you need assistance, all you have to do is say so," Ethan reminded him.

Tal nodded again.

"I also feel the need to remind you that as long as you keep your phone on, I'll be able to track you."

"I realize that," Tal said.

"No complaints?" Ethan asked.

"None. Look, I know what I'm doing is crazy, especially with that storm moving in. But I'm *so* close, Ethan. I know I am. I have no idea what's going to happen when I find her. She might tell me to fuck off, that she doesn't need or want my help. That she's not this Heather girl and she's perfectly happy living how she is. But I *need* to know. If she's not happy with her situation, I can help her."

"What would be crazy is you *not* going out of your way to help her," Ethan countered. "But know that you aren't alone. Even if you're going out there by yourself, you're never alone. Got it?"

It felt great to have Ethan and the others watching his back. It had been one of the best things about being in the military. Knowing no matter how badly a situation might go sideways, he could always rely on his fellow soldiers. He nodded at Ethan.

"Right. Then go on. Get to work. I'll wait until you're gone to tell Rocky that you might not make the ceremony."

Tal winced. "Shit, he's not going to be happy."

"Nope," Ethan said. "And Bristol will be sad too. But I'm thinking all will be forgiven by the crew when you bring the mystery woman back here to Fallport, so Lilly can fawn all over her and bring her into the fold."

Tal chuckled. "She *is* kind of like a mother hen, isn't she?"

"Wouldn't have her any other way."

"You're a lucky man."

"I know," Ethan said with a grin. "Call me every day, Tal. I mean it. If you don't, I'm coming after you...and I won't be happy."

"Got it. Any particular time?" Tal asked.

"Preferably not when I'm making love to my woman," he joked.

"Shit. So not in the mornings, and not in the evenings, and not in the middle of the night. Oh, and not around lunch, because there might be a quickie going on."

Ethan grinned. "When you knock up *your* woman and she's got all these hormones running amok in her body, making her horny as hell, you'll understand."

Tal rolled his eyes, but deep down he couldn't help but feel a pang of jealousy. He was happy for Ethan that he'd found someone as amazing as Lilly. But the lonely future he saw looming ahead for himself made Tal wish for things he'd probably never have.

He was too...old fashioned. Women today were very independent. They didn't necessarily want to be taken care of. And Tal longed for a woman who would let him do just that. He wanted to provide for someone. Didn't like the thought of his woman paying half a mortgage, using her own money to buy groceries, buying her own car, traveling by herself.

Most women would consider that overbearing and controlling, but it really wasn't that he wanted to control someone's every move. He just wanted to see to his woman's needs, make sure she was safe.

He was definitely born in the wrong era. The few women he'd dated in the last decade had let him know in no uncertain terms that what he wanted in a relationship was unrealistic.

Forcing himself back to the present, Tal held out his hand. Ethan shook it. "I appreciate you guys taking up the slack on any searches I'll miss. I'll make it up to you all."

"Whatever," Ethan said. "I'm sure I'll miss my share once my son or daughter arrives. No one's keeping track of hours worked. That's not how any of us operate and you know it."

"I do," Tal said, dropping his hand. "But that doesn't mean I'm not keeping an internal tally. And if you tell me *you* aren't, I won't believe you."

Ethan chuckled. "We're all so alike, it's scary. Good luck, Tal. I have a good feeling about this search."

"I hope you're right." He nodded at his friend and headed down the sidewalk toward the barbershop. He really didn't want to work, but he had taken a lot of time off lately and was about to take more. Fortunately, Harvey was a cool boss. Spent more time chatting with his clients than worrying about how fast he cut hair or how many people came in and out of the door. The laid-back atmosphere was just what Tal needed. He'd worked a high-stress job for long enough, making a vow when he got out of the service that he wouldn't ever subject himself to such pressure again.

Cutting hair wasn't the most stimulating job, but surprisingly, Tal liked it. Listening to the everyday lives of the men, and occasional women, who sat in his chair was a refreshing change from the political and military talk he'd been immersed in before moving to Virginia.

He had a full schedule for the day, but Tal's mind was already on the evening. When he'd leave, how far he might get on the trail before stopping, and what he'd do if he *did* find the woman he was searching for.

As he entered the barbershop, the bell over his head ringing, Tal couldn't help but wonder what she was doing right that moment. Was she cold? Hungry? Scared? Could she tell a storm was coming? Was she prepared?

All he had was questions and no answers. But hopefully soon that would change.

CHAPTER TWO

Sunset Meadowblossom smiled up at the roof of the cave where she was lying. The air outside was chilly, but in here, with her small fire going, wool socks on her feet, legs covered in buttery-soft leggings, and the oversized sweatshirt she rarely took off, she was toasty warm.

The first time she'd taken off the brown dress she'd worn for as long as she could remember, she'd been incredibly nervous. But it had felt so freeing! Women in The Community were only allowed to wear dresses. Never pants. Shirts. Only the brown, shapeless, somewhat scratchy wool shifts Arrow had deemed appropriate.

Of course, the leader of The Community, and the other men, were allowed to wear whatever they wanted. Including warm jackets in the winter and pants that kept their legs from freezing. They all had warm boots and gloves too. Once, she'd heard one of the other wives asking why she couldn't wear pants. The woman was told there was no need, since her place was inside, cooking and taking care of the men.

That would've been an understandable argument if Sunset wasn't required to go into the forest to hunt. She had been one of the best hunters The Community had, and if it wasn't for her, there would've been a lot more nights with growling bellies. But even though she'd been tasked with hunting for meat, she still wasn't allowed to wear pants.

It always seemed unfair to her, though as Arrow had frequently chided, she was simply ungrateful and needed to learn her place. But that was the thing—Sunset had no idea what her place *was*. She'd been Arrow's wife, along with four other women, and even though he was the leader of their group, she was still looked down upon.

The only person who'd sought out her attention was the one man whose attention she didn't want. Arrow's son, Cypress, never hid the fact that he wanted her. But because she was the leader's wife, she was off-limits. She'd gone through her days doing her best to stay under the radar, doing what was required of her and not making any ripples in the difficult existence that was her life.

She still remembered the uncomfortable and painful consequences of speaking out of turn. Of saying whatever she was thinking. Of trying to change the circumstances of her life. She'd been shown time and time again that speaking out, trying to buck against the rules of The Community, would only end in time in the punishment tent, restrained and left alone for days, sometimes weeks on end. Each time Arrow finally came to get her, she was docile once again. Desperate to return to her normal duties for The Community.

Her acquiescence usually lasted for several months before the certainty that this wasn't how life was supposed to be crept back in. And she'd get in trouble all over again. That pattern had continued from her earliest memories, right up until she'd made her escape.

When the time came, Arrow had also insisted she do her wifely duties, just as he demanded of his other wives, but Sunset had never enjoyed those moments. Dreaded when he requested her presence in his tent. In the last few years before he'd passed, it had been a relief when his penis no longer got hard. Instead, he'd fondled her under her dress, which hurt because he was too rough when he touched her. Sunset had learned to pretend it felt good, so he'd stop within a few minutes of touching her.

When he'd died, she'd lost the protection being his wife had afforded. She and his other wives had been given to other men in The Community, and Cypress had wasted no time claiming her as his own.

Being his sixth wife had been hell. He was cruel, violent, didn't care if he hurt her when he took her. In fact, he delighted in her pained cries and relished the bruises he left on her body.

She'd taken to acting out more and more, just so she'd be disciplined with solitary confinement in the punishment tent. At least there, Cypress couldn't touch her. Couldn't hurt her. But inevitably she'd be released to go back to her duties, usually because The Community needed more fresh meat. And she'd end up right back in Cypress's tent, enduring his awful touch.

When the men had decided to move The Community to Florida, where it wasn't as cold, dread had overwhelmed Sunset. She couldn't leave. The feeling wasn't one she could explain, beyond knowing that *this* was her home, and being taken away wasn't something she could endure. She kept her misgivings to herself...not that any of the men would've listened to her anyway.

In the middle of the night, the evening before they were set to leave, Sunset crept into the forest to hide nearby.

Cypress had been furious. He'd yelled for hours, calling her name as he stomped through the woods around the encampment. Ordered her to come back. Threatened her. But still she hid.

She'd waited until she saw with her own eyes all the wives packed into the back of a large truck with no windows and no seats, the door shut and locked behind them. She continue to watch as the men all climbed into comfortable vans and drove off, yet she still didn't come out. She didn't trust that it wasn't a trap. That Cypress wouldn't jump out from behind a tent and grab her, forcing her to go with them far, far away.

She'd lived on her own in the woods for at least a week before she dared go back to the abandoned camp. Cypress had left all the tents, promising they would have new, better homes where they were going. No one questioned him, although Sunset couldn't help but wonder how moving to a new place would work without bringing their homes. She still wasn't convinced Cypress wouldn't be there to grab her when she *did* go back, and when she'd crept into the camp, she ended up watching the tents for two days before she felt brave enough to venture to the only home she remembered.

Most of The Community's belongings had been packed, but they'd also left quite a few useful items behind. Sunset had found a knife and a few stray pots. The straw pallets the women slept on were still there, although she wasn't surprised the beds the men used were gone. She'd found some rice that hadn't been ruined by mice, and even a discarded dress in one of the tents.

Looking back, she realized that all of the men's belongings had been packed up and taken with the group. It was only some of the women's things left behind. Because they weren't as important.

The first few months on her own had been both scary and exhilarating. There was no one telling her what to do. She got to eat all the good parts of the animals she trapped, didn't have to save it for the men. She could sleep later if she wanted, didn't have to get up with the sun to start cleaning and making breakfast. Drank as much water as she wanted, ate as much food as she liked. She'd even gone back to The Community one morning and taken one of the smaller tents, carrying it back to the woods and fashioning the most comfortable bed she'd ever slept on.

Best of all, she didn't have to endure Cypress's touch.

Over the years, many females in The Community had told her how lucky she was to be one of the leader's wives. And when Cypress claimed her, they'd once again told her she should be grateful. But Sunset hadn't been grateful. Not at all.

Now she was free of him. Of her old life. She was making a new life in the woods by herself.

Then, strangely, as the months passed, she'd slowly begun to feel like she had when she was restrained in the punishment tent.

Terribly alone. Isolated.

She longed to see people. Talk to them. Not that she was allowed to talk to the other women in The Community very often; the men frowned on them getting too close. Still, being around others had been a comfort of sorts. And before Arrow died, there were rare times when he was less cruel to her, if not fully nice.

Without cooking and cleaning to do all the time, Sunset also found herself growing bored. There wasn't much to do in the little cave she'd made her home. She'd started venturing out more and more, farther and farther, discreetly following people she came upon in the forest. At first it had been utterly terrifying. The first time she'd heard people talking, she'd fled, running all the way back to her cave, and didn't come out for days.

But eventually her curiosity got the better of her and she ventured out again.

She was now an expert at staying hidden. On spying on people as they hiked the trails of her forest. She'd never felt the need to talk to anyone or interact with them in any way...until the day she'd seen a man holding a woman against him, a knife to her throat.

She'd listened quietly, heard him talk about touching her the way Cypress did to Sunset, when he made her go into his tent.

Something had come over her in that moment. An anger so hot that she'd acted without thinking, running into the clearing and throwing dirt in the man's face.

It had felt *good*. She'd helped save that woman.

Sunset had been all ready to do something to get her away from the *other* man, the biggest one, but as she followed them, she realized the man wasn't hurting her.

He was protecting her.

It was confusing. That wasn't how men were supposed to act.

She didn't understand why he wasn't blaming the

woman for what had happened. Or demanding she make a fire and find them food when they were forced to spend the night in the forest. Instead, he took her into his arms and held her close all night. Keeping her warm. Putting himself between her and the opening of the rock under which they'd slept.

For the first time in her life, Sunset had witnessed a man treating a woman...gently.

For years, when memories of her "before life" had threatened to come to the forefront of her mind, Sunset had pushed them back ruthlessly. She'd been told by Arrow and other men in The Community that if she ever talked about her before life to anyone, she would be severely punished. When she was a child, she *had* been punished. So badly that she'd gone to great lengths to make sure such retributions never happened again...including not thinking about her before life ever again.

But after seeing the man with that woman, vague memories began to slowly trickle back. Flashes that made little sense. Scenes in her head of being warm and happy. Of a tree with twinkling lights. Of a man and woman yelling at each other, but stopping when she came into the room. Of sitting with other children in rows, listening to a woman who was talking to them at the front of the room and writing on a green wall.

The memories were always accompanied by a pounding headache, and even now, that was still the case.

As Sunset lay on her bed, staring at the roof of her cave, she had so many questions. But no way to get answers.

Except maybe by talking to one of the people she saw in the forest.

She knew one of them in particular, Talon—the same

man who'd left the clothes and other items—was looking for her. He'd left her a note, telling Sunset his name and explaining that he was giving her gifts because he was worried about her.

She was scared of what would happen if he found her cave...but she was also wildly curious. He'd given her such lovely gifts. She didn't know what he'd want in return... which was where her nervousness and fright came in. He'd probably want to touch her like Cypress had. It was his right as a man. But she didn't want that.

Maybe she could just give him back the clothes, and then he wouldn't demand anything from her.

But she didn't want to give the clothes back. She *loved* wearing pants. They made her feel safer. Men couldn't just reach under her dress and touch her like they did back in The Community. And her toes didn't tingle with cold at night with the socks on her feet. It was no wonder the men liked wearing clothes so much. She'd never felt as safe or as warm as she did right this minute.

Lifting her head, Sunset brought the material of the sweatshirt to her nose and inhaled. The clean, fresh scent the material had when she'd first received it was almost gone now. But she still remembered vividly how *good* the sweatshirt smelled the first time she'd pulled it over her head. It reminded her of the spring, when the women were responsible for airing out the linens on the men's beds. They used soap Cypress and Arrow brought back from town to clean them in the stream, then hung them up. It was the one duty Sunset always did without feeling the least bit of resentment. She loved that clean smell.

She didn't even mind when Cypress forced her to do her duty after cleaning day. She willingly got on her hands and knees as he took her from behind, because she could bury her nose in the clean material under her and pretend she was anywhere but in his tent.

Turning her head, Sunset looked at the other things the man, Talon, had given her. The chocolate was long gone, but she'd kept the wrapper. She could still smell remnants of the sweet treat on it, which was *almost* as good as when she'd eaten it. She also had the trash from the funny-tasting food. Partly because she had nowhere to get rid of it without risking one of the random hikers in her woods realizing someone had been in the area, and partly because *he* had given it to her.

There was a pink plastic device that had sliced her finger when she'd touched it. There was a blade in the head of the thing, but Sunset hadn't been able to figure out how to remove it without breaking the plastic. And she didn't want to break anything Talon had given her.

He'd also given her a wool hat, which she wore when she left her cave, and a blanket, shiny and silver on one side, that had been folded up into a tiny square. When she'd unfolded it, it made far too much noise for her peace of mind. She couldn't get it folded right again, so it sat off to the side of the cave for now.

He'd also given her some rope, which had come in handy for making traps, and some strips of plastic that she eventually figured out how to use. One end went into the other and, when pulled tight, couldn't be undone again. They made tying sticks together for her traps much easier.

The most recent bag had come with another note. It had been so long since Sunset had been able to read anything—women in The Community weren't allowed to read or write—it was a struggle to figure out what Talon had written, but she'd figured out the general meaning of his words.

. . .

I brought you more things I thought you could use. If you need something specific, please don't be afraid to let me know. I just want to help you. Can you tell me your name? You can trust me. I swear I won't hurt you. Will you stay and say hello to me next time? I'd love to talk to you.

~Talon

Trust. Sunset didn't think she had it in her to trust. She didn't know why, precisely, only that there was something bad lurking in her mind. Something to do with her before life. And it wasn't as if Cypress or Arrow had given her any reason to trust men. But there was something about Talon that made Sunset yearn to be someone else. Someone who could walk up to him and introduce herself. Someone he could learn to like. Someone he wouldn't hit. Or hurt.

Someone who might thank her for the food she made, instead of grunting at her and complaining that it was overdone, or underdone, or too cold.

Sighing deeply, Sunset sat up. It was useless to wish for those things because they'd never happen. She was on her own, and that was how she wanted it. She'd left The Community for a reason, and she'd never felt as free as she did right now. So what if there was dirt under her nails, if she smelled funky, and if she was lonely? She'd take her new life over her life as one of Cypress's wives any day.

With that thought in mind, Sunset crawled out into the chilly air to do her business. Then she needed to get some water from the stream half a mile away, check her traps, and eat something. Later, maybe she'd venture out and see if she could amuse herself by finding some hikers to spy on.

She wasn't going to go look to see if Talon had left another bag of presents. No, she needed to be smart, and she'd already made him far too curious about her. The last thing she wanted was for the man to track her down. To find her little cave. Nothing good could come out of *that*.

CHAPTER THREE

The sun was just beginning to rise, and Tal was starting to think this search would end the same way as all the others. With him going back to Fallport with no more idea where the mysterious woman was than when he'd started.

Last night, his fourth spent in the forest, he'd stopped hiking just before sunset to make camp. When he went to sleep, he woke up again just an hour later, sweating profusely after dreaming of a faceless redhaired woman floating away from him in a river, her arm outstretched, begging for help. In the dream, Tal had run along the bank, desperate to get to her, but she was just out of his reach. No matter what he did, how fast he ran, how long the branches he held out for her, it wasn't enough. He woke up just before the woman plunged over a hundred-foot waterfall.

After that, he'd decided to pack up his little camp and continue walking. It had been slow going in the dark, but walking in the cold evening was better than trying to go back to sleep and having more nightmares.

In the gloom just before sunrise, when he'd been about

to stop for breakfast and try to honestly assess what the hell he was doing, he stepped into a tiny clearing—and stared at the small cave in front of him.

He could just see a wisp of smoke rising into the brisk morning air. The smell of burning wood wafted to his nostrils, and he immediately crouched low to the ground.

This had to be her! There was literally no one else it could be. He hadn't seen or heard any other hikers for three days. He was so far out, so far from any established trail, it was almost impossible for anyone else to be here. Besides, it looked like this small campsite was well used. Tal could see two distinct trails leading away from the cave, and the grass in front of it was trampled down to the dirt.

His heart beat like a jackhammer in his chest and adrenaline coursed through his veins. As he crouched in the trees, Tal frantically tried to figure out what to do next. While he'd wanted to find the woman, he honestly hadn't expected to. And thus he had no plan in mind. Did he just stroll up and say hello?

No, that wouldn't work. He'd freak her out for sure.

Did he backtrack and make a bunch of noise as he walked toward her cave? Giving her advance notice that he was nearby?

No. He was certain she'd bolt if he did that.

Frustration rose within him. Tal had never wanted to meet a person more than he did this one, but he knew without a doubt almost anything he did would frighten her. And that was the absolute last thing he wanted.

He stayed crouched down for what seemed like forever, but was probably only about five minutes, before he cautiously moved forward until he could peek inside the cave. He and his teammates hadn't had a search this far out in the past. He hadn't even known this cave existed. They'd done their best to take note of all the places people might hole up for shelter, but this cave hadn't been on their list.

Yet, it was a perfect location. It was near a stream but not too close. They were probably about half a mile from the closest water source. There was a slight overhang on the cave, protecting the inside from inclement weather. It was densely surrounded by trees, providing shade in the summer and acting as a windbreak in the winter from the blowing snow.

All in all, it was an ideal place to hole up.

The cave was larger than he'd expected, the recesses fully dark without the benefit of daylight. Tal couldn't make out a person...but he knew she was there. He could feel it. Why else would there be a small, smoldering fire inside a cave?

The hair on his arms was standing up and adrenaline coursed through his veins. He stood, walked back about ten feet or so, to the far edge of the clearing, then slowly and silently lowered his pack to the forest floor. Staying as quiet as he could, he leaned it against a tree. He had a clear view of the mouth of the cave...just as the woman would have of *him* when she woke.

He was completely sure she wasn't yet aware of his presence, because if she was, he had no doubt she'd have acted by now.

Tal lowered himself to the ground, keeping his eyes glued to the cave. He leaned back against his backpack, doing his best to look harmless and relaxed.

Of course, being six-three, muscular, and with a beard that was scruffier than he liked after so many days in the woods—not to mention wearing all black and five days of trail dust—he knew "harmless" wasn't exactly the image he was projecting. But that couldn't be helped at the moment.

He still had no idea what he was going to say to try to convince the woman he'd been obsessed over for the last month that he wasn't a threat to her, but he hoped something came to him before she woke up.

* * *

Sunset woke slowly. She'd stayed out late last night checking her traps and having an impromptu feast after she'd arrived back to her shelter. She'd cooked the two squirrels she'd caught and delighted in eating every scrap of meat and licking the juices off her fingers afterward. The difference in her life now and when she was living in The Community was like night and day. There was no one to tell her to be quiet, to lie down and spread her legs, to mend a tent or clothes.

A smile spread across her face as she stretched. For the first time in her life, she was content.

Sunset sat up and crawled forward, glancing outside her cave to gauge what time it was. That was another thing she enjoyed, not having to get up with the sun to prepare breakfast for the men in The Community when they finally rolled out of their beds.

As far as she could tell by the light shining into the cave, it was mid-morning.

But as soon as that thought registered, Sunset froze.

A man was sitting directly opposite the mouth of her cave. He was leaning against a tree, staring at her.

Her first inclination was to leap up and run, but she had no doubt the man would catch her. He was *huge*. She could see his muscles flexing even as he watched her. He reminded her of the men in The Community, but his beard was shorter. She could see that his eyes were blue, because he didn't blink as he continued to stare.

Sunset licked her lips and did her best to control the trembling of her limbs. Who was he? What did he want? Was he a part of The Community? Had Cypress sent him back here to find her and force her to go to Florida? That wasn't happening. She *wasn't* going.

She didn't dare move a muscle, and it felt as if she and the man were in some kind of standoff. The fear didn't leave her...but slowly, another emotion began to rise.

Anger.

This wasn't fair! She was doing just fine on her own. She didn't want a man coming in and telling her what to do, making her do his bidding!

Sunset thought about the knife Talon had left for her. If she moved very quickly, she might be able to grab it before the man could get to her. She'd used it last night to skin the squirrels, and she thought she'd left it by the fire. But she didn't want to take her eyes off the man to look.

"I'm not going to hurt you. You can trust me," the man said. His voice was low and raspy, and sounded completely different from anyone she'd ever heard before. He had an accent of some kind, and it took her brain a moment to process his words.

"I'm Talon. Most of my friends call me Tal. I'm the one who's been leaving the bags of supplies for you."

Sunset's eyes widened. *This* was Talon? In her panic, she hadn't recognized him. As she studied him, she realized that, yes, despite a bit more facial hair, it was the same man she'd seen and stalked in the woods. He looked different sitting down, for some reason.

As he spoke, he hadn't moved. Stayed leaning against a

large pack at his back. His legs were outstretched in front of him and crossed at the ankles. His arms were across his chest, and when she glanced back at his face, he smiled.

Sunset had no idea what to do or say. She was slightly relieved to know this was her mysterious benefactor, but since she didn't know what his motives were, or how he'd found her, or why he'd tracked her down, she was still extremely wary. She didn't want to leave her cave or all her things, but if she got a chance, she would run, leaving everything behind. She'd started from scratch before. She could do it again.

Tal kept talking. And the more he spoke, the more used to his accent she got.

"This is the perfect place to live. I'm impressed. It's well hidden, but close to water and the deer trail I followed for a while to get here. That cave is deep enough to protect you from bad weather and allow you to set a fire inside, but not too big that it would invite animals to join you."

His praise made Sunset feel good. How long had it been since anyone had complimented her? She honestly couldn't remember. Back at The Community, all the men did was complain about the women being slow, or messy, or talking back, or a hundred other things.

"I hope the things I left for you were useful. I wasn't sure what you might need. Although it doesn't look like you actually need *anything*. You've done a wonderful job of surviving out here without help from anyone."

He wasn't wrong. The more he spoke, the more Sunset's muscles relaxed, until she slowly sat on the ground, her knees bent in front of her so she could hug them—and spring up quickly if necessary. She was still wary, and he could be purposely attempting to make her drop her guard before attacking, but for the moment, he looked more than content to stay where he was.

"Will you tell me your name?"

Sunset pressed her lips together as she stared at him.

"Right, too soon. That's okay. Brock and Finley are very thankful that you helped them. Brock couldn't do anything as long as that knife was at Finley's throat. He wasn't willing to make a single move that might've gotten her hurt. Then you were there, throwing that dirt in her captor's face. You gave him a chance to get her away from that knife, and for them to escape."

Brock and Finley. Sunset liked their names. Her lips twitched upward. She knew the man and woman had been able to get away, since she'd followed them to make sure the woman was truly safe.

"I have a feeling not much that happens in this forest gets by you, does it?" Talon asked.

Sunset shook her head slightly.

Talon's lips curled upward in a big smile. Sunset was surprised to see he had a dimple in his left cheek. She could just see it through his beard. It seemed so out of place.

"I didn't think so. Again, they both send their gratitude."

"What happened to the other men?" Sunset asked. Her voice was little more than a whisper, but Tal heard her. His smile widened, as if he was pleased she'd spoken.

"They buried Brock's backpack on their way out of the woods, which my friends found. They were drug dealers, and when they didn't get the information out of Finley that they wanted, that their boss demanded they get, they left Fallport. One of them overdosed and died. The other was caught and put in jail."

Sunset nodded. She wasn't sure exactly what a drug dealer was, but assumed it was something bad. For the first time in years, she considered how little she knew of the world. She could survive here in the woods on her own, knew the best way to catch and skin an animal, could make her own clothes, and had even helped one of the women in The Community give birth, but she knew nothing about the world outside of this forest.

For a moment, shame almost overwhelmed her. She was a grown woman, but she felt incredibly stupid compared to this man.

She'd begged Arrow to let her learn to read and write, but he'd refused. She'd snuck a peek at some of his books when she was sure he wouldn't catch her, but many of the words were long and she couldn't understand what they meant. Years ago, she'd practiced writing with a stick in the dirt, but eventually gave up since there didn't seem to be a point.

She'd learned all she could about other things. Paying attention to the men when they thought she was busy sewing or cooking. She soaked in as much information as possible, but it obviously wasn't enough.

"Sunset," she blurted softly.

"I'm sorry, what?" Talon asked.

"Sunset," she repeated. "My name."

"Your name is Sunset?"

She nodded.

"It's beautiful. It fits you to a T."

Another compliment. Talon must be lying. She wasn't pretty in the least. Arrow had told her often that she was lucky he'd taken her as a wife, since she was so unusual looking. Her red hair was the sign of the devil, and not many men would want to tie themselves to her. He'd made fun of her small boobs and hadn't demanded she undress when she was in his tent for the night. He'd rarely looked at her when lying on top of her.

Talon was just saying nice things because he wanted her to drop her guard.

"You don't believe me," he said. It wasn't a question. "I'm not lying. Your eyes are an unusual shade of bluish-green. Almost turquoise. I swear they're the color of some of the most beautiful waters I've seen in the Caribbean. You've got eyelashes women pay big bucks for in the city. And the intelligence I see swirling in those gorgeous eyes of yours is the icing on the cake."

Now she *knew* he was lying. She might've been swayed by his compliments if he hadn't added that last part. She wasn't smart. Not in the least. Again, Arrow and his son had gone out of their way to make sure she knew just how dumb she was.

"Go away," she said, her voice hard.

Talon blinked in surprise, but she saw a muscle in his jaw flex as he stared at her. In fact, every muscle in his body tensed. She was prepared for him to come after her and beat her now. She knew better than to speak to men like that, but the words had escaped before she'd thought them through. Arrow had hit her countless times for her impulsive behavior, trying to beat it out of her...without success.

But Talon didn't move. He stayed slumped against his bag. "I'm not here to hurt you," he said quietly.

"Why *are* you here?"

Tal moved then. He slowly sat forward, pinning her in place with his gaze. "Because you were barefoot."

Sunset frowned. "What?"

"Brock said you were barefoot when you ran through

that clearing. There was no way I *wasn't* going to try to find you after hearing that."

Sunset was still confused. "I don't understand."

It was Tal's turn to frown. "What don't you understand?"

"Why does that matter?"

"Sunset, it's December. It's cold. I could not and *would* not sit around, warm and toasty in my home, knowing you were out here not properly dressed. Not to mention, I owe you. As do all of my friends. If something had happened to Finley, Brock would never have recovered. He loves her more than anything in this world."

Sunset's mind spun. She didn't understand why Talon cared. Arrow had never cared if she was cold. Or hot. All he cared about was getting his meals on time and having sex when he wanted it. None of the men in The Community cared about the women's comfort. And certainly none of them loved their wives. They were there to serve. Period.

Her belly clenched. She didn't like not understanding, and she had a feeling there was a lot she was missing.

"Do you like the socks?" Talon asked, nodding to her feet.

Sunset stared down at her wool-covered feet. She wiggled her toes, then looked back at Talon. "Yes."

"Good. I brought a pair of boots for you. I hope they fit, I had to guess on your size, but I did estimate based on a footprint I found that I was pretty sure was yours."

She stared at him with wide eyes. Boots? He'd brought her *boots*? Only men got to wear boots. Was this another trick?

"I hate that look," Talon muttered softly, but he leaned

back again once more, as if he had nowhere he needed to be and nothing to do.

For the first time, Sunset noticed that the sky had clouded over since she'd woken up and now a light rain was falling. But Talon didn't make any move to get out of the rain, he simply sat where he was. She was so confused. Literally every man in The Community would've forced their way into her cave by now, pushing her out. They would've ordered her to collect more wood to warm the space, insisted she go out and find breakfast, and probably settled down for a nap on the bed she'd made.

But Talon didn't do any of those things. He sat in the rain, getting wet, acting as if he didn't even notice.

"It's raining," she blurted.

"Yup," he said without moving.

"You're getting wet."

"I am," he agreed.

"Don't you want to get out of the rain?"

"I'm okay."

Frustrated, Sunset said, "Why aren't you coming into the cave?"

"Because I haven't been invited. Because it's *your* cave. Because you don't trust me. Because I don't want to do anything that might scare you even more. Take your pick."

Sunset was so puzzled. Talon wasn't acting like any of the men she'd ever known. She didn't know what was wrong with him. She couldn't deny she appreciated him giving her space, but she didn't understand *why* he was doing it.

"I'm not here to hurt you," Talon repeated. "I'm here to help you. Get to know you. Let you get to know me. I want your trust, but I'm willing to earn it slowly. There's a big snowstorm coming, and I'd like to take you back to

33

Fallport before it hits...but I have a feeling that's not something you'll agree to. So, we'll hunker down and ride it out together.

"I know saying it doesn't make it so, but you *can* trust me, Sunset. I won't touch you without your consent. I won't eat your food, won't enter your home, won't do one bloody thing without your approval. You've been through enough, and I'll be damned if I add one more black mark to your psyche."

Surprisingly, Sunset found herself *wanting* to trust him. But she'd seen more than one man win a woman's trust, only to show his true colors later. "I don't trust anyone," she told him.

"I know," Tal said sadly. "I appreciate you not running when you saw me."

"You surprised me," she said honestly.

"I know that too."

"I need to pee," she blurted, then immediately regretted it.

But Talon simply smiled, that dimple making an appearance again. It disappeared as soon as it appeared. "Please don't run," he told her. "I swear, Sunset, I'd never hurt you."

She *had* thought about running. But she knew he wasn't lying about the storm coming. She'd felt it in the air. Over the years, she'd learned to read the signs. It had gotten colder recently and the wind had shifted the night before. Animals were burrowing in and obviously preparing for what mother nature had in store for them. If she ran now, she'd be at the mercy of the storm without her cave. As scared as she was of Talon, she didn't have a death wish.

Finally, she nodded.

"Thank you," he said. "Do you need water?"

Sunset frowned. "Yes, but I'll get it on my way back."

Talon shook his head. "I'll go. Is that your only bucket?"

She looked at the bucket sitting near the entrance to the cave. It was one of the items she'd taken from The Community when she'd gone back to scavenge after everyone left. She nodded.

"If you throw it over here, I'll fill it up while you're taking care of your business. When the snow starts, if we're still here, we can melt snow for water."

Sunset didn't know what to make of this man. He was offering to do one of the women's chores? It made no sense. But she didn't hesitate to get up on her knees and shuffle over to the bucket. She didn't want him to get too close to her. He was way bigger than she was. He could easily overpower her. And she didn't even want to think of being snowed in with him.

Talon slowly stood, and Sunset swallowed hard. He really was huge. He didn't look this big when she'd seen him on the trails...but she was much closer to him now than she'd ever been before. Yeah. She hadn't been wrong about him being able to overpower her.

She tossed the bucket in his direction.

He picked it up and took a step backward. "If you *are* going to run, take my pack," he said solemnly. "It's got the boots and other things I brought for you. I've also got a tent in there, and rations."

Sunset's head throbbed. He asked her not to run, and now was telling her if she did, to take his backpack? He was so bewildering, and she hated feeling as if she was missing something.

"I don't want you to go," he continued. "But if you

can't help yourself, if you're too afraid of me, I want you to be able to survive the storm that's coming. I'm not lying about that. The forecasts are calling for at least a foot of snow. Maybe more. This cave is the safest place for you... well, that's not true. The safest place is back in Fallport. But I'm thinking that's not going to happen. So the second safest place is right here. You can trust me, Sunset. I'm not going to hurt you. I'll be back with the water."

And with that, he turned and walked in the direction of the stream.

Sunset sat back on her heels and stared at where he disappeared into the forest for a long moment. He kept saying that he wasn't going to hurt her, that she could trust him. He'd said it several times. She'd learned that what men said and what they did, didn't always match. But so far, he'd been nothing but kind.

Sunset slowly stood and looked down at herself. She had on the sweatshirt he'd given her, the leggings, the socks. The knife he'd left for her previously was indeed by the fire. He hadn't grabbed her this morning. Hadn't done anything but sit in the rain and talk to her.

He confused the heck out of her, but he hadn't hurt her.

His instinct was correct. A part of her was screaming at her to run. To get away from him. To grab his backpack and disappear into the forest she knew so well.

But another part, the part that was desperate for a human connection, the part that reveled in being called pretty and smart, wanted to stay. Wanted to trust him.

She was torn. So very torn.

Stepping outside into the light rain, Sunset headed into the forest.

CHAPTER FOUR

It was a risk to leave, but Talon knew he couldn't keep his eye on Sunset every second of the day. Everything within him was screaming to go back. To make sure she didn't run. But she was an adult, and he wasn't her captor.

She was breaking his heart though. It was obvious she was confused. That she'd been treated like shit by the people she'd lived with. The jury was still out on whether Sunset was really Heather Brown, the eight-year-old kidnapped twenty years ago. The odds were against it...but what if she was?

As he walked toward the stream, Talon strained to hear anything other than the rain falling on the leaves around him and his own footsteps. But he wouldn't hear her if she left. She was as nimble and quiet as any forest creature. She was in her element here, and if she was going to leave while he was gone, Talon had a feeling he'd never find her again. The only reason he'd found her this time was because the trail cameras he'd put up had given him a direction to head toward, and because her guard was down and she didn't think anyone was looking for her.

Now that he'd found her once, she wouldn't make the same mistakes again. She'd never come back for another bag of supplies. Would be long gone by the time he made it into the woods again.

Talon hated the look of distrust in her eyes. He could tell her over and over that he wouldn't hurt her, that he only had her best interests at heart, but actions spoke louder than words. He'd have to prove that he was nothing like the wankers who'd taken advantage of her in the past.

He'd never thought much about the commune that lived outside Fallport. He'd been told they were harmless. Kept to themselves. Apparently, the former police chief had talked to the leader of the group on several occasions, and had been reassured that everyone lived there voluntarily. He hadn't seen anything to make him suspicious that anyone was being abused.

But apparently, he'd been easily fooled.

Sunset, and probably all the women in the group, had been treated little better than slaves. The signs were clear. He hadn't missed her surprise at his offer to get water. Her shock that he wasn't barging into her cave.

He'd seen way too many women like her in the past. Those who were oppressed and beaten down and had no idea what a normal life should look like.

Of course, there were some women who didn't mind taking over all the chores in a household. But it was their *choice*, something he didn't think Sunset had. He'd seen a spark of something in her eyes. Discontent? Anger? Frustration? He couldn't tell, but whatever it was, he was glad. She wouldn't have been able to survive on her own in the woods without that inner core of strength and determination.

Walking back to the cave took longer than getting to

the stream, since Talon didn't want to spill the water in the bucket he was carrying. He held his breath as he approached Sunset's hidey-hole. He was fully expecting to see his pack gone and the area deserted—so he let out a sigh of relief when he came around a tree and saw Sunset building up the small fire in the cave.

She hadn't left.

Respect coursed through his veins. She was one tough cookie, even if she didn't see herself that way. Her self-esteem was nonexistent, and Talon made a vow to do whatever he could to show the woman her worth.

"Where do you want this?" he asked softly, not willing to crowd her by getting too close.

"You can put it down there," she said, nodding at the ground where he stood.

Tal gently placed the bucket on the ground. Then he turned his back to her and headed for his backpack. He wouldn't have been surprised if she'd looked inside, but nothing seemed to be disturbed as he opened the pack.

He pulled out his small one-person tent and quickly set it up near the tree he'd been sitting against when she woke.

Sunset watched him without comment. Once he had the rainfly on, Talon sat down at the entrance and rummaged through his bag. He had to hunch over, as the tent was quite small, but he ignored the way his back complained at the position. He pulled out the things he'd brought for Sunset and placed them next to him, then shoved his backpack toward the back of the tent. There wasn't any extra room, but Tal was used to sleeping in tight places.

When he looked up, Sunset had retrieved the bucket of water and she was staring at him. He noticed she'd placed the knife he'd given her in a previous supply bag within reach. He approved. He'd give her no reason to use that blade on him, but he was pleased she was being cautious.

"I brought you some more things. I already mentioned the boots," Tal said. "But I also have another sweatshirt, more leggings and socks, a pair of cargo pants that I really hope will fit...although, now that I can see you, I think they'll probably be too big. I do have some rope that you can use as a belt if necessary. I wasn't sure if you liked to read or not, but I brought a book, some cards, some more chocolate, another knife, some eating utensils and dishes, more flint...Oh, and some stuff for your hair."

Tal looked down at everything and internally winced. Shit, he'd gone overboard. He hadn't meant to, but once he started thinking about what she might want or need, he hadn't been able to stop himself. His pack had been quite a bit lighter once he'd taken out the things for her.

When he looked at Sunset, she was staring at him once more. He couldn't read the expression on her face.

"It's too much. I'm sorry," he said with a small shrug. "I got carried away."

"All that is for me?" she asked.

"Yeah."

Instead of looking happy or excited or intrigued, she looked even more wary and resigned. "What do I have to do for it?" she asked woodenly.

For a moment, Talon was shocked. Then he wanted to swear. Punch a tree. *Something*. But he forced himself to sit still and not move a muscle. "Nothing. Not a bloody thing." He realized the abuse this woman had endured was far worse than he'd imagined. It was more than the physical and sexual abuse he'd already suspected; she'd suffered severe emotional and mental abuse, as well.

Of course she had. Especially if this was actually Heather Brown. There was no way an eight-year-old would assimilate into whatever fucked-up society the commune had been without exploitation, manipulation, threats, and abuse. There was no telling what twenty years of that kind of torture and control would do to a person's psyche.

Knowing he was scowling, but not able to stop himself, Talon stood again. He gathered all of the items he'd brought for her and carried them toward the cave. He placed them just under the overhang, doing his best to keep his distance from Sunset. He needn't have worried though; as soon as he started walking toward her, she'd scooted backward until she was as far away from him as she could get while still being in the clearing.

Talon walked back to his tent and sat once again. He shoved his pack aside and lay down, staring at the roof of his tent. He could hear the light rain against the nylon and usually the sound comforted him, but not right now.

"Anyone who gives a gift with conditions is a piece of shit," he said in a low, controlled voice. "I brought those things for you because I figured you would like them. That's all. I don't expect anything from you. Not even a thank you. I'll keep saying it as many times as you need to hear it. I'm not going to hurt you, and you can trust me."

Tal took a deep breath and continued. "I was a soldier before I moved to the States. I lived in England. I did a lot of things I'm not proud of on behalf of my government. Some of the missions I went on were for the greater good of the world, and others seemed to have no real purpose. But the one that was the last straw was when we were sent to hunt down a suspected terrorist. He was the mastermind behind some of the worst attacks on my country. Cowardly attacks. Chemical bombs on the subways, blowing up night clubs, that sort of thing. We found his hideout, but he wasn't there. He'd somehow gotten word that we were coming. But we *did* find a roomful of women and children."

Tal paused. He couldn't believe he was telling Sunset this story. He hadn't told *anyone* what had happened that awful day. And he wasn't even sure *why* he was telling her. It wasn't as if this would make her trust him. But he couldn't stop now.

"They were scared to death. None spoke English, so we couldn't communicate. They were terrified of us. They were so skinny...the kids were malnourished. Without me having to say a word to my team, we all emptied our packs of every bite of food we had. We tried to give it to them, but no one would take it.

"I didn't realize until that moment, there were a few men in that room too. They were behind all the women, using them as shields maybe. And even though those women and kids were starving, they looked to those men for permission to take the food. All it took was one shake of the oldest man's head, and they lowered their eyes to the floor. The women were bloody starving, their *children* were starving, and yet they wouldn't take the food.

"My team and I wanted to kill those men, but we hadn't been given permission to take out anyone other than our target. And they weren't doing anything overtly threatening toward us or the women. They weren't holding any weapons; they were literally just sitting there. Killing them would've caused an international incident and definitely scarred those women and kids for life.

"I wanted to help them. Do *something*. But other than

reporting to our commanding officers what we'd found, asking them to do something to help those women and children, leaving our rations was the only thing we could do at that moment."

Tal stopped talking once again. He didn't even know what his point was anymore. He was stuck in the past, seeing those kids and women. Desperation in their eyes, and Tal unable to do anything for them.

"What happened?" Sunset asked, now crouched a few feet from his tent.

Tal jerked. He'd actually forgotten where he was for a moment. Once more lost in the horrors of the past.

"They died," he said. "They all died. The terrorist came back after my team gathered up his known men, leaving the women and children. Word was, he wasn't happy we had dared try to overrule his command by leaving food. He didn't kill them. He just left them there...and they all starved to death. The craziest thing of all was, he didn't even lock them inside that room. They could've left at any time. But because he'd told them to stay put, they did. They were obviously scared to death of what would happen to them if they disobeyed.

"One of our commanders eventually notified a local aid organization, but they didn't get there in time to save them. My team and I were allowed to go back to assist in the relief effort...but it was too late," he finished.

"I'm sorry," she said softly.

"Me too. They didn't deserve that. I don't know what I could've done differently, but after that...I was done. I couldn't do my job anymore. All I could think was that I should've done more. Should've tried harder to get those women and kids help. I knew how awful the terrorist leader was. I should've known those women needed help... protection. But I did nothing."

"I'm not sure what a terrorist is," Sunset said after a moment, "but I'm guessing he's a very bad man. And I don't think there was anything else you could have done." She was quiet for a moment. "I've never been allowed to wear pants before."

The abrupt change in topic made Tal lift his head. "What?"

"You gave me these leggings. I've never worn pants. Only the men were allowed. I was scared to put them on at first. Even though I was here by myself, I somehow thought Cypress would know. But after a while, I decided that was stupid. He was gone, and I was by myself. I don't know those women, but I understand their fears."

Tal shifted so he was sitting again. "If you put the cargo pants on over the leggings, I bet you'd be even warmer," he said gently.

"Thank you for the things you brought," she told him.

"You're welcome. I'm not going to hurt you. You can trust me, Sunset."

Her lips twitched. "You've already said that."

"I know. And I'll *keep* saying it until you believe me."

"You make me nervous," she admitted.

He nodded. She wasn't telling him anything he didn't already know. "I'm not like the men you've known in the past."

"I've noticed," she said, before moving back to the cave, out of the light rain.

It was surprising how easy it was to talk to her. That was the last thing Tal expected. He'd kind of expected to have to do *all* the talking. And she wasn't exactly a chatterbox, but she wasn't mute either.

The rain eventually tapered off, but Tal didn't move from his spot in the tent. Though it was still pretty earlier in the morning, he found himself suddenly exhausted. He did his best to stay awake, but the long days and nights of looking for Sunset caught up to him, and he soon dozed off.

He wasn't sure how long he'd been asleep when he heard his name being called somewhat urgently. Coming up on an elbow, Tal looked around in alarm. When he didn't see anything dangerous, he glanced over at the cave. Sunset was standing just under the overhang at the entrance, and she looked alarmed.

"What? What's wrong?" Tal asked, sitting up and reaching for the knife he always kept in a holster on his calf.

"You were shouting," Sunset told him. "I said your name a few times to try to wake you, but it didn't seem to help. Finally I yelled it and you woke up."

Tal ran a hand over his face and sighed. "Sorry. I don't sleep well."

"Are you all right?"

"I'm fine," he reassured her, even though he was anything but. He vaguely remembered the dream. It was the same as the night before, except this time the woman being washed away in the river was definitely Sunset. "Thanks for waking me up." He looked at her carefully for the first time—and smiled. "They fit?" he asked, seeing she'd put on the cargo pants.

She nodded. "You were right. It is warmer with them and the leggings on."

Pleasure swam through Tal. "Good." He looked at his watch. "Are you hungry? It's well past lunchtime."

"I had a large dinner last night, but I can go out and

catch you a squirrel."

Tal shook his head. "No. You don't have to feed me. I'm perfectly capable of hunting for my own food. But I've got some stuff here that will do for now," he told her, reaching for a packet of freeze-dried food. He held it up. "Do you want to try it? It's a different kind than what I left for you before."

He saw her hesitation and wanted to kick himself for pushing her too hard, too fast.

"I don't think so."

Tal shrugged as if he didn't have a care in the world, but inside it killed him to eat in front of her. He used some water from his canteen to prepare the instant meal and ate without even tasting it.

Sunset had moved back into the cave once more, sitting by the small fire a few feet inside the entrance, and Tal saw that she'd moved the pile of things he'd brought for her inside.

Just as he was trying to think of something to talk about, his satellite phone rang.

He'd honestly forgotten all about contacting Ethan, and it had definitely been more than twenty-four hours since his last check-in. He pulled out the phone and looked at Sunset. She had that scared look on her face again, which Tal hated.

"This is my friend, Ethan. I was supposed to check in with him every day, so he knows I'm safe, and I forgot to call him this morning in my relief at finding you. I'm going to answer this and put it on speaker, so you can hear our conversation. I don't want you to think I'm keeping anything from you. You can trust me, Sunset, and I won't hurt you." The last words had become his mantra.

Upon hearing them, Sunset's shoulders lowered a fraction. She nodded.

Tal clicked on the phone and hit the button to put it on speaker. He held it up so Sunset could hopefully hear the conversation. He had nothing to hide from this woman, and every single thing he did from here on out would be with the goal of earning her trust.

"I'm sorry, I forgot," Tal said as soon as he answered the phone.

"Christ, Talon, I had visions of you lying unconscious in the woods and dying when you didn't call. I checked the beacon and you haven't moved for a few hours."

"Sorry, Ethan. I'm fine. I found her. And you're on speaker so she can hear you," Tal warned.

"You did? Holy hell, that's awesome! Is she okay? Are you okay, ma'am? What do you need?"

"She's fine. Her name is Sunset, and she's set herself up in this kick-ass cave," Tal told his friend. "What's the forecast on the storm?"

"Bad news, mate. It's picked up speed. It's supposed to hit anytime now. You gonna be able to get back?"

Tal's gaze met Sunset's. She was looking between him and the phone in his hand. He wondered if she'd ever seen a cell phone before. He was doubtful. "Negative. We'll ride it out here."

"Shit. Okay. Do you need one of us to come out?"

"No," Tal said quickly. "We're okay." The last thing he wanted was for Sunset to have two strange men to fret about.

"You have enough food to tide you over?"

"We'll make do," Tal reassured him.

"Is it her?" Ethan asked.

"Not sure. But you can tell Brock that I've thanked her for him," Tal said, quick to change the subject. He didn't want to bring up Heather Brown yet. He didn't think Sunset was ready to discuss her past.

"I will. Sunset? Can you hear me?" Ethan asked.

Tal looked over at the woman he was quickly coming to realize was perfectly at home in her forest cave. Her eyes were wide, but she didn't respond verbally, only nodded at Talon.

"She can hear you," he said quietly.

"Tal is one of the good guys. You can trust him one hundred percent. I've known the bloke a while now, and while he might sound funny with his English accent, I trust him with my life. And the life of my wife, as well."

Tal appreciated his friend's words, but they were just that...words. Sunset was going to have to learn for herself that he was trustworthy.

"Is everything all set for Rocky and Bristol's wedding ceremony tomorrow? Is the storm going to mess things up?" Tal asked.

"No way in hell is a little bit of snow going to keep Rocky from getting married. He already said he didn't care if they were the only ones there."

"Kind of hard to get married without an officiant," Tal joked.

"Actually, he's already there. He's spending the night at the house, just to be safe. And me and the rest of the team are gonna be there even if we have to walk to their house."

"Is he upset that I'm not there?" Tal asked.

"He's not happy, but he understands you've got more important things to do at the moment."

Tal looked at Sunset. She was studying him intently. "He's not wrong. All right, I'll call you tomorrow. One o'clock, right?"

"Right. Better make it twelve-thirty. I have a feeling

Rocky's gonna be impatient to put that ring on Bristol's finger."

"Will do. Thanks for everything, Ethan."

"Of course. Glad you found her. Sunset? I know you don't know me, but I'm very relieved you're all right. Take care of Tal for us, okay?"

Tal chuckled. "Shut up, you cheeky bastard."

Ethan laughed. "Talk to you tomorrow."

"Later." Tal hung up, then glanced back at Sunset. "What are you thinking about so hard?"

"So many things," she said.

Tal couldn't help but grin. "I bet. You want to tell me?"

"No."

He was extremely curious as to what was going through her head, but he respected her enough not to push. "All right."

"I think I'm going to take a nap," Sunset said.

Tal was surprised, but he nodded anyway. "All right. I'll just stay over here. You can trust me—"

"And you won't hurt me," Sunset finished for him.

Pleased, Tal nodded. "Exactly."

He watched as she settled on her bed near the back of her cave and closed her eyes. He had a feeling she wasn't so much tired as needing some space to think, and he had no problem with that. He was just shocked she was willing to leave herself vulnerable with him so near.

Tal needed time to think himself. The woman was so much more than he'd expected. To be fair, he hadn't known *what* to expect. She was obviously scared and distrustful, but she was also easily the most resilient person he'd ever met.

Sunset wasn't a victim. Even though she'd obviously been through hell.

CHAPTER FIVE

Sunset stared at Talon from beneath her lowered lashes. She'd gotten good at pretending to be asleep. Eavesdropping had been a great source of information for her over the years. She also didn't want to sleep in case Tal decided to do something. She supposed she was testing him... seeing if he'd try to hurt her when he thought she was asleep.

She couldn't stop thinking about that conversation with his friend. She wasn't sure how he was able to talk to the man who was obviously far away from here, but he had.

The longer she lay there, the more questions she had. A year ago, she would've quashed all the thoughts running through her mind. None of the men would answer her questions, and she would've been beaten for daring to ask anyway. But even though she'd only known Tal a short while, she was fairly confident he wouldn't mind her asking about all the things that were rolling around in her head.

The Community had very few electronics. She vaguely remembered some things from her before life, but it had been a very long time since she'd thought about them. She'd been too busy trying to survive. But now she couldn't help but wonder exactly how Tal's phone worked. A memory of a phone on a wall with an extra-long cord sprang into her mind, but she hadn't seen a cord on the device Tal had used.

She watched through slitted eyes as he gathered firewood and neatly stacked it near the entrance to the cave. Every time he walked toward her, she tensed. But he never crossed the imaginary line where the forest stopped and her cave started.

It was odd, and somewhat discomfiting, to watch him do the work that had been her responsibility for so long. She couldn't ever recall any of the men in The Community doing something they considered women's work. Which was basically everything that had to do with cleaning or eating...including chopping and gathering wood for the fires to cook their food.

Sunset didn't have an ax, so it had been difficult to find enough wood to keep her small cave warm, but she'd managed. The ease with which Tal carried and stacked the bigger logs was impressive.

The fifth time he returned with an armful of wood, she could no longer stay quiet.

"How were you able to talk to your friend? I thought phones had to be plugged into a wall to work."

When he calmly looked over at her, not surprised in the least that she was awake, she realized that he probably knew she was watching him the entire time.

"It's called a satellite phone. I don't know every single detail about how it works, but basically, it sends a signal to a satellite up in space, which will then transmit the signal back down to Earth."

Sunset frowned and sat up.

"Have you ever seen a cell phone?" Tal asked.

"Um...I don't know what that is, so I don't know," she admitted. She hated not knowing things. Hated to look stupid.

But Tal didn't look surprised. He eased himself to the ground a few feet from her cave and rested one arm on an updrawn knee. He looked completely at ease in the forest. Comfortable in a way she'd rarely seen, even after all the time she'd spent in the area.

"A cell is another type of small phone that doesn't require cords. It uses signals from big metal towers. The more towers there are, the stronger the signal. There aren't any towers here in the forest, so cell phones don't work. Too many hikers come into the forest thinking they're safe because they have a cell phone, but when they need help, they realize it doesn't work. My search team is often sent out to find them."

"Which is why you're using a phone that uses satellites instead of the towers," Sunset said.

Tal grinned. His dimple was more prominent when he smiled widely. "Exactly."

"And that was your friend? One of the men on your search team?" she asked.

"Yes. Ethan. He's married to Lilly. She came to town to film a TV show about Bigfoot. Did you see the camera crews at all? They were here months ago, tromping all over the woods."

Sunset's lips twitched.

Tal returned her grin. "You saw them."

She nodded.

"Please tell me you messed with them."

"I was so confused at first. They were yelling and

beating sticks against trees. It was very odd. One night, I couldn't stop myself from hitting a tree after they did. They got really excited about it."

"I bet they did," Tal said, laughing. "And by the way, that was literally the highlight of their show. I can't tell you how many times they played that sound footage back. Anyway, so Lilly met Ethan while she was here. She was a cameraperson for the show. It turns out one of the cameramen killed one of the show's stars, and he tried to kill Lilly too. But she's okay now."

Sunset stared at him in horror. "I didn't know about that. I got nervous that they might see me, so I came back here. I didn't go anywhere near those trails for weeks."

"That was smart. If that asshole had seen you, he probably wouldn't have hesitated to get rid of you too," Tal said softly. Then he took a big breath. "Anyway, Lilly and Ethan got married back in October, during Halloween. They're deliriously happy and she's pregnant with his baby. Ethan is kind of the leader of our search and rescue team, and I have the upmost respect for the bloke."

"Who's getting married tomorrow?" Sunset asked.

"Right, so...there are seven of us on the team. Ethan, Zeke, Rocky, Drew, Brock, Raiden, and myself. Zeke and Elsie are already married, as are Brock and Finley...the two who you helped save from those assholes here in the woods. Drew and Caryn are holding off on tying the knot, but they're definitely in it for the long haul.

"Raiden and I are the only single ones left in the group, but Raid and Khloe definitely have something going on, even though they're both tiptoeing around their attraction. She works with him at the library.

"That just leaves Rocky. He's Ethan's brother, and it's his wedding tomorrow. He and his fiancée Bristol bought a beautiful house that had a large barn on the property. They set it up for her to use as a workshop—she makes stained glass—and that's where the ceremony is supposed to be tomorrow. With the storm coming, I'm guessing a lot of people won't show up, but my teammates and their women wouldn't miss it for the world."

Sunset's mind spun with all the names he'd just mentioned, and there was a lot of other things she didn't understand, but because she didn't want to feel stupid again, she simply nodded as if it all made sense.

"Bristol didn't want bridesmaids or groomsmen, but the girls are all supposed to go over to the house early, like they did with Lilly's wedding, and get their hair and makeup done. It's kind of a ritual. Finley, who owns a bakery in town, made their wedding cake, and even if it's just our small group, I'm sure no one is going to let them skip all the usual traditions, like throwing the bridal bouquet, the first dance, or smashing cake in each other's faces."

Sunset was even more confused now. She had no idea what Tal was talking about.

Her cluelessness must've shown on her face, because he said, "I'm sorry. I'm going on and on. What questions do you have?"

It was the first time Sunset could remember a man willingly offering to answer questions. The ceremony sounded important to his friends, and like a very big deal, but she didn't know why. Although she wanted to understand, years and years of conditioning kept her from asking the questions that were on the tip of her tongue.

Once more, it was as if Tal could read her mind. "How about you tell me what you know about weddings?" he suggested.

That she could do.

"When a man decides he wants another wife, he tells the woman he's her husband, then they go into his tent where he makes her lie down and he has sex with her. Then they're married," she said.

Tal stared at her for an excruciatingly long moment before abruptly jumping to his feet.

Sunset flinched when he stood, expecting him to come into the cave and do just what she'd said—declare that they were married and force her to lie under him.

Instead, he looked extremely agitated as he paced back and forth in the small clearing, his hands locked together behind his head.

Finally, he stopped and faced her.

"That is *not* a wedding or a marriage, Sunset," he said quietly. "First, a guy doesn't get to just *tell* a woman that they're getting married. He *asks* her. And two people should only get married if they love each other, if they can't imagine ever being with someone else. Then they pledge to love and honor each other, usually in front of their friends and family. It's a celebration of two people in love. Not the horror you just described."

"How many other wives does Rocky have?" Sunset asked.

Tal took a deep breath, looked toward the sky briefly, then went back to where he was sitting. He eased himself to the ground and stared at her with an intense look in his blue eyes. "It's *illegal* to have more than one wife. A guy might marry someone, then cheat on her with another woman, but the government only allows men and women to have one spouse."

"I was Arrow's fifth wife. And when he died, Cypress immediately claimed me. I was his sixth. All the women in

55

The Community were wives. Many had more than one husband," she explained.

Sunset could see the muscle in Talon's jaw flexing as he stared at her. "Did you want to marry them?"

"No." The word was flat and hard.

Talon shook his head. "I'm so sorry that happened to you," he said after a moment. "But you need to know, Sunset, that what you experienced…it's not normal, moral, legal, or right. Rocky is marrying Bristol because he loves her desperately. He would do anything to keep her safe. He would never hurt her. Ever. He'd never force her to do anything she didn't want to do. Forcing someone to marry is abuse, plain and simple."

Something within Sunset seemed to loosen. She hadn't wanted to be Arrow's wife. And she didn't want to be claimed by Cypress either.

She'd always thought there was something wrong with how many things were done in The Community, but she hadn't been able to question it. Hadn't been able to do anything to stop it. She *hated* not having any control over who she had to have sex with. But she hadn't had a choice. In anything.

Now, Talon telling her that her marriages weren't legal or normal actually made her feel so much better about her circumstances, instead of worse.

She'd been right all along. It was an incredible feeling.

"Do you understand, Sunset? You were never married to those assholes. You were taken advantage of and abused. If you ever see…what's his name? The son? Cypress?"

She nodded.

"Right, if you ever see Cypress again, you do *not* have to go with him. He is *not* your husband, and he has no right to make you do anything you don't want to do. Got it?"

His words made Sunset even more relieved. She nodded.

"Right. And you should know...I have the utmost respect for you. I admire the hell out of you. Surviving in the woods for so long after those assholes left you is utterly amazing."

"They didn't leave me," she blurted.

"What?"

"I hid," she admitted.

To her surprise, Talon grinned. Huge. "Good for you," he said.

"Cypress was moving The Community to Florida. I didn't want to go. I like it here. It's my home. I felt if I left...I don't know...something bad would happen. So I snuck out of our camp and hid in the woods. I know them better than anyone, since I did most of the hunting. He was mad, but I didn't come out when he yelled for me. Not even when he threatened to put me in the punishment tent for a year if he caught me. Eventually he had no choice but to leave. I stayed hidden for a long time, until I was sure no one was hiding in the old camp, waiting for me to come back. Then I went in and got some things, like the canvas I'm sleeping on, and any other supplies I could salvage."

The changing emotions on Talon's face were fascinating to watch. He went from smiling, to scowling, to his brows furrowing, to something that resembled gentleness.

"Again, you amaze me. Someone in your shoes has every right to be completely broken. I can't imagine what you've been through, and yet, here you are, brave enough to talk to a stranger and sitting there as if what you've done isn't anything special. You remind me so much of my friends' women."

Sunset tilted her head in question. "I do?" She'd always wanted a friend, but in The Community, it was frowned upon for the women to get close. If they were caught talking too much beyond what was required for chores and general camp upkeep, they were separated and punished. She'd talked more to Talon than she'd talked to anyone at one time in her entire life. She liked it. A lot.

"Yeah. Elsie's son was kidnapped by her ex-husband. He was going to kill him for insurance money. But Tony's smart, and he got away. Then Elsie put her own safety on the line by agreeing to meet with her ex, taping everything he said, so he would go to jail. I've never known anyone quite as brave as that...until now."

Once again, his compliment fed a hole in her soul she didn't even know was there. "But her son's okay?"

"He's fine. Great, actually. He's nine going on eighteen."

Sunset didn't know what that meant, but she said, "I love kids. Especially the very young ones. They're so innocent."

"You never had any?" Talon asked somewhat reluctantly. "Children?"

"No," Sunset said, looking down at her hands in her lap.

"Were there lots of children in The Community?"

"A few of the wives had babies, but most of the children in The Community were adopted by the men and brought in."

"*What?*" Talon asked.

Sunset looked up at him, surprised by the anger in his voice. "The men adopted children. Mostly girls. Sometimes boys. They were usually really young. Babies. The girls would be promised to some of the boys from the very start. They were raised knowing who they would belong to someday. But mostly the men adopted girls. The population of our group was probably seventy percent women. Which is why there were so many wives for each man."

"Bloody hell!" Talon swore.

Sunset flinched and scooted backward a little. She'd never seen Talon so obviously mad before, not even when he'd been pacing...and it scared her. Reminded her too much of Cypress and the others when she messed up and did something wrong.

Talon took a few deep breaths. "I'm sorry, sweetheart. I'm not mad at you. Do you know where these kids were adopted from?"

She shook her head.

"Of course. Because they didn't want anyone asking too many questions." He shook his head. "How come there weren't many babies born? If each of the men had several so-called wives, I would think there would be lots of pregnancies."

Sunset pressed her lips together. She wasn't sure she should tell him. It was one of the very few things the women talked about to each other. In whispers. When they were sure no one was around to hear them.

"I will never hurt you, and you can trust me," Talon said quietly, the familiar phrase comforting Sunset. "Whatever you had to do to protect yourself...I'm glad. I think deep down, you knew something wasn't right with the way you were living. And you did what you needed to do in order to keep a child from being born into that kind of situation."

He wasn't wrong. "Queen Anne's lace," she said softly.

"What?"

"It's a plant. Many times, swallowing the seeds can prevent a baby from forming. I don't know how. I would crush them up and put them in my tea. One of the older women taught me when I started bleeding the first time."

"Bloody hell," Talon said again, running a hand over his face.

Sunset sat stock still, waiting for Talon to do or say something else. She couldn't read him. Didn't know if he was mad at her, or why he seemed to be so upset by what she'd said. But he was right, after being in The Community for years, and hating it, the last thing she wanted was to have a baby. She saw how the children were raised... remembered how she herself was raised. The babies were taken away from their mothers early. The children were raised by the men. The boys taught how to take control of their women, and the girls brought up to be meek and submissive.

Sunset didn't know why she was so different. Didn't understand why she couldn't be like the other women who'd been raised by The Community. She questioned everything, and no matter how much time she'd been forced to spend in the punishment tent, she'd always been different. An outcast.

"Right, so...as I was saying, you remind me of my friends' wives and girlfriends. Bristol was kidnapped by an obsessed fan. He kept her tied to a bed in an apartment a few doors down from where Rocky lived. She didn't panic and did everything right until we could find her. Caryn used to be a firefighter in New York, she came to Fallport when her grandfather got injured by the guy who kidnapped Bristol. Another crazy man was jealous of her because she's very good at what she does, and he tried to set her on fire...but didn't succeed. And Finley—she's the one who owns a bakery in town, the one you helped save here in the forest—was *also* nearly set on fire by the woman who hired those assholes who tried to abduct her here in the woods. But she was able to get away."

Sunset stared at Talon in disbelief. "Really?"

He huffed out a breath, which kind of sounded like a laugh. "Really. They're all strong women. Survivors. And you're just like them."

Sunset frowned. She said the first thing that came to her mind. "I wasn't kidnapped."

Instead of agreeing with her, Talon just gave her a look. He was silent for so long, Sunset felt uneasy.

Eventually, he dropped his gaze from hers and said, "I was thinking about the upcoming storm."

It was an abrupt change of topic, but Sunset wasn't sorry. While she liked hearing about Talon's friends, she felt wary of the direction their conversation had gone. It felt as if she was missing something. Something big, and she hated not knowing what it was.

"And?" she said.

"I've collected the driest wood I could find, and I'll look for more, but you said your bed is made out of the canvas from one of the tents you used to live in?"

Sunset nodded.

"Your cave seems to be pretty insulated from the wind, but if the storm gets too bad, the snow will still get in. Not to mention it'll be difficult to keep the fire going. What if we found a way to attach the canvas to the mouth of the cave? It'll help keep the heat in and the snow and wind out."

Sunset's first reaction was to disagree. She loved her bed. It was lumpy and smelled kind of funky, but it was better than sleeping on the ground, like she'd done for most of her life. But the more she thought about Talon's suggestion, the more she knew it was a good idea. She should've thought of something like that herself.

"Okay." Sunset stood up to try to figure out how she was going to attach the canvas, but Talon stopped her.

"I've got it," he told her. "If you want, you can move the logs into the cave, along the back wall. That should dry them even more, so they'll smoke less when you need to use them for the fire."

Once again, Talon had surprised her. In The Community, she would've been responsible for everything. Suddenly, she realized the only reason he hadn't brought the wood in himself was because he'd promised not to step foot into her cave unless she invited him.

She picked up the canvas, trying not to be sad about losing her bed, and dragged it over to the mouth of the cave. She dropped it and stepped back, still not completely comfortable being too close to Talon. So far, he hadn't done anything to hurt her, but he could be waiting for the right chance.

"I'm not going to hurt you. You can trust me," he said gently, as he walked closer.

It really did seem like this man could read her mind.

Sunset didn't respond, just backed farther away.

It took about an hour, and Sunset couldn't help but be impressed with Talon's creativity. He didn't have any tools in his pack, but he managed to climb on top of the cave and anchor the canvas with large rocks, some of the rope he'd given to her in the past, and a lot of brute strength. She wouldn't have been able to do what he'd done, and Sunset was surprised to feel a sense of gratitude toward him. She couldn't remember the last time she was thankful for having a man around. Most of the time they were the reason for her discomfort, pain, and uneasiness. But almost everything about Talon made her feel relaxed.

She'd moved all the wood into the back of her cave as he'd suggested, then ventured into the woods to relieve herself and to find more wood and kindling. She'd returned from one of her trips back and forth with a huge armful of grass she'd pulled from the ground, a cushion for sleeping, when she saw Talon backing away from the canvas draped over the mouth of the cave.

For a split second, disappointment swamped her. She assumed as soon as her back was turned, he'd gone back on his promise not to enter her cave.

"I didn't go in. Just dropped something inside for you."

Sunset didn't believe him. He was a man, after all.

But Talon quickly backed farther away and went over to sit in his tent.

Hesitantly, Sunset drew back the corner of her newly formed "door" and looked inside the now dark tent. There was enough light coming through the opening that she could see a mound of something near where Talon had been standing. She pinned back the canvas using a rock, so she'd have light to see, and walked over to the mound.

She was confused when she saw the material Talon had spread inside his own tent, as a bed. He'd given it to her.

She walked back to the entrance and looked over at him. She didn't see more bedding spread out for himself.

"What's this?" she asked, holding up the lightweight, but surprisingly soft and fluffy material.

"My sleeping bag. Since I used your pallet to close up the cave, I gave you mine. It's rated to negative ten degrees, and I can promise it lives up to that, even though it feels thin. There's not much I can do about the hard ground, but at least you'll be warm."

Sunset frowned. She had no idea what the negative ten thing meant, but she was extremely uncomfortable about him giving her his bed. "I'm not lying with you," she blurted.

Talon stood and faced her. "I know."

"Then why...what..." Her voice trailed off.

"Because you need it. Because I took your bed. Because the upcoming storm's gonna be nasty, and I need to know you'll be comfortable and warm."

She couldn't believe she was about to say this, but she asked, "What about you?"

He smiled. The dimple flashed. "I'll be fine."

Sunset was baffled by his behavior, and yet again, she hated feeling so confused.

Talon didn't give her a chance to question him further. "Have you tried the boots on that I brought?"

She shook her head.

"Why don't you do that? You'll need them if we really do get a foot of snow like they're forecasting."

Sunset looked down at the rabbit hides she'd fashioned into shoes. She thought she'd done a damn good job of making them, and they did protect her feet from the cold ground and sharp rocks. But she couldn't deny that the thought of wearing boots was exciting. She couldn't remember the last time she had actual shoes. Again, it wasn't allowed in The Community.

She nodded at Talon, then went back into the cave. She ran a hand down the cargo pants she had on and couldn't help but smile. She loved them. She understood why the men kept the women in dresses. That way, they could touch them and have sex whenever they wanted. It was much easier. But with pants...no one could touch her between her legs quite so easily.

Not understanding her sudden impulse, Sunset picked up the boots and carried them to the cave entrance. She wanted to try on her shoes where Talon could see her.

The smile on his face when he saw her sit, boots in hand, made her feel good. It was obvious he was just as eager to watch her try them on.

"Loosen the laces," Talon instructed when she tried to shove her foot inside the boot, without any luck. "Good, like that. They'll probably feel strange at first, especially the support around your ankles. No, don't frown, it's normal for them to be hard to get on. If they were too loose, you wouldn't have the support you need when hiking."

Sunset stood and used her weight to push her foot into the boot. For a moment, she didn't think they were going to fit. The disappointment was almost overwhelming, but then her foot popped into the leather—and she looked up with a huge smile on her face.

"How does it feel?" Talon asked.

"Good," Sunset whispered in awe. And it did. The leather of the boot hugged her foot, making her feel secure and sturdy. She quickly grabbed the other boot and went through the same process to put it on. Then she stood there in her new boots and couldn't stop staring down at her feet. She had pants on. And boots. Was covered from her wrists to her feet...and it felt glorious.

"Go ahead and tie the laces," Talon told her.

The smile faded from Sunset's face. She didn't know how. Oh, she knew how to make a knot with rope, she had to do that for her traps, but she didn't think tying shoes with a knot that was almost impossible to get untied was a good idea.

"Sunset?" Talon asked from where he was standing near his tent.

She felt like crying. A memory from her before life flashed in her brain. Of her kneeling on the ground, fumbling with laces on a shoe and crying because she couldn't figure out how to do it. Then a pair of women's hands brushed hers away, and a soothing voice told her not to worry, she'd figure it out soon enough.

The vision in her head vanished almost as soon as it appeared, and Sunset felt shaken to her core.

Who was the woman? She'd spoken with such love and affection. And were the shoes hers? As far as she knew, she'd never had shoes since she'd been in The Community.

"Will you let me help you?" Talon asked gently.

Looking up, she saw him standing only about four feet in front of her, frowning.

"I promise not to hurt you. You can trust me."

What was it about those two sentences that made her feel all warm and fuzzy inside? They were just words. They meant nothing. But Sunset had a feeling that, coming from this man, they meant everything.

She nodded cautiously.

Talon took a step toward her, then went to his knees. He scooted forward until he was right in front of her. Sunset could've reached out and touched his hair, put her hand on his shoulder, but she kept her hands fisted at her sides. If he tried to grab her, she'd be ready. She hadn't lied earlier, she wasn't going to have sex with him, no matter how nice he'd been to her up until now.

But he didn't touch her. Didn't grab her hips and try to force her to the ground. He merely reached for the laces of her boots. He tightened them and then looked up at her. "Cross the two laces over each other. Poke one end under the other like you're making a knot, but only do it once. The easiest way to do this next part is to make two loops with the laces, like this." He demonstrated once, then again. "Think of them as bunny ears. Then cross the bunny ears over each other, again, like you did before. But keep the loops intact. Now pull them tight. Voila! Shoes are tied. Now...you try it."

He undid the lace by pulling on one of the ends and it came apart in less than a second.

Talon stood up and took a few steps back, giving her room, which Sunset appreciated. Heck, she was beginning to appreciate everything this man did. It was a strange but not unwelcome feeling.

She leaned over and fumbled with the laces, trying to emulate what Talon had just done. To her frustration, she couldn't quite get the hang of it. The stupid loops wouldn't cooperate, making her want to cry again.

"May I help?"

Sunset dropped the laces and nodded.

He went to his knees again and came toward her. It was weird to see a man on his knees in front of her. That was so not what she was used to.

"Try again," he ordered.

He was close enough once again to touch, and this time, when she took the laces in her hands, his were there to guide her.

It was the first time she'd been touched since her last night of sex with Cypress. But Talon's hands were far more gentle than Cypress's had ever been. There were calluses on his palms, just as there were on hers. She could smell his earthy, musky scent, as well as a hint of the same clean scent that had been on her sweatshirt when she'd first pulled it over her head. It was a comforting smell, and that more than anything had Sunset relaxing as she concentrated on tying her shoe.

"That's it, like that. Good job! I think you're ready for the advanced lesson. Pull on that lace...see how easy it was to untie?"

Sunset nodded.

"Right, now tie it again. Just like that. But now, cross the bunny ears again."

"Into a knot?" she asked.

"Yeah, but not too tight. Now, pull on the lace...see how it doesn't come undone easily? That will help when you're hiking to make sure the laces don't accidentally come apart. As long as you don't pull them terribly tight, you can get them undone. Go on, try it."

She did, and was delighted to find that tying the bunny ears twice didn't make it impossible to untie. She internally rolled her eyes at calling the laces bunny ears, but it did seem to make it easier to figure out what she was doing.

Talon backed up once more, but stayed on his knees as she tied the second boot. When she was done, she once more stared for a long moment. It was hard to come to terms with the fact that she was looking at her feet. In boots.

Talon leaned forward and hesitated with his hand over her boot for a moment. "Can I check the fit?"

There he went again, asking permission to touch her. It was another foreign concept. "Yes."

He pressed on the end of the boot, and she could feel his touch through the leather against her big toe. "Not bad," he said with satisfaction. "Try walking with them, see how they feel."

Sunset stepped sideways, away from Talon, and took a few steps around the area.

"So?" he asked.

The boots felt strange. As if they were strangling her feet. But at the same time, her feet were warm, and even when she purposely stepped on a rock, she didn't even feel it. The leaves crunched under her feet, making her steps louder than when she wore the rabbit hide, but she didn't even care. "They're good," she said, smiling shyly at him.

"I was worried, but I'm glad I got the size right." Talon stood and wiped his hands on his pants. "I need to see what I can find us for food. I've got plenty of freeze-dried rations, but I have a feeling they'll get old fast if the storm lasts too long."

Sunset blinked. *He* was going to go hunting?

"I'll do it," she said.

"Nope. You stay here."

Sunset frowned. It was an odd thing to feel relieved and happy that she didn't have to go hunting, but at the same time, kind of upset that he wasn't allowing her to do so.

Talon sighed. "I know you *can* do it. I'm perfectly aware that you don't need me to help you. You've proven that all too clearly in the last year. But I *want* to. I *like* doing things for you. It makes me feel good to provide for you. You can stay here, get used to your boots, arrange your space the way you want with your new things and maybe even find some more rocks to hold down the canvas here on the ground. If the wind gets going, it'll need to be anchored firmly. Or if you want, you can just relax and read the book I brought for you."

"I'm not good at reading," she said. "Women weren't allowed to read or write."

Talon pressed his lips together for a moment. "Then when I get back, I can read to you if you'd like. Or I can help with any words you don't know."

Sunset stared at the man in front of her. The first reaction when she'd woken up—was that just this morning?—was to be scared of his size and what he would do to her. But the longer she was around him, the more she realized he was one hundred percent different from any man she'd ever known. He really did seem to want to do things for her, instead of making her wait on him. It was awkward... but she didn't hate it.

"Okay."

"Okay?" he asked. "You'll stay here while I go find us something to eat?"

She nodded.

"Thank you," he said in a low, earnest tone.

That was another thing. Had any man ever thanked her before? If so, she couldn't remember.

With that, Talon turned to go back to his tent. He pulled out the satellite phone and walked toward her. "Take this. If I don't come back, or if the storm gets too scary, push the button that looks like a star, then the number one. That will connect you with Ethan. He'll come and help you."

"He knows where I am?" she asked.

Talon looked reluctant to answer, but he finally said, "There's a tracker in the phone. It's expensive, so if we ever dropped the phone in the woods or lost it, the trackers allow us to retrieve it. And it helps us find each other easily during an active search."

Sunset wasn't sure she liked people knowing where she

was, but she nodded and reached for the phone. Their fingers brushed...and tingles shot down her arm.

It startled her so badly, she almost dropped the phone.

Talon stared at her in surprise for a long moment, as if he'd felt the same thing she had, but he eventually turned and went back to his tent. He reached inside his pack and pulled out one of the silver bags he said was freeze-dried food, and a coil of thin rope. He smiled at her and said, "I've found that critters can't resist the sausage. It tastes like shit to me, but who am I to judge?" With that, he winked and set off into the woods. "I shouldn't be too long. I'm thinking the animals around here are very aware of the coming storm and will be happy to find some food to bring back to their dens. Stay safe while I'm gone."

And then he vanished. Fading into the woods around them as if he was born there.

Sunset looked down at the phone in her hands and was suddenly scared to death that she'd push a wrong button or drop and break it. She went into her cave and carefully placed it on the ground toward the back of the space. Then she spread out the material Talon had given her, and pulled the things he'd brought for her closer so she could inspect them more carefully.

She smelled the lotion and hair stuff, and tried to run the brush through her long hair. That turned out to be impossible with all the tangles. Shrugging, she put the brush aside. She longed to cut her hair, but so far hadn't gotten the courage to do so. It was prohibited for women to cut their hair, and the punishment she'd been given a few years ago when she'd decided to cut off just the ends with a knife was still fresh in her mind. Cypress had been the one to wield the whip, and he'd taken great pleasure in making sure she understood that her body wasn't her own. The men were in charge, and she had to follow their rules.

It had taken months for the whip marks to heal, and in the meantime, she'd still been responsible for her regular duties. She hadn't dared to touch her hair since.

Sunset grabbed the book Talon had brought and stared at it for a long while. It felt daring and somewhat scary to even hold the thing. In The Community, doing this would get her whipped just as badly as or worse than when she'd cut her hair.

But she wasn't in The Community anymore. She was on her own and could make her own decisions. With that thought in mind, she opened the cover and turned to chapter one.

CHAPTER SIX

Tal was relieved when he was able to catch three rabbits without too much difficulty. He made his way back to the cave, praying Sunset hadn't left. He didn't think she would, but at this point, he didn't want to make any assumptions.

He hadn't lied when he'd told her he thought she was amazing. She was so bloody strong, it was scary. She didn't need him, or anyone, to survive. She'd been doing just fine on her own. But it made him want to cry—or fucking kill the men who ran that cult she was forced to join—when she struggled with something most kids easily understood. Like tying her shoes. Or reading. Or knowing what a cell phone was. On one hand, she was knowledgeable about things most people had no clue about, and on the other, she was as naïve as a small child.

His gut soured when she'd explained what marriage meant to her. And to hear her talk about children being "adopted" and brought into the cult almost made him puke. Every single man in that cult should be arrested for child abuse, kidnapping, rape, and probably dozens of other charges. Tal had no doubt they were stealing children to bring to the cult. They were raising boys to be rapists and polygamists as well. Everything Sunset had survived made him equal parts devastated and more impressed.

He *hated* the way she tensed whenever he got too close. Or how she'd assumed he went back on his word and entered the cave without being invited. Coming right out and telling him she wouldn't sleep with him made him proud of her, yet bloody well furious that she even had to concern herself with such a thing.

He didn't care how many times he had to remind her that he wouldn't hurt her, that she could trust him. He'd repeat it every day, every hour, until his last breath if necessary. No one would hurt this woman ever again. Not on his watch.

It was an insane thing to think, because there was no guarantee she'd agree to come back to Fallport. And if she did, if she was really Heather Brown—with every minute that passed, he was more and more certain she was—she had parents who would be overjoyed by a reunion with their long-lost daughter. Yes, they'd moved away and then divorced, but they would surely still want their daughter to move wherever they'd relocated.

The thought of Sunset moving away made his heart hurt, but Tal pushed the feeling down. She was an adult, and he was honored to have this chance to get to know her. If he could help her assimilate back into society, not the fucked-up way of life the bloody cult had taught her, he'd be satisfied.

Trying to ignore the voice inside that told him he was full of shit, Tal walked back to the cave. When he arrived, he was somewhat alarmed not to see or hear Sunset.

"Hello?" he called out.

Within seconds, Sunset's head peered around the canvas door he'd fashioned. "You're back."

"I am," he said with a grin. Holding up the three rabbits he'd attached to a sturdy stick, he said, "And with food."

"Yum!" she exclaimed.

For a split second, Tal envisioned the same scene years from now. They were on a camping trip with their kids and Sunset was welcoming him back to their campsite and eager to show their children what their father had brought them to eat.

But then reality set in. This wasn't a fantasy, and he and Sunset didn't have a future together.

"I'm thinking we should probably cook the meat up tonight, before the weather gets too bad," he said.

"I agree," Sunset said, walking toward him hesitantly. "I'll do it."

Tal wanted to protest, wanted to be the one to prepare her meal. But he didn't want to take away any of her hard-won independence. He simply nodded and handed over the rabbits. The smile on her face made his decision worth it.

She quickly set about skinning the small animals. She set their pelts aside and had a larger fire going outside the cave in an impressively short amount of time. By the time they sat down to eat, fat snowflakes had begun to lazily fall from the sky.

As he ate, Tal spoke about nothing and everything. He told Sunset about Fallport, about the citizens he'd gotten to know over the years. He recounted more stories about Tony and about all the men on his team, and their women. She didn't ask many questions, but he could see the interest in her eyes.

He was running out of things to talk about when he finally resorted to telling her about his job at the barbershop.

"When I got to Fallport, I wasn't sure what I was going to do. My job with the search and rescue team is great, I was excited about it, but I knew it wouldn't take up all my time. It's kind of hit or miss. There are some months when we're extremely busy, especially in the summer, but there are other times when we might not get called out for thirty days or more. I knew I needed something to occupy me. Back in England, I was the go-to guy on long-term missions to trim my buddies' hair. So I went into the barbershop on the square and asked Harvey—he's the guy who owns the shop—if he needed any help. I have to give him credit for hiring me, not only a newcomer to town, but a foreigner at that, with no professional experience. I don't work full time, but I do enjoy talking to the men, and the occasional women, who come into the shop."

Sunset stared at him for a moment. "You cut hair?"

Tal wanted to chuckle. Wasn't that what he'd just explained? But when he thought about it for a moment, he realized she might not understand what a barber was. He just smiled and said, "Yup."

She looked down at her now empty plate, the one he'd brought her, then at the fire, then off into the forest. Tal didn't think she was going to get up the courage to ask whatever it was she was thinking...but then he saw her square her shoulders and knew she'd overcome her embarrassment or shyness to ask what she wanted to know.

"Will you cut my hair?"

Tal blinked in surprise. "What?"

"I know women are supposed to have long hair but...I don't like it."

"Women can have whatever length hair they want," Tal countered gently. "Wait until you meet Caryn. She keeps her hair cut *very* short. Says it gets in her way if it's long."

"Really?"

"Yes." Tal hesitated before asking what he was thinking, but in the end decided to just be blunt. "How come you haven't cut it yourself?"

She sighed. "I did once. Just a little bit off the ends. Cypress noticed, and he whipped me as a warning to the other women. We weren't allowed to cut our hair. Ever."

Anger threatened to overcome Tal. The life this woman, and everyone else in that damn cult, had endured was more than abusive. It was bloody sadistic. He took a deep breath in through his nose, praying for calm and the right words to help this woman.

"I don't have any scissors here," he finally said.

Sunset's lips pressed together, and she nodded.

"But I can use my knife. You can trust me, and I won't hurt you."

"I think I'm beginning to believe that," she said softly.

Tal's belly clenched at her admission. No one's words had ever affected him so deeply.

"But...maybe I shouldn't. I mean, I've always had long hair...it's just hard to keep clean and it gets in my way a lot. I appreciate the hair ties you gave me but...I just don't know."

She sounded so unsure when just a moment ago, it seemed as if she was all for chopping off her hair. But the more Tal thought about it, the more he realized she might want to have shorter hair, but the repercussion of what happened last time was obviously still fresh in her mind.

"How about we take things slow. We can start with taking off just a little bit. Maybe the length of the tip of your finger. Then tomorrow we'll see how you feel, and if you wish, we'll do that again. We can continue to take it slow until you're comfortable with the length. It's just hair, Sunset. It'll grow back if you hate it short. And if you decide we're going *too* slow, and you want me to cut more off, we can do that too. Your hair is gorgeous. Absolutely stunning. It reminds me of the beautiful sunsets back home in England. But you're no longer under their thumb. If you want to wear pants, cut your hair, and sleep on a comfortable bed, do it."

Sunset stared at him intensely the entire time he was speaking, and Tal couldn't tear his gaze from hers. There was so much emotion swirling through her eyes.

"I want it shorter…but I'm scared."

Tal was so damn proud of her. The men she'd lived with, and had probably been kidnapped by, hadn't broken her. They'd tried, that was obvious, but by some miracle, she'd been able to retain a shred of independence. She wouldn't have been able to survive the last year alone in the woods if she didn't have a spine of steel.

"You can trust me," Tal repeated softly. "Your hair is your own. Your body is your own. You have the right to decide what to wear, or eat, or say, or who to have sex with. *No one* should force you to do anything you don't want to."

He saw tears swim in her eyes, but she beat them back. "Okay."

"Okay what?" Tal asked.

"Okay, I want to do what you said. Cut a little bit of my hair today. And tomorrow. And the next day."

"So damn brave," Tal muttered, then nodded.

She looked surprised. "You think I'm brave?"

"Hell yes," he said.

"I'm not, you know," she said, as if she was commenting on the weather.

"You're wrong," Tal told her bluntly.

Sunset shook her head. "I wanted to go to town, but it was forbidden. And I've heard so many stories about how the people there don't like outsiders. How they'd hurt me if I dared show my face. I've wanted to cut my hair for the last year, but didn't have the guts to do it myself. I saw a bear a couple of months ago and it scared me so badly, I came back here and hid in my cave for days. I'm not brave, Talon."

Tal wanted to hug this woman so bloody much, but he forced himself to stay right where he was. Though he did lean forward as he spoke. "You've been fed a pack of lies for twenty years, sweetheart. The men you lived with were abusers, plain and simple. They told you lies to control you and the other women. How were you to know what they were doing was wrong? You were simply trying to protect yourself by not going to town or cutting your hair. It's called self-preservation. And the bear? Bloody hell, *anyone* would be scared to come face-to-face with one."

"Including you?" she asked quietly.

"Yes. Where I come from, there aren't any bears. I saw one when I was in Russia once...I thought it was cute until it rose up on its back legs and roared at me. I swear I pissed my pants. My mates all laughed their arses off and said they'd never seen anyone move as fast as I did to get away from it. Self-preservation isn't a bad thing. In fact, it's *the* most important trait to have as far as I'm concerned. That feeling deep down inside you that says 'not a good idea' or 'don't go that way' or 'stay quiet and don't look him in the eye,' has probably saved your life more than once."

Sunset looked at him as if he was giving her the keys to her freedom. She slowly nodded.

"Right, so no more talk about you not being brave. Okay?"

Her lips turned up in a small smile. "Okay."

"Good. Now, how about I clean up our meal, then I'll cut a teeny-tiny bit off your hair. After that, you can settle in for the night before this storm ramps up."

"I can clean up," she said, looking worried.

"I know you can. But so can I. Let me take care of you, Sunset. Please."

Yet again, she looked startled by his words.

"I'm thinking no one has taken care of you in a very long time. Give me this gift, sweetheart," Tal said softly. He was relieved when she gave him a small nod.

The snow was still falling but Tal ignored it as he picked up the pan she'd used to cook the rabbit and headed for the stream. He brought along the bucket as well to refill it. He had a feeling once the storm fully moved in, neither of them would be going anywhere.

He returned and saw Sunset sitting on his sleeping bag with the Narnia book in her lap. She was staring at it, and her lips were moving silently. She hadn't heard him return, so he cleared his throat to avoid startling her too badly.

Her head came up, and she gave him another small smile.

Tal felt as if he'd been given the best gift in the world, seeing her welcoming expression. He placed the bucket of water near the entrance to her cave. She still hadn't invited him in, and he wasn't going to push the issue. He'd be okay in his small tent. He'd weathered storms in it before, he'd be fine with this one too.

"Are you enjoying it?" Tal asked, nodding to the book in her lap.

She sighed and looked down. "It's hard."

Tal wanted to kick his own ass. He hadn't even thought about her not being able to read. If this *was* Heather, she was in the third grade when she'd disappeared, old enough to read, but if the cult she was taken by hadn't wanted the women to read or write, it had been twenty years since she'd seen a book.

As if she didn't want to offend him, she added, "But of what I can understand, it's good so far."

"You want me to read it to you?" Tal offered. He belatedly realized the offer might not be the best idea. He wasn't a reading-aloud kind of guy, and he didn't want her to feel bad about not being able to read and understand it herself.

But she surprised him by enthusiastically asking, "You wouldn't mind?"

"Not at all," Tal said. "If it's okay with you, I want to move my tent closer to the entrance to your cave. If it does start snowing hard, I want to be able to hear you if you need anything. And you'll be able to hear me better too."

She bit her lip and looked back down at the book in her lap.

"No pressure, Sunset. I'm not going to enter your space. I won't hurt you. You can trust me."

Her shoulders straightened in that telltale way she had, and she looked up at him. "Okay."

"Thank you, sweetheart." Tal knew he should probably stop calling her that, but the word just kept popping out. "Give me a few minutes and we'll get started."

It didn't take him long to move his tent, and while the

ground was a bit harder near the mouth of the cave, it seemed more protected from the wind that had started to pick up in the last hour or so, thanks to the surrounding trees. He staked his tent down and pulled out his high-powered flashlight and made sure he had his stove handy for later. It was useful for cooking food, but it would also provide heat for his small tent when the snow really started to fly.

He had a couple extra emergency blankets, and he spread one on the ground before walking over to the entrance of the cave. Not entering, he said, "If you come and sit out here, I'll get the first hair trim out of the way, then we can read."

While he'd been getting situated, Sunset had moved her own bed to one side of the cave nearer to the open canvas flap. He wanted to tell her to move it back to the farthest corner, where she'd be more protected against the elements, but he refrained.

He was glad to see no reticence in her movements as she stood and walked closer. She sat a few feet away from where he was, then scooted backward toward him.

Her back was ramrod straight, and he could see and feel the tension in her body. Tal pulled his razor-sharp knife out of the sheath at his thigh and lowered to his knees behind her. He'd much prefer to do this with the high-quality scissors Harvey had at the shop, but he'd make do.

"I'm not going to hurt you, and you can trust me," he reminded her softly as he reached for a lock of her hair. As he did, he immediately realized this wasn't going to work. Her beautiful but listless red hair was in countless tangles hanging down her back.

"Will you let me brush it first?" he asked quietly.

If anything, Sunset's body got even tenser. She didn't turn her head as she shook it and said, "It hurts."

Tal closed his eyes in frustration and fury. Those fucking men who'd abused her needed to die. A slow, painful death. He swallowed hard and took a deep breath before saying, "Not the way I do it, it won't."

He waited patiently, not rushing her as she considered his words. Then she moved forward and stood, walking over to her things stashed against the back wall of the cave. She pulled out the brush he'd given her and walked back toward him. She looked as if she'd rather be anywhere else, and she was obviously dreading this.

She sat back down after handing the brush to Tal and squeezed her hands together in her lap, focusing her stare on the back wall of the cave. He wanted to reassure her again, tell her that he'd be careful, but he knew actions spoke louder than words, so he picked up a small lock of her hair and went to work on the ends, careful to hold her hair tightly so there was absolutely no pressure on her scalp as he worked.

After a moment, Tal saw her shoulders relax a fraction when she realized no pain was forthcoming. With every tangle he was able to brush out, she relaxed even more.

It took a while, but eventually he was able to tenderly run the brush through her hair from her scalp all the way to the ends. She'd closed her eyes at one point and tipped her head back as he worked.

Tal had never thought brushing a woman's hair could be so...intimate. He continued to run the brush through her hair long after he'd gotten the tangles out. As the light began to fade, the snow continued to fall, and the early evening got even colder, he knew he needed to get this done. Reluctantly, he put down the brush and picked up his knife. They hadn't spoken while he was brushing her hair, but the silence wasn't awkward in the least. It felt...comfortable.

Very carefully, Tal cut off the ends of her hair. As he'd promised, he only took off about half an inch. He gathered the hair in his hand and held it out to her when he finished, so she could see. "All done," he said.

Sunset looked down at his hand, then twisted her neck to look at him. He couldn't read her expression, but he saw her hand shaking as she lifted it to his. Tal put the hair in her hand, and she sat there and stared at it for a long moment.

"It didn't hurt," she whispered.

"What didn't?" Tal asked.

"You...brushing my hair. Every time Arrow made one of his other wives brush it, it always hurt."

Fucking assholes she'd lived with.

"I told you, I won't ever hurt you. Whether it's simply brushing your hair or using words as weapons...I won't do it. And I won't let anyone else hurt you either."

She sighed and looked back down at the ends of her hair. "You really don't care if I cut my hair?" she asked next.

"It's *your* hair, sweetheart. You can do whatever you'd like with it."

"I don't want to be ugly," she whispered, still not looking at him.

Tal wanted to put his finger under her chin and force her to meet his gaze, but he curled his hands into fists instead. "You could *never* be ugly," he said a little too force-fully, taking a breath to try to control his anger.

"They said short hair is ugly," she argued.

"They were bloody wankers who took delight in

crushing others under their thumbs," Tal retorted, the words bursting from his mouth. "They were abusive assholes who took delight in raping defenseless women and children, and pretending it was normal to have six fucking wives. Hair doesn't make someone ugly, Sunset. Neither does the clothes someone wears or the size of their bodies. *Actions* do. And the actions of those you were forced to live with were not only ugly, they were repulsive, criminal, and downright *wrong*." There was so much more Tal wanted to say, but he knew he needed to calm down before he scared the woman.

He stood and stalked away from the cave, not knowing where he was going, just that he needed to get his fury under control.

He didn't go far, and he didn't stay away for long. He was drawn to Sunset like she was the air he needed to breathe. He didn't understand it but didn't want to analyze the feeling. It just was.

"I'm sorry," he said when he returned. Sunset was still sitting, now facing the forest near the front of the cave. She had her arms wrapped around her legs and didn't seem to even notice the snow that was building up on her boot-clad toes.

"You're the first man who has ever apologized to me," she said almost conversationally. "In The Community, the men were always right. Their word was law. Even when they messed something up, they claimed it was on purpose...to teach us women a lesson."

Her words weren't helping Tal calm down any.

"I always thought something was wrong. That it wasn't right how the women and girls were treated. But I couldn't do anything about it. It was my life, and I was stuck there. Thank you for being honest with me. Thank you for finally saying the things I'd always thought deep in my heart."

She was killing him. "You're free of them," Tal told her.

The chuckle that came from her throat wasn't a humorous one. "I'll never be free of them," she said.

"Wrong," Tal told her. "You already are. You've seen through their bullshit and the best thing you can do to make sure they get what's coming to them is to tell your story. With no shame. Because what happened to you, how they treated you, that wasn't your fault. It was all on them. They took advantage of you and abused you for years. Getting away from them and living your life the way you've always been meant to is the best revenge. Show them that they might've held you down for a while, but they have no control over you now. You're stronger than their mind control, and you've come out the other side."

"You make me want to believe you," she said softly.

"Good. I'm not saying it'll be easy. They'll be there in the back of your mind, trying to pull you back. But you're strong enough to push their evil words away and come out of your shell."

Sunset tilted her head as she stared at him. "How do you know?"

Tal nodded at the small pile of hair he'd cut from her head, which was now sitting by her side, and said, "Because of that. You were scared to let me cut your hair, but you did it anyway. It's things like that, choosing for yourself and acting, even when you hear those voices in your head telling you it's wrong, or that you'll be punished."

Sunset looked down at the small pile of hair, then up at him. "You're right."

"I know."

The smile on her lips was more genuine now. "Are all men like you?" she asked. "I mean...outside The Community?"

Tal sighed. "I'm not sure what you mean, but if you're asking are all men as supportive and encouraging toward women, the answer is no. There are just as many assholes out in the regular world as there were in the damn cult you lived in. But the good news is, now you know how to identify them. If anyone tries to force you to do anything, you tell them to fuck off and walk in the opposite direction. And I'll teach you to defend yourself. So if any of those assholes try to use their strength against you, you can fight back effectively."

Tal was practically growling by the time he finished speaking, but the thought of anyone touching this woman against her will made him feel downright feral.

To his surprise, she wasn't frightened of what he was saying. She nodded instead. "Can I wear a knife like you do?" she asked, looking at the sheath strapped to his thigh.

Tal chuckled. "If you want, sure. Although there are laws about being armed in some establishments."

She merely shrugged.

If wearing a knife made her feel safer, Tal would absolutely not only teach her how to use it, but he'd buy her a hundred knives and sheathes to wear.

"Do you still want to read?" she asked.

"Yes," Tal said. He was tired, and heavy emotions still swam in his veins, but if this woman wanted him to read to her, that was what he'd do.

Reaching behind her, Sunset picked up the book and held it out to him. Tal stepped forward and took it, then backed up once more. There was about half an inch of snow on the ground, and, with the way it was still falling, by the time they woke up tomorrow it would be much higher.

He unzipped his tent and scooted inside. He lay down on his belly with his head at the entrance. Looking up, he saw that Sunset had scooted backward until she was sitting on the sleeping bag he'd given her.

"Can you hear me?" he asked.

She nodded.

Tal cleared his throat and began to read.

CHAPTER SEVEN

Sunset woke up slowly the next morning. Tal had read to her for quite a while before he brought the book back over to the mouth of her cave and told her to close up the canvas and get some sleep.

She'd agreed, but she felt guilty about Talon being outside in the blowing snow and wind in his tent, while she was inside the cave. She wasn't ready to share her space though. It was *hers*, and it had been a long time since anything was solely her own.

I won't hurt you and you can trust me.

His words echoed in her head, and while she wanted to believe him, her history had taught her that no man was trustworthy.

As she lay inside the padding he'd given her, Sunset recalled the way he'd brushed her hair. He hadn't yanked at the tangles. Had been extremely careful and worked through them methodically and gently. And when he'd run the brush through the strands from the top of her head all the way to the ends, it had felt so good. Relaxing even.

For the first time in her life, she'd fully let down her guard around a man.

She realized with a start that even though her brain was telling her Talon wasn't to be trusted, that she'd just met him and he probably had an agenda, her heart believed differently.

Sighing, hating how confused she was, Sunset pulled the book over to her and turned on the flashlight Talon had given her. She aimed it at the book and began to slowly try to make her way through the pages. It helped now that Talon had already read them and she knew the story. All of the words weren't familiar, but she was proud when she was able to muddle through the first chapter on her own.

She fell asleep again, dreaming of Aslan and hearing Talon's unique-sounding voice in her head. But she woke up to the sound of the wind screaming outside. Her nose was cold where it was sticking out of the bedding and when she sat up, she shivered. The cave was cold, but not as cold as it would've been without the canvas he'd insisted on tacking up over the mouth of the entrance.

Grabbing a log, Sunset put it on the fire and stoked it, satisfied when the flames caught and a bit of warmth began to spread through her small space.

Grateful for the leggings, pants, and sweatshirt, she crawled to the edge of the cave and lifted the canvas to peek outside. She blinked in surprise at the sight that greeted her. There was white as far as the eye could see. And it was still falling. Snow had built up against the canvas from the wind, and she could barely make out Talon's tent, even though it wasn't that far from where she was kneeling.

"Talon?" she called out.

When she didn't hear him respond, anxiety spiked. She didn't need him, she was perfectly safe here in her cave for as long as the storm lasted, but for some reason she didn't like the thought of him being in that little tent. It didn't seem very sturdy.

As soon as she had that thought, a gust of wind blew through and she watched as the material of the tent fluttered violently. "Talon? Are you okay?" she said a little louder.

"I'm good. Stay in the cave. Keep warm!" he called back.

Sunset bit her lip, torn about what to do. The *right* thing to do would be to invite him inside with her. But she didn't want him to get any ideas. Didn't want to find out he was just like Cypress.

I won't hurt you and you can trust me.

"Talon...the storm is too bad for you to be out there. Come into the cave."

The words came out of her mouth before she could stop them. For a moment, she wanted to take them back. The cave wasn't huge, and having Talon in there might be too much for her. He might take back the bedding he'd given her, or start ordering her around, or try to touch her. He would take away the independence she'd fought so hard for.

But then she shook her head. She hadn't known Talon very long, but she'd watched him in the forest without his knowledge. She'd never seen him do anything to hurt others. He treated the women he rescued with respect, even when they were mean to him.

Then she thought about how Brock had been with Finley. He'd protected her when they were under that rock. He'd put his body between her and the forest.

"Are you sure?"

Sunset jerked in surprise at Talon's words. She'd been so lost in her head, she'd forgotten where she was. Looking out into the blinding white of the forest, she saw he'd unzipped his tent a fraction and was looking at her.

"Because I'm okay in here," he went on.

He didn't look okay. He looked tired. Sunset wondered if he'd slept at all.

"I'm sure. It doesn't look like it's going to stop anytime soon. There was a storm years ago much like this and we were all stuck in our tents for at least a week before the wind stopped enough that we could walk around. We shoveled for ages just to get from tent to tent."

Sunset remembered that storm like it was yesterday. She'd been delighted to have seven full days to herself. She didn't have to cook for anyone. Or clean. Or hunt. She'd simply hunkered down in a tent with Arrow's other wives and relaxed. Of course, when the wind calmed, she and the other women were in charge of shoveling paths, and she had to do her wifely duties with Arrow the second the snow stopped, but it had been worth it to have an entire week of down time.

"Okay. I'm going to pack up my things and take the tent down. In the meantime, close the canvas and stay inside," Talon told her.

Instead of being irritated at him telling her what to do, Sunset merely nodded and dropped the canvas. She realized the difference was that Talon was ordering her to do something for her own good. He wasn't ordering her to go outside and get his stuff together and take down his tent. It was a huge difference, and it felt surprisingly good that he was worried about her when *he* was the one out in the storm.

It didn't take long before Talon appeared at the entrance to the cave. He pulled back the canvas and entered. His head and beard were covered in snow, and it stuck to his clothes as well. He put his bag and the folded tent down near the entrance and sat almost right where he'd entered. He resecured the canvas and sighed.

Sunset sat tensely on her bedding, waiting for him to do something. To start ordering her around, to ask what she was making him for breakfast...*something*. But all he did was sit there with his eyes closed. The snow eventually melted from his face and clothes, and yet still he sat there almost motionless.

If she didn't know better, she would've said he was asleep, but there was no way he could sleep upright...could he? "Talon?" she whispered.

"Yeah?" he said immediately, but didn't open his eyes.

Sunset didn't really have a question to ask, just wanted to know if he was awake or not.

His eyes opened and he stared at her from across the space. The cave was dim, the light from the fire flickering around them. The wind whistled outside and Sunset was once more very glad for the extra protection the canvas gave her. She wouldn't have thought to use it as a type of door if Talon hadn't suggested it. She'd been all right the winter before in her cave, but there hadn't been any blizzards like this one last year.

"You okay?" Talon asked. "You want me to go back outside in my tent?"

"No!" she blurted. "I just..." Her voice trailed off.

"I understand," Talon said calmly. "You can trust me, and I'm not going to hurt you."

Sunset blew out a breath. "Are you sick of saying that yet?" she asked.

"No. And I never will be. I'll keep saying it until you believe it with your heart and soul, and then I'll probably *still* keep saying it. Thank you for inviting me inside."

Sunset nodded. Her throat was tight and she didn't think she could speak.

"May I get up and put another log on the fire?"

He was asking *her*? Sunset felt off-kilter, but she nodded.

Slowly, Talon got up and walked past her to the pile of wood they'd collected the day before. He frowned as he studied it. "On second thought, I think I'll wait. Not sure how long this storm is going to last and I don't want to run out of fuel." Then he looked at her. "Are you warm enough?"

Sunset nodded.

He walked back to his pack and rummaged through it for a moment. He pulled something out, a small packet, and squeezed it in his hands before holding it out to her. "Here."

She reached out without thought and took it from him. "What is it?"

"A hand warmer. A little packet that uses chemicals to heat up. It'll last for a few hours before the heat dissipates. It'll help keep you warm without having to use a lot of the wood right now."

Surprisingly, the packet in her hands *did* begin to warm, and Sunset's eyes widened. "It's like magic," she breathed.

Talon chuckled as he sat once more by the entrance. "I totally agree. And don't ask me how it works, because I have no idea. Just that it's full of chemicals and I was more than grateful for them last night." He tapped his boot and said, "Put one in each shoe last night and my toes thank me for it today."

Now that her eyes had adjusted back to the dim light of the cave after being blinded by the snow outside, Sunset could see the dark circles under his eyes. "You look tired," she blurted.

"I'm okay," he said with a shrug.

It was another way this man differed from those she'd known in the past. Arrow took a lot of naps. Didn't think twice about sleeping while his wives were working. Cypress was just like him. But Sunset had a feeling this man would never sleep while those around him were busy working.

"Do you mind if I change my shirt?" Talon asked. "Mine's damp, and I don't want to risk getting sick."

Adrenaline coursed through Sunset. She shook her head silently, but didn't dare take her gaze from Talon. She clutched the hot packet in her hands and held her breath as her heart beat hard in her chest.

Talon rummaged in his pack and pulled out a long-sleeve shirt. He turned his back and took off the fleece he was wearing, then the sweatshirt, then the skin-tight black shirt. She couldn't help but wonder at the differences between this man and the ones she'd lived with. Cypress and Arrow weren't nearly as lean as Talon. They had pasty-white skin and large bellies that stuck out. Talon's shoulders were broad, and it didn't look like he had any extra fat on his body. She could see the muscles in his upper back ripple as he moved. Even his forearms were muscular.

All too soon, he'd covered himself up with another tight shirt that clung to his body. He also replaced the sweatshirt with another and donned his fleece before spreading the damp clothes on the ground near the fire.

Then he sat once more with his back against the cave

wall. "Feel like listening to more of *The Lion, the Witch, and the Wardrobe?*" he asked.

Sunset nodded. She still felt weird inside. Not scared exactly, more like...excited? It didn't make any sense. She'd been afraid when Talon had taken off his shirt. Scared he was going to want to lie on top of her, but he hadn't even looked her way.

Maybe...just maybe...she *could* trust him.

She tossed the book over to Talon, careful not to get it anywhere near the flames. He smiled at her, opened it, and immediately picked up from where they'd stopped the night before.

Time had no meaning as Sunset got lost in the world of Narnia and Aslan the lion. The wind continued to shriek outside. Trips out to do their business were quick, and she didn't even feel awkward about needing to see to her bodily functions around Talon. He made everything feel easy and normal.

He was in the middle of a chapter when he stopped and said, "Bloody hell, I almost forgot!"

Sunset was confused when he started searching in his pack. He pulled out the satellite phone and gave her a small smile. "Rocky's wedding. I promised to call."

"Will it work?" Sunset asked.

Talon wrinkled his brow. "I sure as hell hope so. Otherwise I'm in deep shit."

He dialed the phone and put it on speaker once more.

"You don't have to do that," she said quickly.

"I want you to hear what a wedding ceremony is *supposed* to be like," Talon countered, just as someone answered.

"It's about time," a deep male voice said.

Talon chuckled. "Hello to you too, Brock."

"We had a bet going on if you were going to forget to call or not."

"No way would I forget something this important." Talon winked at Sunset and put his finger to his lips, as if asking her to keep quiet about how he *had* almost forgotten to call. She gave him a small smile.

"Hi, Tal," a feminine voice said into the phone.

"Got you on speaker," Brock told him.

"Hey, Finley," Talon said.

"Is she there?"

"Yes."

"Her name's Sunset, right?" Finley asked.

"Yes."

"Hi, Sunset," Finley said immediately. "I'm Finley Mabrey. I'm the one you saved when you threw dirt in that jerk's face, the one who was holding me at knife-point. Thank you so much. Seriously, you were so badass, and I was scared out of my mind. You ran through that clearing like Wonder Woman or something. It was amazing, and you gave Brock enough time to grab me and get us out of there. I can't tell you how appreciative I am."

"I think you just did," Brock said with a chuckle.

Sunset sat stock still as she listened to the other woman's praise. Again, she was so unused to people thanking her for anything, she felt uncomfortable. She didn't know what to say or how to react.

"Right, well, I want to make sure you know that what you did was so brave and amazing. I hope I get to meet you soon," Finley went on. "I'm gonna make you my super-special snickerdoodle caramel cake. I don't make it a lot because it's kind of a pain in the butt, but it's sooooo good. It tastes exactly like a snickerdoodle, but in a cake instead of a cookie."

"Wait, how come you haven't made that for me yet?" Brock asked his wife.

"Because. Didn't you hear me? It's a pain to make and the cookies are a heck of a lot easier to whip up. And I want to make something special for Sunset, since she literally saved our lives."

"Right, fine. I can understand that," Brock said.

Sunset looked down at her hands and did her best not to cry. She had no idea what a snickerdoodle was, but the mere fact that this woman, who she didn't know, wanted to make something special for her, had her choked up.

"Is she there? Hi, Sunset, I'm Lilly! We're all here, and we wish you could be here too, but hopefully we'll get to meet you soon and we can all get to know each other."

"Hey, Sunset!" another woman called out from the background. "I'm Elsie!"

"And I'm Caryn. Khloe is here too, although at the moment, she's outside with Duke. *Outside*! In this crap-tastic weather! She's totally using it to escape the hubbub going on...and I think to get away from Raiden for a moment, since he's being especially annoying to her today."

Sunset's brain spun. She didn't know these women, wasn't sure she'd remember all the names, and had no idea why they were being so nice to her.

Talon pushed off the wall he'd been leaning on and scooted a bit closer to her. He was still careful not to get close enough to make her uncomfortable, but he held the phone out in front of him so she could hear more easily.

"Hi," she said after a moment, tentatively, not sure what else she should say.

"Hi!" a chorus of voices said in tandem from the other end of the phone.

"You've all had your chance to say hello, now let me talk to Tal for a sec," Brock told the women.

They all giggled and called out their goodbyes to Sunset.

"You good?" Brock asked. "Not buried?"

"No, we're good. Although I could use a spot of tea," Talon said with a wide grin on his face.

"You Brits and your tea," Brock said with a laugh. "But seriously, you need anything?"

"No. Sunset's cave is perfect. We've got food, fire, and we're hunkered down."

"All right."

Sunset heard music start in the background.

"Looks like things are starting. Gonna shut up now so you can hear what's happening."

"Before you go, everything's all right with everyone there? With the storm and all?"

"Yeah, we're fine. It was a little hairy getting over here this morning, but we're all present and accounted for."

"Good."

The way Talon wasn't afraid to show his concern for his friends made the odd feelings within Sunset flare up again. In her experience, men never thought much about anyone but themselves. She couldn't remember a time when Arrow was worried about those he was in charge of. His philosophy was that whatever happened was meant to be.

She found herself leaning forward when the music coming from the phone got louder. The melody was beautiful, and she tilted her head to hear more easily.

"I saw a picture of Bristol's dress," Talon said softly. "Lilly showed it to me. She made me swear not to give any hints to Rocky on what it looked like. It's form fitting down to her knees, where it poofs out. She didn't want a train, so the veil comes down to her ankles, and I heard she was planning on wearing a pair of sneakers with the dress. She said she wanted to be comfortable on her wedding day. She's short—sorry; the politically correct term is 'petite,' but she doesn't care about that kind of thing—but said she refused to wear high heels and be miserable all day. The colors for the ceremony are red and green, to go with the holiday, and I bet she's got a huge bouquet."

Sunset appreciated Talon trying to describe the scene for her. She wasn't exactly sure about everything he was describing, but she nodded anyway.

"Oh, you should see Rocky's face," Brock said quietly. "He's gobsmacked."

Sunset frowned at the strange word she'd never heard before.

"Rocky's seeing Bristol for the first time in her wedding dress," Talon explained. "Gobsmacked means he's blown away by how beautiful she looks. And probably asking himself how he got so lucky."

Again, the things Talon was describing were so foreign. The last time she got married, she'd been wearing the same brown dress she always wore, was sweaty from the heat of the day and from cooking dinner, and Cypress had taken her by the arm, marched her into his tent, and told her he was done waiting for her to come to terms with his claim. Then he'd pushed her to the ground and consummated their marriage.

"We are gathered here today for the union of this woman and this man," said a deep voice Sunset hadn't heard before. She leaned forward again, eager to hear what the man was saying.

Talon moved closer, holding the phone between them.

She listened in awe, and confusion, and a little bit of disbelief as the man spoke of love and loyalty. Of honor and sacrifice. He spoke about adversity and how it made people stronger, and how together, two people in love could overcome any obstacle thrown in their path.

She was lost in his words and desperately trying to swallow the ball of emotion that had risen in her throat.

This was what marriage was supposed to be? She'd had no idea. Life in The Community was nothing like that. It was about servitude, obedience, and punishment.

The next voice she heard was feminine, strong and steady. "From the moment I heard your voice calling my name in the woods, I knew I was going to be okay. You're my safe harbor, Rocky. The first person I want to see when I wake up, and having your arms around me before I go to sleep is the best feeling in the world. You're my muse, my best friend, and my love. You've changed my life in so many ways, I can't even begin to list them all. I love you so much, Cohen Watson. I'll spend the rest of my life attempting to show you how much, but it still won't be long enough for me to fully demonstrate. I promise to be true to you, to love you and only you, in sickness and in health. To celebrate the good times and be your rock during the bad, just as you've been mine. I love you."

Sunset felt numb. She could *feel* the love in the woman's words. She could picture her looking up to the man she was marrying as she spoke. They were obviously standing in front of a group of people, their friends, and yet the words were so intimate. Sunset felt almost guilty listening.

"You are my life," a man replied. "I wasn't living until I found you. Not really. I've never met anyone so strong. No SEAL compares. I'm in awe of you, Bristol Wingham.

You're smart, beautiful, funny, and you have a core of steel so strong, nothing can bend it. I want to be the man who stands at your side, celebrating each and every victory, and the one holding you up when you need support. Being with you makes me a better person, a better man. I have no idea how to be a husband, but I *do* know how to be the man you can trust one hundred percent, a shoulder you can cry on, and a protector when you need one. When you were missing..."

Rocky's voice broke, and Sunset couldn't keep her tears back anymore. One slid down her cheek as she listened.

"...it felt as if a part of me had been viciously torn away. I never would've given up looking for you. Not *ever*. You are now mine to protect, to cherish, and to provide comfort to. In return, I'm yours, body and soul. There will never be another. How could I even *think* about straying when your hands are the only ones I want touching me, your voice the only one I want to hear late at night, and when your very essence has seeped so far into my psyche, you're with me even when we're apart. I can't imagine not having you by my side. I love you, Bristol, even if those words seem too small for how I really feel."

Sunset's tears wouldn't stop. It was hard to believe what she was hearing. That a man could be so fiercely devoted to a woman. That he had no problem declaring his feelings for her in front of so many people.

With sudden clarity, she fully realized what The Community had done was an abomination. The multiple wives, treating women like slaves rather than partners, the punishments...all of it. It was wrong. Evil.

And just like that, a weight seemed to lift from Sunset's shoulders. Nothing she'd been through was fair or normal or right. But she *was* right to run away, to escape. She wasn't selfish or somehow broken because she didn't want to be "married" to Cypress.

"You may kiss your bride...and your husband," a male voice said, right before voices in the background began to cheer.

Looking up at Talon, Sunset was surprised to see his gaze locked on *her*, not the phone.

Very slowly, he reached out his other hand. When she didn't pull back, his fingers brushed against her cheek, wiping away the tears there with a whisper-soft touch.

"You can trust me...and I won't hurt you," he whispered.

Sunset swallowed hard once again.

"I have the great honor of introducing for the first time as man and wife, Bristol Wingham and Cohen Watson!"

Another cheer went up.

"She's keeping her last name," Talon said softly, as if speaking in a normal tone would somehow ruin the moment. "She's a very famous artist, and while she could've kept her last name for her business only, they decided that would get too confusing."

Sunset's brows furrowed. "Last name?"

It was Talon's turn to frown. "Yes. Do you not have a last name?"

"Many women in The Community had the same one... Meadowblossom. What's yours?"

"Ross. Talon Ross."

She liked it. "Arrow and Cypress's last name is Goodson. I always thought it was funny because they weren't good sons, not at all." She'd never said those words out loud before, even though she'd thought them more than once.

"Tal? Is that you?" an excited woman asked, her words making both Sunset and Talon jump in surprise.

"Yeah, Bristol. It's me. I'm sorry I couldn't be there in person. Congratulations!"

"Thanks, and it's fine. You're doing something more important. This storm is bad. Keep her safe, okay?"

Tears formed in Sunset's eyes once more. These women she'd never met had more compassion and concern for her than the people she'd known her entire life.

"Plan on it," Talon told her. "Make sure Lilly takes lots of pictures so I can see them when I get back."

Bristol laughed. "As if I have to tell her that. I swear she's worse than the paparazzi."

"Hey, Tal. You found Bigfoot yet?" a male voice asked.

"Nope. Sorry, Rocky. But I found something better," he retorted, staring deep into Sunset's eyes.

"Well, the good news is that this storm has chased everyone out of the forest," Rocky said. "Which means I can have a honeymoon without worrying about being called out in the middle of the night to find someone who's lost. Bad news is, I might have to host everyone here if they can't get home. Never thought I'd have a house full of guests on my wedding night."

Talon chuckled.

"Gotta go. Glad you could be here by phone," Rocky went on.

"Same. Cheers, mate. You couldn't have found a better woman for you."

"I'm a lucky bastard, and I know it. Later!"

"Tal?"

"Still here, Brock."

"I'm gonna let you go. I mean, I'd let you hang out for the reception, but I'm thinking that won't be good for the batteries on your sat phone. Stay put," he ordered. "I'll call Harvey and tell him you won't be back for a bit. There's nothing going on here, like Rocky said. We don't expect to be called out, but even if we are, we can handle it. You do what you need to do there. Take your time."

"Understood."

"The storm's supposed to taper off later today, but it's gonna stay damn cold for at least a week. If you need anything, and I mean *anything*, call. We'll all be pissed if you don't."

"Same goes for you. If something comes up, let me know."

"Will do. And, Tal?"

"Yeah?"

"Is it her?"

Sunset saw Talon's muscles tense. She had no idea what his friend meant, but it was obvious Talon did.

"I think so, but I'm not one hundred percent sure."

"Okay. We'll follow your lead on that. Stay safe out there."

"Of course."

"Sunset?"

"Yes?" she said quietly.

"You can trust Tal. He'd rather cut off his own hand than hurt you. I know he sounds funny, but he's an okay bloke."

Sunset knew Brock was teasing Talon, but she couldn't get past his first words. It was just another confirmation that she really could trust the man in front of her. That he *wasn't* going to hurt her. She looked straight at Talon and said, "I know."

She saw his physical response to her words. His shoulders relaxed and the emotion swimming in his eyes told her that he more than appreciated what she'd said.

"We'll play things by ear," Talon told Brock. "Hoping to be back by the end of the week."

At that, it was Sunset's turn to tense up. He was leaving so soon?

"Can't wait to meet you, Sunset," Brock said. "And I think you probably got that my wife and all our friends are anxious for the same. Stay safe out there. Later."

Talon clicked a button, ending the call without another word to his friend.

"Sunset?"

She'd dropped her eyes when he'd said he would be leaving soon.

"Will you please look at me?"

He hadn't ordered her, which she appreciated. So she tentatively raised her eyes.

"I want you to come with me when I go back to Fallport."

She blinked in surprise.

"I have no intention of leaving you out here on your own. No way in hell. I know you can take care of yourself, you've been doing it for a very long time. But...you aren't alone anymore. I want to help you. I know it's probably scary to think about going to town, especially after everything the assholes you lived with said about it. But it's not a dangerous place. The people are actually very nice. Well, most of them. And you can trust me, I'm not going to take you to town and drop you off somewhere. You'll have a place to stay, a safe space to acclimate back into the life you were born to live."

Thinking about going to town was downright terrifying. Even if she was beginning to realize nothing about her life in The Community was normal, she couldn't shake Arrow's lectures about the evils of Fallport.

"At least think about it. Right now, I'm sure all you want to do is say no. It's easier and more comfortable to continue with a life you know, rather than take a chance on the unknown. But you have my word that everything will be all right."

She nodded. Strangely enough, his words made her feel better.

They spent the rest of the day hunkered down inside the cave. The temperature was surprisingly comfortable with the canvas keeping out the worst of the wind and cold, and with the small fire crackling merrily.

Talon read to her some more, then he encouraged her to do her best to read some of the book to *him*. It was embarrassing how often she stumbled over the words, but Talon was nothing but encouraging.

He made them both dinner, which was still weird to Sunset, as she was so used to doing everything that needed to be done to survive. Sharing responsibilities with someone was an odd but pleasant feeling. When night fell, she and Talon continued to sit in the darkness of the cave, lit only by the flames from the fire, and talked.

He told her everything he could think of about Fallport. It was obvious he enjoyed living there, and the people he spoke about sounded interesting.

For the first time in her life, Sunset felt a keen need to go into town. Even though she didn't have a home, Talon had promised to help her figure that out...and she believed him.

She wanted to meet Sandra who ran the diner. Wanted to check out the used bookstore. Wanted to meet Khloe and Raiden, who worked at the library. Talon said she could get a special pass that would allow her to take books home for free.

She was intrigued by his description of the three older men who sat in front of the post office every day and gossiped about everyone and anything. She could almost picture them in her mind. She wasn't sure why her mental image of them was so strong, but just the thought of them made her smile.

And when Talon described the square, the downtown area of Fallport, somehow she knew he was going to mention a gazebo in the middle—which he said locals called The Circle—surrounded by trees. *How* she knew that, Sunset had no idea, but a peculiar longing began to throb deep within her chest. It was an uncomfortable and scary feeling, so she quickly asked a question about Talon's life before he came to Virginia.

The rest of the night was spent talking about Talon's childhood, his parents—who were both alive and well, living back in London—and some stories about his time with the Special Boat Service.

Sunset had already known Talon was completely different from the men in The Community, but by the time her eyes were too heavy to stay open anymore, she knew with certainty that he was also special. He was a warrior. He'd spent his entire life keeping people safe.

The words of trust he kept reminding her of, over and over, penetrated a tiny bit further.

No, that was a lie. They'd already seeped deep beneath her skin. She understood now that she wouldn't have invited him into the cave if they hadn't. No matter how much snow there was outside or how cold it got, if she didn't trust him, she wouldn't have let him get as close to her as he was right now.

He was lying on the other side of the cave, against the wall opposite the fire from Sunset. She hadn't asked him to stay over there; he was doing so to make her comfortable. He'd given up his bedding, had cooked, gone out and forged a trail through the snow to a place where they could both relieve themselves, and constantly fiddled with the canvas, making sure it was secure and wouldn't blow off while also allowing smoke from the fire to escape.

Everything he'd done had been to put her at ease. He hadn't touched her except to cut her hair and the one time he'd brushed her cheek, when she'd been overwhelmed with emotion after hearing his friends' wedding vows.

"Talon?" she whispered. The wind had stopped howling quite so hard, and she hoped that meant the snow had stopped as well, or would stop soon.

"Yeah?"

His low voice seemed to reverberate around the cave, wrapping itself around her like a warm blanket. She'd always preferred to be alone. Her times hunting in the woods were some of her most cherished memories. Back in The Community, she was never alone. There were always other wives around, watching and waiting for her to mess up so they could tell Arrow, and then Cypress, once his father died. Any attention on someone else meant eyes and ears were off *you*, so the other women were quick to point out each other's flaws and missteps.

And of course, the men were always watching as well. She'd often felt their eyes upon her.

She supposed she should be grateful she'd only had one husband, only had to lie with one man at a time. Some of the other women, the younger, more obedient and subservient women, had two or three husbands.

But Sunset realized, lying there in the dark cave, that

she was *glad* she wasn't alone. She'd never liked storms, and if she'd been by herself, she wouldn't have used her bedding as a door. She would've been cold and scared and the snow surely would've piled up inside her cave with the way the wind was blowing.

Not only that, but she liked how she felt around Talon. He didn't talk down to her. Didn't order her to do things. He talked to her as if she was an equal.

With sudden clarity, Sunset realized *that* was what she'd always wanted. She'd never felt as if she was just as important as the men around her. She was a slave, and up until the moment Cypress had informed The Community they were moving to Florida, she'd blindly accepted it.

For months, she'd wondered if she'd done the right thing by running away. By hiding from Cypress. But now that she'd met Talon, even though it had been such a short period of time, he'd validated her actions. Had shown her that she'd been right to stay hidden from The Community when they'd searched for her.

"Sunset? Are you all right?" Talon asked.

She jerked in surprise. He'd been patiently waiting to hear what she wanted to tell him. He hadn't yelled at her for making him wait. Hadn't called her stupid for collecting her thoughts. She sighed. "I just wanted to tell you that I'm glad you're here."

She heard his deep sigh, and braced for whatever he might say.

"You have no idea how much that means to me," he told her. "And I'm so very glad I'm here too."

Warmth spread through her body, and it had nothing to do with the heat coming from the flames of the small fire.

She smiled. If someone had told her a week ago that

she'd be lying in her cave with a man feet from her, and she'd be completely relaxed, she would've laughed her head off. But here she was.

"Sleep, sweetheart. I'll make sure the fire doesn't go out tonight."

For a split-second, she felt guilty for not even thinking about that, but then she closed her eyes and let sleep take her.

* * *

Tal sat up late into the night, watching Sunset sleep. So many emotions threatened to overwhelm him. Happiness for Bristol and Rocky that they were now married. Relief that the storm finally seemed to have abated. Gratitude that he'd found Sunset before the storm hit. And relief that she trusted him enough to invite him into the cave.

The more he learned about her life with that bloody cult, the more he wanted to hunt down every single one of the men who lived there and shove their heads up their arses.

The fact that Sunset had been able to trust him enough to let him within twenty feet of her was a small miracle. She'd been through hell, and yet she was still compassionate and caring. He didn't understand it, but he was grateful all the same.

He thought about the wedding ceremony, about how it had affected her so deeply. If she'd ever received an ounce of affection while living with the cult, he'd be surprised. From what he'd gathered, the men ruled with iron fists, and the women had done all they could to survive.

He could picture how Lilly and the others would take Sunset under their wings when he got her back to Fallport.

They'd show her what true friendship was supposed to be like. She'd see what a loving relationship looked like, as well, simply by watching his friends with their women.

Sunset was a fascinating contradiction of naïve and old soul. She might not be educated in the normal sense of the word, but she was smarter than most people in many ways. Her hunger for knowledge was painfully obvious. She was embarrassed that she couldn't read that well, but that didn't stop her from trying.

Yes, it was safe to say Sunset had gotten under his skin. He admired her, respected her, and was so damn impressed with how she'd been able to take care of herself for the last year. He didn't feel sorry for her or pity her. How could he, when she had more determination and strength inside her than just about anyone he'd ever met...including the most badass soldiers he'd worked with in the special forces.

He ached to give her a hug, to help her experience the first gentle embrace she'd probably ever known from a man...but that wasn't going to happen anytime soon. He'd just continue to use his words and actions to prop her up. To make her understand that her past didn't dictate her future.

With that thought, Tal added a log to the fire, then sat back against the side of the cave and closed his eyes. Sleeping was out of the question, but he could at least rest his eyes for a bit.

CHAPTER EIGHT

With every day that passed, Sunset felt more comfortable in Talon's presence. He still hadn't grabbed her. Hadn't done or said anything that would make her think he was anything like Cypress or the other men she'd known.

Each day, they read more of the book he'd bought her, which she was loving. Each day, they talked. Each day, Talon had cut a bit more of her hair, and with every trim, Sunset felt as if she was shedding some of her painful past. It was also one of the most difficult things she'd ever endured. Because every time Talon touched her hair, memories of her time in the punishment tent resurfaced. Being in the dark, alone, shackled, sometimes blindfolded and gagged, unable to do anything but lie there and shake in fear.

Talon was patient, and his praise was constant. At first she'd dismissed most of the nice things he said, the criticisms of Arrow and Cypress too loud in her mind, telling her she was worthless, a horrible person, ugly, ungrateful. But slowly, the old words began to fade as Talon's pushed them out.

He told her several times a day how unusual and beautiful her hair was. When she made another pair of shoes with the rabbit skins, he praised their craftsmanship. He commended the improvements in her reading, and claimed her thoughts on the book were spot on.

Being around him made Sunset feel...seen. Her entire life, she'd done everything possible to stay under the radar. To *not* be noticed. Because having attention had never been a good thing. It meant having to do her wifely duties. More chores. Getting yelled at and punished for messing up something.

But even when she'd knocked over the water bucket, and Talon had to go back to the stream, through the deep snow and out in the cold, he hadn't berated her. Hadn't said anything but "it was an accident, it's not a big deal." She'd been ready for him to backhand her. But his body language hadn't changed at all. He hadn't tensed. Hadn't frowned. Nothing.

It was as confusing as much as it was a relief.

Every day, Talon also called one of his friends to check in. And every day, Sunset got to talk to one of their wives or girlfriends. It was strange that they were all being so nice and friendly to someone they didn't know, but Sunset secretly looked forward to his daily calls.

Six days had passed since the storm, and Sunset realized she was...happy.

For the past year, she'd simply existed. She'd ventured out and had followed people who were in the forest out of boredom and curiosity, a desire not to feel so alone.

But when the phone Talon had been using rang one morning, Sunset tensed. She'd gotten used to their routine. No one had ever called Talon; he was the one who reached out to his friends.

"Tal here," he said as he answered—then, seconds later, he gasped. "What? When? Is she all right?"

There was a pause as he listened to whoever was on the other end of the line. For once, he hadn't pressed the button that would allow her to hear what was being said. But Sunset didn't think it was because he was being secretive. Talon was just too absorbed in whatever he was hearing to think about it.

"Bloody hell! Why didn't anyone tell me before now?"

Sunset could hear the hurt and worry in his voice.

"Right. Okay, I'm coming in today. I don't know...but there's no way in hell I'm not coming. Tell them I'll likely see them this evening. I have no idea how long it'll take to get out of here, what with all the trails being buried, but nothing—and I mean, *nothing*—is going to keep me from being there to support them."

The emotion in his voice made Sunset's brow furrow and her belly clench. Something was wrong. And it was clear he was going to leave.

She wasn't ready. It was a weird feeling to not *want* him to go.

"I know. I appreciate you telling me. You sure she's okay? All right. Yeah. How's everyone else? How's Finley? She was so looking forward to going through the process with Lilly."

Sunset kept her gaze glued on Talon as he listened to whatever was being said. She sat stock still, not moving a muscle as she waited to hear what was happening.

"Yeah, that sucks. Okay, I'm gonna get off so I can get things sorted here."

As the person talking to him said something else, Talon's gaze met hers. She could see emotion swimming in the blue depths, and Sunset wanted desperately to know what to say to make him feel better, but she was so out of her element.

"Don't know, mate, but I'll do my best. Okay, I'll see you soon."

Talon took the phone away from his ear and hit a button before taking a deep breath. He didn't move from where he was sitting across the cave from her, but every muscle in his body was tense.

"That was Drew. Lilly had a miscarriage...she and Ethan lost their baby."

Sunset inhaled sharply. "Oh no," she whispered. Lilly had been so excited about being pregnant. Just three days ago, she'd told Sunset all about how happy she and her husband were, how Ethan had already started fixing up a room in their house as a nursery. Sunset was a stranger, and yet Lilly had still shared such personal things. The loss she must be feeling right now had to be agonizing.

"I need to go back. Make sure she and Ethan are all right," Talon said.

Sunset nodded immediately.

"I want you to come with me."

She stared at him with wide eyes. Her heart started beating a hundred miles an hour. He'd told her before that he wanted her to go to Fallport with him, but she'd thought that would be way in the future. In the spring, maybe. She wasn't ready to leave yet. She couldn't!

"You can trust me, and I won't hurt you. No one will. I give you my word on that. You're safe with me and my friends. You've gotten to know the other women a bit from their calls. Do you think they'd intentionally do anything to hurt you? No way."

He wasn't giving her time to say anything; in fact, he started talking faster.

"I have to see them. They're my dearest friends. I feel sick that I wasn't there, that I didn't know. Drew told me both Lilly and Ethan ordered everyone not to say anything to me when it happened. Do you know why they did that?"

Sunset swallowed hard and shook her head.

"Because they were worried about *you*. They knew when I heard, I'd want to see for myself that they were okay, but they didn't want you to be left on your own out here."

Sunset frowned. People caring about what happened to *her* was a completely foreign concept. No one ever went out of their way to make sure she was okay.

"Please come with me, Sunset."

Her mouth opened before she thought about what she was going to say. "Okay."

"Okay?" he asked, seeming a bit shocked.

She nodded.

Talon's eyes closed and he sighed in relief, as if her agreement had been important.

Sunset realized with a start that her acquiescence *was* important to him.

"Thank you," he whispered. Then his eyes opened and pinned her in place once more. "It isn't going to be easy to get to my SUV at the trailhead."

"I know." And she did. The snow might've stopped, but there was at least a foot and a half on the ground. And it was still bitterly cold outside. Every time she stepped outside to relieve herself, she was reminded just how fortunate she was to have her warm cave to retreat into.

He eyed her and nodded. "Thank God you've got the boots. I've got an extra shirt you can wear to add an additional layer to what you've got on. I know my way around the forest, but I have a feeling you'll have a better sense of the easiest way to get to the trailhead."

It was a question without being *asked* as a question. Sunset nodded slowly.

"Good. You can lead. Well...I'll go first so I can make a trail, so it won't be as hard for you to get through the snow. But you can tell me which way to go."

Being around this man continued to be utterly eye-opening. No way in hell would any of the men in The Community ever admit that they didn't know something. And they never, *ever*, would've trusted any of the women to take control of an important situation like Talon was. They wouldn't have let her lead the way through the forest, even though she knew it like the back of her hand. They would've wandered around in circles, completely lost, before ever asking a woman for help.

Talon stood and began rummaging in his pack. "I can't leave the tent behind, because if something happens and we need to take shelter, we'll need it, but I want to leave enough staples behind in case we have to use this cave in the future."

"What?" Sunset asked. The way the question came out so easily and without thought made her realize exactly how comfortable she'd gotten around this man. In the past, if she dared question her husband, or anyone else, she would've been backhanded.

"This is your safe space," Talon said, straightening and looking her in the eye. "You can always come back here if you need or want to. I won't ever give you a reason to want to escape me or retreat back into the woods, but I still want you to know you have a place to go if you need it. A safety net."

Sunset stared at Talon in disbelief.

He broke her gaze and looked around. "We'll need to take the canvas down and fold it up, but we'll do that last, right before we leave. I've got some extra freeze-dried meals I can leave, and I'll put the things I brought for you in my pack, so you can have them with you when we get back to my apartment. I'll leave the cards, one of the pocket knives, the cutlery and dishes, and of course your bucket and pots. The flint and the brush can stay too."

Sunset's mind was spinning. This was actually happening. She was leaving, going to Fallport. The one place Arrow had pounded into their heads that they should never go. He seemed especially adamant that *she* never went there. Sunset hadn't understood why it would be so bad for her to be seen by the locals, for her to venture into town, but she'd been so busy trying to survive, she hadn't thought too much about it.

"Are you sure you're all right with this?" Talon asked as he paused in his packing.

Sunset swallowed hard and nodded, realizing she *was* all right. She was scared, terrified actually, but a feeling of anticipation and excitement was also coursing through her veins.

"*Truly* sure?"

"Yes," she told him. "I'm scared," she admitted. "But you need to see your friends. I can do this."

Talon took a step toward her before seeming to catch himself and stopping abruptly. He stared at her from the small distance that separated them.

"I read something once," he began in a conversational tone.

Sunset knew he was anxious to get going, and yet here he was, talking to her, trying to reassure her.

"It's a quote that stuck with me. It was something

about how being scared means you're about to do something really brave. And being brave means you're smart enough to know that despite what you're about to do is scary, difficult, and maybe even dangerous...you're doing it anyway, because the possibility of succeeding is worth the chance of failing."

Sunset let his words sink into her soul.

"I'd be worried if you *weren't* scared, sweetheart. You've been told all your life that Fallport is bad. That the people there are evil. You couldn't know that those were lies. Couldn't know that you were being oppressed by the very people who were supposed to care for and protect you."

"Have you ever been scared of anything?" Sunset asked.

"All the bloody time," Talon said without hesitation. "When I had to leave all those women and kids when I was on that mission, I was terrified. I had a bad feeling about what would happen if we left, but I wasn't in a position to do anything about it.

"And more recently, I was scared I wouldn't find you. Then I was scared that if I *did* find you, you'd run. I'm scared I'll say the wrong thing and you won't trust me. I'm scared that I'll do something that'll make you afraid of me. I'm scared that when we get to Fallport, it'll be too much for you. That you won't want to stay."

"Talon," she whispered, not sure what to say to all of that.

"You can trust me. I won't ever hurt you," he said softly. "If things get too frightening, if you get too overwhelmed, repeat those words to yourself. At any time, if you can't handle something, you tell me, and I'll get you out of the situation. We'll go for a hike. I'll take you back to my place, where you can regroup. I'll do whatever it takes for you to realize that you're safe and no one is going to hurt you ever again."

His words were a balm to her tattered soul. "Okay."

"Okay," he agreed. "You want to help me pack this stuff up so it'll be good to go if and when we come back?"

We. He'd said *we*. Not *you*. They were both well aware that she could come back to this cave by herself in the future, but inferring they might come back together at some point made Sunset's chest loosen. This cave had saved her life. When she'd run from Cypress and the others in The Community who were trying to take her away, she wasn't sure where she was going to go. Finding this ideal shelter had been a miracle, and in many ways, she'd miss it terribly.

But it had also been a prison of sorts. The longer she'd lived here, the harder it was to imagine ever leaving. Talon finding her had been the catalyst she needed to make a change. That change was scary, but she was going to grab onto it with both hands. Knowing she could come back if she wanted to was the last push she needed to get on with her life.

It didn't take long to pack the things she wanted to take with her and secure the rest in the back of the cave. The last thing they did was take down the canvas. She folded it in half and wrapped the supplies they were leaving inside. They put rocks around and on top of the tarp to try to prevent animals from dragging it away.

"Ready?" Talon asked gently as she stood in the mouth of the cave, staring at the empty space.

Taking a deep breath, she nodded. Sunset wasn't sure she was ready, but if Talon thought she was brave, she didn't want to do anything to make him think otherwise.

"If you get too cold, let me know. You've got the last

handwarmer, make sure to switch it between your hands every couple minutes."

"I will," she said. He was extremely worried about her comfort. Sunset didn't have the heart to tell him about some of the times she'd gone hunting in the winter, wearing nothing but the damn brown dress she was required to wear at The Community and her rabbit fur shoes on her feet. Compared to that, in her leggings, cargo pants, long-sleeve shirt, sweatshirt, fleece, wool socks and boots, she was positively toasty.

They started out with Talon in the lead, forging a path through the deep snow, and Sunset walking a few steps behind him. Before too long, Talon realized she was struggling. While warm, the boots were hard to get used to after never having worn shoes before. The wind had picked up, now that they were away from the cover of the dense trees and vegetation surrounding the cave, and it was difficult to hear when they spoke unless they were facing each other.

When Sunset tripped and fell, Talon didn't notice, and he'd actually gotten quite a ways ahead of her before he realized she wasn't right behind him. He returned to her quickly and shook his head. "This isn't working."

Dread raced through Sunset. She'd been clumsy and he was now impatient with her. She braced for his harsh words. But she should've known better.

"I could get out a length of rope and put it around my waist so you can hold onto it, but I'd prefer you not be that far away from me. I'd like you to hold onto my waistband or my backpack as we walk. You can use me as a walking stick of sorts. I can help you stay upright as you walk through the snow. I know you don't want to get that close, but you can trust me, Sunset. I won't hurt you."

Most people would probably be sick and tired of hearing him say the same thing over and over, but each time he uttered the words, they sank deeper into her soul. She didn't reply, instead just stepped closer and slipped her fingers behind the belt around his waist.

"Thank you," Talon told her. He smiled at her, and that damn dimple made her knees weak before he turned back around. "Here we go. If I go too fast, speak up. Let me know which way I should go."

Walking this close to him was actually easier than walking alone. Talon was like a strong, sturdy tree walking ahead of her. When she did trip over her feet, or when they felt as if they weighed two hundred pounds as she dragged them through the deep snow, Talon was there to keep her steady.

They walked for a while, then took a break, and repeated the pattern over and over. Even when she didn't feel as if she needed a break, Talon insisted. Each time, he checked her fingers to make sure she wasn't too cold, then requested she drink to stay hydrated.

That was another thing...he always encouraged her to take her fill of water before he even thought about taking any for himself. The Community men ate and drank first. Without question.

Walking through the snow was more tiring than she thought it would be, even with the breaks. Even though she was in shape, she usually didn't stray too far from her cave in bad weather. It took longer than she thought it would to get close to the beginning of the trail. She was cold, tired, and her nerves were definitely getting the better of her.

"It's okay, Sunset. We're almost there, I promise. And going to town is a good thing."

How he was able to read her mind should've worried her, but instead it was a comfort. "I know." And she did, but that didn't mean she wasn't still apprehensive.

"You really do know this forest, don't you?" he asked as they walked.

"I've spent most of my life in here," she said. "It would be kind of sad if I couldn't find my way around."

"I'm thinking we could use you on our search and rescue team," Talon muttered, then he turned his head to smile at her.

Sunset froze. Her? Working with the other men she'd spied on more times than she could count as they searched for missing people? No, she couldn't. She was a woman. She couldn't be responsible for something like that.

"You'd be really good at it," he said, seeing the disbelief on her face. "But today isn't the day you have to decide what you want to do with the rest of your life. Today's a day to take a deep breath and see that there's a whole 'nother world out there. One that's much kinder and easier than the one you've known."

Sunset wasn't sure about that, but she didn't disagree with him.

Talon laughed. "You so want to tell me I'm full of shit. But you'll see," he said before continuing on their trek toward the trailhead.

This man continued to confuse her...and make her yearn for things she'd never experienced. She liked that he didn't care if she questioned him. And it seemed as if he was amused when she disagreed with something he'd said. He was so different from anyone she'd ever known...and she liked it. A lot.

For the first time in her life, Sunset thought maybe she could be someone different.

"We're here," he said a short while later.

And they were. His car—at least, she assumed it was Tal's—sat in the parking lot, completely buried under feet of snow. But instead of the area being otherwise deserted, a man sitting in a truck with a snow plow mounted on the front smiled when he spotted them from the driver's seat. When they emerged from the woods, he waved and opened the door.

Without thinking about what she was doing, Sunset moved closer to Talon, instead of farther away. Her hand dropped from his waistband and she clutched the hand closest to her.

He looked at her in surprise, but immediately tight-ened his glove-covered fingers around hers.

"Hey, you two!" the man called, stepping out of the truck. "I'm Rory! Ethan sent me. He hired me last week to make sure everyone could get to his brother's wedding, and when he heard you were returning from your camping trip—camping in the middle of a snowstorm is crazy, if you ask me, but then again, most people think I'm crazy for loving what I do, so who am I to judge?—he asked if I'd come out this way and give you a lift back to town. I could try to dig out your SUV there, but it'll be faster if I just take you."

Talon smiled at the man and said, "We'd love a ride, thank you."

"Great. Wow, your woman sure is pretty. If I'd spent a week in the woods, I surely wouldn't look as good as she does. Anyway, it'll be a tight fit in the cab of my truck, but I think we'll manage."

Talon's hand tightened on hers as Sunset thought about the exchange. The man, Rory, hadn't looked twice at her.

Hadn't asked her what the hell she was doing, standing so close to Talon. And he'd called her pretty.

"If it's okay with you, I'd like to go straight to Lilly and Ethan's," Talon said, looking at her.

Frowning, Sunset studied him. It sounded as if he was asking for her permission. "Um...okay?"

"I could take you to my place first. We could change, you could shower and get something to eat before we visit them, if you'd prefer."

She'd heard how worried Talon was for his friends. She knew delaying the visit wasn't what he wanted to do. He wanted to go straight to Lilly and Ethan to offer his support. Make sure they were all right. She'd never experienced that feeling, never had anyone support her, but she wanted to do whatever she could to make Talon feel better.

She shook her head. "No, you need to get to your friends as soon as you can."

He gave her a smile and squeezed her hand. "Thank you, sweetheart."

Then he turned and headed for the man's truck. He threw his backpack into the bed then opened the door and climbed in, scooting over until he was in the middle of the long seat, next to Rory, who was settling back behind the wheel.

Sunset closed the door behind her, noticing how much space there was between her leg and Talon's. He was doing his best not to crowd her. Everything he'd done since she'd first seen him sitting outside her cave had been to try to make her feel comfortable.

The ride to Fallport wasn't silent. Rory didn't stop talking the entire trip. He was friendly and outgoing, and filled the ride with commentary about various topics. He told them all about how Rocky and Bristol had invited him to their wedding, and how much fun he'd had. They learned he was a widower; his wife had died a few years ago and his kids had all moved away. He enjoyed helping out the community by plowing the streets in the winter. In the fall, he drove the truck that sucked up leaves people left on their curbs, and in the spring and summer he traveled.

By the time they started seeing houses along the side of the road, Sunset had begun to relax. But that didn't last as more and more buildings came into sight. She felt as if her heart was going to beat out of her chest.

What was she doing? She shouldn't be here! She was going to have to spend the next year or more in the punishment tent.

Just as she'd worked herself into a frenzy, Talon slowly took her hand in his. This time they weren't wearing gloves, and the feel of his bare hand, calluses and all, settled against her own...it immediately soothed her.

She wasn't in The Community anymore. Cypress was gone. He'd left her behind. She was on her own.

No, that wasn't true. Talon was there.

She could trust him. He wouldn't do anything to hurt her.

She realized she'd internalized the words he was constantly telling her when Rory pulled up in front of a pretty house surrounded by other well-kept and nice-looking houses.

"Here we are," he announced happily.

"How much do I owe you for the ride?" Talon asked.

"Nothing!" Rory said with a shake of his head. "It was my pleasure. When I heard why you were coming back from your camping trip, I was only too happy to help."

The man's voice lowered. "My wife lost a child once, it was the worst thing that ever happened to us. We went on to have three other babies, but I still think of my oldest girl... sad that I never got to know her. Anyway, if you need a lift to your place when you're done visiting, just give me a yell. Ethan's got my number. It was nice meeting you both...but especially you, lovely lady. I know I talked too much and didn't give you a chance to get a word in edgewise. My kids are always telling me I'm too friendly, and I keep telling them there's no such thing. You be safe, okay?"

Sunset nodded automatically. Arrow and Cypress had always claimed the people who lived in Fallport were suspicious of and downright mean to outsiders, but Rory was so far from either, it wasn't even funny. And even though she'd already suspected the people she lived with had lied about quite a few things, Rory was a living, breathing example of how right she'd been.

"It was nice meeting you too," she said softly, after she'd gotten out of the truck.

Rory beamed.

Talon grabbed his pack out of the back of the truck and gave Rory a chin lift. Then he held out his hand to Sunset and said, "You ready to do this?"

She took a deep breath as Rory's truck pulled away. "Yes."

She wasn't ready. Not at all. But she was going to do it anyway. First, because these were Talon's friends and they were hurting and he needed to see them. And second, because she desperately wanted a different life. One where she didn't have to worry about being thrown in the punishment tent, or being claimed by another husband, or where she was beaten if she dared ask a question. She wanted a life like the one Talon had described. One where she could be the person she'd always felt was hiding deep within her. The woman she'd pushed deep down inside for her own protection.

"Brave as bloody hell," Talon told her as she placed her hand in his own. Then he turned and headed for the front door of the house.

She felt as if she was going to puke, she was so scared, but Sunset kept putting one foot in front of the other. Talon was with her. She could trust him.

CHAPTER NINE

Tal was so proud of the woman at his side, he felt goose bumps rise up on his arms. He had no idea where she found the strength to continue to step outside her comfort zone, to overcome the shit her captors had forced into her head, but he couldn't deny he was almost overwhelmed by her bravery.

He sobered as they approached Lilly and Ethan's door. The reason he was here settled on his shoulders like a heavy blanket. He was devastated for his friends. Didn't know what to say to make them feel better.

"I'm sure they'll be happy to see you," Sunset said softly from next to him.

She'd obviously picked up on his reticence.

Nodding, Tal lifted a hand and knocked.

"Come in!" he heard Ethan yell. He pushed open the door and stepped inside, still gripping Sunset's hand.

"That you, Tal?"

"It's me, mate!" Talon called back as he secured the door behind him.

Sunset squeezed his hand, then they made their way

into the main part of the house, where Ethan was sitting in an oversized armchair with Lilly on his lap.

Seeing his friend holding his wife so close made his throat close up with emotion. Lilly had already been through so much, he hated that this happened to them.

Ethan inched out from under Lilly and stood. Without hesitation, Tal stepped forward and hugged him, hard. "I'm so sorry," he said quietly.

"Thanks," Ethan said, returning the tight hug.

Tal stepped back and turned to Lilly, who had stood by the chair. He wrapped his arms around her just as tightly. To his surprise, he felt tears well up. "This sucks," he blurted into Lilly's hair.

She sniffed and nodded against him. He held her for a long moment, wishing there was something he could do for his friends. But there was nothing he could say or do that would take this pain away.

It was Lilly who pulled away first. She gave him a sad smile, then reached up and gently wiped the tears away that had spilled onto Tal's cheeks.

"I'm gutted for you both," he told her.

"I know. But you being here means the world to us," she said. Then she gave him a crooked smile and asked, "Would it have killed you to take a shower before you rushed out of the wilderness to come visit?"

Tal snort-chuckled. He stared down at Lilly for a long moment. Searching her eyes for...something. He wasn't sure what. Maybe to reassure himself that she would be okay. She was hurting, there was no doubt, but as he studied her, he breathed a little easier for the first time since hearing the news. With Ethan by her side, she would make it through this. Losing their child was a blow, but she had so much love surrounding her.

"If you think I was going to take more time than absolutely necessary to get to you both, you're bloody crazy," he told her.

Lilly gave him a sweet smile, then her gaze went past him and she said, "Are you going to introduce us?"

Turning, Tal saw Sunset standing at the entrance to the large living room, looking uncertain. As soon as he backed away from Lilly, Ethan moved back in, curling his arm around his wife's waist and pulling her against him.

Tal walked over to Sunset and said in a low tone, "You okay?"

She nodded.

He wasn't sure if she was being honest, but he smiled at her anyway. "Good. Come on, I want to introduce you to two of the best mates I've got."

She swallowed hard and nodded again. Once more, the thought that she was strong as hell struck him. She was clearly out of her element. Unsure what to do, how she'd be received, and yet she was trusting him to not steer her wrong. She humbled him.

"This is Sunset," he said. "And this is Lilly and Ethan Watson."

"It's so great to finally get to meet you and not just talk to you on the phone," Lilly said warmly.

"Hello," Ethan said with a smile.

"It's a pleasure to make your acquaintance," Sunset said, sounding formal and not at all like the woman Tal had gotten to know over the last week.

"Are either of you hungry or thirsty?" Lilly asked.

"Lil," Ethan warned.

"I'm okay," she said, turning to her husband. "I've been doing nothing but sleeping and sitting around. Nothing bad is going to happen if I go to the kitchen and make a couple mugs of tea."

Tal got the feeling Ethan had been crazy overprotective since Lilly had gotten back from the hospital...not that he could blame him.

"All right. But if you aren't back in five minutes and off your feet, I'm gonna come and get you."

Lilly rolled her eyes, then went up on her tiptoes and kissed Ethan lightly. Turning toward Sunset, she asked, "Would you like to help me make some tea?"

Tal could see Sunset wasn't enthusiastic about the idea, but she nodded anyway, probably too afraid to say no.

He wanted to warn Lilly to go easy, but he bit his lip. He didn't need to caution her, Lilly wouldn't do or say anything that would jeopardize her friendship with Sunset. She was a good judge of character and would know that she needed to tread carefully.

Tal gave Sunset a reassuring smile before she followed Lilly into the kitchen.

Knowing he didn't have a lot of time to talk to Ethan before he went to check on his wife, Tal said, "How are you holding up?"

Ethan ran a hand through his hair and sighed. Tal could see the devastation come over his face that he hadn't allowed to show around his wife.

"Not good," Ethan admitted. "When Lilly screamed for me from the bathroom and told me she was bleeding, bad, I've never been so scared in all my life. Not only for our baby, but for her. I almost lost her once, I couldn't go through that again."

Tal stepped closer to his friend and put a hand on his shoulder, squeezing hard.

"The look in her eyes when the doctor told us...it was

pure devastation. She already knew, really, but to hear the doctor confirm that our baby was gone..."

His voice trailed off. Tal couldn't imagine the pain his friend was going through.

Ethan cleared his throat and did his best to get control over his emotions. "We'll get through this though," he said. "Lilly needs to rest for at least two weeks, then she can go back to work. The doctors said it wasn't anything she necessarily did or didn't do. That sometimes the fetus just isn't developing normally. But I know Lilly's at least partially blaming herself. And that sucks, because there's nothing I can do or say that will change her mind."

"What about future pregnancies?" Tal asked. He didn't know anything about this kind of stuff, but now his mind was spinning, wanting to know all the details.

"Doc Snow came over yesterday, and we had a long talk with him about everything. We were kind of in shock at the hospital in Christiansburg, too much so to ask many questions. He said most women go on to have other children without issue. I think that was Lilly's biggest fear. That somehow her body wasn't built to carry a child or something. So we'll wait until we're both emotionally and physically ready before trying again."

Tal was relieved neither Lilly nor Ethan was going to give up on their dream of kids. They'd both been so excited to have children, it would be a shame if something biological kept that from happening in the future. He knew adoption was always an option, and although he hadn't talked about it with either of his friends, he had a feeling they'd be on board with that. Still, it was obvious they first wanted to see if they could have a biological baby. "That's a good thing," he finally said.

"Yeah. You know, there are times when loving Lilly as

much as I do scares the shit out of me. I am literally not the same person I was before I met her. It's a good thing I'm no longer a SEAL, because I'm not sure I'd be able to do my job as effectively as I did when I was single. When we're apart, I think about her constantly. Wonder if she's okay, if the job she's on is going all right, if she's happy. And when I get a text from her, or she calls, it literally makes my entire day. I'd be embarrassed at how much she means to me if I didn't know she felt the same way. Being helpless to do anything when she's hurting is just awful, Tal. I can't explain it any better than that."

"You don't have to. And if anyone gives you a hard time about loving your wife...tell them to fuck off."

Ethan chuckled. "I will and I have."

The two men shared a smile.

"Enough about that...what's the deal with Sunset? You think she's Heather Brown?"

"I'm ninety-nine percent sure she is. She hasn't talked about her life outside of that bloody cult she lived in."

"Was it bad?" Ethan asked.

"Worse than bad," Tal growled. "From what I gathered, it was a total shitshow. The men were in charge, the women were abused physically, mentally, and sexually. The men had several wives each, and the women had to do whatever they said, whenever they said. Sunset talked about something called a punishment tent, and although she hasn't gone into detail with me about what happened in there, I can well imagine. She was even whipped for cutting her hair."

"Fucking hell, man!" Ethan said with wide eyes.

"That's not the worst of it."

"There's more?"

"Yeah," Tal said grimly. "Sunset said there weren't many

kids born inside the cult. She admitted that the women used Queen Anne's lace seeds to prevent pregnancy, but in order to keep their numbers up, and probably to keep their harems, the men would randomly show up at the camp with children."

"*What?* What do you mean, show up with them?"

"That's what Sunset said, they'd just show up with infants and toddlers that they claimed to have adopted. The boys were groomed to be in charge, and the girls were claimed by different men or assigned to the boys as future wives."

"Holy fuck!" Ethan exclaimed. "They've been kidnapping kids for decades?"

"Apparently."

"You need to talk to Simon."

Tal inhaled deeply. "I know. But I have a feeling Sunset is going to be reluctant...she's scared to death of men, Ethan."

"She seems okay with you."

"Yeah, but only because she didn't really have a choice. That storm moved in fast, and if she hadn't invited me into the cave she's been living in for a bloody year, I would've been in trouble."

"She trusts you," Ethan said.

"I don't think she does."

"She *does*," his friend insisted. "You didn't see her because you were talking with Lilly, but she didn't take her eyes off you. And when Lilly wiped your face, she took a step forward, as if wanting to comfort you herself. She caught herself and moved back to where she'd been standing...but you're in there, brother."

Ethan's words made Tal feel good. Really good. "Still,

I'm not sure how to bring up the fact that she, herself, might've been kidnapped when she was eight."

"You'll figure it out," Ethan said confidently.

Tal didn't have the same confidence his friend had.

"Did she say how old the kids were? The ones the men brought into the cult?"

"Young. She used the word 'babies.'"

"So maybe they learned their lesson with her," Ethan said. "She was older. Probably retained a lot of memories from her old life, and maybe too much of her independence. It was probably difficult to train her to accept her role with the group."

It was the same thing Tal had thought. "I agree. And there have been times I think she remembers some of her life before she was taken, but I've been reluctant to push her. As it is, I suspect she's blocked all her memories for self-preservation."

"Maybe being back here in Fallport will make those memories start to come back."

"I'm not sure if that's a good thing or not."

"It is," Ethan said. "She needs to know that how she'd been living wasn't normal, or even legal."

"I think she *does* know that. I've told her as much. And when the cult up and moved a year ago, she hid in the forest so she didn't have to go with them."

"Good for her," Ethan said fervently.

"She's strong," Tal said. "So damn strong it amazes me."

"She'll fit in perfectly with our women then."

Ethan wasn't wrong. She already fit in with them, even without having met most of the group in person. Tal just hoped she'd eventually be able to put aside the bad experiences she'd had and embrace any new friendships.

* * *

"How are you doing?" Lilly asked.

Sunset blinked in surprise. Why she was asking how *she* was, when Lilly was the one who'd just been through something awful, was bewildering. "I'm fine."

"It couldn't have been easy, living out in the woods. I mean, I like to camp now and then, but from what I understand, you were out there a long time."

Sunset shrugged. "It wasn't so bad." And it wasn't. She was used to living in a tent. The cave was actually more comfortable in a lot of ways.

"Would you like some tea?"

Sunset did her best to hide her reaction. She hated tea. *Hated* it. The leaves the other women in The Community used for tea tasted horrible. She'd never gotten used to the nasty taste, but there'd been no alternative. Women were expected to drink tea, while the men drank beer. "Um... thank you."

Lilly laughed a little. "I take it you aren't a fan of tea."

Sunset wasn't sure what to say. Was this a test? Would she be looked down on if she said she didn't like it? Would she be kicked out of the house?

"It's okay if you don't like it...honestly. But I'm thinking you might like the kind I have. I don't like regular tea. I don't even like iced tea. It tastes like I'm drinking dirt, frankly."

Sunset's eyes widened. That was always how she felt too.

"But I found this stuff recently. It's cinnamon apple. I swear it tastes like you're drinking Christmas. Okay, that sounds weird, but it's fruity, and the cinnamon makes my taste buds tingle a bit. Shoot, that sounds awful too. But I swear it's good. How about if you try it, and if you hate it, you don't have to drink it? I'll get you some water, or juice, or anything else you can use to wash away the taste if you hate it."

A memory niggled at Sunset. A smell she remembered. Cinnamon and other spices. Filling the air, mixed with pine. She wasn't sure where the memory was from, as she couldn't recall ever having any spices while in The Community. The men were allowed to use salt and other spices on their food, but not the women. Arrow claimed spices were bad for the female body.

"Will you try it? I promise I won't be mad or upset if you hate it."

Sunset nodded reluctantly.

Lilly smiled at her again. "The others are going to love you. It's hard to get a word in edgewise when we all get together, and you not being a chatterbox will both endear you to them and frustrate them. Because they're gonna want to know all about you, and when they can't pry any answers out of you, that'll only make them want to know more."

Sunset furrowed her brow. That didn't sound good at all. She was used to being quiet. Though, once upon a time, her penchant for talking too much had to be beaten out of her.

"Oh, shoot, I'm sorry! It's not a bad thing. Not at all. We're all just natural talkers. Well...except for Khloe. But it's perfectly okay if you want to sit back and listen. No one is going to care. Darn it, now I've upset you when I didn't mean to."

"It's okay," Sunset said, not wanting Lilly to feel bad. "I just...it was frowned upon for women to talk, even to each other."

A sad look crossed Lilly's face before she offered another small smile. "Well, now that you're here, you don't have to worry about that. Talking's good. It's the best." She chuckled. "Now I sound like Buddy the Elf when he says 'smiling's my favorite.'"

Sunset smiled politely, but she had no idea what Lilly was talking about.

"Right. I'm confusing you again. Sorry. I just watched *Elf* the other day. It's a Christmas movie. We'll have to watch it together sometime. Anyway, will you fill the kettle with water for me? It's over there."

Sunset glanced to where Lilly pointed and saw a pretty ceramic jug on the counter. She picked it up off the base it was sitting on and brought it to the sink. It had been a long time since she'd had the luxury of running water, and she couldn't help but smile as she filled the kettle.

"That looks like a good thought," Lilly said.

"I was just thinking how nice it is not to have to walk half a mile to the creek to get water," Sunset told her.

"No wonder you're in shape," Lilly said. "I'd die for legs like yours. And hair. And lips. You're really pretty, Sunset."

Sunset's eyes widened as she stared at her new friend.

"And your eyes! Jeez, you're just gorgeous."

The compliments warmed Sunset from the inside out. Yes, Talon had told her she was pretty, but she'd kind of thought he was lying just to try to get her to trust him, so he could have sex with her. She couldn't figure out the motive behind the nice things Lilly was saying. Women didn't compliment other women. At least not in her experience. But she still found herself enjoying the words.

And hadn't she hidden from Cypress in the woods because she was more and more sure that The Community wasn't...right?

"Thank you," she managed to squeak out.

"You're welcome. If you put the kettle back on its base and push that small lever down...yes, just like that. Now it'll heat the water. I could just put the mugs in the microwave, but Tal is always bitching about us Yanks not making tea right. And when he brought over the kettle one day, I figured I might as well try it his way. And you know what? He was right. The tea tastes better when I make it this way."

Once again, Sunset was lost, but she nodded and smiled.

While they waited for the water to heat up, Lilly leaned against the counter, momentarily lost in thought. Sunset frowned. She was being super friendly and doing her best to make Sunset feel at ease, but flashes of sorrow still showed through her happy demeanor.

"I'm sorry about your baby," Sunset offered softly.

"Thanks. I just...it was such a surprise. I hadn't even thought that I might lose my baby."

"A few years ago," Sunset started slowly, "I found a pregnant deer in the woods. I was supposed to be hunting, finding food for The Community. She would've been an easy kill, but I couldn't bring myself to hurt her. She'd gotten her leg tangled in some fishing line from the stream. I knew I'd be punished if I told anyone about her, for not bringing the meat back, so I didn't tell anyone. Every time I went back to that area of the woods, I'd bring some extra carrots from our garden, and the deer was always there. I named her Chloe.

"Anyway, one day I went to our spot, and she wasn't there...but she'd had her baby. It didn't survive. I named her baby Little Chloe and buried her. I never saw Chloe again. I don't know what happened to her. Maybe she was so sad she couldn't go on living, or maybe another hunter got her. But I'd like to think that she ran far away from the sad memories of her baby that didn't get a chance to live and started over somewhere else. I want to believe she found another male deer and got pregnant again. This time giving birth to a happy and healthy Little Chloe, and they're both wandering around the forest, eating leaves and living a beautiful life."

The second she stopped talking, Sunset felt ridiculous. Talking about a silly deer losing her baby wasn't anything like a human losing her child.

But Lilly pushed off the counter and came toward her with tears in her eyes. "Can I hug you?" she asked.

Sunset froze, barely managing a nod.

It felt uncomfortable and weird to have someone so close. She stood stiffly in Lilly's arms, but that didn't seem to faze the other woman.

"Thank you," she said softly, her breath warm against Sunset's neck. "And I agree, I think your Chloe is alive and well with her new little baby doe, and she still remembers fondly the woman who saved her from that fishing line and who brought her carrots to eat."

Slowly, Sunset brought her arms up and wrapped them loosely around Lilly's back.

As she stood there in Lilly's embrace, a memory flashed through her mind. She was a young child, and a woman was hugging her. The scent of flowers on her hair was comforting.

Blinking hard, Sunset jerked in Lilly's arms.

The other woman immediately let go and backed away. "I'm sorry if I overstepped. I'm a hugger," she said with a small shrug.

"It's okay...I just...it's been a very long time since I've been hugged."

Lilly smiled at her. "I think the water's ready." She moved the mugs she'd gotten from a cupboard closer to the kettle and ripped open two little packets.

Sunset was immediately intrigued. The way she'd always seen tea made was with leaves being mashed into a pulp and the hot water poured over the whole mess. The leaves always got in her teeth as she drank and the whole experience was like chewing water. Completely gross.

But the smell coming from the mug as Lilly poured the water over the little packets was delicious. Sweet.

Sunset watched closely as Lilly dipped the bags up and down in the water, turning it brown.

"The longer you leave the bag in the water, the stronger the tea. I don't know if you would like it better weak or strong."

Sunset didn't know either.

"So...how about I make mine strong, because that's how I like it, and we'll do yours a little weaker? You can try them both, and if you like mine better, we'll put your tea bag back in and fix it. Okay?"

Sunset nodded. She was so out of her depth here, she'd leave the decisions about the tea to Lilly. It was pathetic that she had no idea how to even make a cup of tea like this, but she was determined to learn as much as she could. She'd obviously missed out on so much while living with The Community. It was exciting to be learning new things.

"Some people add milk or sugar to their tea, but I think the flavored kinds don't really need either of those things. Again, we can experiment to see what you like." Lilly handed her a mug. The tea inside was lighter than the water in Lilly's cup. "Try that and see what you think."

Tentatively, Sunset lowered her head to the mug and inhaled. The sweet smell was stronger now, and surprisingly, her mouth watered. She sipped the hot drink—and her eyes widened as she swallowed. "It's good!" Sunset said in surprise.

Lilly smiled happily. "Right? Here, now try mine. See if it's better or worse."

Sunset accepted Lilly's mug and took a sip. The cinnamon apple flavor was much stronger...and sweeter.

Lilly smiled. "You like mine better. Keep it. I'll put the tea bag back in yours for a minute or two, then I'll take that one."

Sunset took another sip of the tea as Lilly doctored the other mug. Soon she was sighing in contentment as she drank her own.

She hadn't been in town an hour, and already Sunset was seeing for herself that the people who lived in town weren't the enemies The Community had made them out to be. Lilly and Ethan couldn't have been nicer. And she'd learned that there was pleasure to be had in something as simple as tea. She couldn't help but wonder what other delights awaited her.

For so long, The Community had been her only family. All that she'd known. She'd taken Arrow and the other men's words for what was going on outside her small circle as fact. It had taken Arrow's death and Cypress's meanness to make her want something different.

Drinking this delicious tea in Lilly's kitchen was the first step to her new life, and Sunset couldn't help but feel happy. She was sorry for the reason she was there, for Lilly and Ethan's loss, but she couldn't be sorry Talon had found her. Had shaken her out of the complacency she'd become comfortable with.

"You look like you're thinking really hard," Lilly observed.

"I am," Sunset said simply.

"Well, thinking can be good. But don't get too lost in your head. Believe me, it's not always a good thing," Lilly said with a wince. "You can trust Tal. He's a good man, just as all the men on the Eagle Point Search and Rescue team are. You might hear stories about how he's a killer, how he did whatever his government asked without thinking twice, but that's not true at all. Ethan was a Navy SEAL, and yes, he killed people, but he never did it indiscriminately. If it wasn't for the things he did while in the Navy, a lot of innocent people would've died. I feel the same way about all the guys."

Once again, Sunset was lost. She didn't think of Talon as a killer. He'd told her that story about the women and children he'd tried to save, who'd died because of the men in their own community. That didn't sound like something a killer would do.

"I'm just saying that being here in Fallport might seem scary, but you can trust Tal to do right by you. You're in a different world than the one you've been living in, but that's a good thing. And no matter where you live, bad things happen to good people all the time. Look at me and my friends. But with support, you can get past it."

It felt as if Lilly was trying to tell her something without saying it directly, but Sunset had no idea what it was. She simply nodded yet again.

"Right. So you can trust Tal and all the other guys. Simon too."

"Simon?" Sunset asked.

"The police chief. He's great. Really wants what's best for Fallport. Oh, and Doc Snow is awesome too. When we called him in a panic, he was calm and met us at his clinic. He arranged for the ambulance to take me to Christiansburg, and he sat with me and Ethan and answered all of our questions. I don't think he left here until like midnight the other night. And if you need some girl talk, you can call me, or Elsie, Bristol, Caryn, Finley, or Khloe."

"Um...okay," Sunset said, because it seemed Lilly was waiting for her to agree.

"I'm sure the others are going to want to meet you as soon as possible. Maybe we can meet at The Sweet Tooth. You have to try one of Finley's cinnamon rolls. They're so delicious. Oh! And you'll have to check out Bristol's stained glass at Sunny Side Up! It's totally awesome. Do you like to read?"

Sunset nodded. She liked to read even if she wasn't very good at it, but she didn't say that.

"Good. Khloe works at the library, I'm sure she'd help you pick out some books. Elsie's son, Tony, hangs out there after school, and he's funny and sweet. He'll probably talk your ear off about living in the woods too. He loves camping and hiking and all things 'boy.' And when you meet Caryn, don't be intimidated. She's tough, but a total marshmallow inside."

Sunset's head was spinning. But the more she talked, the more Sunset found herself wanting to meet the other women. She wasn't sure what she might say to them, or how she should act, but if they were half as friendly as Lilly, Sunset didn't think she needed to worry too much.

"You ready to sit back down?" Ethan asked as he entered the kitchen.

Sunset jerked in surprise—and immediately took a step away from the large man coming toward them.

His eyes flicked to her, but he didn't say or do anything

alarming. He merely wrapped an arm around Lilly, pulling her against his side.

"Yeah," she said, looking up at him with love in her eyes.

Sunset watched them closely. Lilly obviously wasn't afraid of her husband. Not in the least. All the relationships she'd seen in The Community, at least from the women's points of view, were driven by fear. Everyone was scared of saying or doing the wrong thing and earning a punishment. When they were ordered to their husbands' tents, an air of resignation surrounded them as they acquiesced. At no time did *any* husband touch his wife the way Ethan was holding Lilly. There were no questions, like the one he'd just asked. Everything was an order. Go here. Do this. Faster. Stop doing that.

"You okay?"

Sunset startled at the question. Ethan and Lilly had left the kitchen and Talon had entered. She hadn't even noticed, she'd been so lost in the past. "Yeah."

"Did Lilly say anything to upset you?"

Sunset quickly shook her head. "No, not at all. I love this tea. It's nothing like I thought it would be."

Talon didn't lecture her on the inappropriateness of her abrupt change in topic. "It smells good."

"You want some?" Sunset asked, holding out her mug. She didn't expect him to say yes, but he reached for the cup and turned it so he took a sip from the same side she'd been drinking out of. For some reason, she blushed, but she couldn't take her gaze from his.

"It's a little sweet for me, but it's not bad," he said, handing the mug back to her.

Shyly, Sunset took it. "There are different kinds?"

"Oh yeah, there're hundreds of flavors of tea."

She frowned. "Really?"

"Yup."

"Wow." She loved how Talon didn't belittle her for her lack of knowledge about things she was sure everyone else on the planet, who didn't live in The Community, already knew. Trying to act nonchalant, she turned the mug in her hands and took another swallow of the tea, drinking from the same place he had.

Talon smiled, but he didn't comment on her actions. Sunset didn't know why she'd done that. It wasn't as if he was interested in her like that...she didn't think. He hadn't touched her except to hold her hand. He'd been very careful to keep his distance, to avoid intimacy...until that sip from her mug.

"You ready to head out? I don't know about you, but I need a shower in the worst way. Lilly was too polite to say more than that one little snarky comment, but I'm sure I don't smell all that great."

Immediately, Sunset thought about how her new friend had hugged her. She had to have been repulsed because she couldn't even remember a time when she'd last bathed. It was simply too cold in the winter to do more than a quick rubdown under her clothes. It was easier to do that when she'd been wearing the brown dress, but she hadn't done it often even then, because of how long it took her to warm up afterward.

She dropped her head in embarrassment.

"Sunset? What's wrong?"

She shrugged and kept her gaze on the floor.

"Will you please look at me?"

Darn it. She couldn't resist when Talon asked her to do something nicely, instead of ordering her. She looked up.

"Lilly's not thinking about anything other than

wanting to make you feel welcome and comfortable. You being here is a good distraction for her. Ethan said she looks happier today than she has since she realized she lost the baby. Don't be embarrassed. If anything, I should be the one embarrassed that I didn't give either of us time to get cleaned up before we arrived."

Hearing a man take responsibility for something he'd done wrong was still a new experience for Sunset. Not that wanting to get to his friends and make sure they were all right was wrong, but still. "She's really okay?" she asked quietly.

"She will be," Talon said firmly. "You really do like that tea?"

She nodded.

He grinned, then reached over and took several packets out of the box.

"What are you doing?" she asked in horror.

"You like the tea, I don't have any of it at my place, so I'm making sure you have something you enjoy drinking until we can get to the store and stock up."

"That's stealing!" she whispered.

"Naw, I'm just borrowing. I'll buy her a new box when we're at the store."

Sunset couldn't believe how nonchalant he was being. Taking anything from someone else meant a week in the punishment tent.

She took a deep breath. No. She wasn't in The Community anymore. Cypress wasn't here. The women who loved to tattle on everyone else weren't here.

"Will she mind?" she asked softly.

"Not at all. In fact, I bet once we let them know we're headed out, she'll offer to give you the entire box. Trust me, Sunset, I'm not going to do anything that would get you in trouble with anyone."

"And you won't hurt me either."

He looked pleased at her words. "Never," he breathed. He put the tea bags in his pocket and said, "Finish up your drink, and we'll go and say goodbye."

Again, his words could've been an order but they didn't sound like one. At least not like an order she'd ever been given by Arrow or Cypress. The tea had cooled enough by now that Sunset was able to drink it down fairly quickly. Talon took the mug from her hands and placed it in the sink.

"I should clean that," she said, but Talon held out his hand.

"Ethan'll take care of it later."

It still surprised her that a man would clean dishes. But she'd seen Talon do it often enough back at the cave that she didn't give his comment too much thought. She stared at his hand for a beat before reaching for it. She realized that Talon hadn't ever touched her without asking for permission first, other than in Rory's truck. But even then, he'd done so very slowly, allowing her to pull away if she wished.

He was so incredibly different from the men she'd known, it might always make her head spin.

They walked back into the living area hand in hand, and Sunset saw Lilly was once more sitting on her husband's lap. It didn't look as if he was forcing her to be there. When she was young, Arrow would hold her on his lap and stroke her hair. It felt uncomfortable, especially when he'd touch her between her legs and tell her she was a good girl.

In contrast, Lilly had her head on Ethan's shoulder and

she was holding one of his hands, while the other stroked his chest. He was holding her tightly against him with an arm around her back. Her legs were off to the side, and they both looked comfortable and content.

"We're going to get out of your hair," Talon told them.

"Oh, do you have to go so soon?" Lilly asked, raising her head.

"Yes," Talon said firmly. "I need to get Sunset home, showered, fed, and figure out what to do about clothes and other stuff."

"She can borrow things from me if she needs to," Lilly offered without hesitation.

"I appreciate that. I'm sure I've got something to tide her over until we can get to a store," Talon said.

"All right, but if you change your mind, just say so. We can bring something over. I mean, it's not like she can borrow something from Bristol."

Sunset was confused as the other three chuckled.

"She's only four-eleven," Talon explained when he saw her confusion.

"And we're around the same height," Lilly said with a smile.

"Feel free to grab food from the fridge to tide you over," Ethan offered.

"Oh! Let me up, Ethan, I want to get that box of tea and give it to Sunset to take with her."

Talon squeezed her hand as if to say "told you so" and replied, "I already pilfered some tea bags to tide her over. We're good."

Lilly settled against Ethan once more. "Oh, okay. Great."

Her response reinforced what Talon had said about taking the tea. Lilly honestly didn't care. And neither did

Ethan. Every minute that went by, Sunset was learning something new and amazing. Her mind was opening up to an entirely different way to live.

"You'll stay in touch though?" Lilly asked. "I'm guessing she doesn't have a phone yet, so I can't talk to her. And the others are going to want to meet her as soon as possible."

"I will. And I'm thinking we'll need to ease her into society. No phone yet, I don't want her to get over-whelmed. I need to talk to Simon, but I'll be in touch and will set something up so all the women can meet her when she's ready," Talon said.

Sunset wasn't sure why he would need to talk to Simon, who she now knew was the police chief. That made her extremely nervous. Was she going to be in trouble for living in the woods for so long? Was she going to go to jail?

"Trust me," Talon said, squeezing her fingers. "It's fine."

She relaxed. His request for trust immediately made her more comfortable, maybe because the words were so familiar now. Or perhaps it was because he hadn't once given her a reason *not* to trust him.

"It was so good to meet you, Sunset," Lilly told her.

"Same," she responded.

"Thanks for coming by," Ethan said.

"I'm sorry I wasn't here when it happened," Talon told them.

"You're here now. Means the world to us," Ethan said.

The deep friendship between Talon and his friends was easy to see.

"Oh, wait. I'm assuming you don't want to walk home?" Ethan asked.

Tal let out a huff. "Bloody hell, I forgot I don't have my vehicle."

"Take my Outback," Ethan said. "I'll call the guys so we can get yours back to you tomorrow."

"Appreciate it. Rory, the plow driver, said he was going to dig it out."

"Perfect. My keys are in a bowl in the kitchen," Ethan said.

"Want me to lock up behind us?" Talon asked.

"Please."

"I'll hopefully see you soon. If you need anything, just ask Tal to let me know. Okay?" Lilly told Sunset softly.

She had no idea what she could want, but she nodded anyway.

Talon steered them back into the kitchen to grab the keys, then to the front door. He locked the dead bolt after closing the door behind them. He picked up his pack he'd left by the door and walked them to the vehicle sitting in the driveway.

It was hard for her to wrap her mind around how easily Ethan had offered his car to Talon. In her experience, men were overly protective about who got to drive their vehicles. Cypress never let anyone drive his van. Ever.

Talon held open the passenger-side door and waited until she was seated before closing it and walking around to the driver's side. He put on his seat belt, then turned to her. "Belt?" he asked.

For a second, she wasn't sure what he meant, then it dawned on her. She reached behind her and pulled the seat belt over her shoulder. In the vans The Community members owned, none of the seat belts worked.

When it clicked into place, he smiled at her and started the engine. As they drove away, he said, "You have a choice to make, Sunset."

The thought of having to make a decision about

anything made her tense up immediately. She didn't like choices. Usually, no matter what she picked, it ended badly for her. Especially when Cypress presented her options.

"I'm taking you back to my apartment so we can both get clean, get something to eat, and maybe even wash our clothes. After that, you can either stay at my apartment by yourself and I'll head to the Mangree Motel, or I can take *you* to the motel. I'm sure Edna would be more than happy to take you under her wing. Or, if you trust me enough, you can stay at my apartment, and I'll stay with you. You can have my room and I'll sleep on the couch."

Sunset stared at Talon as he drove. He looked relaxed, as if he didn't care which option she chose. The thought of being taken to a motel and left alone didn't appeal. She'd gotten used to Talon being around. It was ridiculous, really, as she'd been alone for most of the last year out in the forest. But she knew the woods like the back of her hand. She was in a world she didn't completely understand now. Everything seemed new. Being alone seemed much more frightening than it should.

Being in Talon's apartment by herself didn't feel as scary, simply because it was his home. But she didn't like the thought of being there when he wasn't. What if something happened? What if she broke something? She didn't want to take the chance of him getting mad if she ruined something of his and never talking to her again.

The thought of losing Talon almost sent her into a panic attack. It felt as if he was her lifeline in this strange new world she'd found herself in. "Your place with you there," she finally said.

"Are you sure? You don't sound sure," Talon said.

Sunset took a deep breath. "I'm sure."

"Okay. That's what we'll do. But be warned, I'm going

to be asking you *a lot* if you've changed your mind. At any time, you can choose one of the other options and I won't be mad, okay? I wouldn't be surprised if any of the other women offered for you to stay with them as well. You are *not* a prisoner in my apartment. You can come and go whenever you want. Understand?"

Sunset nodded, even though she couldn't think of a reason why she'd want to leave. She had no money. Had no way of *making* money. Couldn't read or write very well. Talon was kind of stuck with her. She figured he'd want her to leave before she'd ever want to go.

"Don't think so hard," he said gently. "I know this is all new to you, but you're doing wonderfully. Lilly seemed so much happier when we left than when we arrived. I attribute that to *you*, Sunset."

"Me? I didn't do anything."

"Maybe, maybe not. But you being there, letting Lilly take care of you, helped her a lot. And I don't know what you talked about in the kitchen, but whatever it was...it sank in."

What they talked about? Sunset tried to remember. Tea. Her eyes. And the deer she'd named Chloe. Could Talon be right? Could her story have helped, even a little? It didn't seem likely. It was just a stupid story about a deer. But deep down, she felt good. As if maybe she *had* helped her new friend at least a little bit.

"My apartment isn't anything fancy. I've got two bedrooms, one of which is pretty much empty. I didn't bring a lot with me from overseas when I moved here. And I don't feel the need to buy things I don't really need. But maybe now's the time. I can get a bed and a dresser for you. Definitely a bookshelf, and we'll go to Fall for

Books, the used bookstore in town, and see if we can't fill it up."

Sunset stared at him with wide eyes. "You don't have to buy me things."

"You're wrong about that. But we'll play it by ear. You might want your own place sooner rather than later."

Sunset was reeling. Talon had already been nicer to her than anyone else in her life. It was confusing...but so comforting at the same time.

"So, clothes...I've got lots of T-shirts and sweatshirts you can wear, but I obviously don't have any pants that will fit. Sweatpants will probably work for tonight though, although they'll be huge on you. We'll get your leggings and cargo pants washed tonight, and you can wear them tomorrow. I probably should've taken Lilly up on her offer to borrow some things for you, but I didn't want her to get up, and...you deserve your own things. New outfits you pick out yourself. I have a feeling you haven't ever gotten to do so."

He was right about that.

"Right, so tomorrow, we'll go shopping. Then hit the grocery store. Then I need to talk to Simon."

"Am...am I in trouble?"

"No!" Talon said so quickly, Sunset couldn't help but believe him. "But there are things we need to discuss."

"About The Community," she said. It wasn't a question.

"Yes. And how you got there."

Sunset frowned. How *had* she gotten there? She'd always just assumed she'd been adopted like all the other kids.

"But you've been through enough upheaval for today. You had to walk for miles in the cold, then ride in a truck with a stranger to get to town. You saw Fallport for the first time, then met my friends, who're grieving the loss of their first child. It's been an eventful day and it's not even over yet. You've yet to see my flat."

"Your flat?"

"Sorry, that's my British side coming out. My apartment."

"I like your words," she told him somewhat shyly.

"Thanks." He pulled into a parking lot in front of a three-story brick building. "I think this is the tallest building in Fallport." He grinned. "I'm on the third floor, by the stairs. You ready for this?"

Was she? Sunset's first impulse was to say no and ask to be taken back to the forest. At least there, she knew what to expect. It wasn't an especially comfortable life, but it was familiar. But she took a breath and nodded at Talon.

"Strong as bloody hell," he said under his breath. Then he looked her in the eyes and said, "I won't hurt you and you can trust me. This is going to work out. Promise."

What else could she do but believe him?

CHAPTER TEN

Sunset didn't even realize until she'd already showered and changed into the huge pair of sweatpants and T-shirt Talon had given her that she probably should've been a little more cautious about getting naked in what was essentially a stranger's bathroom.

But because the stranger was Talon, and he felt like anything *but* a stranger, she hadn't thought twice about it. Truthfully, she'd been overwhelmed with the newness of everything from the second she'd stepped foot in Talon's apartment.

She'd managed to keep her curiosity and awe at how different and modern everything seemed when she was at Lilly and Ethan's house. She was more concerned about not making a fool out of herself, and worried about Lilly, to think too much about all the new things surrounding her.

But when she'd walked into Talon's apartment, she was sure her eyes were so wide, she had to look like a total weirdo. From his huge television, to the appliances on his countertops...she wanted nothing else but to stop and investigate everything. She'd lived a life devoid of nearly all technology for so long. The men at camp had radios and a few other electronics, but Sunset hadn't had a chance to look at them up close, much less use them or ask how they worked.

But Talon hadn't given her a chance to do much more than follow her to his room, where he said she'd be sleeping, before pulling out some clothes for her to put on after her shower, showing her how his shower worked, then leaving her alone.

Having hot water had also diverted her attention. She couldn't remember the last time she'd showered with warm water. Every now and then, mostly in the summer, the women would boil water to use for bathing, but mostly they made do with sponge baths.

Standing under the shower felt like a rebirth. As the years of filth and dirt washed down the drain, Sunset could practically feel the shadow of Arrow and Cypress sloughing off her skin. She'd felt oppressed and beaten down for so long. Even when she'd been in the forest by herself, she'd feared Cypress's return. He was so mad when she'd hidden from him. If he'd found her, she would've had to spend months in the punishment tent. They both knew it.

The threat of that fate hung over her even though she hadn't seen Cypress or anyone from The Community since she'd fled. Her rebellion had been a long time coming, and even though she was proud of herself for doing it, she'd also lived in a state of fear every day since.

But now? Being treated as if she wasn't less important, less worthy, than those around her? Sunset felt a burst of optimism rise within her. Lilly had been so nice, even while dealing with her own grief for her lost child. She hadn't made fun of her for not knowing there were different flavors of tea. She hadn't looked down on her for anything, in fact.

More importantly, her husband hadn't either. Ethan had greeted her warmly, hadn't ordered her around, and the way he'd acted with concern for Lilly made Sunset truly understand that the kind of leader Arrow had been was just plain wrong. He might've been old, but he set the rules in The Community. He was the one who ordered punishments and taught the children and women how to behave.

When she'd finished her shower, used the softest towel she'd ever felt in her life, and then dressed in the borrowed clothes, Sunset had attempted to brush her hair. She'd used the shampoo Talon had left for her, but it was almost impossible to get the brush through the tangles.

She walked out of the shower and didn't see Talon anywhere. There was a large bed with four pillows on it, and for a moment, Sunset wondered how many wives Talon had to need so many pillows. Then she shook her head. No, Talon said he wasn't married, and she believed him. He hadn't done or said anything that felt like a lie... and she'd gotten very good over the years at reading people. It had gotten to a point where she could tell almost everything Cypress said was a lie.

The bed made her very nervous, even though it looked as if it was more comfortable than anything she'd ever slept on before. The bedding Talon had given her in the cave had been so much softer than the canvas she'd been using, and ten times better than sleeping on the ground like she'd done back in The Community.

But she also remembered the mattress Arrow had owned, which Cypress had used when he'd taken over after his father's death. She'd had to lie on her back on the soft surface when it was time for her to do her wifely duties. She'd come to hate the feel of that softness against her back, because of what it meant she'd have to endure.

Scooting around the bed, Sunset vaguely noticed the dresser against one wall and the window that let in the late-afternoon sun. She walked out of the room into a hall, headed into the room with the large TV, and saw Talon standing in the small kitchen that ran along one end of the room. He had a glass of water in one hand, and he was staring out the small window above the sink.

"I'm done," she said softly.

His head whipped around and he put down the glass. Then he stared at her for so long, Sunset began to feel uncomfortable. As if he realized what he was doing, and how he was making her feel, Talon immediately dropped his gaze and reached for a second glass she hadn't noticed sitting on the counter near him.

He slowly walked toward her with the water in hand.

"I figured you might be thirsty," he said, holding out the glass.

Sunset nodded and took the offered water. She took a sip, surprised at how...clean the water tasted. The water from the streams they used in The Community, like the water she drank while living in the cave, was good, but she could somehow always taste the grit from the dirt that flowed through it.

There was no dirt in this water.

"Do you feel better?" Talon asked quietly.

Feeling shy all of a sudden, Sunset could only nod.

"Good. I'll wash both our clothes after I shower. You want to watch TV while I'm getting cleaned up?"

Sunset nodded eagerly. She knew what TV was. She didn't know how she knew, but she did.

Talon hadn't taken his gaze from her. He studied her from head to toe, then back up again. He winced when he saw the condition of her hair. "You want me to try to brush that out when I'm done?" he asked, nodding to her head.

Sunset's first reaction was to say no, that she could do it. But then she remembered how gentle he'd been with her when he'd brushed it back in the cave. "Will you cut some more off?"

"Do you *want* me to cut some more off?" he returned.

Sunset was finding it difficult to have to make so many decisions. She'd gotten used to being told what to do every minute of every day. When she'd first been on her own in the forest, it had been a struggle figuring out what to do without The Community's rigid schedule to follow, but eventually she'd gotten into a routine of her own. That routine was now thrown out the window, and Talon was always asking her what she wanted to do or if something he was doing was okay. It was hard to get used to. "Yes?" she said tentatively.

"It's up to you, sweetheart. I can take another little bit off, or we could brush it out and you can see how you feel after that. Now that it's clean, and you can wear it however you want, you might change your mind about cutting it."

Sunset didn't think that would happen. Even with the little bit Talon had already cut off, she felt so much better. It was still long, coming down almost to her butt, but it was heavy and reminded her too much of her time in The Community. Of having no choice but to keep it long. "I think I want you to cut some more off," she said, lifting her chin as if Talon would argue with her.

will hide that." He wrinkled his
...ken Ethan up on his offer to take
...ridge. If this doesn't work, I can run
...nd things to tide us over. Maybe I'll
...r something."

...now what a pizza was, but she shook her
...be fine." And it would be. She didn't have
...it, cook it, and she had a feeling Talon
...her wash the plate afterward either. She
...njoy this meal more than he knew, no matter
...like.

"...ut don't be polite for my sake. If you don't like
...you't have to eat it. Same for any of our meals. You
...an te me exactly what you think about it, and I'm not
...oing to be mad if you don't enjoy something. Actually,
that goes for *anything* we do. If you aren't enjoying something, if you get scared or aren't having a good time, all you
have to do is say the word and we'll stop or leave."

He had no idea what he was giving her. She'd never had
a say on literally anything before, food or otherwise.
"Okay," she whispered.

"Good." He tossed a pillow from the couch onto the
floor, then sat on the couch directly behind it. "If you sit
here, I can reach your hair easier. You want to watch the next
episode of this show while I brush your hair and we snack?"

Sunset turned her head so he couldn't see the tears that
welled in her eyes. He was being so *nice*...and it was almost
her undoing.

She scooted off the couch and moved to sit in front of
him. He didn't need to put a pillow down, but he had
anyway, solely for her comfort. He held the plate out.
"Why don't you hold this?"

"Then that's what we'll do. For the record...it's beautiful. Even prettier than before. I didn't realize you had all
those different shades of auburn in it."

Sunset's cheeks felt hot for some reason. Arrow had
always seemed to like her hair well enough, but it was
Cypress who worshipped it. When he made her do her
wifely duties, he'd gather it in a fist and hold it to his nose
as he had sex with her. Sometimes he didn't want to have
sex at all, but he'd make her lie completely still while he
wrapped her hair around his penis and masturbated. She
hated how his eyes would shine when he looked at her.
How he'd tell her how much he loved her hair.

But for some reason, when Talon told her how pretty
her hair was, it felt...nice. Maybe because he wasn't leering
at her like Cypress did. "Thank you," she said softly.

"You're welcome. Come on, let's find something that
interests you on TV."

He turned and reached for a long, flat device and
pointed it at the huge screen on the wall. Sunset jumped
when two people suddenly appeared on the screen,
laughing loudly about something.

"Bloody hell, sorry. I forgot to turn it down when I
shut it off last time," Talon said sheepishly. "Let's see...
what's on...a true crime show...no. Football? Doubt that
would interest you. A cooking show...maybe...hmmmm.
Shit. I have no idea what you might enjoy."

The pictures on the screen scrolled by quickly, but
Sunset was delighted by the bright colors and how many
shows there seemed to be. "What about that one?" she
asked, pointing as Talon scrolled through the images.

He stopped and turned to her. "Which one?"

"Um...that one that had the purple background and the
cute little green guy?"

Talon looked back at the screen. "*StoryBots?*" he asked.

Sunset shrugged. "I guess."

Talon didn't declare her choice stupid. He immediately pushed a button and the purple picture suddenly filled the screen. "I won't be too long, so if you don't enjoy this once it starts, we can find something else," he told her.

But Sunset was already enthralled by the pictures moving across the screen. She vaguely heard Talon chuckle but didn't take her eyes off the TV. He gently steered her toward the couch and urged her to sit, but she was already lost in the world of Beep, Bing, Boop, and Bo, the cute little robots who were trying to figure out how computers worked. Sunset wanted to know the same thing.

By the time Talon returned, the show was just ending.

"I take it you liked the show."

She smiled. "I know it's for children, but I actually learned so much! And the songs were fun."

When she finally looked up at Talon, she blinked in surprise. She'd gotten used to his scruffy beard, but he'd trimmed it up while she'd been watching the show. He was wearing a T-shirt that clung to his muscular chest. He had on a pair of sweatpants just like she did, but he definitely filled them out much better. Even from where she was sitting, she could smell his fresh, clean scent.

In short, this man was completely different from Arrow, Cypress, or any of the other men in The Community. He was...beautiful. It was the only word that came to mind as she stared at him.

"Are you okay?" Talon asked.

Sunset lowered her eyes and nodded.

"Good. I put our clothes in the washer. You want a snack before we get started on your hair?"

Butterflies swam in Sunset's belly. They were alone, and

he could do anyth... know. But instead keeping his distance, with her hair.

She might be naïve a... world, but she knew all a... between two people. Before ... The Community had educat... describing how the man would li... his penis inside her. Abstractly, sh... people actually enjoyed sex, but she wa...

For the first time in her life...she understand. She *liked* looking at Talon. L... smelled. And the thought of his hands on ... her nipples tingle on her chest.

Instead of being scared or freaked out, Su... relieved. She actually *wanted* Talon to touch her. She w... sure she wanted to lie under him, but if *he* wanted tha... would do it. She could trust him, and he wouldn't hurt...

With that thought in mind, Sunset smiled again.

"Sunset? Does that smile mean you want something... eat?" Talon asked.

It wasn't, but she nodded anyway. She forced herself to stay seated on the couch as Talon walked to the small kitchen that was next to the large open room. He'd told her more than once that she didn't have to wait on him, that he'd been looking after himself for a long time. She liked that he didn't expect her to do all the chores.

So with that thought in mind, and because he hadn't asked her to help, Sunset stayed where she was.

It didn't take him long to walk back toward her with a plate. "There's not much to choose from, but I had some crackers and cheese. The crackers might be a little stale,

She took hold of the plate and stared down at it through blurry eyes. A plate of food, clean clothes, letting her watch the silly show for kids, and Talon brushing her hair. It was overwhelming.

Holding the plate with one hand, she picked up a cracker with the other. She felt Talon lean toward her, and the heat from his chest brushed against the back of her head as he reached for a cracker himself. She froze for a second, thinking he was going to grab her, but when he sat back, she let out a long breath.

How could she both *want* him to touch her and be scared of it at the same time? It was confounding. But more than that, it made her mad. She wasn't going to let Arrow and Cypress keep her from what she'd always wanted—to belong. To have friends. To be accepted. To have a family. A *real* family. Not the messed-up one The Community tried to claim they were.

She'd been so scared to come to town. Fallport had always been made out to be dangerous and its citizens portrayed as monsters. But she was quickly discovering the monsters were the people she'd been living with.

Sunset knew, however, that she was probably feeling things for Talon simply because he was the first man who'd ever been kind to her. Despite that, she wasn't going to feel bad about how much she liked him. As she saw for herself, his friends respected and enjoying being around him. That went a long way toward helping her to trust her own feelings.

"Tell me if I hurt you," Talon said as he ran a hand lightly over her hair.

A shiver ran through Sunset, and she nodded. He started the next episode, which wasn't quite as entertaining as the first; she already knew she couldn't eat dessert all the time.

Talon was gentle as he brushed her hair. Even though she'd seen all the tangles, it was as if they didn't exist as he ran the brush through her strands. He got up at one point to get a pair of scissors, and she was so relaxed, even the sight of them didn't make her tense up.

Talon cut off another tiny amount from the ends of her hair. She wanted to tell him he could take more off than he did, but he was being so careful, so gentle with her, that she didn't want to do or say anything that might upset him.

Long after the sun went down, Sunset was as comfortable as she'd ever been in her life. Her belly was full, she was clean and warm sitting on one end of the comfortable couch, and Talon had let her watch several episodes of the kids' show. She'd learned all about different animals in the world, how ears and volcanos worked, and what electricity was. The show was informative without going into too much detail. The problem was, now she wanted to know *more*.

Her brain was soaking up as much information as it could, and still she needed more.

"Tomorrow we'll go to the library," Talon told her from the other side of the couch, as if he could read her mind.

"I thought we were going to go to the store to get food?" she said in confusion.

"We are. We'll go to the library afterward. Tony's on holiday vacation from school, but Elsie still usually drops him off in the afternoons because he enjoys hanging out there…and of course, she won't leave him home alone when she and Zeke go to work at On the Rocks."

"Then we'll talk to Simon?" she asked. She dreaded

that. The police were corrupt. Mean. Liked to put people in jail.

"Maybe," Talon said nonchalantly.

Sunset breathed out a sigh of relief. She'd put off talking to the police forever if she could. She still didn't even know why Talon wanted to have a meeting with the man.

He smiled over at her. "Are you all right?"

Sunset nodded.

"Comfortable?"

She nodded again.

"Good. Anything you need or want, you only have to tell me and I'll bend over backward to make sure you get it."

"Why?" The question popped out without thought, and Sunset cringed. It was that kind of question that always got her in trouble in the past. But Talon wasn't a Community member. He didn't seem upset or irritated with her in the least.

"Because you've been dealt a raw hand. Because you deserve it. Because I like seeing you happy. I like *you*, Sunset. You've been through a lot, and I know it's way too early for you to even be thinking about any kind of relationship, but...when you're ready..." His voice trailed off.

Her heart started beating fast in her chest as she stared at Talon. Was he saying what she thought he was?

"I'm sure a psychologist would be pissed that I'm even bringing this up, but I've seen firsthand how short life can be." He pinned her in place with his intense blue gaze. "I like everything about you, sweetheart. Your strength. Your determination to survive despite what you've been through. Your pragmatic ability to take things one day at a time. Your physical looks. Your huge heart. I didn't miss how worried you were for Lilly, a woman you just met and had no reason to feel any kind of way toward. And yet you let her take care of you, allowing her to feel somewhat normal again. I know all the other women are going to love you, and they'll help you acclimate to Fallport, to life not under the thumb of a bunch of assholes.

"So...when you feel as if you're ready...I'll be here. I want to be your man, Sunset. I want to have the *privilege* of being yours."

Sunset swallowed. "Um...okay."

"Okay," he said easily, as if he hadn't just rocked her world.

This man wanted to be hers? That wasn't how it worked, was it? Shouldn't he have said he wanted her to be *his*? She was confused...but inside, she was also jumping up and down like Beep did on the *StoryBots* show she'd just watched.

"It's getting late. We've got a busy day ahead of us tomorrow. Think you can sleep?"

Sunset nodded immediately. She was exhausted but hadn't wanted to end the night because she was having such a good time.

"Good. Because I'm so tired, I think I could fall asleep standing up," Talon said. "Come on, let's go make sure you've got everything you need for the night."

He was tired too. That was something else Talon frequently did that she'd yet to get used to—admitting a weakness. It was nice to know she wasn't alone.

She followed him to his room and saw the clothes she'd been wearing earlier were folded neatly on the dresser. He'd washed and dried them for her. It was one more way he took care of her that sent warm feelings throughout her body.

"We'll find you more things to wear tomorrow." He pulled the blanket back and took a step away from the bed, backing toward the door. "Sleep well, Sunset. This is the first night of the rest of your life, sweetheart." Then he turned before she could speak and closed the door behind him.

Sunset looked at the bed and smiled.

She didn't take off the sweats she was wearing, simply climbed onto the mattress and pulled the covers up to her chin. The light on the ceiling was still on, but she didn't mind. She liked the light. Closing her eyes, she did her best to relax. To appreciate the luxurious mattress. Her bones didn't hurt from poking into the hard ground. She was warm.

But the longer she lay there, the more uncomfortable she got.

She shouldn't be here. This wasn't her bed. It was Talon's. She could smell him on the blankets and on the pillows under her head. He'd given her his bed, and it felt wrong. As much as she tried to tell herself it was all right, it didn't *feel* all right.

Having no idea how long she'd been staring at the ceiling, Sunset climbed out of the bed and headed for the door. She opened it, thankful it didn't make any noise. She tiptoed down the hallway, past the empty room Talon had promised he'd furnish for her, and entered the TV room.

Talon was lying on the couch they'd sat on all night. He was frowning in his sleep, and even as she watched, he turned onto his side with a grunt.

As silent as a deer moving through the forest, Sunset took a step toward him. Then another. She felt safer near Talon. He wouldn't hurt her, and she could trust him.

With the words he'd said so many times repeating in

her head, she lowered herself to the floor next to the couch and closed her eyes.

She could hear him breathing above her, and she felt content. This felt more right than being alone in the other room.

* * *

Tal woke with a jerk. Damn it. He repeatedly hoped the nightmares he'd suffered since that fucked-up final mission would eventually go away completely. But years later, they still hadn't.

Sighing, he ran a hand over his face. His couch was comfortable enough to sit on and watch a ball game, but sleeping on it was a different story. He stretched—then froze as a sound hit his ears. Deep breathing.

Moving slowly, and cursing the fact that he didn't have a weapon nearby like he did in his bedroom, Tal turned his head and strained to see what he'd heard in the darkness.

There was a glow coming from the hallway...giving him just enough light to see a shape lying on the floor by the couch.

Sunset.

She was lying on her side, facing him, fast asleep. She didn't have a blanket or a pillow.

Tal had no idea why she was there and not in bed where he'd left her.

The thought of her lying in his bed had haunted him long after he'd closed his eyes. He shouldn't have said anything about wanting a relationship. It was too soon, he knew that. But he hadn't been able to stop himself. Without a doubt, once she started getting out and about, other men would take notice. She was bloody beautiful.

And she had a sweet disposition, despite what she'd been through.

She probably saw him as her savior or something, which wouldn't bode well for a healthy romantic relationship. And even though he knew all that, he still couldn't stop himself from declaring his interest.

Sighing once more at his own stupidity, Talon sat up, careful not to step on the sleeping woman as he stood, then immediately kneeled down next to her. He didn't want to scare her by touching her, so he whispered her name instead. "Sunset."

She didn't move.

Tal's lips quirked up. She was adorable all the time, but especially so right now. Still, the sight of her using her arm as a pillow and lying on the hard floor wasn't cute at all. He said her name again, a little louder.

This time she jerked—and immediately she rolled into a small ball, putting her arms over her face.

Mentally swearing—and vowing to avenge her, no matter how long it took—Tal quickly stood and took a giant step away from her. Giving her space.

"It's me, Talon. I'm not going to hurt you. You're safe here."

She immediately came up on an elbow and turned her head to the side, as if that would make her see in the dark better. "Talon?"

"Yes, it's me. We're in my apartment. Why are you sleeping on the floor?" he asked.

"Um...it seemed appropriate."

"Explain," Tal ordered. His voice sounded a bit too harsh to his own ears, but he needed to understand her thinking.

"The bed was soft...almost too soft. I wasn't used to it.

Then I got to thinking that it wasn't right that I was there and you were out here. That's not how things work in my world. So I came out here to tell you to switch places with me, but when I saw you sleeping, I didn't want to wake you up."

"So you decided to sleep on the floor?" he asked incredulously.

"It's not a big deal. I'm used to it."

He didn't move closer to her, but he knelt down so he could look her in the eyes. The room was still dark, and even with the light that he now realized was coming from his bedroom, he couldn't see her clearly. But he needed her to understand the kind of man he was.

"You're used to something that isn't acceptable," he told her firmly. "The life you've known, it's done. You're starting a new one. Where women are treated like gold. Where you will always get your food first, your bed will always be the softest, you'll shower first to make sure you always have hot water, and I'll protect you from anyone who dares to even *look* at you wrong."

"That's...I don't know what that is," Sunset said, sitting up.

"This is Tal's world, and you're now living in it. I was raised to treat women and children as precious. You've had the misfortune to have met the worst of humanity, and I'm going to do whatever it takes to help you unlearn everything they taught you. In my world, you can ask as many questions as you want, you can disagree as much as you want, you can even tell me to go to hell, and you won't be disciplined for any of it.

"In my world, you have friends who will have your back, no questions asked. Because you see, they live in

Tal's world too, and you can trust them just like you do me, and they will never hurt you either.

"But the one thing you *can't* do in my world, is treat yourself as if you're not as worthy as me or anyone else. The way I see it, you're so far above most people in this world because of what you've survived. You deserve a crown of gold, but all I've got is a comfortable bed, shows on the TV that you enjoy, and a promise that your life just got a hell of a lot easier."

He was breathing hard by the time he was finished speaking, but Tal didn't move. Not one inch. He was probably freaking her out, but she needed to understand that under no circumstances was he going to allow her to sleep on the bloody floor.

"I think I want to live in your world," she whispered.

"Good. Because you already are." He slowly stood and took a step toward her and held out his hand. "Come on, I need you off the floor and back in bed."

She put her hand in his, and every muscle in Tal's body relaxed. He helped her to her feet then put a hand on the small of her back and turned her toward the hallway. He immediately dropped it as soon as she started walking but kept close to her.

He saw the mussed covers, as if she'd tossed and turned before getting up. He straightened them out then gestured for her to climb back in.

She did, then said, "I don't know if I can sleep knowing you're out there on the couch and I'm in here."

He didn't like her obvious guilt, but he'd promised she could say whatever was on her mind without him getting upset. He wrestled with what to do and say for a long moment before walking around the bed and lying down on top of the covers next to her. "Is this okay?"

"Yes."

He heard the heavy relief in that one word.

"Light on or off?" he asked.

"Would you mind if we kept it on? I should be used to the dark, but I prefer to be able to see."

"Of course I don't mind," Tal told her.

"Talon?" she said after a minute.

"Yeah?"

"I don't want a crown of gold. I just want to feel safe."

"You *are* safe," he said immediately. "It might take you a while to truly believe that, but it doesn't make it any less so."

He heard her sigh, but she didn't comment.

"Good night, sweetheart. Sleep well."

"You too," she replied quietly.

It took a while for Tal to fall asleep, partly because he was savoring the sound of Sunset's deep breaths next to him. Of the feel of the mattress moving as she turned in her sleep. But when he did finally succumb, he'd never slept as soundly as he did now, knowing the woman who'd changed his life for the better was safe and content next to him.

CHAPTER ELEVEN

Tal was well aware he'd been putting off Sunset's meeting with Simon. On one hand, he wanted her to give them as much information about the cult leaders as possible so they could be found and prosecuted, but on the other, he was loving watching her relax more and more and come out of her shell. He didn't want to do anything that would hurt the progress she'd made in the few days she'd been in Fallport. And he had a feeling bringing up her past and telling her she'd been kidnapped when she was eight would be a massive blow.

In the last four days, the other women had completely stepped up. Tal had brought Sunset to The Sweet Tooth, where she'd met Finley. No one could resist Finley's outgoing personality and friendliness, and Sunset had been no exception. He'd driven her out to Bristol and Rocky's place, and she'd been dazzled by some of the amazing stained-glass creations Bristol had made that hadn't been shipped off yet. She also got to see where the wedding she'd listened to had taken place.

He and Sunset had eaten lunch at On the Rocks the

day after she'd arrived in town, so she could meet Elsie and Zeke, and later, Tal had taken her to the library to meet Tony. Needless to say, *that* had gone extremely well. At first, Sunset had been shy, but Tony being Tony, he was oblivious to her reticence and had quickly won her over with his nonstop chatter.

She'd been overwhelmed with all the book choices, but Raiden had helped—after a word from Tal—by picking out some books he didn't think would be too hard for her to read, taking into account she probably only had a third-grade education or so.

Khloe had come out to say hello too, and while Sunset seemed shy around both her and Duke, Raiden's blood-hound, she still seemed to enjoy meeting them.

They'd gone over to visit with Lilly again, and this time Caryn had been there. It seemed to Tal that Sunset hadn't been able to take her eyes off Caryn's short hair. And when Drew had arrived, proving beyond a shadow of a doubt with a too-long kiss in front of everyone just how beautiful he thought she was—short hair and all—Tal could practically see the wheels turning in Sunset's head.

Escorting her around town and showing her all the things he'd always taken for granted was both heart-breaking and fun at the same time. They'd gone to the big box store to get a bed for his empty guest room, a small set of drawers, some clothes to tide her over until the other women could outfit her more appropriately, and to stock up on food he thought she'd enjoy, as well as things he wanted her to try. Sunset's eyes had been as wide as saucers the entire time they'd shopped. She hadn't said much at the time, but it was easy to see she was both overwhelmed and excited.

Yesterday, they'd walked around the square, getting a

feel for the town in general. They'd stopped into Grogan's General Store, and Tal couldn't resist buying Sunset one of the "Home of Bigfoot" shirts Harry Grogan had made to sell to tourists. They'd also said hello to Silas, Otto, and Art, who, even though it was early January and not exactly warm, were in their usual spots outside the post office. Then they'd had lunch at Sunny Side Up, where Sandra warmly welcomed Sunset to town.

He'd even brought her into the barbershop and introduced her to his boss, Harvey. While there, she'd let Tal take a little bit more off her hair. All in all, he'd enjoyed showing Sunset the town. He hadn't been born or raised here, but he'd come to love the small town and its mostly friendly residents.

They spent their evenings watching television, making dinner together, and talking about nothing in particular. He'd read more chapters of *The Lion, the Witch, and the Wardrobe* to her, and he loved seeing her excitement over learning things, and the way she embraced this new, sometimes confusing and scary way of life.

Nighttime was both heavenly and frustrating as hell for Tal. Sunset had yet to spend a night in the bed he'd bought for her in the guest room. When it came time for bed, Tal could read the fear in her eyes. She never admitted to being scared to sleep by herself in the other room, but it was obvious that, while she might enjoy the newness of everything, it was also overwhelming.

So they were still sleeping together in the queen-size bed in his room. Her under the covers on her side, and him on top on his side. He hadn't been sleeping well, but for the first time in his life it wasn't because of nightmares. It was because as he lay there next to her, listening to her breathe, he was content in a way he hadn't ever been before...and he didn't want to miss a moment.

Sunset made him want to be a better man. She'd been so mistreated by others in her past, he wanted to protect her from anyone who would dare do anything to burst the safe bubble she was in now.

And he knew without a doubt that telling her she'd been kidnapped when she was eight would definitely put a dent in the happiness she was experiencing. As far as he knew, the people in the cult were the only parents and life she remembered. If she recalled anything about her life before age eight, she didn't share it with him. He was more and more certain she'd probably blocked it out as an act of self-preservation...and Tal didn't blame her.

So making her talk to Simon would definitely ruin the happy vibe she had going on, and Tal was reticent to do that to her. But he knew he couldn't put it off. Cypress needed to be found and locked away so he couldn't continue to hurt other women and children.

Tal quietly slid out of bed without disturbing Sunset. It was early still, and he wanted to let her sleep in. Living in the forest wasn't an easy life, but with all the things she'd been doing lately, her body was still getting used to being even more active.

Looking down at her before he left the room, Tal smiled. Her temperature ran hot. Every night she went to sleep under the covers, but by morning she'd kicked them off. The cold didn't seem to bother her, and she didn't mind that he kept his apartment on the cool side. He supposed she was used to the cold after living outside her entire life. It was one more thing he loved learning about her.

Tal grabbed a change of clothes and slipped into the

bathroom silently. When he was done, he couldn't keep his gaze from going to the bed once more. Sunset's hair was spread out on the pillow in disarray, the auburn strands looking bright against the white of the pillowcase. She was spread-eagle on the bed, as if her subconscious was reveling in the ability to stretch out on a comfortable mattress.

He realized he was still smiling minutes later as he prepared a cup of tea for himself and set out a mug for Sunset, for when she woke up and joined him. Her wide eyes when she'd taken in the tea aisle at the store had been comical, and when she couldn't decide which to try, Tal had bought twenty different boxes. She'd also tried coffee —and hated it. He could drink it, but he was English through and through, and he loved his tea.

He sat on the couch, sipping his tea as he opened his laptop to read the day's news. He was halfway through an article about the increasing tensions in the Middle East when there was a knock on the door. Surprised, because it was still early and he hadn't made plans with any of his friends to hang out, Tal got up to answer it.

His stomach clenched in discomfort as he realized his time was up. Simon had given him some space, but he was obviously done.

"Morning," Simon said with a nod.

Tal returned the nod and stood back, giving the police chief room to enter the apartment.

"I need to talk to her," he said gravely, without preamble. He had a folder under one arm and a serious look on his face. He wasn't wearing his uniform, which Tal appreciated. He hadn't missed how skittish Sunset was with anything that had to do with the police. Simon currently wore a pair of jeans, a polo shirt with the Fallport Police Department logo on the front left pocket, and a leather jacket.

"Can you give me a chance to talk to her first?" Tal asked as he closed and locked the door behind Simon.

"From what I understand, you've been back in town with her for days," he replied.

It wasn't a no, but it was obvious the man had reached the end of his patience.

"We need to go easy on this," he insisted.

"Do you think she's Heather?" Simon asked.

Tal sighed and nodded.

"She has a right to know," the chief told him.

"I'm not disagreeing with you. But she's terrified of the police. Those assholes she lived with told all the women that if they went to town, they'd be arrested. That the people here were gunning for them. That they'd be abused and treated like shit...which is ironic, considering their living conditions."

"All the more reason for me to talk to her," Simon argued. "So she can see for herself that I want nothing but the best for her and everything she learned was bullshit. I also need as much information as I can get, so I can find everyone involved and get justice for her and the other women."

Simon's voice dropped. "She was right under our noses the entire time, Tal. I should've found her. I should've done more for all the women and children who were living out there. I wasn't here when she was kidnapped, but I went with the former chief's gut feeling that the men and women living in that camp were harmless. That they were kind of hippies who were living off the land and doing nothing wrong. If what Ethan has already told me is true, they were as far from harmless as people can get. I want them to go *down*, Tal. And I need her help to do it."

He sighed. Simon was right, he knew he was, but he hated that talking about this was going to hurt Sunset. "Can you at least let me give her a heads-up? Give me half an hour to talk to her before you interrogate her?"

"I'm not going to fucking interrogate her," Simon retorted. "Give me some credit here. Jeez."

"Sorry," Tal said. "I just hate this for her."

"You and me both. Take your time. Tell her what you need to. I'll be out here when you're both ready."

"Meaning, you're not leaving until you talk to her," Tal said with a resigned smirk.

"Yup." Simon looked toward the kitchen and frowned. "Shit, I forgot you don't drink coffee."

Tal chuckled. "No, but I've got lots of different kinds of tea you can choose from."

Simon's lip curled. "There's something wrong with anyone who doesn't start the day off with a big cup of joe."

For some perverse reason, irritating Simon right now felt pretty good. Then he sobered. He didn't want a non-caffeinated Simon to take his frustration out on Sunset. "You've got time to run to Grinders if you wanted to. I promise not to go on the lamb with her."

Simon turned his intense gaze to Tal's. "I'm gonna go easy on her," he said softly, but with a thread of steel in his tone. "No matter how tired I am or how badly I want or need caffeine, I'd never take my frustration out on an innocent woman."

Tal knew that. Simon was a bloody good police chief. He was just worried about his upcoming talk with Sunset.

"Talon?"

As if his thoughts had conjured her out of thin air, Tal

turned to see Sunset standing at the end of the hallway. She had on another one of his sweatshirts, even though he'd bought her clothes of her own that fit much better. She was wearing a pair of the jeans he'd gotten for her, and her hair was hanging around her shoulders. It was still long, down to the middle of her back now instead of her butt, but she still hadn't gotten used to brushing it when she got up. It was messy, which only made Tal want to run his hands through it.

"Am I in trouble?" she asked, her voice shaking.

"No," he said immediately, turning his back on Simon. The man could make himself comfortable; he needed to reassure Sunset more than he needed to be a good host.

When he got to Sunset, he reached for her waist and gently turned her back toward the hall. In the last few days, she'd gotten more and more used to his touch, which thrilled Tal. She no longer flinched when he got close to her.

"Come on, back to our room."

Our room. He'd used the words without thought.

She didn't protest and walked quickly back to the safety of the room she'd just left. As soon as Tal closed the door, she turned back to him. Her arms were around her waist protectively and her brows were furrowed. "Talon?" she asked again.

"Come on, sit," he said gently, gesturing toward the bed.

Sunset shook her head and said, "No. Just tell me what I did wrong and what's going to happen."

Tal couldn't help but smile.

"Why are you smiling?" she asked, sounding pissed.

"I think that's the first time you've told me no," he told her.

Sunset froze as she stared at him with wide eyes.

"And for the record, I'm proud of you. If you want to stand, or pace, or whatever, you can. I just wanted you to be comfortable while I talked to you about something serious. You aren't in trouble. Simon's just here to talk to you. He's not going to arrest you. He's not going to yell at you. I promise. You can trust me."

He saw Sunset take a deep breath and let it out slowly. Then she gave him a small smile. "I did tell you no, didn't I? And I demanded an answer to a question too."

"Sure did."

"So? Are you going to answer it?"

Tal's good mood vanished. He sat on the edge of the mattress and hiked one leg up. He didn't take his gaze from Sunset's as he asked, "You haven't talked much about your childhood. Do you remember anything?"

Sunset frowned as she stared at him. "No."

"Are you sure? Not even flashes here and there?"

It didn't seem as if she even blinked as she continued to stare at him. "Why?"

Tal sighed. He wasn't doing any of them any good dragging this out. "Sunset...I'm pretty sure you grew up here in Fallport. Your name was Heather Brown, and you were kidnapped when you were eight years old. I think you were taken by that bloody cult. There were searches for months, but there were no signs of what happened to you."

Sunset had gone so still, Tal wasn't sure she was even breathing.

When she did finally move, it was toward the bed. "I think I'll sit now," she whispered. She sank onto the edge of the mattress and stared off into space. Tal didn't like that she wouldn't meet his eyes, but he continued to speak.

"I don't know for sure, but from what you've told me, I'm thinking they took you just like they did all those babies and toddlers. They raised you to believe what was happening to you was normal. They made you and all the other women and children afraid of town, to keep you away so no one would suspect they were anything but the harmless hippies they pretended to be...and so no one would recognize you. They made you think polygamy was normal, as was abusing children by 'marrying' them. *Nothing* about how you lived when you were with Arrow and the others was normal or right, which I've already mentioned. And it wasn't your fault. You were just a kid when you were taken."

Sunset looked up at him then. Instead of the devastation he expected to see in her eyes, he saw...relief?

"How do you know I'm her? This Heather girl?"

"Well, we won't know for sure until we do a DNA test. Your parents gave your DNA sample to the police when you were taken, just in case."

She blinked. "I have parents?" she whispered.

"Yes. Although...I recently found out that they passed away. I'm *so* sorry. I guess they moved away a few years after you were taken, when you weren't found. From everything I've heard, they were devastated. They just couldn't continue to live here without you. Everywhere they looked, they were reminded of their heartbreak. Not knowing what happened to you ate at them, and they weren't able to move on. Your mom started drinking to cope with your loss, and she was in a car accident about a decade ago. Your dad had a heart attack almost five years ago."

"Did I have any brothers or sisters?" Sunset asked quietly.

"No. But from reading the archives of the news articles from that time, the entire town kind of adopted you as their own. So in many ways, you're everyone's sister, daughter."

When she didn't say anything, just turned her head to stare off into space once more, Tal clenched his hands into fists. He wanted to take her into his arms. To tell her everything would be all right. But he didn't want to do anything that might scare her. Or make her lose the tenuous hold she had on her emotions at the moment.

Then she shocked the hell out of him by straightening her back and turning her head toward him. "So Simon is here to talk to me about this? To see if I'm Heather?"

"Yes. And to see if you'll be willing to tell him about Arrow and Cypress and everyone else you lived with. They shouldn't get away with kidnapping you and who knows how many other kids. It's illegal, immoral, and they need to be punished for their crimes. Are you okay? Talk to me, Sunset."

"*Heather*. My name is Heather," she said firmly.

Tal blinked in surprise. "We don't know that for sure yet."

"I do," she insisted. "All my life, I've felt as if I didn't belong. All the other women and kids simply accepted how they were treated. I didn't. I was constantly getting in trouble. I spent more time than anyone in the punishment tent, even as an adult. I couldn't understand why I had to test their limits, why I was always saying the wrong thing at the wrong time, asking questions. You have no idea how big of a relief it is to know my suspicion that something wasn't right was correct all along. I have a last name," she said as her eyes filled with tears. "One that isn't shared by every other woman around me."

"Well, you should know that Brown is a common name here in the States. Millions of people have that last name," Tal couldn't help but say.

She let out a huff of breath that was partly a laugh. "I don't care. It's still mine. I'm Heather Brown."

It was Tal's turn to close his eyes and let out a sigh.

"Talon?"

He opened his eyes immediately. "Yeah?"

"You were scared to tell me."

"I was," he agreed. "I didn't know how you'd react. If you'd be mad, scared, or if you'd deny it outright."

"I *am* mad," she said with a shrug. "And scared. I can't deny it. I don't remember when I got to The Community, but I remember spending a lot of time in the woods. There were times when I'd be picked up and carried into the trees without warning, a hand over my mouth and someone whispering threats in my ear about having to spend more time in the punishment tent if I called out. Maybe that was when people were searching for me? I don't know. But the more time I spend walking around Fallport with you, the more...familiar it seems."

"How so?" Tal asked.

"Like with Mr. Grogan. When he talked to me, I had a flash that I'd been there before. Walking up and down the aisles seemed very familiar."

"Harry was around when you were here," Tal said with a nod. "What else?"

"Art. I don't have a specific memory with him...but it felt as if I already knew him before you introduced me. And the gazebo in the square. Will you...will you show me the house I lived in?"

"If you want me to," Tal said.

"I'm sad that my parents didn't live long enough to know what happened. But...I don't really remember them. I think I've remembered flashes of things here and there, but I thought they were dreams. Or wishful thinking."

"It's okay," Tal soothed.

"Is that why you wanted to find me so badly?" she asked.

Tal shook his head. "No. When Brock and Finley told me about what you did, how you saved them, I was so intrigued—and worried. You were in the cold woods in a dress and no shoes. I *had* to find you...to help you. It wasn't until I was already well and truly obsessed with finding you that I found out about Heather, about her kidnapping. It doesn't matter to me if you're Heather or Sunset or someone else. I like you for who you are now. I admire you for your strength and fortitude and intelligence. And I'm so proud of how you've dealt with all the changes you've experienced in the last few days."

"I'm not smart," she said hesitatingly.

"The hell you aren't," Tal returned. "There's book smarts, and then there's life smarts. And you have more common sense and knowledge about the things that matter in life than anyone I've ever met. Besides, you can always take classes and learn the things you missed after being taken. The ability to survive in the woods and self-preservation are much harder to learn."

"I think you're just being nice," she said after a moment.

"I'm not," Tal insisted. "I admire you more than just about anyone I've ever met."

She swallowed hard and whispered, "I'm Heather

Brown. Not Sunset Meadowblossom. Wait—am I still married?"

"You were *never* married," Tal growled. He took a breath and tried to calm himself. "We talked about this. Those cowards who kidnapped you were child molesters and completely evil. To be legally married, paperwork has to be submitted to the courts. I can guarantee they didn't do that. Not to mention, it's not legal to be married to more than one person at a time."

"Good."

It *was* good.

"So...is Simon still here?"

"Yes."

"What's he doing out there?"

"Don't know, don't care. But I wasn't going to let him break the news to you about your past. I wanted to do it myself."

"Why?" she asked.

"Because you don't know him. You know *me*. You can trust me. And if you didn't take the news well, I would've gone out there and told him you weren't up to talking to him today."

Her eyes widened. "You would've sent him away?"

"Yes."

Tal couldn't read the emotion behind her eyes. He hoped it wasn't fear.

"Are you willing to talk to him now? If not, if you need to let this settle, that's okay. I can take you to see the house you grew up in and anything else you want. We can go visit Lilly and you can talk to her about all this if you want."

"I want to do all that," she told him. "But I want to talk to Simon. I know I'm Heather, I feel it inside, but I want proof. And I want to tell him as much as I can about Cypress and The Community. It's not right, what they did. To me and all the other kids who suddenly appeared. They deserve to know who they are for real too."

"I'm so bloody proud of you," Tal said, his voice cracking. He should've known this woman wouldn't buckle after hearing about her past.

"I'm still scared," she said softly. "But now that I know the feelings I've had inside for so long were right, that I wasn't a misfit, that I wasn't just a bad wife and Community member...I feel as if I can breathe again."

Tal stood and held out his hand. "Come on then, let's go talk to Simon."

She stood and put her hand in his. "Talon?"

"Yeah, sweetheart?"

"Can I...do you think..." Her voice faded off.

"What? You can ask me anything. You can trust me, and I won't hurt you."

"Can I have a hug?" she blurted.

Without another word, Tal pulled her closer and wrapped his arms around her. They stood like that for a couple of long minutes. Soaking each other in, finding comfort in one another. He felt her take a large breath right before her arms loosened around him.

"I'm ready," she said with determination.

Tal twined his fingers with hers and headed for the door.

CHAPTER TWELVE

Heather's mind spun with everything she'd learned. Simon had shared everything he knew about her abduction twenty years ago, including all the efforts that had gone into finding her. She was satisfied that the police and townspeople had done everything they could to track her down and figure out what had happened.

Arrow might have been old, but he wasn't dumb. He'd kept her well-hidden after she'd arrived at The Community. He'd let the police search through the tents and grounds several times, until they were satisfied she wasn't there. Then it was just a matter of brainwashing her into thinking everyone in Fallport was the enemy, that going to town would be the worst mistake she'd ever made.

She couldn't feel guilty that she hadn't tried even once to escape. She'd been so traumatized after her kidnapping and subsequent beatings and threats, that her brain had blocked out her past in order to cope. To survive.

Simon explained all that to her, and he went into great detail about the psychology of kidnap victims, and she was grateful for how hard he was trying to make her not feel bad about her actions, her acquiescence to her new circumstances.

When he'd tentatively asked her to tell him what she knew about Cypress and the other men, and where they were going, Sunset...no...*Heather*, had told him everything. She didn't hold anything back. She felt no loyalty toward the people who had taken her from everything she knew and loved.

Thinking about the other children who had appeared, who everyone had been told were adopted, made her want to throw up. Cypress and everyone else who was aware of what was going on needed to pay for what they'd done. To her and everyone else.

Simon had swabbed the inside of her cheek to get her DNA and said he'd ask the lab to put a rush on the results, so they'd know for sure if she was truly Heather. But she already knew she was. He'd warned her that once the results were back, and if it was confirmed that she was Heather Brown, it was likely word would get out. He'd said that children who were kidnapped generally didn't show up twenty years later, alive and well. There had been a few cases, but the odds were overwhelmingly against it. So if the press got a hold of the story, she might be inundated with requests for interviews.

Heather didn't like the sound of that, but Talon had reassured both her and Simon that he'd watch out for her. Knowing he'd have her back made the idea of word getting out a lot less stressful.

Before the police chief left, he asked what she would prefer to be called. Without hesitation, she'd said Heather. In her mind, Sunset no longer existed. She was a made-up person Arrow had conjured, and everyone else who'd gone along with his sick schemes accepted it.

She wanted to be Heather, the woman who'd defied Cypress by hiding in the woods when he'd left for Florida. The woman who'd survived for a year on her own. The woman who Tal had found, and who he seemed to like. *That's* who she wanted to be.

Three days after her talk with Simon, after finding out who she really was, Heather was sitting on Bristol's back porch, drinking a cup of hot flavored tea, talking with Bristol and Elsie while Tony, Zeke, Talon, and Rocky threw a football in the yard.

It felt surreal. She'd never had the luxury of sitting around chatting before, especially with women. She was expected to remain busy. There had always been something to do in The Community. Repairs to tents, sewing, hunting, cooking, cleaning, taking care of the children... something. It felt nice to be able to just sit and enjoy the company of other people, especially since it was becoming easier and easier to talk to the women.

The air was crisp but sunny. Heather was completely comfortable in her sweatshirt, jeans, and the boots Talon had brought to her when she was living out in the cave, while Elsie and Bristol were bundled up like it was absolutely freezing, including in blankets Rocky had brought for them from inside.

"Tony felt so important when you asked him for help with the book you were reading," Elsie told her.

Heather blushed and looked down at the mug in her hands. "I was having trouble with a word. I didn't recognize it. But when he said it, I realized I knew what it was. I'd just never seen it written down. There are so many words that look nothing like they sound."

"What was the word?" Bristol asked.

"Sword," Heather said. "I don't know why it has a W. It makes no sense."

"You're so right. What about lasagna? Why is the G in there?" Elsie asked.

"There's a G?" Heather asked.

They all chuckled.

"This is probably a conversation better had with a pen and piece of paper," Elsie said. "Yes, there's a G in lasagna. Just like there's an L in the word salmon and a K in knife."

"I'm never going to be able to learn all this stuff," Heather mumbled.

"Yes, you are. I have no doubt. But if you don't...who cares?" Bristol said with a shrug.

"I think I do," Heather admitted. "Women weren't allowed to read or write in The Community. We weren't allowed to know *anything*. All we were supposed to do was chores. And I mean all of them," she said a little bitterly. "The men could drive, read books, go to town...all the things they said were off limits to us women. It wasn't fair, and I hated it."

Bristol reached over and put her hand on Heather's arm. "I'm so sorry."

"Me too," Elsie said. "Our situations weren't the same, not at all, but my ex was horrible to me too. Called me stupid all the time and made fun of everything I wanted to do that didn't involve catering to him."

Heather took a deep breath and turned to her. "But you married Zeke?"

"Zeke is *nothing* like my ex," Elsie said without hesitation, her voice hard. "I admit I was reluctant to get involved with anyone ever again. I wanted to put Tony first in my life and never let another man get close to either one of us. But Zeke slowly knocked down the emotional walls I'd put up around me. He was kind, to me *and* Tony, and he proved over and over that we could trust him. That he'd never hurt us the way my ex had."

"When I was being held hostage, I had the utmost confidence that Rocky would find me. I didn't know how or when, I just knew he would. All I had to do was stay smart and not do anything that would make my captor lose his shit. It took longer than I'd hoped, but in the end, Rocky *did* find me, and he's taken care of me ever since," Bristol said.

"The first thing Talon said to me was that I could trust him and he wouldn't hurt me," Heather admitted.

"I'm not surprised," Bristol said with a small smile.

"That sounds like something Tal would say," Elsie agreed.

"And do you?" Bristol asked.

Heather frowned. "Do I what?"

"Trust him?"

She was nodding before she'd thought about her answer.

"Good. Because if you said no, you were going to get a lecture," Bristol said with a small smile.

"I...It's...*weird*, because all my life I've been scared of men. I haven't been treated well by them. They've hurt me over and over. And yet when I'm with Talon...I feel safe."

Bristol turned her chair so she was facing Heather fully, then leaned forward. "Has he told you what he used to do?"

"About being a killer? Yes."

Heather frowned when both Elsie's and Bristol's eyes widened.

"What? Was I not supposed to say that?" she asked.

"Well, they usually prefer to say they were soldiers. Killers has a negative connotation."

"Connotation?" Heather asked, hating that she didn't always know the words people used.

"Yeah, it's kind of how a word makes you feel inside."

Heather nodded. *That* she understood. Hearing the word "marriage" made her cringe inside, where these women obviously had only happy feelings about it.

"Anyway, my husband and his twin, Ethan, were Navy SEALs together. They did a lot of things they still struggle to come to terms with today," Bristol said.

"Wait, Ethan and Rocky are twins?" Heather asked.

"Yeah. Fraternal, so they don't look alike."

"Oh, that's kind of neat," Heather said.

"It is. Anyway, men like ours—like all of the guys on the search and rescue team—they take being a hero to a new level. They feel as if it's their duty to protect others. They get angry when something bad happens and they weren't able to stop it. It's kind of in their DNA. They all get *really* mad when women and kids are abused or hurt."

"Talon told me about a mission he was on once, when lots of women and kids died. He said it really hurt him inside," Heather admitted.

"That makes perfect sense," Elsie said with a nod.

"Totally," Bristol agreed.

"What does?" Heather asked, feeling lost.

"Tal has a deep need to take care of people. Deeper than even the rest of our guys. I'm guessing it's partly because of whatever happened on that mission. What I'm trying to say is, you're perfect for him," Bristol said.

Heather stared at her new friend, not fully comprehending her meaning.

"I'm not saying you might feel any particular way about

him today. Or tomorrow. Or even a month from now. But if you keep an open mind, I think you could find yourself falling in love with Talon."

"You can trust him. You *already* trust him," Elsie added. "And believe me, I know trust is the first step to deeper feelings."

Heather wanted to be surprised by what they were saying. Wanted to protest and say she wasn't ready to be with another man. Might not *ever* be ready. But all of that would be a lie. The more she got to know Talon, the more she liked and respected him. And now that she knew how wrong and perverse—another new word she'd learned—The Community men were, the better she felt about her enjoyment of spending time with Talon.

Deep down, Heather wanted what Elsie and Bristol had. Wanted a normal life. Family. A husband who might treat her nicely. Who could love her.

Bristol eyed her for a long moment then sat back, turning her seat around so she could see the guys playing catch once more. She smiled at Heather when she said, "I'm thinking we don't need to give you encouragement. You already know how great Tal is."

"I do," Heather agreed. She was blushing, but she couldn't help it.

"Let him take care of you," Elsie added gently. "Don't feel bad about it. He needs to do it, and I'm sure it makes him feel really good when he does."

"It makes me feel good too," Heather admitted softly. "No one has ever done anything for me before...well, that I remember...and my belly feels all swimmy when he does something like hold the covers for me to climb underneath, or when he makes food for me that I commented I might like to try."

"Wait—he holds the covers for you?" Bristol asked.

Heather nodded. "Yeah. When we go to bed."

"You're sleeping with him?" Elsie asked, eyes wide.

"Yes. Am I not supposed to?"

"Nope, it's fine. Great. Perfect!" Elsie said quickly, with a huge smile. "Right, Bristol?"

"Yup," Bristol said with a firm nod. "You do whatever feels right. No matter what anyone else says."

Heather finally realized what her new friends were thinking. "We aren't doing sex," she blurted.

Elsie patted her arm reassuringly. "I'm thinking you and I both know better than a lot of women that having sex doesn't mean you're intimate together. My ex would have sex with me, and it meant nothing. Tell me this: Do you like sleeping next to Tal?"

"Yes." It was an easy question to answer.

"Then don't worry about what you should be doing, or what other people think you should be doing or not doing. You and Tal should *always* do what feels right."

Heather nodded. "Okay."

"Okay," Elsie agreed.

"And now that we've awkwardly tried to butt into your personal life to give you advice you apparently don't need... when do you think you'll hear from Simon about the DNA results?" Bristol asked.

"I don't know. He said he'd call Talon when he knew something. But...I thought maybe he's just forgotten to call, since everyone I've met in town since then has started calling me Heather, saying how happy they are that I'm home and have been found."

Both Elsie and Bristol laughed.

"That's just Fallport. Nothing stays a secret here for long," Bristol said. "Thankfully. That's how *I* ended up being found. Because people paid attention and spoke up when I turned up missing."

"Does the attention bother you?" Elsie asked. "I have to admit, it took me a while to get used to everyone talking about what happened to me and Tony."

Heather shrugged. "It's kind of weird, but I just smile and thank people. I think it helps that Talon's usually there. He's kind of intimidating to others."

"But not to you," Bristol said. It wasn't a question.

"Not to me," Heather agreed.

Elsie and Bristol shared a smile, and Heather felt as if she was missing something yet again, but she wasn't sure what. She didn't want to ask in case it was something bad. Although she didn't think it was, with the way her friends were smiling at each other.

She had the brief thought that having friends was confusing sometimes, but she never wanted to go back to the way things were at The Community. Where the women wouldn't hesitate to tattle on each other if it meant they'd avoid negative attention.

"Heads up!" a voice called out.

Bristol and Elsie immediately ducked in their chairs, but Heather wasn't sure what "heads up" meant, so she was slow to react to the warning.

A football slammed against her shins, making her cry out in surprise more than pain. She also dropped her cup, spilling tea all over her lap.

Before she even registered what had happened, Talon was there. Heather vaguely noticed that Elsie and Bristol had stood and backed away, giving him more room. He smacked the cup off her lap and pulled her to her feet. "Hang on, sweetheart, I know it probably hurts." He whipped off his sweatshirt and began to dab at the spilled tea on her belly and thighs.

The shock of what had happened was wearing off, and Heather realized that the tea she'd been drinking had cooled off quite a bit. While she was wet, it hadn't burned her.

"I'm okay," she said in a somewhat shaky voice.

"Let me take care of you," Talon said as he knelt in front of her, his tone clearly illustrating that he was upset. He gingerly lifted the pants leg of her jeans, scowling when he saw a red mark on one of her shins.

"I'm so sorry!" Tony whispered. He was standing at the bottom of the three stairs leading up to the porch with tears in his eyes. "I thought you'd catch it."

"She was too far away," Talon explained. "And she was busy talking to her friends. That wasn't smart, Ton."

Dreading what would happen to Tony, how he might be punished, Heather did her best to brush off what had happened. "I'm fine," she said firmly. "No harm done. What are our plans for the rest of the day?"

Talon looked up at her, and Heather could feel everyone else's eyes on her too. "He's not going to get in trouble," he said gently.

"You're mad," Heather whispered.

"I'm upset that you could've been injured. That he didn't think twice before he threw that football. But I'm not going to *hurt* him. Neither is Zeke or Rocky. I think his remorse is punishment enough."

Heather looked away from Talon to Tony, and she saw tears coursing down the little boy's cheeks. Talon wasn't wrong. Tony looked miserable.

"I really didn't mean to hurt you," he said, his voice cracking. "I'm so sorry."

"It's okay," she told him. "I should've been paying better attention."

"No, you were minding your own business on the porch," Zeke corrected mildly. "This was Tony's mistake."

Heather felt so bad for Tony.

"Heads up is code for duck," Bristol said from next to her.

"I'll remember that for next time," Heather said with a small smile.

"I'd give you something to change into, but I don't think my stuff will fit you," Bristol fretted.

"I'm gonna take her home," Talon said firmly.

"I'm really okay, just wet," Heather protested, not sure she wanted to end her time talking with her friends.

"Your leg is red from the football. It might become sore. I'm taking you home."

Heather opened her mouth to protest some more, but Elsie spoke first. "Let him take care of you, Heather."

Looking at her new friend, she remembered what they'd been talking about. How they'd suspected Talon needed a woman he could care for. So she simply nodded.

"Thank you," Talon said softly as he stood.

Elsie threw her arms around Heather before she could move. "I'm so sorry Tony hit you. Thank you for not making him feel worse than he already does about it."

"He didn't mean it," Heather soothed. And of course she couldn't help but think back to the times she'd gotten in trouble in The Community. Many of those incidents had been accidents as well. She hadn't meant to burn the fish for their dinner and ruin it. Hadn't meant to set the shirt she'd been sewing on fire. She'd gotten too close to the flames because it was freezing outside, and sparks from the fire landed on the material. Both times, she'd had to spend two full weeks in the punishment tent.

She came back to the present when Bristol hugged her and said she'd see her soon.

Then Talon picked her up, his arms under her knees and around her back as if she weighed no more than a feather. She would've been scared if it had been anyone but Talon holding her.

Relaxing in his arms, she smiled tentatively at Zeke and Rocky. "Maybe we can talk more next time."

Both men grinned and nodded, then she was being ferried toward the SUV by a clearly impatient Talon. He gently placed her in the passenger seat and buckled her seat belt for her. He jogged around to the driver's side and they were pulling down the long drive, away from Bristol and Rocky's house, before she knew it.

"I really am okay," she told him again.

"I'm glad. But we'll go home, you can change, and I can look at your shins to make sure."

She could've kept insisting she was fine. That he didn't need to look at her legs. The football hadn't hit her all that hard. She'd been more surprised than anything. But remembering her friends' words, and deciding that it felt really good to be taken care of...Heather merely nodded.

CHAPTER THIRTEEN

Tal scowled as he paced his living room and thought about what had happened the night before. He hadn't slept well, and this morning Heather had asked him if she'd done something wrong. He'd said no, of course, but hours later, he knew he needed to talk to her, reassure her that he wasn't upset because of *her*...but because of how helpless he'd felt with what she'd gone through last night.

Yesterday, Heather had spent the day with Finley in the kitchen of The Sweet Tooth while he took a shift at the barbershop. Harvey had been more than cool with the time he'd taken off, but he didn't want to take advantage of his boss's generosity. And Heather always enjoyed spending time with Finley.

But he'd taken her to Sunny Side Up for dinner—and it had been a disaster. Word had definitely gotten out about her return.

Since Simon had confirmed her DNA matched that of Heather Brown's, the locals had gone a little crazy. The mayor even wanted to put together an impromptu parade, but Heather had been utterly horrified by the idea, so the plans had been scrapped.

But there had been stories in the online *Fallport Gazette*, and anyone and everyone who'd ever known little Heather had been interviewed. Details about where she'd been and the ordeal she'd suffered had been scant, but that hadn't kept people from speculating.

Not only was Heather now a celebrity according to the citizens of Fallport, word had officially traveled outside their little community.

As a result, while they'd been trying to have dinner in Sunny Side Up, she'd been suddenly mobbed by reporters from near and far. Everyone wanted an interview with the girl-turned-woman who'd been miraculously found after twenty years.

Sandra had done her best to run interference, but after the fifth person rudely interrupted their dinner by walking up to the table and sticking a recorder in Heather's face, and after the umpteenth picture had been taken, Talon had definitely had enough. He'd wrapped an arm around Heather's shoulders and, with the help of a few locals, he'd not so gently shoved his way through a dozen or so reporters to his SUV.

They were safe in his apartment, but Tal had a feeling it wouldn't be long before the reporters were knocking on his door. Heather's situation was unique, and the entire world loved to hear about a missing child being found after so many years.

"I'm sorry about last night," he told Heather as she sat on the couch.

"It's not your fault," she said in a tone that was flat and a little distant.

He ground his teeth together and sighed. He'd known

this would happen. Known everyone would want her story. They'd ask inappropriate questions, want to know every detail about her captivity...because that was what it was. Even though she didn't have chains around her ankles, she'd still been a prisoner.

He went into the kitchen and got her a Sprite. She didn't like the taste of wine or beer, but loved the sweet, bubbly soft drink. He sat next to her on the couch and handed her the can.

She gave him a smile and took a sip. "Maybe I should go back to my cave."

Tal was shaking his head before she'd even finished the sentence. "No!" he blurted—then he took a deep breath to try to control the fear coursing through him. "Do you really want to go back?" he asked a little more calmly.

It was Heather's turn to sigh. "No." She stared down at the soft drink in her hand. "I like it here. I don't have to worry about finding my own food or chopping wood. I love my new clothes and everyone's been so nice. And now that I know how I ended up with The Community, I don't want anything to do with them, ever again. If I went back into the forest, I'd be letting them win."

Tal reached over and took one of her hands in his. His intention was just to squeeze her fingers, letting her know he was here for her, but when she tightened her own fingers around his almost desperately, he couldn't let go. "They aren't going to win. Simon's going to find them and make them pay for what they did to you."

She shrugged. "I wish I could change the past," she said quietly. "I hate thinking about how awful my disappearance had to have been on my parents. I wonder how many other families went through the same thing because Arrow condoned the stealing of babies." She looked up at him. "How could he be so...horrible? So immoral? Believe it or not, he was kind of nice to me at first. I think I saw him as a grandfather or something."

"Until he forced you to have sex with him," Tal muttered with disgust.

Heather's nose wrinkled. "Yeah, until that. But still, out of all the men in The Community, he was the least mean. Though in reality, since he was the leader, he was probably the most depraved. He had to know what the others were doing. He might have even ordered them to find more girls. He always took it upon himself to teach the boys who joined our group." She shivered. "He knew what he was doing, and he didn't care."

Tal felt helpless. All he could do was sit there and let Heather dig her fingernails into the back of his hand. Of course, she had no idea she was hurting him, but he'd felt far worse. He'd sit there as long as she needed him.

Heather looked at him then, but instead of seeing tears in her eyes, he saw determination. "I *hate* them. I hate them all. They took me away from a family who loved me. From my life. They denied me food, made me a slave, raped me, didn't give me proper clothes, and did their best to beat me into submission."

"But you didn't let them," Tal soothed.

"No, I didn't," she said, sitting up straighter. "But only because I was so old when they took me. If I had been even a few years younger, I wouldn't have remembered anything about my old life. I would've believed everything they tried to teach me, everything they said about women being unworthy and how men were to be obeyed without question."

She wasn't wrong. And Tal *hated* that.

Doc Snow had suggested Heather talk to a psychologist who lived in Christiansburg, and she'd agreed, but Tal hadn't had a chance to set up the first meeting. He was fully on board with her talking to someone about what she'd gone through, even if he had a feeling she wasn't going to need long-term counseling. Just in the short time since she'd returned to civilization, he'd seen her blossom so much. The time she spent with the other women had helped immensely too.

His Heather was strong as hell.

Wait...*his* Heather?

Yes.

Yes, that was exactly what she was.

He'd been obsessed with finding her, helping her, ever since Brock and Finley had told him about the mysterious woman who'd saved them. Now he understood the year she'd spent by herself in the woods had been an excellent kind of therapy in and of itself. She'd realized she could support herself. Didn't need a man. She could do what she wanted, when she wanted, and it had to have been liberating for her.

Tal wasn't sure her hatred for Cypress was entirely healthy, but he'd take that over her feeling sorry for the man or wanting to protect him. "We need to talk about something."

Her big blue-green eyes stared at him expectantly.

"Now that your story is out, I'm afraid the media frenzy we saw last night is going to be just the tip of the iceberg. There's a very good chance Cypress or others you used to know will see it. Will know you're alive and here in Fallport."

He watched as the color leeched from her face. Her fingers tightened around his hand once again.

"You're safe here," he said quickly. "But you need to

know so you can protect yourself. Do you think anyone would come here and try to talk you into leaving with them?"

Heather nodded, but didn't speak.

Tal didn't want to ask this, but he felt he needed to. "Do you think they could say or do anything that would convince you to leave? I know it's been a while since you've been in that world, but they manipulated you for twenty years. If Cypress came back and started yelling at you, threatening you with the punishment tent...do you think you'd go with him?"

Even though she had fear in her eyes, she straightened as she said, "I will never, *ever*, go with Cypress Goodson. No matter what he says, no matter what he does, I won't go to Florida with him," Heather vowed.

"He might try to force you," Tal warned.

"Then I'll fight. I'm not the same person he knew. I'm not Sunset anymore. I'm Heather Brown. I *like* my life now. I have friends and a soft bed. I'm warm and don't have to wear that awful brown dress. I can wear shoes and look men in the eye, and I'm learning to read and write better. I like living in your world, Talon. I don't ever want to leave."

His heart swelled in his chest. He couldn't resist bringing their clasped hands up to his lips and kissing the back of her hand reverently. "And I like having you in my world, sweetheart."

Then Heather surprised him by leaning over and putting the can of soda on the end table by the sofa, and scooting closer to him. She let go of his hand to put her arm around his stomach...and *snuggled* against him.

As natural as breathing, as if they sat like this every night.

Tal inhaled slowly, loving the feel of this woman against him, the scent of her shampoo and sweet lotion in his nose. He put his arm around her shoulders, and neither of them spoke, just enjoyed the closeness of another human being.

"I missed this," she said quietly after a few minutes.

"What?" Tal asked.

"This. Hugging. Human contact. No one in The Community touched outside of sex. No hugs. No handshakes. Arrow used to touch *me*. But I wasn't even allowed to touch during my marital duties. I just had to lie there until he was done. Same with Cypress."

"No more talking about that," Tal said gruffly. "They weren't marital duties because you weren't fucking married."

"All I'm saying is...this feels good."

Tal did his best to put her words behind him. He was glad she didn't seem completely broken and traumatized by what she was forced to do, but it still bothered him greatly. "To me too," he reassured her.

"Talon?" she asked, lifting her head so she could meet his gaze.

"Yeah?"

"Do you think anyone will want to be with me after they find out what happened? You know...that I was kidnapped?"

He frowned in surprise at the question. "Of course. Why wouldn't they?"

"I don't know," she said with a shrug.

Tal waited a beat, and when she didn't say anything else, he said, "You can talk to me about anything, Heather. Say what's on your mind."

She'd dropped her gaze after asking her question, but

with his words, she looked at him again. "Do you think *you* might ever feel anything for me beyond friendship?"

He almost choked at her question. He thought he'd been pretty clear when he'd told her how much she was coming to mean to him not that long ago. But she either needed reassurance or hadn't understood what he'd meant.

He needed to tread lightly here. He wasn't sure if she was ready to talk about a future relationship...or even if he should pursue one with her, no matter how desperately he wanted to. Though, two things were very clear in his mind...

One, he didn't want to even *think* about her with another man. And two, he didn't want to do or say anything that might scar her more than she already was.

He'd obviously paused too long in answering, because she began to pull out of his arms.

Tal tightened his hold, refusing to let her go. In the end, he simply said, "Yes."

She stared back. "Yes?" she asked with a small tilt of her head.

"Yes," he repeated. "If I hadn't felt a deep connection to you, I would've brought you straight to Simon. He could've found you a place to live, worked with women's organizations to get you clothes and other necessities. I wouldn't have introduced you to my friends, or encouraged you to befriend them. I wouldn't be sleeping next to you every night. I wouldn't be so worried that someone from that damn cult will hear about you being here, and do or say something that will make you want to go back to them.

"You've gotten under my skin in a way no other woman has before, Heather. It scares me to death. *You* scare me. I don't want to do anything that will make you want to leave. I lie awake at night and listen to you breathe and thank God that I found you. That you're mostly all right. That you've somehow managed to retain a beautiful, sweet personality even after the Devil tried to beat it out of you.

"So, do I think I can feel something for you besides friendship? Sweetheart...I already do."

The last three words were whispered, but Tal couldn't lie to her. Refused to.

She stared at him without blinking. At his last words, her lips drew up in a beautiful little smile. "I do too," she said.

Her words sent lightning bolts straight to his heart, but he didn't react in any way. "You need more time. You haven't been out of the woods for that long. I'm the only man you've really been around."

She shook her head firmly. "I've been around plenty of men," she argued.

Tal brushed a lock of hair off her cheek and behind her ear. He loved how silky and smooth her hair was now. He'd cut off enough so that it now fell to her shoulder blades, and she hadn't told him she wanted to stop yet. The more weight he cut off, the curlier the strands got. It was all he could do not to thrust both hands into the gorgeous waves. "Around normal men," he clarified. "Good men."

A stubborn look flashed over her features, and Tal instinctively braced.

"I watched you," she said. "In the woods. I followed you and your friends as you did your searches, though I didn't really understand that's what they were at the time. But I saw how you laughed with them, how you were serious when you should be, how careful you were with people who were lost and hurt. I listened to your conversations. And I watched other hikers in the forest. Heard how men talked about women when they were with their buddies. Listened to them bragging about all the sex they've had. How they hated their jobs, how they stole things from their employers. It's amazing the things you can learn about people by watching and listening when they think they're alone with their friends.

"I've been around men other than those in The Community, and you, Talon, are the one I want. You told me that I was now living in your world, and I want that. I *want* to be in your world. You aren't going to hurt me, and I can trust you. You've told me that over and over, but you've proven it too. I know I'm not that smart, that I'm different, but if you give me a chance, I can learn. I can be like other women you've dated."

Tal's heart nearly broke at her self-deprecating words. Without thought, he reclined on the couch, taking Heather with him. She ended up straddling his stomach as he lay under her. "You *can* trust me, and I will *never* hurt you," he told her earnestly. "And you're the smartest woman I know. I don't know anyone else who would've been able to do what you did. You outsmarted Cypress and the others. Hid where they couldn't find you. Forced them to leave without you. You saved yourself, and that's incredibly amazing...and sexy as hell. Remember when I told you about those women and children? The ones I couldn't save?"

She nodded. Her hands were flat against his chest, propping herself against him.

"If they'd been half as brave as you, they would've found a way to save themselves. That's probably not fair of me to say, because I don't know their situation, but by saving yourself, being able to survive in the forest—in a fucking dress and bare feet, no less—you've touched me in a way no other woman ever has.

"If you want me, I'm yours," he promised. "I still think after more time has passed, you'll see that you have an entire world in front of you. Men who would line up to be able to call you their woman. But until you no longer want me, I'm happy to be yours. To help you navigate a world that still seems a little overwhelming."

Her eyes teared up again, and she asked, "You're mine? Don't you mean I'm yours?"

"No. You've got me wrapped around your little finger. Anything you want, I'll bend over backward to give to you. You'll never *belong* to anyone ever again, Heather. Unless you *choose* to give yourself to someone. You're free of that shit. From this point on, you decide your fate. Not me, not anyone else. You make the decisions about what you want. I'll be happy to guide you, to give you whatever info you need to make those decisions, but you're in charge. Of where we go from here...of everything."

A tear fell from her eye, and she reached up and swept it away impatiently. "I want to kiss you," she told him quietly. "I've seen Lilly, Elsie, and the others kiss their husbands. But I've never been kissed."

Talon's heart lurched in his chest. He forced himself to let go of her hips and brought his arms up and over his head, trying to seem as unthreatening as possible. "Then kiss me," he said softly.

She smiled—then immediately frowned.

"What's wrong?"

"I've never...Being above you is weird."

The anger toward the men she'd known in her past threatened to overwhelm him. He understood what she was saying all too clearly. "It's not weird," he reassured her. "In normal relationships, sometimes the man is on top, and sometimes the woman. There are lots of different ways couples can be intimate together. This is just one of them."

He saw understanding register in her gaze. She nodded. "So I can kiss you?"

"You can kiss me anytime, anywhere, whenever you want," Tal said fervently.

"Will you tell me if I do it wrong?" she asked.

"You can't do it wrong, sweetheart," he told her. "I promise."

He knew he shouldn't do this. Should give her more time. She was very likely latching onto him because he was the first man who'd been nice to her in twenty long years. But he couldn't deny her. He was too far gone. The only thing he could *ever* do was give her what she wanted. Let her experiment. Give her back her freedom and independence...and pray she'd want to stay with him in the end.

Her leaving would destroy him, but ultimately, he'd let her go with a smile on his face if that was what she wanted.

As she slowly leaned toward him, Tal's heart was practically beating out of his chest. He kept his eyes open, as did she, as her lips tentatively brushed against his own.

She pulled back a fraction and stared down at him. "Like that?"

"Like that," he agreed. "Try again, harder."

She leaned down and this time, her lips pressed flush to his. He couldn't stop himself from opening his mouth and licking her lower lip.

She jerked up and looked at him with wide eyes.

"Some kisses involve tongues. Licking, sucking, nipping," he told her.

Heather's tongue wet her lips, and Tal nearly groaned.

When she kissed him again, some of her reticence had

already disappeared. She licked *his* lip this time, and it was all he could do to keep his hands where they were. He wanted to tangle his fingers in her hair and hold her still as he ravished her. But he'd told her she was in charge, and he'd be damned if he went back on his word.

Her long hair fell around them as a kind of curtain, cocooning them from the world as the kiss went on and on.

She learned quickly, following his lead. Every time he did something, she repeated the move. When he nibbled her lower lip, she did the same. When he groaned, so did she.

It wasn't long before she no longer needed to mirror his actions, she took full control of the kiss. Her tongue entered his mouth, and soon their heads were tilting and they were full-on making out.

She tasted like the sweet soda she'd been drinking, and Tal had a feeling he'd never be able to taste Sprite again without remembering this moment. One of her hands moved to his cheek as they kissed. She ran her fingers lightly over his short beard, and the quiet rasping sound of his facial hair against her skin made goose bumps break out on his arms.

She pulled back to take a breath, and Tal realized he was panting as hard as she was.

"I like kissing," she told him with a blush.

"I like kissing *you*," he replied.

"I like being on top too," she said innocently.

Images of what else they could be doing with her on top swam through Tal's brain. It took all his self-control not to thrust up against her. His cock was rock hard, but luckily she hadn't felt it yet. It was only a matter of time though. She was innocent in a lot of ways, but she'd surely know what his erection meant, and he didn't want to bring back any bad memories for her.

As soon as he had the thought, Heather moved. She sat up a little, and as she did, moved backward enough that she nestled her apex against his cock.

They both froze.

CHAPTER FOURTEEN

"Ignore it," Talon said.

Heather's first reaction was fear. She knew what a hard penis meant. She'd felt Cypress's and Arrow's often enough between her legs. But she'd always been under them. The simple change of being above Talon made everything seem remarkably different.

Without thought, she rocked lightly on Talon's body, just once. Being on top felt...empowering. She liked it. A lot.

"Heather," he warned, but he didn't otherwise move. He didn't grab her. Didn't force her to stop or turn so she was under him. The power she felt from his acquiescence was heady.

Looking at the man under her, she saw his hands were clenched into fists over his head. His lips were swollen from their kisses.

Kissing had been *nothing* like she thought it would be. It had been...almost overwhelming. The first time Talon had touched his tongue to hers, it felt strange. But then he'd nipped her lower lip, and it felt like electricity had raced all the way down her body. Through her nipples and down between her legs. She'd never experienced anything like that feeling.

And now she was endlessly curious. She'd seen a penis before, but only quick glances in the dark. When Arrow and Cypress had sex with her, everything had been over so quickly. And they hadn't ever felt as big or as hard as Talon.

She scooted back so she was sitting on Talon's thighs and stared at the bulge in his jeans. She reached for him without thinking, wanting to touch it.

"Heather!" Talon repeated sharply when her fingers touched the denim.

She looked at his face. A muscle was ticking in his jaw, and every inch of his body had tensed. She could feel his thighs stiffen under her butt.

"Do *not* open my jeans," he ordered.

She tilted her head in confusion.

"It's too soon, sweetheart. I don't want to scare you. Or send you into a flashback. You can touch me if you really want to...but only through my clothes. Okay?"

She nodded immediately. Being given free rein to touch this man was thrilling. She tightened her hand around the large bulge between his legs, and he moaned loudly, even as he pressed his hips up subtly.

The power she felt at that moment was just as foreign as being on top, yet oh so satisfying. When had she last felt as if she was in charge of anything? Never. In The Community, she had to do as she was told, at all times. She had no control over what she wore, what she ate, who she could talk to, or what she could say. But here? With Talon? She was allowed to do whatever she wanted, whenever she wanted to do it. She could have chocolate without having to do painful things first. She could eat whenever she was hungry. She could wear any clothes that she liked.

And she could touch, instead of just *being* touched.

"Does that feel good?" she asked.

"You have no idea how good, sweetheart," he panted.

Talon clearly thought she wouldn't want him once she'd met other men, but he was wrong. She'd tried to explain it, but she had a feeling he didn't believe her. Yes, she hadn't known him for that long, but she'd *seen* him. Had watched him. He was a good man, and nothing she'd seen or heard since he'd appeared at her cave had changed her opinion.

If he thought she was dumb enough to want to be with someone else, he was sadly mistaken. She was more worried about him getting tired of *her*. She was well aware of how much she had to learn. It was likely Talon would tire of having to explain things, of tiptoeing around her so as not to upset her.

The truth was...Heather was more than ready to move on. She'd been denied a normal life for two decades, and she no longer wanted to waste a single moment.

She wanted what Lilly had. What Elsie, Bristol, Caryn, and Finley had. She wanted a man who loved her, like their men loved them. And she wanted Talon to be that man.

She continued to trace his penis through his jeans, her nipples getting tight as she boldly learned the size and shape of him. "You're big," she blurted, then grimaced. She sounded stupid.

"Not *too* big," Talon said, not seeming offended or shocked by her words.

Heather squirmed over him.

"Kiss me again, Heather," he demanded.

She had no problem with that order; she wanted more of his kisses.

Scooting up, she had to let go of his penis, but she flattened herself against him so that she could still feel it between her legs as they kissed.

She had no idea how long they'd been kissing, but eventually she raised her head and frowned at him.

"What? What's wrong?" he asked immediately.

He was so in tune with her. It might've scared her if it didn't feel so good.

"Will you... You're not touching me," she said tentatively.

"I don't want to scare you," he said. "You're in charge, Heather."

"You don't scare me. You won't hurt me. I...I'm not sure I want to be under you, but you can touch me...if you want."

"Oh, I want," Talon breathed.

His arms lowered slowly, and one of his large palms moved up her arm, from her wrist to her shoulder. The fingers of his other hand brushed down her spine before settling on her lower back, and he pressed her harder against him.

The backs of his fingers trailed down her cheek and went around her neck, where he gripped her tightly. "Kiss me again," he said.

Her head was lowering before he'd finished speaking. This time when they kissed, Talon held her tightly in his arms. His thumb brushed back and forth on the sensitive skin of her neck as he kissed her, and he ravished her even from his position beneath her.

Heather couldn't keep still, her hips grinding against his hard penis. It felt so good! She wanted more. Wanted to get closer.

After several minutes, he broke the kiss but kept his

hand on her nape. He rested his forehead against hers and whispered, "Harder, sweetheart. Rub against me harder. Take what you want."

So she did. Loving how hard he was holding her against him, though unsure why. Any other time she'd been held tightly by a man, it had been terrifying.

Tal's fingers slipped under the waistband of her cargo pants, and she could feel them against the sensitive skin of her butt. Heather continued to grind on him, staring into his eyes as he thrust his hips against her again and again—then stopped abruptly.

A long groan left his mouth before he huffed out a sigh and finally closed his eyes.

He stilled under her, and Heather froze. She wasn't sure what just happened. She was confused, and her body was a riot of tingles inside.

"Damn, woman," Talon said a few seconds later, as he opened his eyes and stared at her in wonder.

"What happened? Are you all right?" she asked.

Talon looked confused himself for a second, then he sighed again. "You don't know?"

She shook her head.

"I came."

Heather frowned.

"Do you know what that means?"

"Yes. But I thought it could only happen when a man was inside his wife."

A spark of anger flashed in his eyes before he got himself under control. "No. Both men and women can experience pleasure, can orgasm, at any time with the right stimulation. We can masturbate, touch ourselves to feel that pleasure, just as someone else can touch us and do the same thing."

Heather's mind spun. "We can touch ourselves? It's not illegal?"

"No."

"And we don't have to be married to do that?"

"No."

"And...women can do it too?"

"Yes."

She was amazed. And pissed all over again. There was so much The Community had forbidden, it wasn't even funny. "And you just...you liked that?"

Talon chuckled. She felt his belly move under hers. "I didn't like it, I *loved* it," he reassured her. "I can't remember the last time I came in my pants like that. All it took was the feel of you kissing me, rubbing against me...I just couldn't hold back."

Pride swam throughout Heather. *She'd* done that for him. She leaned up and looked down between their bodies. He was no longer hard, but she could see a dark spot on his jeans between his legs.

"You look proud of yourself," Talon said with a smirk.

"I just...I didn't know it could happen without you being inside me."

"You've never had an orgasm, have you?" Talon asked gently.

Heather shook her head, not feeling embarrassed. This was her Talon, after all.

He smiled, the dimple visible through his beard. "We're going to have fun."

If someone had told her sex could be fun, Heather would've laughed her head off at them. Sex wasn't fun. It wasn't comfortable, or nice, or any other positive adjective. It was a duty. Most of the time it hurt. It was something to get through quickly.

"But not right now. I think that's enough sex education for one day," he said, sitting up, holding Heather on his lap with ease.

The way he moved her without any problem whatsoever made Heather realize for the first time just how powerful Talon really was. He could've forced her under him at any time. Could've grabbed her and really hurt her. But he'd let her have control. Had lain under her docilely without any hesitation.

Talon framed her face with his hands. "Are you okay?"

Her brow furrowed. "Why wouldn't I be?"

"Things got pretty intense there. And you did things you've never done before."

There he went, being all sweet and protective again. Heather reveled in his concern. "I'm okay."

"Good."

"I...do you really like me?" she asked.

She liked the soft look that came over his face. "I really like you."

She smiled.

"But I need to go change," he said.

Heather giggled. "Yeah, you do."

"You're definitely proud of what you did," he said.

"A little," she agreed.

"You should be. I'm known for my control. On the battlefield, control over my emotions, and control sexually. But with you, sweetheart, I have no control over *anything*."

"I'm sorry?" she said tentatively.

"Don't be. I'm putty in your hands. And I love it."

With that, he stood and her feet landed on the floor. He waited until she was steady, before leaning down and kissing her gently on the lips. It wasn't a passionate kiss like before, but it felt just as nice deep down inside. "I won't be long."

Heather watched as he headed for the hallway. She smiled and hugged herself as he disappeared from view. She'd noticed Talon right away when she'd spied on him in the woods, even if she hadn't known he was the one leaving her gifts. How she'd gotten so lucky for *him* to be the one to find *her*, she didn't know.

Determination to take control of her life rose within her. Arrow always hated when she got something in her mind. She was stubborn, and he'd never been able to beat it out of her completely. Talon might think that she'd decide she wanted someone else after getting to know other men, but he was wrong.

Later, after Talon returned from his shower, things between them seemed...easier. He touched her more... little caresses, his fingers brushing against the small of her back as he passed her in the kitchen, running a hand down her arm, sitting right next to her on the couch while they watched TV, instead of sitting on the other end, that kind of thing.

They were relaxing after eating dinner—he'd taught her how to make eggplant parmesan, which she loved— when Talon's phone rang.

"Tal," he said as he answered. "It's getting late...right... okay. We'll be waiting." He hung up with a sigh.

Heather turned to him with apprehension. "What?"

"That was Simon. He wants to come over to talk to you about something."

She couldn't help but tense.

"It'll be okay. I'm not going to let anything happen to you."

Breathing slowly through her nose, Heather nodded.

225

Ten minutes later, there was a knock on the door. Talon got up to answer it as Heather stood nervously next to the couch. He came back into the room seconds later with the police chief at his back.

"It's good to see you again," Simon said with a nod.

Heather gave him a small smile, but reached for Talon's hand at the same time.

The other man didn't miss the intimacy between them, but Heather didn't care. She wanted everyone to know this man was hers. She wasn't giving him back...he'd said he was hers for as long as she wanted him to be, and she wanted him for all time.

"I wanted to talk to you about the press," Simon said after they'd all sat down.

"They're out of control," Talon grumbled.

"You haven't seen anything yet," the chief said with a shake of his head. "Since dinner, when you guys fled the diner, more have shown up. They've parked all around the square and along Main Street. The hotel near the interstate is packed. Whitney and Edna have refused to rent rooms to anyone who even looks like they might be a reporter, which is nice, but I'm thinking these guys aren't going to leave until they get some sort of statement."

"We aren't parading Heather around like some freak for them to gawk at," Talon said heatedly.

"And I'm not asking you to. The town's closing ranks," he replied.

"What does that mean?" Heather asked.

"It means the surprise and excitement everyone felt when they found out who you really are is wearing off fast, since so many reporters are being all rude and pushy. You're Heather Brown, longtime resident. And with the way the reporters are acting, talking to anyone and everyone they can find, asking invasive questions about you and what you went through, the good people of Fallport are quickly becoming disgusted. They're firmly on your side. I think you'll find if you venture out, they're more than willing to stand up for you. To provide a wall between you and the reporters if need be. But..." His voice trailed off.

"It's not going to be enough," Talon finished for him.

"Exactly. The reporters aren't breaking the law by being here. They're a pain in the ass, but it's not illegal to hang out, waiting to catch a glimpse of you."

"So what do I do? Should I leave? Go back to my cave for a while?"

"No!" Talon blurted. He turned to her. "This is your home now. And those assholes aren't going to chase you away."

Again, his protectiveness sent warmth throughout her body. "Then what?"

"I think if you picked a couple respected people to tell your story to, the curiosity would die down," Simon suggested.

"No," Talon said with a shake of his head.

"Hear me out," the man cajoled. "I'm not saying you should have a huge press conference or anything, but the world is dying to know more about Heather and where she's been. Face it, Tal, this is big news. And think about the parents out there whose children are also missing. They'd do anything to have their children found alive. Speaking out, telling her story, it could bring hope to people with missing kids."

"And it could crush them further if they get no new information," Talon countered. "You know as well as I do how unusual it is that Heather's alive. Unfortunately, most children who are taken aren't as lucky."

"I *do* know. But that's why everyone is so intrigued. Remember when Elizabeth Smart was found? It was a damn miracle, and she quickly became America's darling. But after a few interviews, she was able to settle back into a normal life. Then there was Jaycee Dugard. She was held captive for eighteen years, had two children by her captor, and is now free. Not to mention Shawn Hornbeck, Katie Beers, Carlina White, Elisabeth Fritzl. Then there's Michelle Knight, Amanda Berry, and Gina DeJesus..."

"This is different," Talon insisted.

"It's not," Simon said gently.

"Wait, who are all those people?" Heather asked.

"They were all kidnapped, held for months or years before being found. They've been able to lead relatively normal lives since, and they aren't hounded by the press relentlessly," Simon said.

"They were like me? And they're okay?" Heather breathed.

"They're okay."

Heather turned to Talon. "Can I meet them?"

He sighed. "I don't know."

"Right now, you could probably ask Opal Williams herself to interview you and she'd agree," Simon said.

"Who?" Heather asked Talon in a whisper.

"She's a very famous actress turned talk show host. Lately, she's known for interviewing celebrities and other people who have been involved in highly publicized incidents."

"Like mine?" Heather asked.

Tal nodded, then turned his gaze back to Simon. "I don't like this."

"Neither do I, but the bottom line is that those reporters aren't going to go away until they get what the world wants. And if she meets with a reporter of her choosing, and tells her story…maybe the others will lose interest since someone else got the scoop."

Talon sighed. "The more attention she gets, the more likely it is that one of the assholes who took her in the first place will come after her."

"And that will allow us to arrest them. We can get more information about other children they took and where they're living now," Simon returned. "I've contacted the authorities in Florida and told them about The Community, and that it's likely they've relocated to the state. The FBI, Bureau of Criminal Investigations and Intelligence, and the FDLE…the Florida Department of Law Enforcement. But if Heather's story goes nationwide, it would put everyone, civilians included, on alert, and hopefully they can be found and stopped sooner rather than later."

Heather kept her eyes glued to Talon. He was having a stare down with Simon and refused to look at her. "Talon?" she whispered.

He squeezed her hand again, but didn't turn his head.

"Talon," she repeated. "If telling my story can help other kids get away from them…I want to do it."

He took a deep breath and looked at her finally. "I don't want you to rush this. And I don't want you to do anything that might hurt you."

"Will you stay with me?"

He frowned. "Of course I will. Why would you even doubt that?"

Heather shrugged. "I don't know. I guess because you're so mad right now. I thought maybe all this was too much. That you wouldn't want to deal with everything."

He turned to face her fully now and brought his hands up so he was framing her face. "I'm not mad at you. I'm pissed at those assholes who kidnapped and abused you. I'm mad at the reporters who don't even think twice about targeting a real-live person who's still traumatized by what happened to her. All they want is a salacious story."

"I've had time to come to terms with what's happened," Heather said, reaching up and holding his wrists. She brushed her thumbs back and forth, wanting to somehow comfort Talon. "I'm free now, but the other women and kids I lived with aren't. They might not remember any other kind of life, like I did. They don't know how they're living is any different from anyone else in the world. That's not right. If telling my story helps them, I have to do it."

Talon closed his eyes and sighed. Then he opened them again and pinned her in place with his gaze. "You are the strongest person I've ever met in my life. You have every right to be bitter and broken, and yet your first thought is to help other people."

"I'm scared," she admitted. "I don't like talking about my life with The Community. It wasn't good. But I like Fallport...the way it was when you first brought me here. I like being able to walk around the square. Going to the library with Tony. Talking with Art and his friends outside the post office. I really loved spending the day with Finley in her bakery and learning how to make sweet treats. I can't do any of that if someone's yelling questions at me and taking my picture every time I walk around town."

"Fuck," Talon said.

"I don't know who the right person is to tell my story to, but I trust you to find him or her. To set it up. I don't want Cypress or anyone else to take any more of my life away from me. I want to move forward, and if that means having an interview, that's what I'll do."

Talon stared at her for a beat, then leaned in and kissed her softly. With another sigh, he dropped his hands from her face and turned to Simon. "Call Opal."

The other man chuckled. "What, you think I have her on speed dial or something?"

Talon's lips twitched. "I'm guessing it won't be too hard to get her attention. Send her an email, post on her Facebook page...I don't know, *something*. But she's savvy. She'll know how big this is. She'll respond."

"I'll do what I can."

"And the sooner you can set it up, the better. And we want to do it here. In Fallport. Where Heather's got a support system."

"Not asking for much, are you?" Simon said sarcastically.

"She'll do it," Talon said. "And now it's late. We're tired, and Heather needs to get some sleep."

"Right. For what it's worth...I'm not thrilled with the situation either. I'm pissed that those abusers were here in my community for years and I didn't know what was going on right under my nose."

"Don't feel bad," Heather said immediately. "They were very good at what they did. Keeping track of all of us. Making sure we wouldn't say anything. Even if you did come into The Community to ask questions, they would've hidden the children they didn't want you to see, like they did me, and the rest of us would've said what we were trained to say to outsiders. We were told all sorts of awful and scary things about what would happen to us if we were taken away. It's not your fault."

Simon sighed. "It's kind of you to say that, but it

doesn't assuage my guilt. I'll talk to you both soon. In the meantime, I recommend laying low."

"Was planning on it," Talon told him.

He stood and walked the police chief out and when he returned, Heather asked before he could say anything, "What does assuage mean?"

Talon stared at her for a long moment before shaking his head. "After everything you just heard and with the upcoming interview about what happened to you hanging over your head, that's what you're focused on?"

"I can't change what happened to me. I can only move forward. And I don't want to be the stupid woman who doesn't understand what people are saying."

"You aren't stupid," he said gruffly, coming toward her.

He sat next to her on the couch once more and took her hands in his.

"So...what does assuage mean?"

"To make an unpleasant feeling less intense," he said.

Heather thought about that for a moment, then frowned. "I feel bad that he feels guilty. Arrow knew what he was doing, and he was good at it. Very good."

"Doesn't matter. Men like Simon and myself...we consider ourselves to be very observant and able to see through people's bullshit. It doesn't sit well with us when we find out we're wrong."

"What can I do to help him not feel that way?" Heather asked.

"You can live a long, happy life," Talon said without hesitation.

"Okay. I'll do that." She couldn't read the expression on his face. But before she could ask what he was thinking about, he stood, still holding her hand.

"Ready for bed?"

Heather nodded. He helped her up and they walked toward his bedroom.

After changing into a pair of boxers Talon had given her and one of his large T-shirts, Heather crawled into bed. Every other night they'd slept, Heather had stayed on her side while Talon was on his—above the covers. Tonight, he slipped beneath the blankets with her, but was still on his side of the bed. After what they did on the couch, she no longer wanted to be so far away from him. He'd said he liked her, and that he was hers.

So she scooted over until she was against his side. He didn't ask her what the hell she was doing or shove her away, so Heather rested her head on his shoulder. She was thrilled when he wrapped his arm around her and pulled her even closer.

"Is this okay?" she whispered.

"Yes."

"Is it weird? Do married people touch each other while sleeping? I mean, I've never slept with a man before, so I don't know."

"It's not weird, and yes, people who care about each other often sleep in each other's arms, married or not. There are no rules when it comes to sleeping though. Some people don't like when others touch them at night. They can still care, but they might not need this."

"What about you?" she asked. "Does this bother you?"

"I've slept better since I've been next to you than I have in a very long time," Talon said softly. "I haven't had any of the nightmares that have plagued me since that mission I told you about. I have a feeling holding you will make me sleep even better."

"Me too," Heather said happily. "Although…"

"What? What's wrong?" Talon asked.

"You're very warm," she admitted.

Talon relaxed under her and chuckled. "I am. And you run hot. Must be all that time you spent living in the great outdoors."

"Probably. Will it offend you if I roll away in my sleep?" she asked.

"No. Will it bother *you* if I still need to touch you in some way? Like touch my foot to yours, or keep my hand against your back?"

She smiled up at him. "No."

"Good. Because now that I've kissed you, and have your permission to touch...I don't think I can stop."

He always seemed to know the right thing to say. "I like when you touch me. You'll teach me to orgasm at some point, right?"

Talon choked, then let out a slow laugh that Heather felt against the hand lying on his chest. "Yeah, sweetheart. Although I have a feeling you'll be a quick study, just like you are with everything else. It really doesn't bother you? To have me touch you?"

"No. Your touch is *nothing* like theirs. I know the difference between what they did and what we did earlier on your couch. I trust you, and you won't hurt me."

"Damn straight. But even so, if at any time you get scared or nervous, tell me. I won't get mad. Won't get offended. We'll stop and give you time to process what's happening. Okay?"

She nodded against him. "I was serious earlier, I don't want to give them any more of my life. I want to move on. With you. I don't feel the same when you touch me as when they did. I feel tingly inside when I'm kissing you. My chest is tight, in a good way. I want to *live*, Talon."

He turned his head and kissed her forehead before

giving her a tight hug. "We're moving on together," he reassured her.

They were quiet for a while before she asked, "Talon?"

She heard the humor in his voice as he said, "Yeah?"

"Were you serious? Do you really belong to me?"

"I was dead serious."

"I've never been allowed to own anything before," she mused. "I'm gonna take really good care of you, so you never want to stop belonging to me."

She heard his breath hitch but didn't dare look up at him.

"I'm gonna take real good care of you too," he said. It sounded like a vow, one Heather let sink into her soul.

"Sleep well, sweetheart. We'll take each day as it comes from here on out."

"Can I go see Bristol and her new kitten tomorrow?" she asked.

"Yes."

"And will you cut some more of my hair?"

"I could bring you to A Cut Above...they're probably better at cutting women's hair," he said.

"No. I trust you."

"Okay, then yes, we can do that too."

"I think I like the length it is now, but maybe just a tiny bit shorter."

"All right."

"When I talked to Finley, she said there was one more kitten that Khloe was feeding that needed a home."

Another chuckle rumbled through Talon's chest. "You want a kitten?"

"Maybe?" she said, even though she totally did.

"All right. I'll talk to Rocky tomorrow and see if he'll pick up the stuff we need to make a cat comfortable.

Litter tray, scratching post, food, toys, that kind of thing."

Heather picked up her head. "Really?"

"You want the kitten?"

She frowned. She'd already told him she did. "Yes."

"Then I'll talk to Rocky tomorrow."

A contented feeling spread through Heather. This man was...she didn't know. All she knew was that she'd never felt so cared for. So loved.

Love. Did she love Talon? Did he love her? She wasn't sure what love was. Had lived without any kind of true affection for so long. All she knew was that she felt safe around him. Felt wanted. Pretty. Smart. As if she mattered.

As she lay there against him, she realized that when she was around his friends, she felt very similar, so it *wasn't* that she was feeling things for Talon because he was the only man who'd been nice to her. No, she just felt all those things more *deeply* with Talon. She couldn't imagine kissing or having sex with anyone else. The thought made her shiver in fear.

"You okay?" Talon asked sleepily as he felt her shake against him.

"I'm glad *you* found me," she whispered.

"Wouldn't have stopped looking until I did," he said.

Not too long after that, his breaths evened out and his arm around her relaxed. He'd fallen asleep with Heather lying against him. He'd let himself be vulnerable with her... as if he really did belong to her.

"Mine," she said in a barely there whisper. She fell asleep with a smile on her face and the knowledge deep in her heart that despite all the bad she'd been through, she'd somehow found the one person she was meant to be with.

* * *

Cypress Goodson read the article online with a scowl on his face. He *knew* the bitch had been hiding from him! Everyone had assured him she must've had an accident while hunting and had died. They couldn't fathom that a woman would dare disobey any of the men in The Community, much less the leader of their group. Not after how they'd trained them.

But deep down, Cypress had known Sunset was out there.

His father had done his best to beat the disobedience out of her again and again, but Cypress knew Arrow hadn't succeeded just by looking into her eyes. He'd seen the discontent swimming in her gaze.

She'd been brought into The Community too late. Everyone had learned their lesson with that one. It had taken way too long to make her forget her old life and acclimate to her new role. It was why they'd stopped taking children as old as Sunset. Now, they only accepted kids who were four years old or younger. They were easier to mold. To teach.

Despite her wild streak, Cypress had *always* coveted Sunset. After his father's failure to train her properly, Cypress had been thrilled to get his chance upon Arrow's death. He'd immediately declared Sunset his wife...and had done everything he could think of to prove he wouldn't tolerate her insubordination the way his father had.

And still the bitch had *hidden* from him!

He'd had no choice but to leave her behind when it was time to head for Florida...but now that he knew she was alive? Now that the world knew how badly she'd disobeyed him and that he hadn't been able to control her?

He was determined to bring her back into the fold.

He'd keep her in the punishment tent for a goddamn year, only visiting her to prove who owned her...and maybe bring her food once a day, if she behaved. By the time she was released, she'd be the perfect Community wife.

The move to Florida had been difficult for Cypress. He was used to being in charge, and now he had to co-lead two newly combined communities. Though moving *had* allowed him to get six new wives, a good thing, since he'd tired of his old ones. They were also continuing to grow The Community, which was exciting. In the last year, they'd brought in three new girls, ages six months to three years. He'd already claimed the three-year-old as one of his future wives and her training was going well.

There were also two new boys, who would eventually become upstanding members of The Community and take their own wives. They were already learning that girls were second-class compared to men, showing great promise in that regard.

Now, it was Cypress's turn to provide another future wife for their fold. The members took turns acquiring new recruits. Three of the Florida wives were pregnant, which was good, there hadn't been enough children born into The Community in Virginia. Cypress knew those bitches had been doing something to prevent pregnancy, but since moving to Florida, that had somehow stopped. They needed to keep their numbers up in the meantime, and the whole ordeal of pregnancy took far too long...which was why he was heading north.

Cypress knew exactly where he was going to go. He had unfinished business in Virginia. He would find a little girl, then he'd fetch his wayward wife.

Sunset would regret defying him. She'd beg for his

forgiveness by the time he was through with her. He'd take her back to the place where he'd first made her his wife, reassert his dominance. He could kill two birds with one stone by showing the new child what her future duties would be, all while bringing Sunset to heel.

She'd embarrassed him in front of The Community. For that, she had to pay.

No woman said no to Cypress. Ever.

CHAPTER FIFTEEN

The next week went by without any huge incidents between Heather and the press. They were still in town, camped out and eager to get any scrap of information they could. But the citizens of Fallport had indeed closed ranks.

They spread false rumors about where she might be hanging out, to get the reporters to leave their parking spots around the square. Then those spots were taken by locals, who simply left their cars so the reporters had to park elsewhere. The owners of the businesses refused service to any reporter, going so far as to have them escorted out of their stores.

Everyone except for Whip Johansen, who owned The Cellar, but since no one had any respect for him and the people who patronized the pool hall didn't have any inter-actions with Heather, no one expected otherwise.

As a result, Heather was able to continue her visits to the library with Tony, she and Tal had eaten a couple of meals at Sunny Side Up, she'd had a long talk with Henry Grogan about the years when her parents lived in town, and she'd even stopped into Fall for Books and picked up an entire grocery bag full of books.

The furniture he'd bought for her still sat unused in his guest room. He'd intended to give Heather her own space, figuring she might enjoy it after everything she'd been through, but she hadn't spent even one night in there. Not that he was complaining.

Falling asleep with Heather in his arms was everything. He'd literally never slept better. The nightmares he'd been plagued with for so long had all but disappeared. The only problem was, the more time he spent with her, the more he wanted her. *All* of her. It had nearly broken his heart when she'd said that she'd never been kissed or held. He'd wanted to kill the abusive assholes who'd kidnapped her in the most painful way possible.

But he had to believe that Simon and the FBI were doing the best they could to find Cypress and his followers down in Florida. It shouldn't have been hard to find a group of men and women as large as that damn cult, but it was turning out to be surprisingly more complicated than Tal thought it would be.

In the meantime, he spent as much time with Heather as possible. And every day that went by, she seemed to blossom more and more. Meeting new people still intimidated her a little bit, but inevitably after ten minutes or so, she'd loosen up and win over the hearts of everyone she came into contact with.

She was resilient, kind, and had a disarming personality that drew people in. The townspeople who'd been so excited by her return were now extremely respectful of her privacy, not asking invasive questions and treating her as one of their own.

And not surprisingly, Heather's old memories were beginning to surface.

One day, while they were shopping at Grogan's General Store, an older woman had been standing in the middle of one of the aisles. Heather stopped in her tracks and stared at her with wide eyes. It turned out the woman had been her teacher the year she'd disappeared. Both women had cried after realizing who the other was.

Today, they were meeting Khloe at the apartment so she could deliver the final kitten she'd been trying to find a home for. Rocky had hooked Tal up with anything and everything a kitten could need or want. His apartment had cat toys all over it. Along with a cat tree, forty cans of cat food in his pantry, a large bag of kibble, and three litter boxes. It all seemed like overkill to Tal, but since each and every thing Rocky brought over made Heather smile, he didn't care. He'd fill his apartment with things for the cat if it made her happy.

"What time did Khloe say she was going to be here?" Heather asked, interrupting Tal's thoughts.

He smiled. "Around one."

"Should we make her something to eat?"

"Relax, sweetheart. She's not going to expect us to feed her. She's just running over here on her break at the library."

"What if she doesn't like me?"

"Khloe? She already likes you," Tal said in confusion.

"No, the kitten," Heather said with a frown.

"She's going to love you," he assured her.

"I've always wanted a pet. But it wasn't allowed," Heather said, looking off into the distance.

As much as Tal hated hearing about all the various ways she was abused, the psychologist she'd been seeing online said that talking about her time in captivity was an important part of her recovery...as long as it was at her own speed and she wasn't forced. Tal never wanted her to be ashamed to talk about the last twenty years. "I can't think of anyone more suited to being a pet owner than you," he said honestly.

Luckily, the faraway look in her eyes faded away as she turned to him.

"You have more love to give than anyone I've ever met. You drink in affection like a sponge and give it back tenfold. It doesn't matter if it's animals, kids, or people you meet on the street."

"Is that a bad thing?" she asked quietly.

Tal couldn't stay away from her any longer. It was physically impossible for him to keep his distance. When she was near, he felt a deep-seated need to touch her. He stepped closer and wrapped an arm around her waist. She immediately placed her hands on his chest and snuggled into him, making Tal sigh in contentment.

"Not at all," he said. "I think because you were denied love, friendship, and human touch for so long, you're making up for it now. And you also weren't able to give any of that back to anyone, so you're doing it in spades. I have no idea how in the world you can be so damn sweet after what you went through...but somehow you are."

"I'm not sweet. The other day, I laughed when that reporter tripped and fell over the curb when he was trying to take a picture of us."

Tal shook his head. "He deserved it," he said firmly. "You be you, Heather. Don't worry about how you think you *should* act. I think that's what's so awesome about you. Because you don't have any preconceived ideas about what you should say and do, you're more natural. More open.

You haven't spent the last twenty years on social media being influenced and judged by millions of strangers...and that makes you more authentic."

"Naïve, you mean," she mumbled, not meeting his eyes.

"There's nothing wrong with that," Tal told her. "I love the way everything is so new to you. The way your eyes widen when you taste one of Finley's amazing creations. How excited you get over every new book from the library. How everything is an opportunity for you to learn something new."

"I want to be someone you can be proud of. Not someone you have to constantly be teaching how to do things...like use a microwave."

"I *am* proud of you," he said immediately. "You're incredible, sweetheart. You could be bitter and broken, but instead you hold your head up high and embrace new experiences. It's a miracle. *You're* a miracle." Deciding he was done talking, Tal lowered his head.

Heather immediately tilted hers and met him halfway. Kissing had never been something Tal had spent much time thinking about. It was just something to do before getting to the "good stuff." But after the last week of kissing Heather every chance he could, he'd changed his mind. Kissing Heather was incredibly intimate. It meant so much more than sex had with other women.

As soon as they began to kiss, Heather's hands roamed. It was torture to feel her hands on him, but he wanted her to explore. To feel comfortable with him. Her fingers slipped under his shirt and moved upward. She was fascinated with his nipples, and without fail, her fingers went straight to them. Brushing, pinching, and flicking. As usual, they hardened under her ministrations and his cock lengthened.

Kissing Heather was an exercise in restraint. Every time she touched him, he wanted her more. Tal pulled his lips from hers with difficulty. As much as he wanted to make out for hours, he knew Khloe would be here any minute. And the last thing he wanted was to have an erection when she arrived.

Heather smiled up at him as her thumbs gently rubbed his nipples. "I love touching you."

"And I love you touching me," he said, remembering the night before when she'd finally convinced him to let her touch his cock without his boxers in the way. He'd nearly exploded when her warm hand had wrapped around him. It hadn't taken long for him to come, and the way she'd licked her lips and stared at him only made him orgasm harder.

It ate at him that *he'd* come, and she hadn't—twice now —but they'd talked about it, and she'd admitted that she was still nervous about sex, which didn't surprise Tal in the least. He was more than happy to simply hold her, to give her all the time she needed in order to heal.

It was only a matter of time before they made love, and as nervous as Tal was about bringing back bad memories for her, he couldn't wait to make Heather his. Or should he say, for Heather to make him *hers*?

The small smile on her face made Tal think she was remembering the night before as well. She'd helped him clean up and had spent a good amount of time exploring his cock with her hands and eyes during the process, explaining that she'd never seen a penis up close before. After hearing that, there was no way Tal could deny her need to satisfy her curiosity...even if it *had* turned him on all over again.

He had no idea if he was moving too fast or not. The

last thing he wanted to do was harm her recovery. Maybe living with him and getting into a sexual relationship was too soon. If he'd sensed the slightest bit of hesitation on her part, he would've put the brakes on by now. But giving her control of their physical intimacy seemed to bring out her confidence. Lowered her fear of an act that had always been too clinical and unemotional and painful in the past.

A knock on the door broke the intimate bubble they'd been in.

"She's here!" Heather said excitedly with a huge smile on her face.

Tal watched as she spun away from him and ran toward the door. He took a deep breath, praying his erection would subside before Khloe got a good look at him. Just in case, he stayed in the kitchen behind the counter.

By the time Heather walked into the room off the kitchen, she already had a small black kitten in her arms. Tal could hear the thing purring from where he was standing.

"I haven't named her yet, I figured I'd let you do that. I'm so relieved you wanted to take her. She was lonely out behind the library without her siblings. But Bristol and Lilly could only take one each, and I can't have pets where I live."

Tal heard the longing in Khloe's voice and forced his attention away from Heather and the kitten to study her.

"She's the friendliest of the bunch too, which is why I thought she'd be a better fit to be an inside cat. The other two were happy playing and chasing mice, bugs, and other animals, but this little girl just wanted to snuggle when I was there to feed them. She's also kind of picky, so you'll want to keep your eye on her and if she's not eating, you might need to get creative. Try mixing kibble with different brands and flavors of soft food. Bristol told me Rocky brought over what I've been feeding her, but I've noticed she gets tired of the same thing all the time and turns her nose up after a while. Oh, and she's favoring her back right leg. I've looked at it and I don't think it's anything serious, but if it gets worse and she stops putting weight on it, definitely have it looked at. She's up to date on her shots, but you'll need to get the boosters starting when she's around one."

Khloe's insights into the kittens she'd been taking care of were more in-depth than Tal would've thought. He supposed since she'd been taking care of them for weeks, maybe it wasn't too unusual...but he still felt she was way more knowledgeable about the health of kittens than someone who'd simply been feeding a bunch of strays.

"I've been taking them to a vet in Christiansburg. I know driving all the way out there isn't ideal, but Dr. Ziegler's a hack. I wouldn't even bring an animal I *hated* to see him."

Heather was stroking the kitten's head, staring at Khloe and nodding at everything she said.

Tal was aware that Khloe didn't care much for the vet in town, but at hearing the vehemence in her tone, he wondered what exactly the older man had done to earn such ire.

"You're gonna be a wonderful cat mom," Khloe told Heather. "I see you guys have a lot of stuff for cats already, which is great. I suggest putting her down and letting her get a feel for the place. Show her where the litterbox is, play with her a bit, then let her nap. This is an exciting day for her, and I'm sure she'll be exhausted soon."

"Thank you so much for letting me have her," Heather said.

"No, thank *you* for wanting her. I gotta go. My break's up and Raiden will be pissed if I'm too late getting back."

"I doubt that," Tal said, finally coming out from behind the counter. He wrapped an arm around Heather and pulled her against his side as she continued to love on the little kitten. "From what I've heard, you've been a huge help to him. You always volunteer to work out on the floor, you read to the kids who come in, and you're one of very few people Duke seems to love other than Raid."

Khloe smiled. "Duke's great. He's such a typical bloodhound. Food driven, slobbery, loves to sleep, and when it's time to work, he can track a scent for literally miles and miles."

It hit Tal then. Khloe loved animals more than she liked people.

She and Raiden were more alike than he'd thought.

"Anyway, if you have any questions, don't hesitate to call or text me. Wait, has Tal gotten you a phone yet?"

Heather nodded. "Although I'm not that good at using it yet."

"Not a big deal. Tal can get in touch with me if you need anything. But seriously, if you have any questions at all, I'm happy to answer them."

"Thank you so much," Heather said again.

Khloe smiled at her. "You're welcome. And I have to say it...I'm so glad you're here with us and not living in the woods by yourself anymore."

"Me too," Heather said simply.

The two women shared a smile, then Khloe turned and headed toward the door. "I'll see myself out. Later!"

Tal heard the apartment door open and shut, but his attention was on Heather and the kitten.

She was staring raptly at the thing, and he could see

she was already completely in love with the little creature in her arms.

"What do you think of Boots for a name? She's got these white patches on each foot, it almost looks as if she's wearing shoes."

"I think it's perfect."

She turned her gaze up to him. "I'm happy," she said simply. "I don't think I've been happy even once in the last twenty years. And now I've got a man, shoes, clothes I got to pick out myself, a warm place to sleep, a soft bed, food I don't have to kill myself, friends, and now a pet! If you'd have told me a year ago when I was hiding from Cypress in the woods this was where I'd be right now, I would've laughed in your face. Thank you for coming to find me, Talon."

His heart melted. If he hadn't loved her before, there was no doubt he was madly and completely in love with her now. She was so grateful for things most people took for granted. She'd been through hell, but was still able to see the good in her life. He would do whatever it took for her to keep her positive outlook. "You're welcome," he said, his voice cracking.

But she didn't seem to notice how overcome he was with emotion. She looked back down at the kitty and said, "Hi, Boots. You're home now. You're safe. You can trust me and Talon, and we'll never hurt you. How about a tour of your new place?"

Tal stood there, taking deep breaths and trying to get control over his emotions, as Heather began to walk around his apartment, showing Boots every corner. Hearing her use the same words he'd said to her over and over to reassure the kitten hit him harder than he'd expected it might. He hadn't been sure she'd ever be able to trust again. But watching her smile and coo at the small kitten, completely relaxed and at home in his space, made him sigh in relief.

She was going to be okay. Her kidnappers had done their best to change her. To mold her into a sex toy, a subservient, unthinking, uneducated slave they could bend to their will. But they'd failed spectacularly. It had taken her twenty years to escape them, but she'd done it.

He hoped he could be even half the man she deserved. He'd do whatever it took to be worthy of her, and he'd protect and take care of her to the best of his ability. *This* was what he'd spent all those years in the service for. To be able to keep evil from touching his woman ever again.

"Oh! I think she likes it!" Heather exclaimed. "Come look, Talon! She's climbing the tree thing!"

With a smile on his face, Tal walked over to where Heather was watching the kitten with awe in her expression. He didn't care if his friends teased him or thought she had him in the palm of her hand. Because it was true. And he was one hundred percent all right with that. He was hers. Plain and simple.

* * *

The next evening, Heather sat next to Tony on Talon's couch and did her best to pay attention and follow along as he read aloud from the book he'd brought over. She hadn't left the apartment since Khloe had dropped off Boots, but she didn't even care. She was madly in love with the kitten, and last night when she'd fallen asleep in her lap, Heather had burst into tears because she was so happy.

She could tell Talon wasn't thrilled when she wanted

the kitten to sleep with them in bed, but he hadn't said no. He was so good to her. She'd never been treated as good by anyone. He didn't talk down to her. Listened to her when she spoke, as if her opinion and thoughts mattered. It was thrilling, and she didn't know if she could ever give him up.

She loved Talon.

She'd had a few online sessions with a therapist and had admitted as much to the woman. The doctor had asked a ton of questions about what she was feeling, enough to make Heather think the therapist suspected her feelings for Talon weren't real. That she was simply grateful for his help, and overwhelmed because he was the first man to show her affection.

But Heather knew that wasn't true. She was grateful for Talon's help…but she was also thankful for *Simon's* help, and she didn't feel for him what she did for Talon.

Heather wasn't an idiot. Not all men were like Cypress and the others in The Community. She wasn't *settling* for Talon. Not even close. She'd seen how all his friends treated their women. Exactly how Talon treated her. She'd met other single men in Fallport and not one made her heart beat faster, didn't make goose bumps break out on her arms when they looked at her. And she couldn't imagine kissing or touching any of them.

Heather knew what she felt. Talon was hers. He'd said it. She wasn't giving him up…well, not unless he decided he didn't love her back.

That thought was so painful, she pushed it to the back of her mind and did her best to concentrate on the here and now—including on their guest.

Elsie had asked if it would be okay if Tony spent the night. She and Zeke wanted to take the evening off from working at the bar and spend it together. Talon had asked if she minded if Tony stayed over, and of course she said she didn't.

Heather loved being around the little boy. He was so different from the children she'd known from The Community. He was curious, asked a million questions, and was so respectful toward her. That was new. She was used to all males ordering her around, being condescending, and generally thinking they were better than everyone else. It didn't matter if the male was six years old or sixty. As a female, she was required to do whatever was asked of her, no matter a male's age.

Tony still went to the library every day after school, and Heather loved sitting with him as he did his homework. She was learning vicariously through him, and it was exciting and fun. Of course, Tony didn't think homework was fun, so he was thankful for her help.

They frequently read together after his homework was done, until it was time for him to go home. Even in the short time she'd been in Fallport, Heather felt as if her reading ability had improved considerably.

"Heather?" Tony asked, and she blinked, realizing that she hadn't been paying any attention to what he was reading. Searching the room for Boots, she saw the kitten was fast asleep on the cat tree in a patch of sunlight shining through the window. She could hear Talon in the kitchen, preparing dinner.

That was something that had taken a long while to get used to. The way Talon frequently insisted on being the one to cook and clean, letting her read, or practice math problems, or now play with Boots. He didn't seem to mind in the least that he was doing what Community members would call "women's work."

"Heather?" Tony asked again, and she forced her attention to the boy next her.

"Yeah?"

"Did you like living in the woods?"

Heather heard all sounds from the kitchen cease. As if Talon was listening to their conversation and ready to step in if he thought Tony asked something that might upset her. He did that all the time, and Heather appreciated it more than she could say. Many times when they were out and about in town, he'd stopped her from answering a potentially offensive question from someone.

Like the time one of the women she'd been told were notorious gossips asked how she'd managed to never get pregnant.

"Yes and no," she told Tony honestly.

He frowned. "How can it be both? I mean, I love camping. Everything about it. If I could live in a tent in the woods, I *so* would. But I have to go to school and my mom doesn't like bugs and being dirty. So it wouldn't work. When I get old, I'm totally gonna live in a tent though."

Heather smiled at his enthusiasm and naïveté. "Well, I love nature, and waking up to the birds chirping was always the best part of my day. And seeing the other critters minding their own business, going about their lives, was awesome too."

"Did you see Bigfoot?" Tony asked, his eyes wide. "I mean, you were out there a long time. Zeke said you lived in a cave for a whole *year*! You had to have seen him!"

"What's Bigfoot?" Heather asked, knowing full well what the boy was talking about, but curious as to how he'd explain the legendary creature. Lilly had told her all about how she'd come to Fallport to film a TV show about trying to find Bigfoot. Heather remembered seeing the people with cameras, hollering in the woods every night. That had also explained the increase in people hiking in the Appalachians, and why she'd seen Talon and his friends more in the last six months than she had in the years prior.

"You don't know what Bigfoot is?" Tony asked, eyes wide. "He's epic! He's like an ape, but human. He's tall, like over eight feet, which is taller than even Raiden! And he's hairy and has *huge* feet! He growls and grunts and hides from people."

"Oh. You mean Darryl?"

Tony had scooted to the edge of the couch in his enthusiasm, and now he stared at her in wonder. "You know his name?!" he asked.

Heather giggled and decided to let the poor kid off the hook. "I'm teasing you, Tony. I saw a commercial on TV where a woman was talking to a Bigfoot, and when she told him people called him 'Bigfoot,' he looked confused and said, 'But my name's Darryl.'"

Tony stared at her with a frown, then turned to look into the kitchen. "Tal, have you seen that commercial?"

"Yeah, bud. I have. You want me to find it on the internet and show you?"

"Yes!"

Heather forgot that most things she saw on TV could be replayed on Talon's phone. She watched with a small smile as Tony ran into the kitchen to see the commercial Talon had pulled up.

After, the boy laughed and ran back to where Heather was sitting. One thing that wasn't different about the boys in The Community and Tony was that they very rarely walked anywhere. They were always a bundle of energy, running here and there.

"That's funny," Tony informed her with a huge smile.

"But you really didn't see Bigfoot?"

Heather shrugged. "Sorry, no. Deer, squirrels, raccoons, opossums, bats, skunk, turkeys, mice, woodpeckers, rabbits, snakes, hawks, chipmunks, foxes, porcupines... even an occasional black bear."

"Wow, really?"

"Really."

"I want to see a bear," Tony said wistfully.

"I'm sure you will someday," Heather told him.

"All that sounds awesome, but you said you also *didn't* like living in the woods," Tony said. "Why not?"

"Well...it was lonely," Heather told him honestly. "I was by myself, and I didn't have anyone to talk to."

Tony thought about that for a moment, then nodded. "Yeah, I'd miss my mom. And my friends. And all the guys."

"And in the winter, it was cold. I didn't have a nice soft bed like I do now. I couldn't take a shower or bath until the weather warmed up."

Tony scrunched up his nose. "I wouldn't miss not having to take a bath."

Heather laughed. "I smelled," she whispered. "It wasn't good."

Tony didn't look convinced, and Heather guessed that smelling yucky wasn't exactly a deterrent for a little boy. She went on. "I had to find and prepare all my own meals. And when I wasn't able to catch a fish, or rabbit, or anything else, I went hungry."

"You didn't have snacks?" Tony asked.

"No."

"I'd totally bring snacks," he said confidently.

Heather smiled at that.

"And I guess you didn't have TV, huh? Or a phone?"

Tony asked.

"Nope. None of that. I didn't even have any books," Heather said.

"Well, that sucks," he agreed, looking down at the book he'd put aside. "Maybe instead of living in the woods, I can just take lots of shorter camping trips," he said after a minute. "But I'm totally bringing snacks and a book. Oh, and a warm sleeping bag. And maybe I'll let Zeke come with me so I can talk to someone."

"That sounds like a great plan," Heather told him.

"You know, some people have jobs where they work in the forest all the time," Talon said, joining them from the kitchen and leaning against the back of the couch.

"Yeah, like you and Zeke and the others do. Looking for lost people."

"Well, yes, but there are also full-time jobs where people get paid money to be in the woods," he told the boy.

"There are?"

"Uh-huh. Like wildland firefighters, forest rangers, lumberjacks, game wardens, and even some research jobs where people study animals in their natural habitats."

"Cool," Tony breathed. "I want one of those."

"Then you need to be sure to study hard so you can be smart enough to get one."

"I will!" He turned back to Heather. "Do you want me to read more or can I play with Boots?"

She smiled at him. "I think Boots would love to play." She wasn't sure about that, as the kitten looked completely comfortable sleeping where she was. But even though the kitten had only been with them a single night, Heather had already learned how important it was to tire her out before they went to bed, otherwise she'd end up with a kitten on her face while trying to sleep. Or worse, Talon would. And while it was obvious he liked the little creature well enough, she didn't want to press her luck.

After dinner—which was delicious; Talon had made them cheeseburgers and Tater Tots—Tony was babbling about Silas, Otto, and Art arguing over who was ahead of who in winning their chess games.

"Chess?" Heather asked.

"Yeah, that's all they do. Sit out there and play chess and gossip," Tony said gleefully. "In the winter they have a little heater, so they don't freeze to death. They sit out there no matter how cold or hot it is. Although they tend to hang out at Sunny Side Up longer for meals when it's too hot or cold."

Heather smiled. She felt Talon's gaze on her. He was sitting next to her on the couch and had pulled her legs over his lap. She was comfortable, warm, and content.

"Chess is played on a board with white and black squares. There's kings and queens and they each have their own rules on how they can move on the board," Tony explained. "I like checkers better, but Zeke's trying to teach me how to play chess."

Heather swallowed hard and said something she never, ever would've admitted in her old life. "I think I know how to play."

"You think?" Talon asked with a small tilt of his head.

"Only the men and boys were allowed to play games in The Community. But I watched them. I've never actually played chess, but I think I know how."

"Why were only boys allowed to play?" Tony asked.

Heather turned to look at him. He was sitting on the floor in front of the couch, watching TV, but he'd spun around to look at her when he asked the question.

She shrugged. "Because those were the rules."

Talon continued answering the question. "Because she had to live with men who didn't respect women. Didn't understand how amazing they are and that they're just as smart, or smarter, than men. Because they were abusive jerks. They had to oppress women to make themselves feel better about their own shortcomings."

Heather swallowed hard. He wasn't wrong, but somehow it felt weird to say all that to Tony.

The little boy just nodded solemnly. "It's a good thing she's here with us now then, isn't it?"

"Yes, Tony. It definitely is."

Talon squeezed her leg, and Heather couldn't help but close her eyes and be thankful she was right where she was. And that Talon was hers.

"You good?" he asked softly several minutes later, after Tony's attention was focused back on the TV.

She nodded.

Talon stared at her for a long moment before nodding back. "Maybe I should bring you over to the post office and let you practice your chess-playing skills with Art and the guys."

Heather shook her head. "Oh no, I'm sure they're so much better than I am. I've never even actually played before."

"Doesn't matter. Maybe you'll kick their butts and shake them up a bit," Talon countered. "Although sitting out in the open like that wouldn't be a good idea. Even though some of the reporters have left town, there are still plenty left who wouldn't be able to resist taking pictures or trying to get a statement. I'll talk to Sandra and see if we can set up a table when they come in for lunch."

This was one of the many things Heather loved about

Talon. He was always looking out for her. Wanting to protect her and give her experiences she'd never had before. She smiled at him.

Later, as she stood just outside the guest room, she watched Talon tuck Tony into the brand-new bed. The room looked a little bare, with only the twin-size bed and the small dresser, but her eyes were focused on her man and the little boy. This was yet another new experience. In The Community, the boys all slept in the same tent and there was no "tucking in" or tenderness involved.

Talon sat on the edge of the mattress, talking quietly to Tony. "You have a good day?"

"Yeah. Boots is so cute. And the hamburgers were awesome. Do you really think I could get one of those forest jobs? I totally love camping."

"I'm sure of it."

"Will you go camping with me again?"

"Of course. But maybe we can wait until it gets a little warmer?" Talon asked.

Tony sighed but nodded. "What are we having for breakfast? Can we go to The Sweet Tooth and get some cinnamon rolls?"

Talon chuckled. "Sure, bud."

"Tal?"

"Yeah?"

"I don't think I'd like to live in the woods all the time. I'd miss my mom too much. And Zeke. And you."

"It's okay, you don't have to."

"Do you think Heather was sad living out there by herself?"

Talon took a deep breath. He knew she was standing by the door listening, but he didn't hesitate to answer the little boy. "I'm sure she was. But sometimes we do things not because we want to, but because we have to."

"Like me driving all the way back to Fallport, even though I knew I could get in big trouble."

"Exactly like that."

Heather had heard the story about how Tony's biological father had planned for the boy to be kidnapped and killed for money, and how Tony had stolen his car and driven back to town to get help. She'd been heartbroken and impressed all at the same time.

"There are people you meet in life that you just know are extraordinary. People who have survived things no person should have to go through and somehow are still kind and loving."

"Like Anne Frank. I mean, she died, but I have a feeling she would've been an amazing grown-up," Tony said.

His class was studying World War II and the Holocaust, and the boy was fascinated by the young girl and what she'd gone through. Heather had been just as intrigued, as she didn't remember anything about history that she'd learned before she was kidnapped.

"I think so too," Talon agreed. "Heather is one of those people, bud. She was treated very badly by the people she lived with, and yet she's still wonderful, inside and out."

"Did she really get stolen when she was around my age?" Tony asked.

"I'm afraid so."

"And she doesn't have parents anymore, does she?"

"No. They died."

"Well...she has us, right?"

"Right," Talon said.

"She's pretty. I like her hair," Tony said.

"Me too."

"And she's really smart. When I first met her, she didn't know a lot of words. But now she knows a ton of them."

"She's a fast learner."

"She should stay," Tony said with determination. "You should marry her. Zeke's got my mom, and your other friends all have girlfriends and wives. But you don't. She could stay here with you, and you guys can get married."

"You think?" Tal asked.

Heather had a feeling her cheeks were bright red, but she couldn't bring herself to step away from the door.

"Yeah. It's either you or Mr. Smith from school. But he's old, and he makes a funny noise when he sneezes. So I think *you* should."

Talon chuckled. "I'll take your recommendation under advisement."

"Does that mean you will?" Tony asked.

"It means it's late and you need to get some sleep. I don't want your mom and Zeke to think we let you stay up past your bedtime," Talon said.

"That's not what it means," Tony complained. "But fine."

Talon leaned over and kissed Tony's forehead. "Sleep well, bud."

"I will. Talon?"

"Yeah?"

"I'm glad you found her and brought her back."

"Me too, Tony. Me too." With that, Talon stood and Heather stepped farther back so she was out of Tony's sight.

"Sleep well. If you need anything, Heather and I are right down the hall."

"I know. I'll be fine. If I wake up before you, I'll read. That's what Mom makes me do."

"Sounds good. Love you."

"Love you too, Talon. Good night."

With that, Talon exited the room and closed the door almost all the way, leaving a small crack. "You okay?" he whispered.

Heather nodded.

"He's a curious kid," he said, continuing to whisper.

"I don't mind his questions," she said honestly.

"Good."

For a second, she was afraid he was going to bring up Tony's last question. But he simply asked, "You want to watch more TV or head to bed? We can read or something if you aren't tired yet."

"Bed," she said without having to think about it. While the television was interesting, it was also overwhelming sometimes. She liked the silence of the night and not being bombarded with words and music and people trying to sell stuff in all the commercials.

"Sounds good. You head on in and get ready, and I'll go grab Boots."

Smiling, Heather nodded.

By the time she was done brushing her teeth and changing, Talon was in bed with Boots. The kitten had settled in her usual spot on Heather's pillow. Since she always fell asleep with her head on Talon's shoulder, she didn't really need it.

She petted Boots and listened to her purr while Talon took his turn in the bathroom. When he exited, he turned off the light and crawled under the covers on his side. He immediately pulled Heather against him and sighed in contentment when she got settled.

"I thought we were going to read?" she asked.

"We can if you want. I just wanted to hold you for a second first."

She couldn't argue with that.

She wanted more kisses, but suddenly was too tired to move. As much as she enjoyed having Tony around, his endless energy was a little bit exhausting. He asked nonstop questions and needed to be entertained. Again, Heather loved doing so, but wasn't used to the constant stimulation.

"For the record," Talon said after a moment. "I think Tony's suggestion was an excellent one."

Heather stilled as he continued speaking.

"I think you should stay too. And I seem to be a better option than poor Mr. Smith, who sounds weird when he sneezes."

"I haven't heard you sneeze," Heather reasoned.

He chuckled, and she felt the sound reverberate against her.

"True. But you're already here, you might as well stay. But no matter what, there's no pressure. If you decide you need your own space, I'll help you find an appropriate place to live. If you want to see other people, I'll do my best to step aside, although I'll hate every second of it. No one will ever control you again, Heather. I'll make sure of it. But for the record...I like having you here. I like falling asleep with you in my arms. I like everything about you. I don't *want* you to leave, and I certainly don't want you kissing anyone else. But if that's what you need, or what you want, I'll support you one hundred percent."

"I don't want to leave, and I don't want to kiss anyone else," she said softly.

"Good."

The relief in his voice was easy to hear.

"Tomorrow, I'll talk to Art and Sandra and see if we can't set up that chess game for you. You want to go with me to pick up cinnamon rolls from The Sweet Tooth? Or do you want to stay here with Tony?"

"I'll stay."

"Okay. You know Boots will be okay if we leave her in the apartment by herself, right?" he asked with a small chuckle.

"Yeah," she said, not sure if she sounded convincing.

"Sleep well, sweetheart. I know *I* will. I'm knackered. Tony's a spitfire."

"Knackered?" she asked.

"Sorry, British slang. Means tired. Exhausted."

"I like your words," she told him. "And I'm knackered too."

"You want one someday? A kid?" he asked.

Heather stiffened against him. She hadn't thought much about it. While living in The Community, she'd done everything she could to prevent pregnancy. She didn't want a daughter being treated like she and the other women were, and the thought of her son being brought up to hate her, or to treat other women and girls like they were trash, was abhorrent.

But now that she was free? Wasn't living in a cave in the forest? After meeting Talon and seeing how gentle he was with her, with Boots, with Tony...

The thought of having a baby didn't seem so scary anymore.

"Never mind," he said when she didn't immediately answer. "It's too soon for me to be asking."

"I think so," Heather blurted. "But I don't know anything about being a mother."

"Hogwash," Talon said. "You'd be an amazing mom."

He didn't say anything more, but now that he'd asked the question, Heather couldn't stop thinking about it.

He turned his head and kissed her temple before sighing and closing his eyes.

That night, Heather dreamed of a little red-haired girl holding her arms up to her and calling her mommy. And by her side was Talon, looking at them both with an expression so full of love, Heather's heart felt as if it might explode.

CHAPTER SIXTEEN

The chess game couldn't happen the next day, but Heather didn't mind. Tal could tell she was content to hang out in the apartment with Boots. He finally convinced her to leave the apartment three days later to meet up with Lilly and Ethan. Lilly was cleared to return to her normal activities, and they all met over at Bristol's house for a loud, chaotic lunch.

And three days after *that*, Talon finally got Heather over to Sunny Side Up to visit with Art and his friends, and to try out her chess-playing skills.

The first few games were difficult, but once she got the hang of how each piece moved, Heather was a formidable opponent. She'd obviously paid very close attention when the men in The Community played, and that, along with her intuition, served her well. She didn't win any games, but came very close the last time. Even Art seemed impressed.

They were eating a late lunch and Heather was reveling in her successful chess games when Talon's phone rang. Seeing it was Simon, he answered, hoping the police chief would have more information about the whereabouts of Heather's kidnappers.

"Opal Williams will be here tomorrow morning. I thought you could talk here, at the station."

Talon's heart skipped a beat. This was so out of the blue! Sure, he'd suggested Simon call Opal about talking to Heather, but never in a million years had he expected it to actually pan out.

"No way, not there," he said immediately. His mind spun as he tried to come up with an appropriate setting for the interview.

"Well, you have until tomorrow to think of a better place and to get Heather there. I'm sure Opal's people will help her with makeup and shit."

"A heads-up would've been nice," Talon said, the frustration easy to hear in his voice.

"This *is* your heads-up. I didn't find out until just now. Last I heard, it was in the works. Apparently Opal's got an unexpected break in her schedule, so this is the only time she can get here. I figured you'd like to get it done sooner rather than later."

He wasn't wrong. "Fine. I'll call you back soon."

"This is going to work out," Simon said, in an uncharacteristically gentle tone.

"I hope so," Talon countered, then hung up.

"What? What's wrong?" Heather asked.

Grateful they were almost finished eating, he stood and held out his hand.

Heather took it without missing a beat and he helped her to her feet. He waved at Sandra and thanked her for the meal, then led Heather outside. It was chilly, but not unbearably so. After the monster blizzard and the extremely frigid weather that had come with it, the temperatures had leveled out and been more normal for this time of year.

"Talon?" she asked as he walked her to his SUV. Looking around, Tal didn't see any reporters lurking, which he was thankful for. Many had given up, going back to wherever they'd come from. But a few were still lurking, and every now and then, someone new came to town hoping to get a scoop.

After he'd gotten her into his SUV and he'd climbed behind the wheel, Tal took a deep breath and turned to her.

"What's wrong? You're scaring me," Heather said.

Shit. That hadn't been his intention. "I'm sorry. I'm just thinking. That was Simon."

"Did he find The Community?" Heather asked.

"No. I mean, I didn't ask. He was calling to tell me that Opal is on her way to Fallport. She'll be here in the morning."

Heather blinked in surprise. "Really?"

"Yeah."

"Okay."

"Okay?" he questioned.

Heather shrugged. "Yeah. You said she's the person I should tell my story to, so everyone else would forget about me. I'm ready to do that."

She never failed to surprise and impress him.

"You're upset," she added, frowning. "Should I not do this?"

"It's not that. I just...you've been doing so great lately. The therapist says you're adjusting extremely well. The last thing I want is you talking about everything and regressing."

"I think I *want* to talk about it," Heather said. "Maybe

if someone hears my story, they'll recognize if other people like Arrow and Cypress have set up in their towns. My parents didn't live to find out what happened to me, to see that I'm alive and well...but if I go on TV and talk about my experience, it could give *other* parents hope that their kidnapped children are still alive somewhere. Like Simon said. I can't lie, I'm nervous, but you'll be there, right?"

"Of course. I wouldn't let you do something like this on your own."

"Then I'll be okay," she said firmly.

Tal was impressed all over again. "I'm in awe of you," he said. "You're so bloody strong, it's not even funny."

"It's not that I'm strong," Heather said. "I'm *mad*. Arrow and The Community stole so much from me. It took me twenty years, but I was able to get free. And there are so many others who haven't been as lucky. We talked about the boys and girls who simply appeared at camp... where did they come from? Where are *their* parents? I'm hoping that by speaking up, it will help the police find Cypress, and all those kids can be returned to their families."

Tal leaned over and gently palmed the back of her neck. He pulled her closer and kissed her forehead gently. "I hope so too," he said quietly.

They sat like that for a long moment before he took a deep breath and let his hand fall from her nape. "We need to figure out where we're gonna do this. Maybe the girls can help you find something you'll feel comfortable wearing. I need to call the guys and let them know what's happening. Shit, I was supposed to work tomorrow. I hate to ask Harvey for another day off, but it can't be helped. I should—"

He stopped talking when Heather put her hand on his arm. "It'll be okay," she said.

Taking a deep breath, Tal nodded. She was right. It would. And he didn't miss the irony of Heather being the one to assure *him* this time. He gave her a smile and turned the key in the ignition.

* * *

The next morning, Heather was nervous. She didn't know this Opal person, but last night, Talon had shown her one of the woman's interviews online, so she could see what would likely happen when she sat down with the extremely famous TV host. In the recording she watched, Opal was interviewing a prince from Talon's country, and his relatively new wife. They were living in the United States now and apparently there was a lot of controversy over that. After watching the entire thing, Heather felt better. Opal asked some difficult questions, but she wasn't rude about it and she seemed...nice.

Talon had arranged for the interview to take place at the Chestnut Street Manor Bed and Breakfast. Lilly had suggested it. She'd stayed there when she'd first come to Fallport while she was a cameraperson on the Bigfoot show, and had gotten close to the owner, Whitney Crawford. Apparently, Brock, Raid, and Drew had spent the afternoon at the B&B yesterday, transforming the dining room into a makeshift studio. They'd helped Whitney clear out furniture, clean, and had done what they could to help her get ready to have TV royalty come to her house.

Heather and Talon had arrived at the B&B around six-thirty that morning. She'd met with a producer, and the woman had gone over some of the questions Opal was going to ask. Heather appreciated being able to prepare for some of the more difficult things she might discuss.

Then she'd been brought into one of the guest rooms, where one woman worked on styling her hair and another had put makeup on her face. Heather had never even worn lipstick before, and her face felt funny and oddly heavy by the time the woman was done.

And now it was time. Time to meet Opal. Time to tell the world her story.

"You can still back out," Talon said gently as he rubbed his thumb back and forth over the back of her hand. He hadn't left her side for even a minute. When she'd gotten overwhelmed with all the attention, Talon was there to help her get through it.

"No, I want to do this," she said, although her voice wasn't as strong as she wanted it to be.

Talon led them away from all the hustle and bustle and leaned against a wall, turning Heather so her back was to the room. All she could see was him as he put his hands on either side of her face and tilted her head up.

"You're going to be great," he told her softly. "The world's gonna take one look at you and want to personally hunt down Cypress and everyone else who dared hurt you."

Heather put her hands on Talon's sides and gripped his shirt tightly.

"You look beautiful. But you should know...the makeup, clothes, and the hairdo are nice...but I was attracted to you back when I first saw you in that cave. Hair in tangles, dirt on your face, and wearing my clothes that hung off your smaller frame. I wasn't drawn to you because of your looks, but because of your warrior spirit. You could've quit trying a long time ago. Given in to your circumstance. Given up. But you didn't. You kept fighting, even when you were hurt. Even when things seemed hopeless. That's the Heather I'm falling in love with. Go out there this morning and be yourself. Don't be afraid to tell the truth. You're safe here. Protected."

"I can trust you, and you won't hurt me," Heather whispered. How many times had she repeated those words to herself? More than she could count. They'd been a lifeline for her. And even when she hadn't trusted him fully, she still clung to his promise.

"Those words are just as true now as they were when I first said them," he vowed.

"You're falling in love with me?" she asked softly, realizing what he'd just said.

"Yes."

One word. Simple and to the point.

She smiled up at him. "I think I'm falling in love with you too," she admitted.

His lips curled up, and she could just see that dimple in his cheek through his trimmed beard. "It's time. You've got this."

Heather nodded and closed her eyes when Talon lowered his head. He kissed her oh so gently, and while she loved the feel of his lips on hers...it suddenly wasn't enough. She wanted all of this man. He'd already taught her so much when it came to sex and intimacy, and she was ready for him to show her everything.

"Heather?" a melodious voice asked from behind them.

She turned, ever aware of Talon's hand on the small of her back, to see a beautiful dark-skinned woman standing behind them. She recognized her from the show she'd watched the day before. "Hi," she said somewhat shyly.

"I'm Opal Williams," the woman said, holding out her hand. "It's so good to meet you."

"It's nice to meet you too," Heather said.

"I'm so glad you're all right."

"Me too," she agreed.

Opal's lips twitched. "I think we're going to have a good chat. Sometimes people are so overwhelmed with meeting me that they tense up. They can't think of anything to say."

Heather shrugged. "I know you're famous, but I wasn't allowed to watch TV for the last twenty years, so to me... you're just another person."

At that, Opal's smile widened. "So I am," she agreed.

"And Talon wouldn't let me do anything that would make me look stupid, or talk to someone who would hurt me, and that's why I agreed to talk to you. That, and because I want things to go back to normal here. I want to go to The Sweet Tooth without having to worry about someone with a camera jumping out from behind a car. Or go to Sunny Side Up and not have someone yell questions at me from across the room. Everyone says that if I let you ask me questions, I can go back to being boring old Heather Brown."

"I'm not sure you could ever be boring," Opal said. Then she turned and gestured to someone behind her. Another woman approached. "And so you aren't blindsided during our interview, this is Lilac Lee."

Heather nodded politely at the other woman.

"She was kidnapped when she was twenty-one and held for eleven years."

Heather inhaled sharply and stared at the woman in front of her with wide eyes. She was older than Heather, but she looked healthy. And happy. She had tattoos on her

273

arms and on her chest, which were peeking out from the V-neck of the dress she was wearing. She had short dark hair, close to the same auburn shade as her own. There was also a piercing in her lip and eyebrow. Heather had never seen anyone like her.

"Hi," Lilac said, holding out her hand.

Heather shook it and licked her lips nervously. This woman looked so...normal. She knew a little bit about her story, and while she was taken when she was already an adult, she'd suffered in the house she'd been held in just as much, if not more, than Heather.

"If you'd like, I'd love to talk once your interview is over."

Heather nodded immediately. She had so many questions for this woman.

Both Opal and Lilac turned away, and Talon leaned down. She felt his beard brush against her cheek before he whispered, "I didn't know she'd be here. Are you all right?"

Heather nodded and turned to look at him. She appreciated his support more than she could say. She remembered Lilly telling her that Talon was a man who was born to take care of a woman, and she was so grateful she *was* that woman.

The producer motioned for her to come forward and sit on the small couch in front of the many lights that had been set up. Talon kissed her temple, then she lifted her chin and headed for the couch.

Three hours later, Heather was mentally and emotionally exhausted. She felt tired in a way she'd only ever been after hunting for days. It was strange, because those days felt as if they were so long ago, but in reality, it hadn't even been a month since she'd been living in that cave in the woods.

Opal had asked some difficult questions, but seeing Talon standing behind the lights and cameras, his steadfast presence never wavering, had given her the courage to answer every question with complete honesty. It wasn't easy, but when it was all over, she felt...lighter. As if sharing her experience and everything she'd been through—how she'd felt while restrained in the punishment tent, being declared a wife without her consent, the terrifying decision to hide in the forest when The Community had been packing up to move...and why she hadn't tried to run away sooner—was well and truly over.

After the lights were shut off and the cameras stopped rolling, Opal approached Heather and asked, "Can I give you a hug?"

Nodding, Heather closed her eyes as the older woman's arms closed around her. She smelled like some kind of expensive perfume, her hair tickled Heather's cheek, but other than Talon's, the hug was one of the best she'd ever received. She'd opened herself up completely. Had shared things she'd never told anyone, not even Talon. And yet Opal still respected her. Still liked her. It was a heady feeling.

Opal pulled back, put her hands on Heather's shoulders and stared at her for a long moment before nodding firmly. "You're going to be all right." Then she said goodbye and headed for the door to the room, the producer by her side the entire way.

Turning—Heather blinked in surprise. Standing behind Talon was Lilly and Ethan. And everyone else too. Elsie, Zeke, Bristol, Rocky, Caryn, Drew, Finley, Brock, even Khloe and Raid were there. Duke was sound asleep on the floor, oblivious to all the commotion around him.

Tears filled Heather's eyes. "What...you all came?" she stuttered.

"Of course we did!" Caryn exclaimed as she strode forward and hugged Heather tight.

"You thought we wouldn't? Friends stick together," Finley said softly.

"Besides, it's *Opal*!" Elsie said, the excitement easy to hear in her voice.

Everyone laughed.

"Don't cry," Lilly ordered. "If you start, we'll all be blubbering."

It was hard to get used to so much support after being on her own for so long. She no longer blamed the other women in The Community for being the way they were. They'd all been conditioned not to talk to each other. Not to make friends. Fear of what would happen to them if they were seen getting too close to someone else was too real.

They'd all been surviving, in any way they could.

Movement to the left caught Heather's eye, and she saw Lilac watching her with a small smile on her face.

"Will you guys give me a minute?" Heather asked, not wanting anyone to be offended if she left to talk to Lilac.

"Of course. Take all the time you need," Bristol said. "Whitney made a late lunch for us, but we need to wait until all the cameras and lights and stuff are cleared out before the table can be brought back in and we can eat."

"Heather?"

She looked up at Talon, knowing what he wanted to know without him saying it. "I'm okay. I just want to talk to her for a minute."

"Okay. If you need me, I'm here."

"I know." And she did. Talon was her rock.

She was nervous to talk to the other woman, but she took a deep breath and walked over. "Hi," she said as she approached.

"Hi back," Lilac said with a welcoming smile. The hoop in her lip was hard to get used to, but she was so friendly, Heather quickly forgot about it.

"I'm sorry for what happened to you," she said.

"I'm sorry for what happened to *you*," Lilac countered. "But after listening to your story, and seeing all the support you have...you're going to be just fine."

Her positive words made Heather feel good. "I...can I ask you something?"

"You can ask me anything you want," Lilac said.

"I didn't know much about your story until today. Until Opal talked about it. She said you got married?"

Lilac nodded. "Yes. I met him through some of my friends, and we got married three years to the day after I was rescued."

"That's great."

Lilac tilted her head and smiled slightly. "What do you *really* want to know?" she asked gently.

"I...how did you know...after what happened...were you nervous?" Heather knew she was messing this up, but she didn't know how to make the right words come out.

"Yes and no," Lilac answered. "I was nervous because I really liked him and wanted him to like me back. I was worried he wouldn't be able to look past what happened to me. That I'd always be the poor girl who was kidnapped and held hostage for over a decade. But being around him felt *right*. I felt safe. He never made me feel different. To him...I was just Lilac."

With each word out of the other woman's mouth,

Heather relaxed. That was exactly how she felt when she was around Talon.

"Was it hard to...Do you have sex?" she blurted, then immediately regretted asking the question.

"We do," she answered with a smile. "And it wasn't hard to fall in love with him at all. What the asshole who kidnapped me did was completely different from making love with my husband...my then boyfriend. It was as different as night and day. I'm not going to say it's always easy, that I don't have some bad days where my memories overwhelm me, but never when I'm with my husband.

"I made a choice not to be a victim. Not to let him ruin the rest of my life. I'm a survivor, and I'm stronger with my husband. We adopted a little boy, and my family is what keeps me going. If you're asking if it's wrong or weird that you're attracted to the handsome guy who hasn't taken his eyes off you in the last three hours...it's not. Live your life, Heather. Love. Laugh. Don't let those assholes keep you from falling in love, having children...moving on."

Her words freed Heather in a way nothing else could have. She loved Talon. It didn't *feel* too soon, but she was worried she'd be judged. That it was somehow abnormal to *want* to be with a man after what had happened to her. Hearing that Lilac was happy and living a normal life, now married, after the horrific abuse she'd suffered...made Heather feel so much better.

The two women exchanged a long, heartfelt hug. "Do you want to stay and eat with us?" Heather asked.

"Thank you, but no. I'm headed home. My son has a birthday party tomorrow, not his, but a friend's, and we need to get a present for him to bring. I also miss my husband very much."

Heather understood. "Okay. It was so good meeting you."

"Same. You're now a member of a select club," Lilac said solemnly. "It's not a club anyone wants to be in, but here we are. If you need anything, I mean *anything*...to talk, to cry, to vent about the unfairness of life...you let me know. You aren't alone. There are quite a few of us out there, women who were kidnapped and held hostage for months or years and lived to tell about it. When you're ready, I can get you in touch with others like us."

"I...I think I'd like that," Heather said.

"Good. Take care of yourself...and don't be afraid to *live*."

With that, Lilac smiled at Heather and followed a man carrying a large light out of the room. Even before Heather turned back to her friends, Talon was there.

He stared at her for a long moment before smiling. "You look...settled."

"I am," she agreed. "But I'm hungry."

"Then let's get you fed," he said easily.

The relief Heather saw on his face made her realize how stressed he'd been about her interview. He'd been worried about her, and it showed.

How she'd gotten so lucky to have this man find her, she didn't know. But she was grateful. He was hers now... he'd said it. And she wanted to show him how much he meant to her. But first, she wanted to revel in the company of her friends.

Live...as Lilac had suggested.

Heather wasn't fooling herself. She knew as soon as her interview aired she'd have to deal with another influx of people wanting to talk to her, get interviews...just as they had when word got out that she'd been found after all those years. But she was fairly certain the citizens of Fall-port would support and protect her, just as they'd been doing.

If she had to stay inside for a while, so be it. She could handle that. Whitney Crawford had even offered to tutor her, something Heather really wanted to take her up on. There was so much she wanted to learn. She wanted to make Talon proud of her, but more than that, she just wanted to know about things most other adults took for granted.

Feeling good about how things were going, Heather leaned into Talon as he squeezed her waist with his arm. He leaned down, kissed her, then went to help the rest of the guys move the large table back into the room so they could eat.

* * *

Four days later, the Opal Williams special aired.

Cypress Goodson was sitting in a hotel room in a small town in North Carolina, planning on how he was going to acquire his next wife, who he'd seen today at a Head Start Center and followed home.

It was on prime time, and he came face-to-face with Sunset talking about her time with The Community. Spilling all their secrets on national television. Fury made his hands shake as he reached for the remote to turn up the volume.

The first thing he noticed when he saw her on the screen was that she'd cut her hair.

Sunset *knew* that was against the rules. That women should never, *ever* cut their hair, and yet, there she was for all the world to see, half of her glorious hair gone. Memories of how he'd jacked off into the thick strands, how his jizz would still be there hours later, marking her as his property, swam through his brain.

She'd *pay* for defying him.

Hatred swam through his veins as Sunset complained about how she'd been treated. Telling the world about the punishment tent, about the children who appeared in camp without warning, how many wives each man had.

Cypress knew without a doubt that his life had just changed. He wouldn't be surprised if the new Community down in Florida was raided and disbanded within the week.

It wasn't dumb luck that he wasn't back home with the others right now though—he was destined to persevere. To obtain and train the first of his many new wives.

Thinking about the little red-haired girl he'd seen today made him smile. She was perfect...just one of way too many foster children in an overcrowded, rundown home. No one would miss her. She was expendable, as were all the children they'd acquired over the years.

Sunset had been one of the first they'd ever taken...and the most difficult to train. A great many beatings and more time than anyone else in the punishment tent eventually made her more obedient. But she was never fully subservient. Always asking questions, despite the consequences, even when Cypress was more heavy-handed with her than Arrow had ever been.

After Sunset, they'd stuck to grabbing toddlers or babies. Children who wouldn't remember life before The Community. It took longer for them to age enough to be claimed as a wife, but that couldn't be helped.

Now Cypress was on his own, and he knew it. He

couldn't go back to Florida, not with all the information Sunset had blabbed in her interview.

It didn't matter. He'd take the girl he'd found today and start anew.

Not only that, he was still going to return to Fallport... just long enough to show Sunset that *he* was still in charge. That she'd never be free of him. Make her submit to him once more. And what better place to force her to accept she'd always be his, than where it had all started?

The more he thought about the plan, the more obsessed he became. It was risky, yes, but he'd avoid talking to anyone in town. He'd wear a disguise to be sure he wasn't recognized. He'd return to where The Community had thrived for all those years, where his father had taught him that men were inherently superior to women in all ways.

No one would expect him to be crazy enough to return, not with a huge spotlight now on the town of Fallport. But he wouldn't be there long...

Just long enough to start his new Sunset's training, and show the bitch on TV that she was nothing but trash.

She always was and always would be.

Satisfied with his plans, Cypress grinned. He didn't even hear what Sunset was saying on the television any longer. Instead, he thought of how thrilling it would be to watch his future wife cower on the floor of his car. How she'd do whatever he told her to do, as soon as he told her to do it. She'd learn. They all learned. And the one who hadn't?

She'd die, regretting that she'd never fallen in line like all the others.

No woman said no to Cypress Goodson.

Sunset Meadowblossom wasn't allowed to live a happy

life. She'd defied him, hidden from him, and now she might as well have spit in his face. That kind of insolence wasn't tolerated. After he'd shown her who was boss, and after she'd apologized and pledged her loyalty—he'd end her. Once and for all.

Then he and his new Sunset Meadowblossom would live happily ever after, far away from Fallport, Virginia. Maybe he'd go to Idaho. Or North Dakota. Or Montana. Where people were few and far between. He'd stay away from cities. Gather enough wives to serve him so he could live a comfortable life.

Cypress shut off the TV and turned off the light next to the bed. He could hear two people fucking in the room next to his own, the loud noises turning him on. His hand slid down his body as he imagined how that bitch would beg for forgiveness. Beg for her life. But in the end, she'd reap the consequences of saying no to him. To *any* man.

CHAPTER SEVENTEEN

It had been seven days since Heather's interview aired, and with every day that passed, she seemed to come out of her shell more and more. Tal had been worried the interview would make her regress. Would traumatize her. But instead, she seemed happier and lighter than ever.

It was the end of February, and even though a cold front was moving through the area, bringing a little bit of snow, Heather seemed like a ball of sunshine, spreading warmth in his life like Tal had never experienced.

The search and rescue team hadn't been very busy, which suited Tal just fine. He had no doubt the Bigfoot hunters would be back in force once spring arrived, but for now he was content to work at the barbershop in the mornings, and chauffeur Heather around in the afternoons.

Before his shifts started, Tal dropped Heather off at Whitney's B&B, where she spent the mornings learning about all the things she should've learned in school. Her reading was getting better at an astonishing speed. She was currently studying history, and learning about everything from the Civil War to what happened at Pompeii.

In the afternoons, Heather was busy with her new friends. One day she might spend with Finley at the bakery, and the next she'd hang out with Bristol while she was making another stained-glass piece. Lilly had gone back to work, and Heather assisted her when she'd gone to take pictures of the softball team at the Fallport High School.

She'd even gone with Caryn to one of the junior fire-fighter meetings, and that had led to Tal sitting next to her on the couch in the evening while she watched firefighting video after firefighting video.

Another afternoon, Heather had shadowed Elsie on one of her shifts at On the Rocks. She'd admitted that night that she hadn't really enjoyed being on her feet all day, but that she *did* enjoy meeting so many people.

Yes, his Heather was like a flower blooming after being denied the sun for too long. Everything was fascinating and interesting to her, and almost everyone she met was respectful. Only a few people had tried to pry into what she'd been through, but they were always shut down by others standing nearby.

Tal was so proud of her. There were times, late at night when she lay in his arms, when she admitted she was scared. Worried about the future, if she'd be able to get a job since she didn't have even a high school diploma. Where the memories of the things she'd been through occasionally overwhelmed her. All Tal could do was hold her. Tell her how proud he was. Remind her of the friends she'd made, and that she could do anything in the world she wanted. She was free.

They fell asleep in each other's arms every night, and

woke up with her having kicked the covers off and Tal still touching her in some way. His hand against her back. His leg wound around her own. His nose buried in her hair.

Today had been busy for them both. The team had been called out on a search for a missing twelve-year-old boy with Down syndrome. He'd wandered away from his house and it had been a half hour before anyone noticed. Raid and Duke took the lead in the search, and thankfully it had only taken an hour to find the boy. He was cold and scared, but otherwise fine. A neighbor's dog had followed him when he'd left the house, and they were discovered inside a shed four doors down from his home, huddled together.

The missing child had brought back bad memories for Heather, and she'd been distraught until the boy was found. She'd hung out with Elsie and Khloe in the bar until news had reached them that the boy was alive and well...and reunited with his parents. Realizing that holing up in their apartment might not be the best thing for her, Tal had brought her to Art, Silas, and Otto afterward, who'd successfully distracted her with several games of chess.

After that, she'd helped Finley make a cake for a fiftieth wedding anniversary. Khloe had then come to the apartment to visit with Boots, and she'd ended up staying for dinner.

The more Tal was around the prickly woman, the more he realized she wasn't so much standoffish...as she was likely hiding something. She was friendly enough, but whenever questions were asked about her past, where she came from, what she did before coming to Fallport, she'd clam up and change the subject.

She was a mystery, and Tal couldn't help but be

intrigued by and worried about her at the same time. But his hands were full with Heather and making sure she continued to thrive in her new world. He made a mental note to talk to Raiden though. He worked with her day in and day out, and Khloe seemed to have bonded with Duke. Raid was the best person to get to the bottom of any secrets Khloe might be hiding.

After Khloe left, he and Heather relaxed on the couch. Heather had a book open on her lap but she wasn't reading. Her mind was somewhere else, and Tal couldn't help but worry.

"You feeling okay after what happened today? About hearing the boy was missing?"

She turned to look at him, and Tal could see surprise in her gaze. "Yeah. I'm glad he's all right."

"Me too. So if that's not on your mind...what's worrying you?"

She closed her book and turned to face him. "I'm not worried...I'm nervous."

"About what? You don't have to be nervous with me, sweetheart. You know I'd never hurt you, and you can do or say anything around me."

"Last night was..." She paused.

Tal's cock immediately began to harden, and he clenched his teeth, trying to control his body's reactions.

Last night, when they'd gone to bed, she'd begged him to let her touch him again. He couldn't refuse her anything, and so he'd taken off his boxers and let her...play. He wasn't sure what other word to use. She'd kissed him until his head spun, then wrapped her warm hand around him and jacked him off until he came all over his stomach and her fingers.

Most of the time, he managed to end things there...but

last night, she'd been eager for him to touch *her* too. Tal had been nervous *and* excited. He'd longed to give her as much pleasure as she'd given him.

At first, things had been good. Great, actually. He'd caressed and licked her nipples, pleasing them both. But as soon as he began to ease a hand into her panties, she stiffened.

As much as Tal had wanted to show her how much he loved her, that he wasn't like the assholes who'd abused her, he couldn't risk anything that might hurt her recovery. That would turn her happy, cheerful disposition into something else.

They'd both been disappointed, but Tal had reassured her over and over that she was making great progress. That he'd wait as long as it took for her to feel comfortable with him.

Now, Heather licked her lips and met his gaze as she finished her sentence. "Frustrating."

Tal wished he could do more for her. Take away the hurt she'd experienced. But the only thing he could do was reassure her over and over that he wasn't like the men she'd known in her past.

Heather went on. "Lilac is married. I looked up some of the others too. Elizabeth Smart is married, with several kids. They're in happy relationships. They've been able to move on. I want to as well."

Tal had never felt as out of his comfort zone as he did right then. He was the toughest of the tough. Had faced the most deadly enemies. And yet he was practically shaking in his shoes at the moment. "You *are* moving on," he said after a moment.

"I don't feel like I am," she told him. "I'm honestly not scared of you," she went on. "You won't hurt me. Last night, I was ready. The feel of your hand...*there*...it surprised me. But I wasn't afraid of you. But then you stopped. I want to know what an orgasm feels like."

"Sweetheart, I—"

She shook her head stubbornly. "I love you, Talon. I want to have sex with you. I'm not scared. You've let me have control, and I never knew sex could be as exciting as it is with you. But I know I'm still missing out. I talked to Lilly, and she told me how it feels when she has sex with Ethan. She says it's amazing. That he makes her feel as if she's flying. I want that too."

With every word that passed her lips, Tal's cock got harder, until he could almost feel it throbbing in his pants. "How many times have I told you that I won't hurt you?" he asked.

She frowned. "I don't know. Too many to count."

"Right, but if I move too fast, I *could* hurt you. I wouldn't mean to, but I still could. And if that happened, I'd never forgive myself."

"And you think having sex with me will hurt me?" she asked with a furrow of her brow.

"It could bring back bad memories. And that's the last thing I want to do."

"Are you going to make me wear a dress, then shove it up over my hips and enter me without making sure it won't hurt?"

"What? No!" Tal exclaimed.

"Are you going to make me get on my hands and knees and take me...back there?"

"Fuck no," Tal said, low and hard.

"Then how in the world could being with you bring back bad memoires? Talon, you are nothing like those other men. *Nothing*. None of them ever let me touch them

289

like you do. None of them let me be on top. None of them ever kissed me. The last thing I'm thinking about is all those other times when I'm with you. All I can smell is you. All I see is you. All I can feel are your hands on me. Your lips on mine."

Tal stared at her for a beat...and realized that while he thought he was doing the right thing in going slow, letting her touch him without the pressure of being touched in return, that was clearly no longer what she needed.

He'd been selfish, and he was ashamed of his actions. He'd gotten pleasure, but hadn't given her any in return. But the thought of touching her, and having her uncertain or uncomfortable in the slightest, still scared him to death, despite her reassurance.

"Are you absolutely sure?" he asked.

"Yes."

"If I do *anything* that scares you or brings back bad memories, you have to promise to tell me."

"Okay."

"I mean it, Heather. Promise me. Right now."

"I promise to tell you if anything feels wrong."

Tal could feel himself breathing way too hard. His cock was throbbing in time with every beat of his heart. He wanted nothing more than to bury himself inside this woman, but he needed to go slow. Make sure she experienced pleasure. Make sure she was one hundred percent with him every step of the way. Despite being horribly abused, she might as well be a virgin, having never experienced how intimate and tender lovemaking could be—and he made a mental vow to make her first time romantic and memorable.

He stood and immediately reached for the woman

who'd owned his heart from almost the first time he'd seen her. Without a word, he walked toward his bedroom.

No, *their* bedroom.

When he got to the side of the bed, he turned to Heather and saw a huge smile on her face. She looked eager. Excited. Definitely not worried or scared. He let himself relax a fraction.

"You need to use the loo?" he asked.

"The what?"

"Sorry, another English word. The bathroom?"

She shook her head.

Without hesitation, he stripped his shirt off over his head. Then he shoved his sweatpants over his hips, shucking his boxers at the same time.

He stood in front of her, naked as the day he was born. His cock bobbed slightly, and when her gaze roamed down his body to land on it, a bead of precome leaked out of the tip and lazily rolled down his shaft.

Knowing he was way too close to losing it, Tal swept the covers back and climbed onto the bed. He lay back, put his arms over his head and stared at Heather. "I'm all yours," he said in a low, gruff tone.

She smiled and began to disrobe. Tal didn't take his eyes off her. She'd seen him naked in the past, but he'd never pushed her to take off her own clothes. She hesitated a beat before taking off the oversize shirt she slept in, but he saw the determination in her eyes right before she grabbed the hem and pulled it upward.

Tal hadn't forgotten to turn off the light. He'd left it shining bright on purpose. He was selfish enough to want to see her. All of her. To see her face when she came for the first time. To watch her eyes widen as he entered her. He was a greedy bastard, and he wanted it all.

His eyes drank her in as she stood next to the bed. The auburn curls between her legs made his mouth water. He wanted to taste her. Wanted to run his fingers through the soft hair until he found her clit. Her tits were a perfect handful, with pink nipples that, even as he watched, hardened under his gaze. She also had freckles. Not many, but he had a feeling when she was in the sun, they'd multiply like a field full of dandelions.

She'd gained some weight since leaving the forest, and her belly was rounded, her hips lush, her thighs touched as she stood there. A lock of hair curled around one of her breasts, as if beckoning him to suckle.

Every muscle in his body tensed, and it took every ounce of control he possessed not to leap out of bed, grab her, and have his wicked way with her.

"Talon?" she whispered, sounding unsure.

Which was unacceptable. She shouldn't feel even an ounce of trepidation with him.

"Beautiful," he said softly. "You're so utterly perfect, I can't even put into words how much I want you." His cock jerked against his belly, and her eyes were drawn to the movement. Another spurt of precome leaked from the tip.

"See that? I think I could come just lying here looking at you."

Her surprised eyes came back to his. "Can I…I want…"

"Yes," he said, not needing her to finish her sentence. "Touch me. Make me yours, sweetheart."

With that, she slowly moved toward him. She raised one knee and climbed up onto the mattress next to him. She sat next to him on her heels and stared at his body laid out before her.

"You're in control," he told her. "Anything you want, it's yours."

"Anything?" she asked.

Tal nodded.

"I want you to touch me," she said without hesitation. "I want your hands on me. Showing me how this is supposed to be. I understand why you haven't touched me before...and I appreciate it. I don't think I was completely ready. But I am now. I want you to make me come. Then I want to feel you inside me."

"Fuck," Tal muttered. He slowly lowered his arms. "Straddle me," he growled. For a second, he thought he'd sounded too bossy, that she wasn't going to like the way he'd ordered her around. But then a small smile formed on her face and she lifted one leg until she was straddling his thighs.

"Come up here," he said, gently holding onto her hips and pulling her forward. He felt her pubic hair brush over his cock as she moved, and it was all he could do not to spill right then and there. He placed a hand on her back and urged her to lean over him.

Her tits hung down, gently swaying with her movements. He smiled up at her and lifted his head, then he took one of her nipples into his mouth and sucked—hard.

"Oh!" she exclaimed. She went perfectly still for a moment before she arched her back, pressing herself into him.

Tal sighed in relief. He took turns feasting on her nipples. First the right, then the left. She moaned low in her throat, and he felt her squirming over him. She was holding herself above him with her palms flat on the mattress by his head.

He liked being in charge during sex. And while she might be on top, he was definitely leading this encounter. He smiled before continuing to suck on one of her nipples.

Tal ran his other hand over an ass cheek. He had to admit, he liked her being on top. He had both his hands free and didn't have to worry about crushing her beneath him.

Tal could smell her arousal as he ran his hands all over her body. Heather had begun to gently sway back and forth over him, and he could feel her wetness spreading on his belly. His mouth watered.

"Scoot up, sweetheart."

"What?" she asked, opening her eyes and looking at him. She looked dazed. Lost in the pleasure of what he was doing.

Tal was still hard. Still way the fuck turned on. But pleasing Heather was much more exciting and erotic than he ever dreamed it would be. While he'd always made sure women he shared his bed with were satisfied, he'd definitely focused on the end game...namely, the fucking. With Heather, he was desperate to make sure she enjoyed herself. Tal wanted *her* to get off. Wanted to watch her orgasm. Honestly, he didn't even care if he got inside her tonight. This, listening to the little sounds she made as she discovered her sexuality for the first time, was a dream come true.

Tal put his hands on her hips and urged her to scoot farther up. "Straddle my face," he said.

"Talon, I don't think—"

"Trust me, I'm not going to hurt you." When he'd first started saying those words, it had been to calm her down. To reassure her. Now they felt like old friends. When he said them, he was really telling her how much he loved her. How he'd spend the rest of his life making sure she was content and happy.

Heather swallowed hard but slowly put a knee on either side of his head. Looking up her body, Tal groaned.

She was so damn beautiful, he was the luckiest man in the world. He shifted under her, bunching his pillow under his head to give him the extra height he needed, then he used one finger to trace her soaking-wet folds directly in front of his face.

"Talon?"

"I've been dreaming of this for longer than I care to admit," he said. "You smell fan-fucking-tastic. So wet. This is gonna feel so good, sweetheart." Then he lifted his head and licked her slit.

She jerked above him and let out an adorable little squeak.

Tal put one hand on the small of her back, and the other gripped a thigh roughly. He closed his eyes and proceeded to show his woman the joys of oral sex.

At first she seemed shocked and uncertain, but slowly she began to relax, undulating over him, chasing his tongue. Tal smiled as he pleasured her. She was extremely sensual...and highly aroused. He could feel her juices all over his face, coating his beard. All he could smell was her musky scent, and the more he licked and sucked, the wetter she got.

Moving the hand that had been holding her thigh, Tal used his fingers to play with her opening as he concentrated on her clit.

"Talon, I..."

She didn't finish her thought as he eased his index finger deep inside her body. The angle was bad and it was difficult to stimulate her the way he wanted, but he could feel her inner muscles tightening against his finger over and over again, and he figured for now, this was enough.

He lowered his head and looked up at her in awe. His cock was leaking nonstop now, and he could feel his precome all over his belly. He really could orgasm just like this, without any stimulation. The sight of her spread out over his face, his finger deep within her body, and her juices dripping down onto his hand...he was more than satisfied.

"You ready to come, sweetheart?" he asked.

"I'm not sure," she breathed. "This is...it's overwhelming!"

"It is, but I promise your first orgasm is going to rock your world."

Looking down, Heather met his gaze bravely. "I trust you."

To keep himself from spurting there and then, Tal had to reach down and grip the base of his cock. Earning her trust had been the most rewarding experience of his life. He refused to let her down.

"Close your eyes and just feel," he told her softly.

She immediately obeyed, and Tal lifted his head and licked her clit once more, before latching his lips around it and using his tongue to flick the small bundle of nerves hard and fast. He kept his finger deep inside her body, loving the feel of her muscles fluttering around him. All he could think of was how she'd feel squeezing his cock as she came.

His jaw and tongue tired, but he didn't slow down his pace as he worked her clit. Her thighs began to shake and he used his free hand to hold her steady above him. He kept his eyes open as he stared up her body as she approached the pinnacle.

* * *

Heather had never felt like this before. It was overwhelming and scary, but she'd never experienced so much pleasure either. Her heart was beating out of her chest and every muscle in her body felt tight. She was on the verge of coming out of her skin.

She had no idea men actually did this to women. Lilly hadn't said anything about *this*. But it was obvious Talon didn't think it was weird or unusual, so she'd gone with it. His tongue between her legs felt totally foreign, but oh so pleasurable. And when he'd inserted his finger inside her, she'd tensed for a moment, remembering the pain of other times, but she hadn't felt even an ounce of hurt when he'd entered her.

She was so wet. Again, she had no idea if that was normal or not, but since Talon greedily licked up the fluids she was leaking, she assumed he had no problem with it. And her wetness allowed him to put his finger inside her without pain.

New sensations and experiences were coming faster than she could process them. For a moment, she got scared of what she was feeling. It was too much. Too intense. But then she looked down and met Talon's gaze. He was staring up at her even as his tongue flicked against a very sensitive place between her legs.

The reassurance and love she saw in his gaze made the fear morph into anticipation. He wouldn't let anything happen to her. As she stared down into his eyes, she felt pleasure swamp her and the most amazing feeling jolt through her body. Every muscle locked and she felt just like Lilly said—as if she were flying.

One hand gripped his hair as he continued to suckle at her, and she used the other to brace herself on the mattress. How long she trembled and shook in his arms,

Heather had no idea. Talon's touch between her legs gentled until he was merely nuzzling her. All the while, he kept his eyes on hers. It was intimate and overpowering... and she'd never felt closer to another human being in all her life.

Talon eased his finger out of her body—and shocked her by immediately sticking it in his mouth and licking off her juices. "Delicious," he told her. Then he palmed her hips and slowly helped her scoot back down so she was lying on his chest. She could feel wetness on his belly and his penis was hard between them. But he didn't insist she touch him. Didn't roll her over and stick it inside her. All he did was stroke her hair down her back and lie still.

When her breathing had returned to almost normal, Heather lifted her head. "That was..." She didn't know what that was, and she struggled to find the right words.

"Beautiful," Talon finished for her. "Seeing you orgasm for the first time was an amazing gift. I've never seen anything so beautiful in all my life."

"Are you...you didn't..." Talking about this was more difficult than she thought it would be.

"Shhhh," he murmured. "There's no rush."

It occurred to Heather then that Talon was going to be noble. He wasn't going to enter her because he didn't want to hurt her. She'd seen him orgasm in the past, when she'd stroked him with her hand, and he obviously enjoyed it. But the memory of how his finger felt inside her was fresh. It had felt good. *He'd* felt good. She wanted more.

Sitting up, Heather went to slide off him and get on her back so he could enter her with his penis.

"Where are you going?" he asked, stopping her with a hand on her hip.

"I want you inside me," she said, knowing she was

blushing but trying to ignore it. "So I'm getting on my back so you can have pleasure too."

He stared at her for a long moment, as if assessing where her head was at.

"I'm okay. I loved that...and it didn't hurt. I want more," she admitted.

"Are you sure?" he asked.

His constant need for assurance might've annoyed her if she didn't know he was doing everything in his power to protect her. To take care of her. Another man wouldn't have cared how she was feeling right about now. The men in The Community always said that males had needs and they couldn't be denied. She'd already learned just about everything they'd ever said had been a self-serving lie. Still, the proof of Talon's need was throbbing against her belly.

The need to please him was overriding the bad memories of what it meant to be intimate with a man. "I'm sure," she said as firmly as she could.

"All right, but you don't need to be on your back."

Heather frowned. She didn't?

"Sit up," Talon said.

She did, and Heather couldn't stop herself from looking down. Talon's penis was long and hard. Much bigger than Arrow's or Cypress's. The head looked almost purple and was wet and shiny from his own excitement.

"Shit," he said after a moment.

Surprised, Heather took her gaze from his penis and looked into his face. "What's wrong?"

"I don't have a condom. I...wasn't expecting this."

"A what?"

Talon sighed and pressed his lips together. She recognized the frustration and anger in his expression, but she wasn't scared. He wasn't upset with *her*, but with the reason behind her ignorance.

"A condom. Men wear them on their cocks to catch their ejaculate, to prevent getting a woman pregnant."

Heather stared down at him with wide eyes. "Really?"

"Yes. But I don't have one."

She swallowed hard. "This isn't the right time for me to get pregnant," she told him.

"How do you know?"

This was embarrassing, but she figured not as embarrassing as sitting on his face while he licked between her legs. "I've always kept track...so I knew when to use the Queen Anne's lace."

Talon closed his eyes for a moment and let out a long sigh. Then he opened them again and brought a hand up to her face. He gently brushed the backs of his fingers down her cheek. "Condoms are also used to prevent sexually transmitted diseases. But I don't have any...haven't been with a woman in years."

Every day, Heather learned new things about the world, but she couldn't say she was liking what she was learning now. She recalled a few of the women in The Community having rashes between their legs, and it being very painful. She wondered if that was one of the diseases Talon spoke of. Wanting to reassure him, she said, "I haven't been with anyone in over a year either."

He gave her a small, sad smile. "I know."

Neither spoke for a moment, then she asked in a quiet voice, "So you don't want to have sex with me then? Because you don't have one of these condoms?"

"I want to *make love* with you more than I've ever wanted anything in my life. I want to feel every inch of your warm, wet pussy on my bare cock. But there's no guarantee I won't get you pregnant."

"It's not my time," she repeated. "I promise."

Taking a deep breath, Talon nodded. "I'm way too weak to resist you," he said. "I'll buy some condoms tomorrow. Touch me, sweetheart. Get me ready for you."

Looking down, Heather saw that his cock wasn't as hard as it had been before. She felt bad that things had slowed down while they'd had their talk. But she was eager to feel him again.

Scooting back so she was hovering over his thighs, she reached down and gripped his penis the way she knew he liked. She literally felt him harden in her grasp. It was an odd feeling, but powerful too.

Using the wetness he'd leaked on himself earlier, she ran her hand up and down his shaft, marveling in the way she could feel his blood pumping through his skin.

"Okay, that's enough. Any more and this will be over before it starts," he said dryly. "Hold the base, good, just like that, now...scoot up and put me inside you."

Heather blinked in surprise. She understood how this was supposed to work now. A heady excitement blossomed inside. She wouldn't have to be under him. He wouldn't squish her. Wouldn't sweat on her. Moving slowly, she hovered over him. He lay still beneath her, not grabbing her hips and forcing her down.

The head of his penis brushed against that sensitive part of her when she was trying to figure out how to make this work, and she jerked.

"Oh, yeah," he said on a long exhale. "Put me in, sweetheart. Slow and steady. Take your time. Oh, *fuck*...you feel so good."

Feeling powerful and in charge, Heather was still tentative as she fed his length into her body. In the past, this had always hurt. But surprisingly, she didn't feel any pain, even with how big Talon was. There was a small pinch of discomfort, but as she lowered herself onto him, mostly what she felt was awe.

Talon was clenching his teeth together so tightly she could see a muscle in his jaw flexing. "Damn, Heather...you are...perfect."

Once he was all the way in, she sat on top of him with a small smile on her face. She'd done it! She was having sex with Talon and it didn't hurt! Then her brows furrowed. It felt nice, but not as exciting as it had when she'd orgasmed earlier. Was she doing something wrong?

"You good?" Talon asked.

Heather nodded.

"Think you want to try moving?"

Moving? Oh! *That's* what was different about this. But she wasn't sure how to move since she was on top.

"Lift up, then lower yourself back down," Talon said gently.

Sweat had beaded on his brow, but he still hadn't grabbed her. He was in control of his emotions, and seeing that made her confidence rise. She lifted herself off his lap, and his penis almost slid out of her body before she quickly lowered herself again.

"Oh!" she exclaimed. "That felt good!"

"For me too. Again," Talon told her.

It didn't take long for her to get into a rhythm. She lifted herself up and down on Talon's penis, faster and faster. It felt good, but she was still disappointed that she didn't feel that rush of excitement that she had earlier. And her thighs were beginning to get tired.

Just when she didn't think this was going to work,

Talon gripped her hips and took much of her weight as she moved up and down on him.

"This okay?" he asked.

"Oh, yes," she said.

When she'd gotten into a good rhythm again, one of his hands moved upward and he pinched her nipple. She jerked and moaned. She felt sparks fly from her nipple down between her legs as he did it again.

"You like that," Talon said. It wasn't a question.

She quickened her pace on him. The sound of their skin slapping together seemed loud in the room, but Heather ignored it.

Talon played with her nipples as she rode him, and she couldn't help but feel disappointed when his hand moved downward once more. But instead of gripping her hip again, he began to touch her in that sensitive spot between her legs.

Her pace stuttered as she jerked at his first touch.

"Keep riding me," Talon ordered. "As hard as you want. Do what feels good, sweetheart."

So Heather closed her eyes and undulated on top of Talon as the exciting feeling she'd had earlier began to return. Trying not to think about how silly she must look, she simply enjoyed the pleasurable feelings coursing through her veins.

She didn't realize when she'd stopped moving altogether and simply sat down hard on Talon, thrusting her pelvis forward into his hand as he continued to stroke that spot. The orgasm came quicker this time and wasn't nearly as scary, now that she knew what to expect.

She quivered and shook as pleasure overcame her.

She vaguely heard Talon apologize before he took her hips in his hands once again. But instead of helping her move up and down, he simply held her above him as he moved. He lifted his ass over and over as he thrust his penis in and out of her. But again, it didn't hurt; instead, the stimulation on her already sensitive lady parts felt incredible.

Then he groaned, jerked her down on him once more, and shook.

A red flush formed on his chest, and Heather realized that he'd taken his own pleasure deep inside her body. Satisfaction filled her to see him so overwhelmed.

Feeling boneless, she let herself fall on top of him, and his arms immediately came around her, holding her against him. His heart was beating hard and their bodies were slick with sweat. He was still inside her body, which was another new thing for her. She had to admit she liked it. No...*loved* it. Loved feeling this close with him.

"Bloody hell, woman," Talon said after a long moment.

For some reason, Heather giggled.

"I didn't hurt or scare you at the end when I took over, did I?" he asked.

Heather shook her head against him. Her eyes felt heavy and it was impossible to keep them open. "I liked it. Can we do it again?"

He chuckled under her, and she felt his penis slip out of her body. She frowned and said, "I like when your penis is inside me."

He laughed again and shifted her so she was lying against his side, her head on his shoulder. His arm was still around her back and one of her legs was hitched over his thigh. "First lesson, it's a cock or dick, not a penis."

Heather lifted her head at that. "You don't call it a penis?"

He smiled at her and brushed a lock of hair off her

forehead. "Technically, it *is* a penis, but a sexier word is cock. Boys have penises, men have cocks."

Heather nodded as she lay her head back on his shoulder. "Okay. And you're right...cock sounds more manly. Talon?"

"Yeah, sweetheart?"

"I don't want to upset you, and I know you don't like it when I talk about this...but that was *nothing* like I experienced in the past. It was...I like orgasming. And you felt so good inside me."

He didn't tense under her, as she was afraid he would. "I'm glad. And you should know...that was nothing like I've ever experienced in the past either."

His words bloomed and filled all the empty spaces she had in her soul, spaces she wasn't even aware were there. Talon obviously had more experience than she did, but to hear him say that being with her was special...it meant a lot.

"I love you, Heather. But there's no pressure. I know this is your first relationship after what you went through, and I'll take things as slowly as you need me to. I probably should let you go, let you experience life to truly know what you want...but after tonight...I can't. I can promise never to hold you back. Whatever you want to do, I'll do my best to give it to you."

"I love you too," Heather said, snuggling deeper into him. "All I need you to do is be there for me. To explain things I don't understand. To love me."

"Done," Talon said, the satisfaction and contentment easy to hear in his voice. "People will tell you that we moved too fast. That you need to experience more before you settle down with someone after all you've been through, but—"

"If they do, I'll tell them to mind their own business," Heather said, not letting him finish his thought. "I might be naïve, but I know a good man when I see him."

Talon tightened his arm around her and sighed. "I love you."

"I love you too."

They fell asleep like that, molded to each other. And as usual, sometime later, Heather rolled over, kicked off the covers, and Talon reached out and rested a hand against her back...keeping the connection between them.

CHAPTER EIGHTEEN

Cypress looked down at little Sunset and smiled. He hadn't had any problems at all snatching the little girl. In his estimate, she was around four, a little older than he'd wanted, but he'd make it work. She'd gotten off the special bus in front of her house and like all the other times when he'd watched, no one came out of the house to greet the girl.

As soon as the bus was out of sight, Cypress had grabbed her.

She was sitting on the floor of the passenger seat with a blindfold on, a pair of headphones over her ears, a gag over her mouth, and her hands tied together with rope that was attached to the bottom of the seat. His father had taught him that sensory deprivation was the fastest way to get a girl or woman to comply. As usual, he wasn't wrong.

He'd informed the little girl that her name was now Sunset Meadowblossom, and she belonged to him. She was going to be a good girl, nice and quiet, otherwise she'd pay the price. She'd cried and screamed and begged to be let go, but after four days on the road, she'd finally learned her place. She sat huddled in a ball wearing the brown dress that all women in The Community wore, quiet as a mouse.

Cypress grinned and turned his attention back to the road. The first part of his plan was finished...now he needed to complete the second. Then he could drive west with his future bride and find a new place to start over. He'd find likeminded men and he'd start a new Community.

He passed a sign informing him that he'd crossed the border into Virginia, and his heart began to beat faster. Soon he'd see Sunset...the bitch now trying to call herself Heather Brown. He'd make sure she understood that she was nothing. That she regretted hiding from him.

From *him*. Her husband, her leader, her superior.

Arrow had been too easy on her. Hell, Cypress had been too easy on her too. Obviously. He couldn't wait to see the fear on her face when she saw him. Couldn't wait to have her submit to him one last time.

Then he'd kill her, leave her body to rot in the precious forest she seemed to favor over him, and live his life the way he was supposed to.

CHAPTER NINETEEN

Tal had kept a close eye on Heather for the last week. He was still worried that he'd moved too fast. That being intimate would somehow hurt the progress she'd made. But he needn't have worried. Similar to sharing her story with the country, their intimacy had made her even more confident and outgoing. He'd never been so relieved.

Her days were spent doing her own thing. She still spent time with Whitney in the mornings, learning all the things she'd missed from not being in school after she'd been kidnapped, and the afternoons were divided between all of her new friends. And her small circle had quickly expanded. Everyone she came into contact with was eager to befriend the woman who'd been so mistreated and cheated out of twenty years of her life.

Her evenings and nights were spent with Talon. He opened up and told her things about his job in the military that he'd never told anyone before. She never judged him for the decisions he'd made or the lives he'd taken. She also talked more about her time in the cult. While Tal hated learning of the hell she'd been through, he listened willingly.

She'd even gone on a search with the team. A couple had gone for a hike and hadn't returned. Luckily, they'd left word about where they were going and when they should be back. When they still hadn't shown up hours later, their friends called the police. It had been a quick search, as Duke had picked up the scent of the couple right away.

Raiden and Duke, Tal and Heather, and Drew and Caryn had been the first wave of the search, while the others stayed back to relieve them if needed. It was obvious Heather was in her element in the forest. She'd been right on Raiden's ass as he followed the bloodhound, giving suggestions as to where the couple might be...and it turned out her instincts had been dead on.

Seeing Heather blossom was both inspiring and humbling at the same time. Tal went through phases where he was so angry about what happened to her, he thought he might burst. There was no telling the good she might've done in the world if she hadn't been robbed of twenty years. But she was making up for that lost time now, and Tal couldn't have been prouder.

Tony's teacher had asked if Heather might be willing to come to the school and give a talk to the class about personal safety and being aware of their surroundings at all times. Talon hadn't been sure it was a good idea, but Heather had agreed without hesitation.

He'd taken her to the school and watched as she gave her talk...and he was impressed all over again by her resilience. She didn't tense up when the kids asked questions that were borderline offensive. She didn't scare them with stories of strangers lurking in the dark to steal them away. She was frank but positive, firm in telling the kids to trust their instincts. To be cautious. And to never give up if they ever found themselves in a scary situation.

"I'm so proud of you," he told her later than night. They'd eaten dinner and were snuggling on the couch, relaxing before heading to bed.

"I'm proud of myself," she said a little shyly. "I was told that I was a piece of trash so many times, that I wasn't as important or as good as men, that I'd begun to believe it. But that year in the woods made me see I was capable of a lot. I wasn't stupid. I didn't need a man to survive. And now? Being free? Being here with you and your friends—"

"*Our* friends," he interrupted firmly.

"Right, sorry, our friends," she corrected. "And from talking to Lilac and reading about other women's experiences after being taken captive...I've realized I have a lot to contribute to the world. I might not ever be a rocket scientist, or understand Algebra, but what I said today to those kids...I think it sank in. I could tell. If my story can help even one child overcome some bad thing that happens to them, everything I went through was worth it."

"You know, Lilac makes a living giving motivational speeches around the country. Elizabeth Smart does too. You could always do something like that."

Heather's eyes lit up. "Really?"

"Yes. And a bonus would be that you'd get to travel... see more of the world than this corner of Virginia."

She frowned then. "But I like Fallport."

"I do too. I'm not saying that you'd move away, but you'd get to travel to places you might not otherwise see."

"Will you come with me?"

Talon's heart skipped a beat. "If you want me to."

"I want you to. But I don't know how to get into something like that."

"We can talk to Lilac. And Elizabeth. Get their advice. I'm sure they'd be willing to help you out."

"Talon?"

"Yeah, sweetheart?"

"I feel so lucky."

Talon could only stare at her in awe. She never failed to surprise him. He shook his head. "You went through hell for two decades. You were lucky to survive, yes, but you were not lucky to have gone through that."

"But it led me to you," she said quietly. "There's no telling where I would be right now if I hadn't experienced what I did. I might have moved away. Might have met someone else and gotten married. Or you might've hated the person I became if you met me when you came to town.

"I know there's a lot of stuff in the world I don't understand, but I have you to teach me. To protect me. To help me figure it all out. If it wasn't for you...I know I wouldn't be doing as well as I am now. You make it easy for me to take chances. When I'm scared of something, I know you're right there, ready to catch me if I fail. I just...I feel like the luckiest woman in the world because I have you at my side."

Tal's throat felt tight. He swallowed hard. This woman slayed him. He was all hers.

And she was his.

Women weren't supposed to want to be taken care of, and men weren't supposed to *want* someone they had to take care of, someone to claim. These days it was more acceptable to be independent. How Talon had found the perfect woman for him, he had no idea. All he knew was that he'd do whatever it took to keep her.

"I'm the lucky one," he finally got out.

"Fine, we're *both* lucky," she conceded with a smile. "And now that we've settled that...I was talking to Caryn today, and she was telling me about a sex position called the G-Whiz, where I put my feet over your shoulders while you kneel in front of me and—"

Tal didn't give her a chance to continue explaining. He stood and grabbed her hand and stalked toward their room. The giggle that left her mouth made him smile even as his cock throbbed. Now that she'd experienced what making love *should* feel like, rather than the abuse she'd suffered through, she was eager to explore. Tal was both embarrassed and grateful her friends were doing all they could to educate her.

They'd both gone to see Doc Snow in the last week, and he'd run several tests before declaring her healthy and inserting an IUD. They'd had another talk about children, and Tal couldn't wait to have a family with her, but he also wanted her to live a little first. She'd been robbed of her childhood, and most of her early adulthood to boot. He didn't want to rush her into having children before she was ready.

While teaching her how to use condoms had been fun, Tal was relieved he could take her bare once more. He'd never felt anything as pleasurable as being deep inside her without anything between them.

As soon as they were by the bed, Heather smiled at him and reached for the hem of her shirt.

This woman meant everything to him, and Tal would never stop being grateful she was in his life.

* * *

Heather smiled as she left the Chestnut Street Manor. Today was science day with Whitney, which she much preferred over math. Everything she learned was so fascinating.

Instead of calling Talon to pick her up, she'd told him that she'd walk to the square and meet him at Sunny Side Up for lunch. It was a nice day, not too cold, and Heather figured she could use the exercise. She'd gained quite a bit of weight since she'd left the forest, and while Talon seemed to love her curves, she didn't think it would be good to get too overweight.

She just couldn't seem to resist the cinnamon rolls Finley made. Or any of the other foods she'd been exposed to. Eating smoked meat and fish and leaves as salad for so many years had dulled her taste buds. The new world of spices and flavorful food was one of the greatest joys of Heather's new life.

She was smiling as she walked, thinking about all the things she wanted to tell Khloe about Boots and how she was doing. This morning, just when things between her and Talon were getting interesting, the kitten jumped on the bed and dug her little claws into Talon's ankle, letting him know in no uncertain terms that she was ready for her breakfast. He hadn't gotten mad though, had simply winced, leaned down, and plucked the kitten off his leg and plunked her into Heather's arms. He'd kissed her and told her to take her time getting up; that he'd get breakfast ready.

He spoiled her, and never seemed to show any sign of getting tired of doing so. She loved him so much.

Lost in memories of how wonderful her life was, and how grateful she was to be alive and with as many friends as she had, Heather jerked in surprise when a car pulled up next to her on the side of the road.

She smiled as she turned, expecting to see someone she knew. Most of the time when she was out trying to get some exercise, one of the guys on the search and rescue team, or their women, would pull up and offer her a ride.

Her smile died when she saw the person behind the wheel of the car.

None other than Cypress Goodson.

She turned to run—and stopped when he said, "Don't you want to meet the newest Sunset Meadowblossom?"

Chills ran down her spine, and Heather slowly turned around. Many of the women in The Community had the same name. It made things confusing at times, but the men didn't seem to care or notice. She'd talked to Talon about it, and he'd said that it was just another way to dehumanize the women. She totally agreed.

She wanted to run away, get to Talon. He'd protect her, she knew it without a doubt. She wanted to tell Simon where Cypress was so he could be arrested. But his words made her freeze in her tracks. She shivered at his evil grin as she faced the nightmare of her past.

"Go on...look in the window. See? She's so pretty...red hair just like you...but unlike you, she's going to be taught to obey the way a woman should."

Heather's heart nearly broke when she approached just enough to look in the window of the front passenger side of the car. A little girl was sitting on the floor, hunched over, her hands tied together as she stared unseeingly into space. Her hair was mussed and she had visible tear tracks on her little cheeks. She also was wearing the horrible brown dress that The Community made all the women and girls wear. Just the sight of it made horrible memories rise to the front of Heather's mind.

Cypress chuckled. "She's such a good girl. Hasn't made a sound in the last few days. She's a fast learner...much faster than you ever were." His voice lowered as he said, "Get in the car, Sunset."

Even hearing her old name made bile rise in her throat. "No," she said as firmly as she could.

Cypress leaned toward the passenger window. "Get in. *Now*. Or little Sunset will be punished in your stead. You remember the punishment tent, don't you? I'll tie her down, blindfolded, gagged, and her ears covered, and beat her until her back is nothing but a bleeding mess. Then I'll leave her there for a week, only coming in once a day to give her water and explain she's where she is because of *you*."

More memories threatened to overwhelm Heather. Her time in the punishment tent had been unbearable. Beyond frightening.

But instead of feeling fear toward Cypress, anger rose hot and fast inside her.

Looking at the little girl on the floor of the car once more, she made the only decision she could. She had no idea if it was the right one or not, and Talon would probably be furious with her, but there was no way she was leaving the little girl in Cypress's hands. She didn't know where he planned to take them, but she'd protect the child with her life if need be.

A conversation she'd had with Talon flashed through her brain as she reached for the door handle. She'd said nothing would make her go with Cypress if she saw him again. She hadn't been lying at the time...but she'd had no idea the lengths he'd go to in order to force her obedience.

Little did Cypress know, she was a completely different person than he'd once known. She wasn't Sunset Meadowblossom anymore. She was Heather Brown. She had a life, friends, and a vision for her future. And she had Talon.

There was no doubt in Heather's mind that when she didn't show up when and where he expected her, Tal would immediately be on the lookout. Finding people was what he did. Several cars had driven by while she'd been talking to Cypress. One of them would report what they'd seen and who she was with. It was simply a matter of time before Talon tracked her down.

Heather had survived years of abuse by this evil man, she could survive another hour. Two. Three. She'd take whatever he wanted to dish out...as long as it meant the precious little girl who was obviously scared out of her mind was spared.

She sat on the front seat, careful not to step on or jostle the girl, and closed the door.

Cypress didn't say a word, simply smirked and put the car into gear and pulled back onto the road. He headed west out of town...toward where The Community used to live.

Heather knew she should be scared. Should be freaking out about where Cypress was taking her and what he was going to do. But instead, she felt...focused.

Talon's love, support, and protection had fundamentally changed her. She'd heard enough of his stories about his time as a soldier and had understood that many times, he was successful in what he'd set out to do because he'd been patient. Waited for the right time to act. That was what she'd do now as well. Cypress was arrogant, and he already thought he'd won.

Well, he'd find out that Heather Brown was stronger than Sunset Meadowblossom had ever been. He wasn't going to get away with another kidnapping. The little girl needed her, and when Cypress made his move...Heather would be ready.

CHAPTER TWENTY

Tal looked at his watch for the umpteenth time. Heather was late. Whitney had called and let him know she'd left. But she hadn't arrived. With what had happened to Bristol last year still fresh in his mind, Tal didn't hesitate to raise the alarm.

He called Simon first, then Ethan, who'd agreed to call everyone else. Then he'd immediately driven to the Chestnut Street Manor. He spoke briefly with Whitney, who confirmed the time Heather had left and what direction she'd walked, then began to walk the same direction she would've taken, looking for any signs of where she might be or what could have happened to her.

Raiden joined him within minutes with Duke at his side. The bloodhound immediately picked up Heather's scent and took off down the sidewalk. He only tracked for two blocks before beginning to walk in circles with his nose in the air. Both Raid and Tal knew what that meant. She'd gotten into a car.

The question was...had she gotten in voluntarily or involuntarily?

If someone she knew had just offered her a ride, she would've shown up at the diner to meet him for lunch much faster than if she'd walked. But that hadn't happened.

"She swore she'd never go with him," Tal said, the fear clear in his voice.

"We don't know if this is Cypress or anyone from that cult," Raid said, trying his best to keep his friend calm.

"It's him," Tal argued.

"It could be someone who saw her interview and got obsessed. Someone who feels the same way about women as the assholes in that cult who raised her," Raid suggested.

But Tal shook his head. He didn't think so. He racked his brain trying to come up with a reason why Heather would go with the man who'd caused her so much pain. As he was trying to figure it out, Simon's cruiser pulled up next to them.

"What did Duke find?" he asked.

"Followed her trail to here, where it disappears," Raid said succinctly.

Tal blocked out his friends' conversation and stared into space, trying to figure out what Heather could've been thinking. He closed his eyes for a moment, picturing her walking down the street. A car pulling up, someone rolling down the window to talk to her...and she simply got in? Why?

Was it really Cypress? Or maybe someone else from that bloody cult she'd grown up in? A stranger? He supposed it didn't matter who it was at this point, just that she'd gotten into the vehicle. He didn't think anyone had grabbed her and forced her into the car, because someone would've noticed. She would've screamed her head off.

So...why?

Tal frowned as Simon called his name.

He held up his hand, stopping the police chief from saying anything more to him as he furrowed his brow and thought of everything he knew about Heather. She'd promised she would never go back to Cypress. Had seemed adamant that she wanted nothing to do with him ever again. What might he have used as incentive to get her to comply?

Somehow, Tal *knew* this was Cypress. All the publicity on Heather's kidnapping and subsequent return had lured him back to town, just like they'd been afraid of, because he wanted her back. She hadn't been kind when she'd talked about her life with the cult on TV. Had been especially harsh regarding Cypress and his late father. It was most likely he was back for revenge.

Tal's eyes popped open as a horrible thought occurred to him.

He turned to Raid and Simon. "He's taken another child."

Both men stared at him in confusion.

"We don't know that," Simon started, but Tal shook his head.

"It's the only thing that makes sense. Heather swore she'd never go back to Cypress. Think about it...even when she was scared to death of Fallport, of anything outside the world that she knew, she still defied him by hiding in the forest when they were ready to leave. Deep down, she *knew* if she left this area, she'd lose her one connection to people who used to know her. To her home. And after she realized what was really happening in that cult, she was appalled. She especially hated that children younger than her had been taken to raise as future wives for the men in the group.

"I'm thinking Cypress came back for her. For revenge. He's spent his entire life with subservient women. He probably truly believes he's superior to all females. How do you think he would've felt after learning he'd been outsmarted by one? Probably outraged—and even more determined to show her that she didn't win. And how best to do that?"

"Kidnap a kid and bring her here," Raid answered with a grim look on his face.

"Exactly. I know in my bones, the only reason Heather would *ever* get into a car with him was if he was threatening a child," Tal said.

"So where would he take them?" Simon asked.

"To where it all started?" Raid guessed.

"I agree," Tal agreed.

"Shit. There's nothing out there. The tents have all been removed, the toilet pits filled in, and even the broken-down shells of vehicles have been towed away for scrap," Simon argued.

"I don't think he's planning on staying. He probably just wants to show Heather that she hasn't beaten him. That he's still in control. And that camp is the place she fears the most," Raid reasoned.

Just then, the sound of a car accelerating down the street sounded. Turning, Tal saw Ethan's Subaru flying down the street toward them. Right behind him was Zeke's truck and Drew's Jeep. All three vehicles screeched to a stop and the remaining five members of the SAR team emerged from the vehicles.

"Sitrep," Ethan barked.

"We think Cypress might've taken Heather to his old camp," Raid summarized. "Duke tracked her to this spot, then her scent disappears."

"Right," Ethan said. "Let's go."

"Shit. All right. Tal, you're with me," Simon said quickly. "Everyone else, *stay behind me*. The last thing I need is all of you going all spec forces on me."

Tal didn't argue, especially since Simon was taking point. But the police chief actually did need them using their special forces training. There wasn't enough time for him to call his officers off whatever tasks they were doing. Every second counted when it came to Heather's life being in danger—and it was. No way would Cypress risk staying in Fallport for long.

Tal knew without asking that as soon as they arrived, his friends would go into fight mode. They'd take positions around the camp to make sure Cypress didn't flee into the woods when everything went down. They were all in professional soldier mode...too much shit had happened to their own women. The thought of evil touching Heather again, after what she'd already been through, was unacceptable.

Every mile they drove toward the abandoned cult grounds felt like an eternity. Tal prayed they were right, otherwise they were wasting a lot of time for nothing. And he couldn't even *think* about what might be happening to Heather or it would completely overwhelm him, and he wouldn't be able to help her when she needed him most.

Hang on, sweetheart. Just a little longer.

* * *

By the time Cypress pulled into the long driveway of The Community, Heather had blocked everything out except the man sitting next to her. She kept her eyes in her lap, as was expected. She didn't want to give Cypress any reason to suspect she was anything other than what he wanted to see...a subservient, scared, very well-trained female.

"I can't say the time away from us has been good to you," Cypress said as he reached the camp, stopping the car. "Look at you...wearing pants, shoes...and you cut your beautiful hair." He made a tsking noise. "You know none of that is allowed. You're going to have to be punished. Severely."

Once, those words would've made Heather cringe. She would've apologized profusely, done anything necessary in order to lessen her time in the punishment tent. But now, all they did was make her madder.

She swallowed her anger...channeled it. Stared down at the lowered head of the child at her feet. The little girl hadn't moved. She sat as still as possible, as if trying to be invisible.

Memories of when she'd done the same, out of self-preservation, threatened to throw Heather back into the past. But she brought up a memory of that morning...of sitting on the bed with Talon as they played with Boots. Drinking tea together while they watched TV. Of the adoring expression on his face as she made love to him.

Seeing the man she loved in her mind calmed her further. Made her even more focused.

"You belong to me," Cypress went on. "You always have and you always will."

He was wrong. She didn't belong to him. Not even close.

She was Talon's...just as he was hers.

"Take off your shoes," Cypress said as he leaned forward and pulled a knife with a serrated blade out of a holster at the small of his back. "You know you aren't allowed to wear them."

Wanting to lash out, scream at him, tell him he was nothing but a pathetic, sick old man who preyed on children, Heather took a deep breath before leaning down to untie her boots. She had to bide her time. At the moment, Cypress had the upper hand with that knife. But she would be ready to make a move when he let down his guard. Her life, her future, and that of the child at her feet, all depended on her making her captor think she was submitting.

Heather wanted to reassure the girl. Wanted to tell her to hang on, that help was coming. But she couldn't, not if she wanted Cypress to let down his guard.

She removed her shoes and socks and left them on the floor behind the child.

"Get out," Cypress ordered. "And don't try anything or I'll take it out on *her*," he warned, gesturing to the girl with the knife.

Bitterness threatened to overcome Heather's good sense, but she managed to nod and reach for the door handle. She stepped onto the ground and immediately shivered. She'd forgotten how cold it could be, walking around the forest without shoes on her feet. But she controlled her involuntary reaction as best she could. She didn't want to give Cypress the satisfaction of knowing she was uncomfortable.

She shut the car door, not wanting the girl to hear or see what was going to happen next. Forcing herself to stand still, looking at the ground, Heather saw Cypress's feet appear in her line of vision. He grabbed her arm tightly, nearly wrenching it out of its socket as he pulled her toward a lone tent in the middle of what used to be a bustling Community.

"Recognize it?" Cypress asked as he hauled her closer. He didn't give her time to respond, which wasn't unusual. All the men in The Community tended to answer their own questions...as if the women weren't capable of thinking for themselves. "It's the punishment tent. I took it when I left Florida, in anticipation of bringing you home. But plans have changed, thanks to your TV interview," he spat. "You spent quite a bit of time in this tent, didn't you? I thought it would be an appropriate place to reacquaint myself with my wife. Then, for old time's sake, I'll give you a short punishment session...before I kill you and head out to start my new life with my little future wife."

This time, it was almost impossible to push the memories aside. The smell of the canvas as they neared threatened to bring Heather to her knees. She *hated* this tent. Somehow it smelled differently than all the other canvas tents that used to be here. Maybe it was because of the suffering that had taken place inside, she wasn't sure. All she knew was that there was no way she was letting Cypress tie her down, blindfold, gag, and deafen her while he had sex with her, then beat her with his belt. She wasn't ready to die. Not when she'd just begun to live.

Cypress flipped back the opening of the tent, and it took every ounce of strength Heather had to calmly step inside. She saw the ropes he'd already prepared to restrain her. There was a single blanket on the ground, obviously where he planned to have sex with her.

Adrenaline coursed through Heather's veins. She wanted to run. Wanted to lash out. But Cypress was still holding the knife. She had to wait until just the right time. He'd have to put it down in order to tie her up. To have sex with her. The second he did, she'd make her move.

"I'm not surprised you've recalled your training so well," he said with a smirk. "You're nothing without The Community. You can't think for yourself, never could. Take off those obscene pants. Now!" he ordered.

The last thing Heather wanted to do was disrobe. But she turned to face him and undid the button on the cargo pants she wore. Then she sat on the blanket, leaned back on her hands and opened her legs. From experience, she knew what Cypress expected of her. This was the position he ordered her into most often when he wanted to exert his husbandly rights. She was still wearing the pants he hated, but she simply couldn't make herself remove them.

If he wanted them off her, he was going to have to do it himself.

Watching through her lowered lashes, Heather waited anxiously. She wasn't sure how far this was going to go before he let down his guard. She held her breath as the seconds ticked by...

To her relief, he got on his knees and scooted closer.

"Fine. I'll take 'em off for you. I'm going to enjoy punishing you for defying me."

Then it happened.

He put the knife down in the dirt next to him as he reached for the opening of his pants.

Heather didn't hesitate. She lunged for the knife.

Cypress hadn't been expecting it, had assumed he was in complete control, like always. Never in his experience had any of the women he'd abused ever fought back.

Gripping the knife firmly, Heather plunged it into his gut, right where she knew it would do the most damage.

She extracted the knife and leaped to her feet, exploding out of the tent and taking her first deep breath since she'd been forced to enter. The whole attack had taken seconds. Now, she immediately turned and waited for Cypress to follow.

And he did, exiting the tent almost immediately. He was stumbling a bit, which made Heather smile.

"Hurts, doesn't it?" she asked, her chin high, meeting his gaze directly. He'd hate that, which made it feel all the more satisfying.

"Bitch!" he growled. "You're going to fucking suffer!"

She was ready when he charged, standing her ground for a heartbeat before jerking away...

And plunging the knife into his back as he ran by.

The howl of pain and outrage that escaped Cypress's mouth wasn't unlike that of a wounded bear.

Heather felt a little sick, but she couldn't stop yet. Not until he was down.

Before he could even spin to come after her again, Heather leapt forward and stabbed him on the other side of his lower back, close to his side.

He fell to his knees.

Moving quickly to finish what she'd started, Heather plunged the serrated blade once more into his body, this time into the back of his thigh, ensuring he wouldn't be able to run...or walk.

As he fell forward into the dirt, screaming in pain and anger, Heather finally took a step back. It felt as if she was watching the scene from high above. She felt detached and unemotional about what she'd just done...except for a small bit of satisfaction. She now had the upper hand.

Cypress wouldn't be able to hurt her, or the little girl who was probably scared out of her mind in the car.

"You *bitch*!" Cypress spat, glaring at her with hatred.

Heather stared down at him in contempt. "Your words can't hurt me," she told him.

"Maybe not, but when I get my hands on you, you're gonna hurt like you've never hurt before," he seethed.

She laughed. Flat-out laughed. Then shook her head. "You aren't going to get your hands on me, that girl, or anyone else, ever again. You taught me well, Cypress. I might not have fully embraced life as a Community wife, but I definitely learned how to use a knife to take down my prey."

Cypress stilled as her words sank in.

"What was it you taught me? Oh, yeah...a gut wound was always preferable because perforating the intestine would spread infection amazingly fast. It would weaken the animal, make them less of a threat. And a kidney shot? Yeah, that would ensure a slow and painful death.

"I remember exactly what you said, Cypress...why kill them quickly? It's always good to let an animal know who's in charge, that they're nothing but fuel for those more powerful and smarter. I always felt it was cruel. Why shoot an animal in the gut when a head shot or through the heart would be quick and painless? Of course, you didn't give me a gun to hunt with, did you? No, you only allowed me a knife. I learned to be very quick with a blade. Unlike *you*, when I trapped an animal, I killed it quickly.

"But because I wanted you to know that I listened, I did to you *exactly* what you taught me."

"Oh, shit..." Cypress said, slowly rolling to his back. "I need help! Go get help!"

Heather didn't bother to respond. She'd been very

precise with her stabs. Even now, he was bleeding to death inside. She felt no regret.

Turning, she headed for the tent that held such awful memories. Using the bloody knife, she slit the canvas from top to bottom. She tore the tent down and continued to slice the damn thing to ribbons.

It was cathartic. And she also didn't want to provide Cypress anywhere to take shelter. It was cold, and soon it would be dark. He would freeze if he didn't bleed to death first.

Cypress alternated between threatening her and begging for help. She ignored him.

He'd stupidly left the keys in the ignition, and she opened the driver's-side door and sighed. She wanted to drive herself out of there. Ached to do just that. But she had no idea how to drive. Talon had talked about teaching her, but they hadn't gotten around to it yet.

Even as she stood there, looking into the car and trying to decide what to do, Cypress continued to scream, moan, and threaten both her and the girl. Seeing the child wince, Heather made her decision. She didn't regret what she'd done to Cypress, but she didn't feel good about it either. She'd killed a man; even if he wasn't dead yet, he *would* be within hours. And the last thing she wanted was this little girl having nightmares about seeing him die.

She pocketed the car keys, then walked around to the passenger side. She sat on the seat and reached for her socks and boots. As she put them back on, she spoke quietly to the girl.

"It's okay. You're safe now. You can trust me, and I'm not going to hurt you. We're going to take a little trip into the forest. But don't worry, we're going to a place I know well. Somewhere Cypress will never find us. He wouldn't be able to follow us anyway, but I don't like the sound of his voice.

"Talon will come for us. I have no doubt of that. He'll know where we are. Soon we'll be home, and I'll introduce you to my kitten. Her name is Boots. She's black with white fur around her feet. I know you're probably cold. I'm sorry. I'll check the trunk and see if your real clothes are in there."

Heather knew she was babbling, but she kept up a steady stream of calm, gentle words. When she reached for the girl's hands, she visibly recoiled.

Heather paused and said, "I won't hurt you. I'm just going to cut that rope off your hands, then we'll leave. Okay?"

She waited patiently, rewarded when the girl dipped her chin the tiniest amount.

"Good girl," Heather praised. "You're so brave. And strong. I'm proud of you. Hang on just a little longer, and hold very still." She sliced through the rope holding the girl hostage and quickly removed the excess from around her tiny wrists. "There, that's better. Do you think you can stand up? Are you hungry? There's some food where we're going. We'll fill our bellies, and when Talon takes us home, we can have something more yummy. You can trust me, I'm not going to hurt you."

To Heather's surprise, the little girl lifted her head and stared at her for a beat with beautiful hazel eyes—then reached her arms up.

Her heart soaring with the trust and bravery the child was showing, Heather picked her up. Immediately, the girl's arms wrapped around her neck in a surprisingly strong grip. Her legs went around her waist and she held on as if she'd never let go.

Putting a hand under her rump, Heather stood, turning so the little girl couldn't see Cypress lying in the dirt. She opened the trunk and frowned when all that was inside was canvas. Slamming it shut, she refused to think about how close the precious bundle in her arms had come to living a life like Heather had. Cypress's desire for revenge had been his downfall, and she'd never been so relieved in all her life that he was so predictable. He could've disappeared with this precious bundle. Could've killed Heather without any warning. But instead, he'd been so sure of his superiority over her that he'd made a fatal mistake.

Heather went back to the passenger door she'd left open and knelt down in front of it. She put the girl on the seat—after very gently breaking her hold—and reached for the sweatshirt she'd pulled over her head this morning, after her shower with Talon. It had been plenty warm earlier when she'd planned a brisk walk to town. Heather would be cold without it, but the little girl needed it more. She wanted to strip off the offensive brown dress Cypress had made her wear, but decided to leave it on.

"Lift your arms, sweetie. Good job. This will make you warmer. Talon will get you some shoes as soon as he can. And warm socks too. There, don't you feel better now?"

The girl stared at her but didn't speak.

"It's okay to talk. I promise. I won't hurt you. You can talk, and cry, and smile and laugh. The mean man will never touch you again. I swear. What's your name?"

"Sunset," the girl whispered.

Heather grimaced. "No, your *real* name. The one your mommy and daddy call you. The mean man tried to change my name too, but it didn't work. I'm Heather. Heather Brown."

The girl didn't respond, just stared at her with fear in her eyes.

"It's okay. You can tell me later, when you're more comfortable. For now, how about we get out of here?"

The girl gave her another small nod, and Heather gathered her into her arms again. And just like before, the child held on as if Heather was the only thing between her and certain death.

She pushed the lock button, then slammed the car door. The sound echoed throughout the trees.

"Where are you going? You can't leave me here! Come back! Right now! I'm talking to you, Sunset! Get back here. At least leave me the keys! I'm going to freeze if you don't!"

Heather ignored Cypress's pleas as she turned and headed for the trees.

* * *

Tal's eyes were fixated on the road in front of Simon's car as they raced toward the place where the cult had lived. They didn't pass any cars, which was both a relief and scary as hell. If Cypress was still in the woods with Heather, he didn't want to think about what she was going through right that moment. But then again, if they'd passed Cypress fleeing the area, and Heather wasn't with him, Tal knew it would be because he'd killed the only woman Tal had ever loved.

Pushing away the thought that Heather could be dead, Tal gripped the dashboard as Simon finally pulled into the dirt road that led to the old settlement, barely putting on the brakes as he did so. The car bottomed out in a few potholes, and Tal winced. Simon was probably taking out the entire undercarriage of his car with the way he was driving, but Tal had never been more appreciative.

Dust surrounded the car when Simon finally hit the brakes several yards from the encampment, coming to an abrupt halt. Tal had the door open even before the tires stopped spinning. He couldn't see through the dust and he coughed as the particles of dirt lodged in his lungs.

Tal heard his friends' cars coming in fast and hard behind them, but he didn't wait. He had no plan. No goal other than finding Heather and killing the son-of-a-bitch who'd taken her.

Up ahead in the clearing, Tal saw a four-door white sedan parked right in the entrance to the camp. Just as he'd taken that in, he saw a pile of what looked like shredded canvas on the opposite side of the camp, between some trees.

Then he heard a pitiful moan from somewhere between the canvas and the sedan.

His heart in his throat, Tal quickened his steps.

"Damn it, Talon, wait for me!" Simon ordered from behind.

But Tal wasn't waiting. If that was Heather moaning, he needed to get to her.

He'd taken several steps into the encampment, the dust in the air from the four newly arrived vehicles following on the wind.

The moan had come from a person, but it wasn't Heather.

A man lay on his back on the ground in a pool of blood. His face was ashen gray, and he stared blankly at the trees swaying over his head.

"Holy shit!" Ethan exclaimed as he approached.

"Is that Cypress?" Zeke asked.

"I would assume so," Talon said.

"What happened to him?" Brock asked.

"Any sign of Heather?" Raid asked. He'd left Duke in the car, which the bloodhound wasn't happy about. Everyone could hear him baying sorrowfully.

"Everyone spread out. See if you can find any signs of her," Drew ordered.

Simon came up beside Talon, and they stared down at the obviously dying man. It was taking everything within Tal not to reach for Simon's sidearm and shoot the bastard in the head. He was frozen with indecision. He needed to know Heather was all right, but he also needed to make sure this asshole would never touch his woman ever again.

"Help me," the man moaned. His head was turned toward them, and he reached a hand out, his fingers opening and closing.

Tal crouched on the balls of his feet, out of the man's reach, and sneered. "Help you? You're kidding, right? You raped and abused my woman for *years*! Who was there to help *her*? You? Your father? No. *No one* helped her. As far as I'm concerned, you got exactly what you deserved at Heather's hands. A slow, painful death. I hope you rot in hell."

"He doesn't look good," Simon said conversationally.

The completely relaxed tone of his voice was so surprising, Tal turned to stare at him.

The chief met his gaze. "You're probably wondering why I'm not doing something. Calling this in. Getting the ambulance rolling."

Tal *had* kind of wondered that, but he merely shrugged.

"After hearing what Heather went through, I'm not too inclined to help him. Besides, it looks like he's done for... not sure anything can save him now."

Tal turned his attention back to Cypress, only to see his eyes staring sightlessly at the sky. Simon was right. He was dead already. Good riddance.

He stood and turned his back on the man. He nodded at Simon, renewed respect for the chief filling Tal.

"She's not here," Rocky said as he jogged back toward Tal and Simon. "We've looked everywhere. The canvas is just that, a ripped-to-shreds tent. There are some footprints, but she isn't here."

"The car?" Simon asked.

"Ethan broke in, it's empty. Nothing in the trunk either."

"There's no other footprints," Zeke said as he approached. "No sign of anyone other than him," he nodded at the man behind them on the ground, "and Heather."

"Bare feet around the tent," Brock said. "But boot prints heading away from the car, toward the trees."

"I'll get Duke," Raid said, heading for the car where he'd left his bloodhound.

"No need," Tal called out.

All seven men turned to stare at him.

"What do you mean? We need to track her in the forest. She's probably running scared," Simon said.

But Tal shook his head. "I know where she's headed."

"The cave," Ethan said.

"Exactly. And she's got the child with her."

"There aren't any other footprints," Zeke reminded him.

"She'd have carried her. Females weren't allowed to wear shoes in The Community, so Cypress would've taken them from the girl."

"There was rope on the floor of the passenger seat. It's

been cut with a blade," Drew said. "The child was probably restrained as Cypress drove."

"How far is the cave from here? Will it be closer to
bring her back this way, or to the trailhead where you were
parked when you first found her?" Simon asked.

Tal itched to get going. To get to Heather. "I don't
want her coming back here. I never want her to see this
place again," he said in a low, gruff voice.

"Right, so Rocky and I will go with Tal," Ethan
decided. "Zeke, you and Drew go to the trailhead and start
walking, you can meet us on our way back."

"Brock, if you can stay with me as a witness, I'll call in
what we found here in a bit," Simon said.

Everyone nodded in approval.

"That leaves me," Raid said. "I'll take Duke back to
town and rally the troops...otherwise known as your
women. They're going to want to be there for Heather
when you bring her home."

Tal was almost overwhelmed by the support from his
friends. When he'd made the decision to get out of the
service and move to the United States, he'd had no idea
what was in store for him. He figured he'd spend a few
years here then go back to the UK. But he'd found the
best friends a man could ask for...and the love of his life as
well.

Gratitude for his friends made his throat close up and
his chest tight, but Tal took a deep breath and turned to
the trees. He was so proud of Heather. He didn't know
exactly what happened here, but he could imagine. She'd
done what she had to in order to protect herself and the
child he was positive was with her. She wasn't running,
wasn't planning on hiding from him...instead, she was
going to the one place she knew with one hundred

percent certainty he'd be able to find her...and Cypress couldn't.

His Heather was smart, and he was the luckiest man in the world.

"Come on, let's go bring your woman home," Ethan said, thumping Tal on the back.

Without hesitation, he headed toward his future.

CHAPTER TWENTY-ONE

The walk to the cave was long but uneventful. Heather knew these woods like the back of her hand. She'd spent nearly her entire life out here. Hunting was when she'd felt the most free. She didn't have to watch what she did or what she said...even if she just talked to herself as she wandered around the forest.

The little girl never loosened her grip around Heather's neck as they walked. She continued to talk to her as she headed for the cave. "Talon is going to be with us soon. He'll figure out what happened and where I am, and he'll come. He's very protective. It feels really nice to have him look out for me. You'll like him. And you'll like our friends. It might be a little overwhelming at first, it was for me, but they're such good people. Finley is pregnant and she practically glows. And wait until you taste her cookies and cinnamon rolls! They're so good. Like, melt-in-your-mouth good."

She went on to tell the girl in her arms a little about all of her other friends. When she was done bragging about her girlfriends, she went on to describe their men. "Don't be afraid when you meet them. They're all big and muscular and can be intimidating, but they won't hurt you. You can trust them. They're like giant teddy bears... standing in the way of anyone who might want to be mean, and yet snuggly and warm when you need them to be."

She was laying it on a bit thick, but Heather didn't care. The girl was very young—she didn't know her exact age—and needed reassurance. "And the rest of the people in town are just as nice. Art, Otis, Silas, Tony, Whitney, old man Grogan, Harvey, Rory, Sandra...even Davis. He's kind of smelly, but he has a huge heart."

She was running out of things to talk about, and just when Heather was taking a breath to mention Boots again, the little girl in her arms spoke.

"Marissa."

Heather smiled. The one word was whispered, and she didn't elaborate, but it was a huge step forward.

"Marissa. That's a beautiful name. Just like you. Much better than the one the mean man insisted on calling you."

"Our hair matches," Marissa said after another moment.

"It does," Heather agreed with a grin. It was crazy how happy she felt right then. Her arms trembled with the unaccustomed weight of Marissa, and she felt a little shaky as the adrenaline that had gotten her through the confrontation with Cypress receded. But she was free of her past once and for all. Yes, there were still other men who'd lived in The Community who could come after her, but Heather doubted they would.

She did worry what Talon would say when he learned that she'd gotten into Cypress's car after she promised she wouldn't. But she hoped once he met Marissa, and understood what was at stake, he'd forgive her.

Marissa didn't say much more as they walked, but she did eventually pick up her head and look around as they neared the cave. Heather approached cautiously; the last thing she wanted was to surprise a bear or some other animal that might've decided the cave was a perfect place to spend the remaining winter. But she didn't see any sign of wildlife.

Seeing the place where she'd spent an entire year made Heather smile once more. She didn't ever want to live here again, but seeing it brought back some pretty good memories. This was where she'd finally tasted freedom for the first time. She'd been able to survive on her own, and that felt amazing.

And this was where she'd met Talon.

Inside the cave, she leaned down and put little Marissa on her feet. The sweatshirt Heather had put over her head touched the ground. It was huge on her, and she couldn't help but smile again. The first thing she did was go to the mound of supplies she and Talon had left, just in case. She pulled out the rabbit-fur slippers she'd once worn. Looking at them felt a little bittersweet.

She sat on the ground, and Marissa came over and plopped herself in her lap without hesitation. Heather picked up one of the knives that had been left in the cave and quickly cut the fur so the makeshift shoes would fit Marissa's feet. Then she spread out the canvas so they wouldn't have to sit in the dirt.

After telling Marissa to stay put, she gathered some sticks and a few dry logs and made a small fire using the flint left behind. She got out a small pot and one of the freeze-dried meals. There was even some water left in the bucket. It wasn't fresh, but Heather didn't think Marissa would mind.

She guessed it was late afternoon by the time they'd finished eating, and she had no idea how long she might be in the woods with Marissa. But Heather wasn't worried. Talon would be here soon. With her belly full, Marissa closed her eyes and her head bobbed. Heather cradled her close as she leaned against the side of the cave. She stared out into the waning daylight and sighed.

She was safe, Marissa was safe, Cypress was dead or dying, and even though she'd been scared out of her mind, Heather was proud of how she'd handled things. She hadn't panicked. Hadn't fallen under Cypress's control. She'd been worried about that. That a man would order her to do something and she'd revert back to her old self without thinking, just because it was how she'd been raised.

But because of Talon, his support and love, she'd been able to think past her panic and not only save herself, but this precious child in her lap. She kissed Marissa's forehead and whispered, "You're safe. You can trust me and Talon, and we won't hurt you."

The words had been her mantra, and while merely saying them didn't automatically mean she'd trusted Talon, his reassurance had eventually seeped deep into her soul. She wanted the same for Marissa. She'd been through a horrific ordeal, but hopefully if she heard the words enough, she could learn to trust again too.

Heather didn't know how much time had passed, but the sun had almost set when she heard footsteps approaching the cave.

She didn't panic. It wasn't Cypress, she'd made sure he wouldn't be in any shape to follow them. Besides, he didn't know where this cave was. There was only one person who did.

She couldn't keep the smile off her face when she saw the beam of a powerful flashlight through the trees outside. Heather stayed where she was, letting Talon come to her.

When he appeared around the edge of the cave wall, Heather smiled even wider, despite his light nearly blinding her. She heard him swear, then he was there. Next to her, cradling her face with his large palm.

"I knew you'd come," she told him. He wasn't alone. Heather sensed someone behind Talon, but she didn't take her gaze from his to see who it was.

"I'll always come for you," he said, kissing her. It wasn't a chaste kiss, it was deep, passionate, and all too short. "You're okay?" he asked quietly, so as not to wake the little girl in her arms.

Heather nodded even as Marissa stirred. She opened her eyes and looked up at Talon with fear in her eyes.

"Marissa, this is Talon. I told you about him on our way here," Heather said softly. "He's here to take us home."

"I can trust him and he won't hurt me," Marissa said, her voice wobbling.

"You can trust me. I won't hurt you," Talon agreed. He looked at Heather, and she could see the tears in his eyes. "I love you."

"I love you too."

Then he helped her stand and led her out of the cave. Rocky and Ethan got to work putting the cave back the way she'd found it. They doused the fire, packed up the supplies she'd used, then the five of them slowly and carefully made their way toward home.

* * *

343

When they arrived back in Fallport, Simon wasn't the only one waiting for them at Talon's apartment. Every single one of their crew was too. Almost twenty people filled every nook and cranny of the small space. Marissa was frightened and overwhelmed, and as much as Heather appreciated everyone's support, she just needed to be alone with Talon.

She'd gone into their bedroom shortly after arriving and removed the offensive brown dress Cypress had forced Marissa to wear, and had pulled another one of Talon's huge sweatshirts over her head. The little girl seemed to like being swaddled in the oversized shirt...either that, or the scent of Talon that had permeated the fabric comforted her. Heather figured it was probably a little of both.

Talon seemed to know exactly what she needed. When she and Marissa had returned to the living room, before she'd even blinked, he had shooed everyone out the door —except for Simon, who wouldn't budge.

Marissa had allowed Talon to carry her through the woods, but as soon as they got to the car, the little girl burrowed back into Heather's lap and refused to let go. Ethan had called Simon during the drive and given him as much information as they knew about the child, so he could begin the search for her parents.

As soon as everyone cleared out of the apartment, after promises to bring by clothes for Marissa in the morning, food, and toys, Simon didn't hesitate to speak.

"So far, we haven't had any luck in finding where he took her from," Simon said, gesturing to Marissa. "Could be anywhere from here to Florida."

"Will she have to go into foster care until her family can be found?" Talon asked. He was standing protectively next to Heather, with one hand around her waist and the other on Marissa's lower back.

"Technically, yes. But I've already put in an emergency request to approve the two of you...if you'd be willing."

"We're willing," Heather said immediately. She felt Talon squeeze her waist as he nodded his agreement.

"All right. And since it's just the three of us...we'll talk about this once and then never speak of it again," Simon said.

Heather tensed, knowing what he wanted to talk about.

"Tell me what happened," Simon said gently.

Looking down, Heather saw Marissa had fallen asleep. She was glad, she didn't want the little girl to hear. As concisely as possible, Heather described the day's events. How she'd planned to run in the opposite direction when she saw Cypress behind the wheel, but then she'd seen Marissa, who Cypress had threatened, and she couldn't leave the child alone with him.

When she got to the part where she'd stabbed him, Heather's voice faltered for the first time. She took a deep breath before starting again.

"I knew where to hit him, where it would do the most damage but wouldn't kill him. Not right away. Gut, kidneys...leg so he couldn't walk. I destroyed the tent so he wouldn't be able to take shelter there, and locked the doors to his car and took the keys with me. Was he dead when you got there?"

"Not yet," Simon said. "But it didn't take long."

Heather knew she should probably feel guilty for taking a life, but Cypress Goodson had already taken so much of hers.

"It was self-defense," Simon said firmly. "Even if I'd

called an ambulance before we'd arrived, it wouldn't have mattered. You have nothing to worry about, Heather. With your past...what happened was self-defense. Period."

"Simon, I—"

But the police chief didn't let her finish her thought. "I took his fingerprints before the coroner transported him. Sent them in and got a hit before I even got back to town. His name is really Alfred Winterborne."

"Was he...was he kidnapped as a child by Arrow? Brainwashed?"

Simon shook his head. "No. He was a peeping tom, someone who got off on looking through women and girls' windows. He was caught and kicked out of his college when he was a freshman. That's how his prints got into the system. And that's apparently when he hooked up with The Community."

"He wasn't Arrow's real son?" Talon asked.

"I'm guessing no. But since we don't have DNA to compare, I don't know for sure."

Heather closed her eyes. Her entire life had been a lie. Even the identity of her last captor. She was stunned, and sadness threatened to overwhelm her.

But then Marissa moved against her shoulder. And she could feel Talon squeezing her waist...

After tonight, she was truly free. Cypress, or whatever his real name was, wouldn't bother her again. She wasn't going to go to jail for killing him, and she was reunited with the man she loved.

"You're free," Simon said, echoing her own thoughts. "I'm going to make sure you have a happy life from here on out. You need anything, I'll do what I can to make sure you get it."

"Sorry, Simon, but that's my job," Talon said.

Surprised at the growl in his tone, Heather turned to stare up at him. Talon's gaze immediately met hers and gentled. She smiled at him, then turned to Simon. "He's mine, and I'm not giving him back," she blurted.

Simon's lips turned up into a smile. "He's a lucky man."

"I am," Talon agreed. "Now, are we done? I need to get my girls tucked in. It's been a long day...and I have a feeling we're going to be busy entertaining our friends tomorrow."

"And probably half the town too," Simon said with a chuckle. Then he nodded at them both and headed for the door. He turned around before opening it and said, "I'll be in touch about Marissa."

The thought of having to say goodbye to the precious bundle in her arms made Heather want to cry, but she nodded anyway. She must have parents who were beyond worried, wondering what had happened to their little girl. Maybe they'd let her have some sort of relationship with her once she returned home. Though it made her sad that Marissa was now a member of that club Lilac had mentioned...the I've-been-kidnapped club.

Talon went to the door and made sure it was locked behind the police chief, then he led Heather to their room. There was no discussion about having Marissa sleep anywhere but next to them tonight. After taking the quickest shower of her life, Heather returned to the bedroom to see Talon lying on his side, his head propped up on a hand as he stared at a sleeping Marissa.

As Heather climbed into bed on the other side of the girl, Talon rolled over and got up. "I'll be right back."

Then it was Heather's turn to stare at Marissa. She was so innocent, so vulnerable. Thinking about how close she'd come to ending up under Cypress's thumb made Heather tear up, lost in thoughts of her own past.

She jerked in surprise when the mattress dipped under Talon's weight.

"Scoot over," he ordered softly.

Heather moved closer to Marissa, and Talon climbed under the covers behind her. He put an arm around her waist and pulled her against his body. She was surrounded by his heat. His comfort. He sighed behind her, and she closed her eyes.

"I was so scared when you didn't show up," he said softly. "Duke tracked you to where you got in the car and for a moment, I panicked. I had no idea where to start the search for you."

"I know I said I wouldn't ever go with him, but I had no choice."

"I know," Talon said. "You saw Marissa and couldn't leave her with him."

Heather nodded. This man knew her better than anyone ever had...than anyone ever would.

"Once I figured that out, I knew exactly where he was taking you. Back to where he'd lost control of you. He wanted to reassert his dominance...but it didn't work."

"It didn't work," Heather agreed.

"I'm proud of you. So damn proud," Talon said. "Arrow, Cypress, and all the other men in that bloody cult tried to make you reliant on men for everything. Tried to take away every scrap of independence. Tried to strip you of any choices regarding your life and your body. But in the end...you broke free. Not only that, you faced your demons, literally, and defeated them on your own. Without help from a man. You're a warrior, and I'm so proud to be yours."

Heather's eyes filled with tears. Happy tears.

"I know that marriage is a tough thing for you to think about with any kind of positive feelings, but I'd like you to think about it nonetheless. I want to belong to you legally. I want to wear your ring, so the world knows who owns my heart."

There were so many ways this man could've asked her to marry him, but he'd done so in a way that she would always remember. By emphasizing her hold on *him*, he'd effectively removed any reticence she might've had.

Turning her head, Heather said, "Yes."

Talon looked shocked. "Yes?"

Heather nodded. "I can trust you, and you aren't going to hurt me. So...yes. And I want to belong to you too. I know it won't be in the way that The Community tried to own their wives."

"No, it bloody well won't," Talon agreed. "I love you. So much. You don't even know."

"I *do* know," she countered. "Because I love you the same way."

Talon leaned down and their lips met in a kiss. She winced when her neck muscles protested the stretch, and she reluctantly pulled her lips from his and rested her head on his arm, which he'd put under her head when he'd pulled her close.

"She looks like what I imagine *you* would've looked like at her age," Talon said quietly. "She's got your red hair, and her eyes are even the same blue-green shade."

"I'm sure that's why he picked her," Heather said.

Talon's arm tightened around her waist for a moment. He nuzzled the hair by her ear.

"What if they can't find her parents?" Heather whispered.

"Then we'll see about keeping her," Talon said matter-of-factly.

Heather's head whipped around to look at him again. "Really?"

"Really. We won't stop looking for her parents. I can't imagine having a child disappear and not knowing what happened to him or her. But we can be her foster parents for as long as she needs a home."

Heather beamed. "I love you so much!"

Talon lifted a hand and brushed her hair off her face, smiling back.

Heather turned over and sighed in contentment. And just like that, she was suddenly exhausted. The day had finally caught up to her, and she fully relaxed for the first time.

As she reclined against him, Talon simply gathered her closer. "Sleep, sweetheart. I'll keep watch over you both."

And with his words echoing in her head, Heather fell into a deep sleep, devoid of bad dreams, content in the embrace of the man she loved.

EPILOGUE

For the first time in three weeks, Heather felt as if she could finally breathe easy. She'd been meeting with Simon, the FBI, child protective services from two states, and she'd even agreed to give more interviews. She'd been thrust right back into the spotlight since she'd been sort of kidnapped again. Talon insisted that even though she got in the car willingly, she'd only done so because of the threat against Marissa...so technically she *was* kidnapped.

As it turned out, Marissa's biological parents weren't in the picture, and she'd been in foster care for a year at the time of her kidnapping. And that situation hadn't been good. Her guardians hadn't reported her missing for a full twenty-four hours after she'd disappeared. They simply hadn't noticed. Between all the other children they had under their care, and the fact that they were both drunk most of the day and night, they'd had no idea Marissa hadn't returned home from school at the normal time.

Because of that, and other violations child protective services had found at the house, Heather and Talon were granted emergency approval to be temporary foster parents. It helped that they already had a room set up and ready for her.

The other big thing that happened—Heather had asked *Talon* to marry *her*. Of course, he'd already told her he wanted to be her husband. But when she realized CPS was dragging their feet about approving their permanent foster status because Talon was in the US on a work visa, and she learned that marrying him would grant him citizenship, she practically dragged him down to the courthouse.

They'd had their wedding. It was nothing like Bristol and Rocky's ceremony, but it was still a dream come true for Heather. All their friends had attended as witnesses, and Caryn had thrown them a party afterward. Heather couldn't remember ever being happier. Being Talon's wife was nothing like what she'd become accustomed to while living in The Community, but then, she'd already known it wouldn't be. For one, this marriage was actually *legal*. Second, it had been her decision.

And third—she and Talon loved each other.

Every time she caught a glimpse of the ring on Talon's finger, she couldn't help but smile. He was hers. And not in an abusive, demented way that Cypress claimed she and all the women of The Community belonged to them. In a loving, respectful way.

When they'd first decided to get married, Talon had explained how names worked. How the woman usually took the man's last name as her own. But he quickly assured her that he didn't care if she changed her last name to Ross or kept Brown. After thinking about it carefully for a few days, Heather made the decision to change her name to his.

Lilac's example had actually influenced her decision.

The other woman had completely changed her name after what had happened to her. Her old name had become synonymous with her ordeal, and people recognizing her name every time she introduced herself made it more difficult to move on.

So Heather Brown officially became Heather Ross. And she couldn't have been happier.

She was currently sitting on Bristol's porch with the other women as the guys entertained Tony and Marissa. Elsie's son had fallen in love with Marissa from the moment he'd seen her. He'd become her little protector, and Marissa had slowly begun to emerge from her shell.

She'd been seeing a child psychologist, but Doc Snow had commented that he thought the little girl was doing as well as she was because of the love she was experiencing since moving in with Talon and Heather. She had a roof over her head, food in her belly, and two adults who showered her with affection. She finally felt safe.

"She's amazing," Lilly said softly from next to Heather. The guys were throwing a large plastic ball back and forth, and Marissa was right there in their midst, laughing every time she dropped it...which was often.

Tony stayed next to her, trying to give her tips on how to best catch and throw the ball, and the men all had goofy grins on their faces as they played with the kids.

"She is," Heather agreed. There were times when memories of Cypress overwhelmed the little girl, and when that happened, they'd crawl into bed or under a blanket on the couch and simply snuggle. Heather would reassure Marissa that she was safe, and loved, and that no one here would hurt her. The words that had become her mantra were quickly becoming Marissa's as well.

"Tal's so good with her," Bristol said. "Watching him, you'd think he was a father ten times over already."

Heather understood what she meant. He seemed to know exactly what to do and say to make Marissa relax, laugh, and simply be a kid. Of course, at night, when they were alone in bed, he confessed to not having a clue as to what he was doing.

"What's the long-term plan with her?" Caryn asked. "I mean, are you guys going to adopt her?"

Heather nodded and stared out at her husband and the little girl in the yard. "We want to," she said softly. "But we're at the mercy of the system."

"That's bullshit!" Caryn exclaimed quietly. "I mean, seriously. Look at her. She's happy...much happier than she was in that fucking foster home she was in. They didn't even know she didn't come home from school! What the hell is *that* all about?"

"Have you talked to Nissi?" Elsie asked. "She helped me so much when my ex was being a douche...even before he became exponentially douchier by trying to kill Tony and me for life insurance money, I mean."

"Not yet," Heather admitted.

"Do it. Soon," Lilly said firmly. "I'm thinking that there's no way the system will deny Heather Brown's—I mean, Heather *Ross's* petition to adopt the child she saved from going through the same hell *she* did, from the very same kidnappers. You're currently one of the most famous women in the world, and possibly the kindest person alive."

Everyone chuckled and agreed immediately.

"But...that's not very ethical," Heather protested. "Using what happened to me like that."

"You want to give her up?" Elsie asked, gesturing to

Marissa, who was giggling uncontrollably as Raiden dramatically and purposely fell to the ground after getting hit in the face with the ball. Duke immediately trotted over from where he'd been lying in the grass to slobber all over his human, making Marissa laugh even harder.

"No," Heather said firmly.

"You might as well get something good out of your notoriety," Finley agreed.

"Other than huge groups of people coming to Fallport to gawk at you," Lilly said with a roll of her eyes. "Seriously, it's worse than all the tourists coming to look for Bigfoot."

"They'll go away soon," Bristol soothed. "Just keep ignoring them."

Heather agreed with her friend. She should know about being a celebrity, because she basically *was* one. It had been a surprise to find out that her down-to-earth friend had more money than she'd ever be able to spend in several lifetimes. She was famous in her own right, a renowned artist, but she ignored people who wanted to befriend her solely because of her work.

"This is the first time we've all been together in a while, and with the news that Talon and Heather are going to petition to adopt Marissa—and win—I think the situation deserves a toast!" And with that proclamation, Caryn pulled a flask from the side pocket of the cargo pants she was wearing.

Everyone laughed, except for Heather. She was somewhat confused.

Finley explained, "Caryn is friends with Clyde Thomas, who's Fallport's resident moonshiner."

When Heather still didn't understand, Lilly added, "Moonshine is alcohol. Really *strong* alcohol. And Clyde makes the best stuff around. Our favorite is his caramel apple flavored stuff. It tastes exactly like the pie."

"Okay, everyone, I don't have cups, so we're just gonna have to swap spit. Take a swig and pass it along," Caryn ordered before tipping the flask up to her mouth. She took a swallow, wiped her lips with the back of her hand, then handed it to Bristol.

When the flask got to Finley, she passed it along without drinking any, on account of her being pregnant. Lilly took a large swallow, coughed, then smiled at Heather when she handed it to her.

Not sure if she'd like the drink, but not wanting to look as if she was chickening out, Heather took a cautious sip.

The flavors exploded on her tongue, and she couldn't help but choke a bit as the strong drink went down. But she smiled and said, "It's actually really good!" before taking another, larger sip.

Everyone laughed and cheered as she handed the flask to Elsie—who immediately passed it back to Caryn without drinking.

"Wait, you didn't take any," Caryn protested.

Elsie shrugged, her cheeks flushed. "I don't really feel like it today."

Lilly turned to her with narrowed eyes. "Wait...*why?*"

"I just don't. You guys can have a second go."

Lilly leaned forward and asked in a low voice, "Are you pregnant?"

She didn't immediately deny it.

Lilly sat back. "You are! Why didn't you say anything?"

Everyone began to congratulate Elsie...but when her eyes filled with tears, the group stared at her in concern.

"You aren't happy? I mean, out of all of us, you're the

one who wanted more kids the most," Bristol said in confusion.

"I *am* happy," Elsie protested. "I just...I didn't want to make you sad," she said, looking at Lilly.

The other woman took a deep breath, even as her own eyes filled with tears and spilled down her cheeks. "That's...I don't know if I should hug you or smack you."

Heather tensed. She'd seen way too many fights between women in The Community. Even though they were submissive around the men, with each other, the women were downright mean sometimes.

"I love that you're worried about me, but it pisses me off that you're not celebrating your pregnancy. My miscarriage shouldn't keep you from being over-the-moon happy about your own baby," Lilly told Elsie.

"I'm just still so sad about what happened to you. It didn't feel right to be all happy and want to celebrate so soon after you lost your baby," Elsie said with a sniffle.

"Okay, it's good we're talking about this," Lilly said, wiping the tears from her face. "What happened to me *sucked*. It was devastating. I'll mourn the baby we never got to hold or even see for the rest of my life. But Ethan and I aren't giving up. The doctor says the chance of us getting pregnant again is high. So we're waiting a bit, but then we're definitely going to try again...and for the record, I'm going to enjoy the hell out of the process."

Everyone giggled at that.

"But in the meantime, that doesn't mean I want you guys to keep your excitement about Finley's baby, or Elsie's pregnancy, a secret from me. I want to be happy *with* you and *for* you. Am I sad that Finley's child and mine won't get to be twinsies? Yes. But that doesn't mean I'm not excited for Finley's kid to be a big brother or sister to mine sometime in the future. I mean, look at Tony with Marissa," Lilly said, gesturing toward the yard. "Why wouldn't I want that for my child?"

Heather's own eyes filled with tears. Both in sorrow for Lilly's loss, but also because her optimism was so beautiful.

"So no more keeping baby secrets. Anyone else have anything they want to share that they've been keeping from me?" Lilly asked.

"Don't look at me. I swear I didn't run off and secretly get married," Caryn said with a laugh, even as she wiped tears from her cheeks.

"I'm having quadruplets," Finley deadpanned.

Everyone stared at her for a moment—before roaring with laughter when she finally grinned, proving she was teasing.

Lilly smiled at everyone, then raised her glass of iced tea. "To the best friends I've ever had. I don't think I would've made it through what happened without each and every one of you. Thank you."

Heather's eyes filled again, but she smiled and raised her own cup along with everyone else. Caryn passed the flask of moonshine around again, and by the time Talon and the rest of the men climbed the stairs when Tony and Marissa finally got bored with throwing the ball around, they were all a little tipsy...except for Finley and Elsie, of course.

"You good?" Talon asked as he propped his hands on the arms of the chair Heather was sitting in and leaned over her.

"Great," she said with a big smile.

"You drunk?"

"Nope."

His grin widened and he lowered his head. "We haven't had drunk sex yet," he said for her ears only.

"Is it better than regular sex?" Heather asked, her voice not quite as low as his.

She heard Caryn chuckle from next to her, right before she said, "Hey, you guys want Drew and me to take Marissa to the fire station and let her see the trucks?"

"Yes," Talon said, before Heather could open her mouth. He grabbed her hand and pulled her to her feet. "Can you bring her home when you're done? In say...an hour? Or two?"

Caryn beamed. "Sure thing."

"Great. Thanks." Then Talon wrapped an arm around Heather's waist and steered her toward the stairs.

"Wait!" Heather exclaimed...but she was already tingling between her legs. "I want to say bye!"

Talon turned without letting go of her so she could see the other women. They were all grinning at her, their men standing by their sides. Raiden had taken Tony and Marissa inside to get a snack, Duke as close as ever, obviously hoping he'd get a snack too.

"Bye!" Heather said, giving them a cheesy wave.

"Bye!" they all said at once. The guys now had grins on *their* faces, and they each gave a chin lift. It was alpha in the extreme...and so sexy, it was all Heather could do not to jump her own man right then and there.

Talon turned her once more and headed for his SUV. He got her buckled into the passenger seat, then jogged around to the driver's side. Because Fallport wasn't that big, they were pulling into the parking lot at the apartment complex in minutes.

Talon all but dragged her through the front door and down the hall. Heather flopped back on their bed and smiled up at him. Her head was swimming pleasantly and she felt kind of floaty.

"Elsie's pregnant," she informed him.

"I know."

Heather frowned. "You do?"

"Yup. Zeke told me the other day."

"Humph," she said with a frown.

"Any other huge announcements you want to make before I make love to my wife?" he asked.

"Elsie said we should talk to Nissi about adopting Marissa, and that we'd probably have no problem because of what happened to me."

Talon's eyes sparkled. "We'll get on that tomorrow."

"Really? Are you sure?"

"You want to adopt Marissa?" he asked.

Heather nodded. "Yes."

"Then I'm sure."

She loved this man so much. "What if I said I wanted to adopt twenty more cats, fourteen dogs, a goat, and have twelve children?"

"Then I'd say I need to increase my shifts at the barbershop, buy a bigger house, and get you pregnant as soon as possible, so we can get on with having those twelve children."

Her eyes widened. "You *want* twelve children?" she asked.

Talon threw his head back and laughed.

She loved seeing him happy. So uninhibited.

He was still grinning, that dimple she loved so much in full force behind his beard. "I love you," he said, still smiling. "You think you might want to have kids with me someday? I mean, other than Marissa?"

"Yes."

He sobered, and his gaze bored into hers.

"What?" she whispered.

"I have no idea how I got so lucky. You've been through hell and yet you're still so open, so trusting, and so willing to live your life. It's bloody beautiful."

"It's because of you. The first thing you ever said to me was that I could trust you and you wouldn't hurt me. Those words reverberate in my mind every single day. I'm only strong enough to get through everything because I have you to lean on. To trust. To love."

"You'll always have me," Talon said. "Now...anything else you want to talk about before we get naked? World peace? Curing cancer? Fixing the hole in the ozone?"

"There's a hole in the ozone?" Heather asked with a straight face. But she couldn't hold it and immediately started giggling.

"I'll take that as a no." Talon took his clothes off in record time, and Heather did her best to keep up, but the alcohol swimming through her veins made her clumsy and by the time she was as naked as Talon was, he was already under her, and she was straddling his thighs.

"Are you ever going to let me be on the bottom?" she blurted.

Talon studied her. "You'd be comfortable with me on top?"

"You? Yes. I trust you. You won't hurt me. Anyone else...I doubt it," she said with a shrug.

Excitement and arousal shone from his eyes. His cock lengthened even though she hadn't touched him yet. "Then the answer is yes...but not right now. I want to see my drunk wife take her husband."

Lust swamped Heather, and she grinned, scooting forward so his cock was between their bodies. Looking down, she could see a bead of precome on the mush-roomed head against her belly. She was soaking wet, even though he hadn't touched her. Just being around Talon, seeing how much he wanted her, was enough for her body to immediately prepare itself for him.

Reaching down, she gripped his cock and went up on her knees. As she sank down onto the man she loved, Heather closed her eyes...and she thanked her lucky stars for her new life.

* * *

Khloe sat at her desk in her office in the library and stared off into space. Frowning, she tried to figure out where her master plan had gone wrong. She was only supposed to be here in Fallport for a few months, while her lawyer gathered evidence against Alan Mather...the man who'd actually tried to kill her after she hadn't been able to save his prize coonhound. It had been her lawyer's suggestion to lay low—to basically hide—while the case was pending.

She'd since gone back home for the trial, and while Alan had been convicted of attempted murder, animal cruelty, and stalking, his sentence had been way too light for Khloe's peace of mind. Seven years. And he'd probably get out in three to four.

It wasn't enough. The man had upended Khloe's entire life. She'd lost her veterinary clinic, her health, her friends...and he'd barely gotten a slap on the wrist.

Khloe's leg throbbed, even though she was sitting and doing nothing. It wasn't fair.

Moving to Fallport was supposed to be very temporary. She'd done her best to stay disconnected, to not get close to anyone...but it had been impossible to keep her distance from Lilly, Elsie, Bristol, Caryn, Finley, and now Heather. They'd all accepted her, grumpiness and all, and did their best to include her in all their shenanigans.

Khloe had made the decision *not* to join her friends at Bristol's house the other day. Everyone had been there, including Raiden. But she had to start distancing herself. She was leaving Fallport soon.

Alan had made her life a living hell back home, and she had no doubt even though he was behind bars, he'd do whatever it took to continue to do so. He *hated* her. For something she'd had no control over. Alan hadn't seen it that way, and he'd made it his mission in life to make her pay for what he felt was her negligence.

But even though she'd made up an excuse, a lame one, as to why she couldn't go hang with everyone at Bristol's house, she'd heard all about how Lilly had lit into their friends for tiptoeing around her, not wanting to upset her regarding Elsie's pregnancy. She'd also learned that Heather and Talon hoped to adopt Marissa, and she had no doubt they'd be successful, and amazing parents. After seeing how Heather was with the kitten she'd adopted, Khloe knew she was a natural nurturer.

Sighing, she closed her eyes. Yeah, it was time to leave. If Alan started fucking with any of her friends, she'd never get over the guilt. They'd all been through their own kinds of hell, it wouldn't be fair to bring her problems to their doorsteps.

Deep down, Khloe had a feeling they'd all be extremely pissed if they ever found out about what happened to her, why she'd been trying to keep her distance from everyone.

Especially Raiden.

She sighed again. Raiden Walker was...

What was he? At first, he'd just been her boss, but as

she slowly got to know him, she realized he was such a crazy dichotomy. Badass former Coastie, book nerd, marshmallow when it came to his dog. He was stubborn, loyal, and completely unaware of his own appeal. He thought he was the outcast of his SAR team...the funny-looking redhead...when that couldn't be further from the truth.

Khloe had always been a sucker for a nerd. For the guys who sat back and observed, then singlehandedly solved the case. For the men who didn't brag about their accomplishments or looks.

For guys exactly like Raiden.

On the outside, he was crusty, standoffish...just like *she'd* been since moving to Fallport. But she knew the real Raid. The one who baby-talked to his dog. Who was a sucker for Duke's sad eyes, always giving him extra snacks. The man who made sure his dog was taken care of after a long search before he even considered himself. He also worried about his friends, about regulars who came into the library...

She was head over heels for her boss—which was the *real* last straw.

She had to leave. Before he found out and rejected her. Before Alan somehow learned how important Raiden was to her. Before Duke's life was in danger. And Khloe had no doubt the bloodhound would be Alan's first target.

He'd take great pleasure in hurting her through the dog.

A strange sound interrupted Khloe's depressing thoughts. She turned to look at the very bloodhound who had been on her mind...and frowned as she watched him. He stood up, paced, then lay back down on the dog bed she'd bought for him and kept in her office. But as soon as he lay down, he stood once more.

He was panting, and more drool than usual dripped from his jowls.

Sitting up straighter, Khloe stared at the dog for another moment—then stood so fast, her chair crashed to the floor behind her. She raced past the still-pacing blood-hound and out the door. She stuck her head into Raiden's office. He jerked in surprise as she spoke, but she couldn't feel bad for scaring him.

"Call Doc Snow and Simon!" she ordered, then turned and ran back to her office. Her leg throbbed, but she ignored it.

She headed for Duke, who whimpered as she approached.

"I know, boy. We're gonna get you fixed up."

"What's going on? What's wrong?" Raiden asked urgently as he appeared in the doorway.

"Duke's bloating," Khloe said bluntly as she took a deep breath, squatted to put her arms around Duke's chest and his back legs, then stood, lifting the dog. He wasn't light, probably around a hundred pounds, but Khloe had adrenaline on her side. She didn't even feel the arrow of pain shooting down her bad leg. Duke needed medical attention. *Now*.

"Shit!" Raid swore. He obviously knew the dangers of deep-chested dogs bloating. When their stomachs twisted and cut off the blood supply. They could literally die if it wasn't fixed surgically. "We need to call Doctor Ziegler!" he said.

"He's out of town," Khloe muttered as she staggered toward the door with Duke in her arms. "Besides, he'd fuck up the surgery for sure."

"Why the hell do you want me to call Doc Snow and Simon? What are *they* going to do?"

"Simon's gonna help me break into Ziegler's vet clinic, and Doc's gonna assist me."

"*What?*" Raiden said, staring at her in shock even as they headed for the back door of the library.

"Get your ass in gear, Raid. I mean it! Duke's critical here, he needs surgery immediately!"

Khloe was grateful Raid didn't argue further. She heard him talking to someone as he put a hand under her arm, assisting her as she carried the bloodhound to her beat-up old Honda Accord. She gently placed Duke on the back seat, then took a few precious seconds to lean down and kiss his snout and tell him everything would be okay, before she slammed the door and got behind the wheel.

Raid jumped into the car right before she peeled out of the parking lot behind the library on the square. He turned to her, his face white, his expression tortured as he worried about his dog...

And asked, "Who the hell *are* you, Khloe?"

She didn't answer. She wasn't sure he'd like what she'd have to say, anyway. Just as they had all along, her plans were going awry yet again. Revealing who she was—at least, who she'd been in her old life—was going to change everything. But saving Raiden's constant companion and best friend was more important than her secrets.

She'd deal with the consequences of her actions after she saved Duke.

And there was no doubt in her mind that Duke would live...she hadn't been voted the best veterinarian in the state two years in a row for nothing. There would be a lot of questions she'd have to answer, a lot of hurt feelings because of all she'd kept from her friends, but she'd pay that price gladly if it meant using her expertise to save a life.

Khloe could feel Raid's gaze on her, but she didn't dare return it. She kept her eyes on the road. She couldn't bear to see suspicion, distrust, or fear on his face. He had every right to be pissed at her, but at the moment, she needed to prepare for surgery.

* * *

One of Khloe's secrets might be out, but there are still more revelations to come. Things are about to get very rocky for her and Raiden...find out how they overcome their past and look to the future in the last book in the Eagle Point Search & Rescue series, *Searching for Khloe*!

Also by Susan Stoker

Eagle Point Search & Rescue Series

Searching for Lilly
Searching for Elsie
Searching for Bristol
Searching for Caryn
Searching for Finley
Searching for Heather
Searching for Khloe (May 2024)

The Refuge Series

Deserving Alaska
Deserving Henley
Deserving Reese
Deserving Cora
Deserving Lara (Feb 2024)
Deserving Maisy (Oct 2024)
Deserving Ryleigh (TBA)

Game of Chance Series

The Protector
The Royal
The Hero (Mar 2024)
The Lumberjack (Aug 2024)

SEAL of Protection: Alliance Series

Protecting Remi (July 2024)
Protecting Wren (Nov 2024)
Protecting Josie (TBA)
Protecting Maggie (TBA)
Protecting Addison (TBA)

Rescuing Mary
Rescuing Macie (novella)
Rescuing Annie

Delta Team Two Series

Shielding Gillian
Shielding Kinley
Shielding Aspen
Shielding Jayme (novella)
Shielding Riley
Shielding Devyn
Shielding Ember
Shielding Sierra

SEAL of Protection Series

Protecting Caroline
Protecting Alabama
Protecting Fiona
Marrying Caroline (novella)
Protecting Summer
Protecting Cheyenne
Protecting Jessyka
Protecting Julie (novella)
Protecting Melody
Protecting the Future
Protecting Kiera (novella)
Protecting Alabama's Kids (novella)
Protecting Dakota

Badge of Honor: Texas Heroes Series

Justice for Mackenzie
Justice for Mickie
Justice for Corrie

Justice for Laine (novella)
Shelter for Elizabeth
Justice for Boone
Shelter for Adeline
Shelter for Sophie
Justice for Erin
Justice for Milena
Shelter for Blythe
Justice for Hope
Shelter for Quinn
Shelter for Koren
Shelter for Penelope

Ace Security Series

Claiming Grace
Claiming Alexis
Claiming Bailey
Claiming Felicity
Claiming Sarah

Mountain Mercenaries Series

Defending Allye
Defending Chloe
Defending Morgan
Defending Harlow
Defending Everly
Defending Zara
Defending Raven

Silverstone Series

Trusting Skylar
Trusting Taylor
Trusting Molly

Trusting Cassidy

Stand Alone
Falling for the Delta
The Guardian Mist
Nature's Rift
A Princess for Cale
A Moment in Time- A Collection of Short Stories
Another Moment in Time- A Collection of Short Stories
A Third Moment in Time- A Collection of Short Stories
Lambert's Lady

Special Operations Fan Fiction
http://www.AcesPress.com

Beyond Reality Series
Outback Hearts
Flaming Hearts
Frozen Hearts

Writing as Annie George:
Stepbrother Virgin (erotic novella)

ABOUT THE AUTHOR

New York Times, *USA Today* and *Wall Street Journal* Bestselling Author Susan Stoker has a heart as big as the state of Tennessee where she lives, but this all American girl has also spent the last fourteen years living in Missouri, California, Colorado, Indiana, and Texas. She's married to a retired Army man who now gets to follow *her* around the country.

She debuted her first series in 2014 and quickly followed that up with the SEAL of Protection Series, which solidified her love of writing and creating stories readers can get lost in.

If you enjoyed this book, or any book, please consider leaving a review. It's appreciated by authors more than you'll know.

www.stokeraces.com
www.AcesPress.com
susan@stokeraces.com

facebook.com/authorsusanstoker

twitter.com/Susan_Stoker

instagram.com/authorsusanstoker

goodreads.com/SusanStoker

bookbub.com/authors/susan-stoker

amazon.com/author/susanstoker